THE WHISPERS OF HIDEAWAY HOUSE

ALEXANDRA BARBER

Storm
PUBLISHING

Ebook ISBN: 978-1-83700-222-1
Paperback ISBN: 978-1-83700-223-8

Cover design: Rose Cooper
Cover images: Shutterstock

Published by Storm Publishing.
For further information, visit:
www.stormpublishing.co

For Friendship
Past, Present and Future

'The wound is the place where the light enters you.'
Rumi

FORTITUDE

Eliza paused to look at the view. The cottage garden was in full bloom, Hidcote lavender with its dense purple flowers abuzz with bees, some new soft pink roses called Gertrude Jekyll which Guy had planted in the border and her own favourite, the deep blue delphiniums swaying in the breeze. Isaac stepped outside and placed an arm around his wife's waist. Instinctively Eliza leaned into him.

'This is a magical place, isn't it, Isaac? A place where dreams can come true.'

'Indeed.'

Momentarily a shadow passed across his face.

'If those dreams are meant to be. Life can't give us everything we wish for, my love. We have to accept our fate then and now.'

Eliza squeezed his hand.

'I sense that we're still needed here, Isaac.'

She felt his resistance.

'There's another guest on their way to Hideaway Cottage. Someone who is in need of this place as much as we've needed it.'

'Then we shall remain to welcome this person,' Isaac said with a hint of a sigh, 'and watch over them, keep them safe and endeavour to guide them towards happiness and contentment.'

Eliza dipped her head in gratitude and as the summer breeze whisked at her skirts she felt a frisson of anticipation.

Isaac dropped a kiss on the top of her head.

'Except this time, Eliza, there must be no meddling.'

Eliza adopted her most innocent expression.

'What you called meddling was merely a helping hand.'

The slightest wrinkle of a frown crossed his forehead.

'Your plan may have worked with our last guest, but it could also have got us into trouble.'

'I know, I know,' she replied, turning her face to the sky, 'but you worry too much, Isaac.'

'I worry that we can't stay here for ever,' he said, dampening her spirit a little with a stubbornness that she recognised so well. 'It is not...'

Eliza stared at the blades of grass around her feet. The gardener, Guy, would be here soon to cut the lawn. Maybe his girlfriend, Carrie, would come with him. Maybe she would remove the little mahogany box from beneath the floorboards again and take out its contents. How Eliza longed to see those precious objects once more. Because precious they obviously had been to someone. Isaac was still searching for the right word and seemed to find inspiration from staring at the sheep in the adjacent field.

'...appropriate,' he declared with a nod of approval and righteousness.

A wave of panic washed over her. He meant well, but she couldn't leave, not until she had seen that box once more. To confess that, however, would incite his wrath again. Isaac was not prone to bursts of anger. She could count on one hand the number of times he had raged during their many years together, but only once had he stormed off and that was after the discovery of the box. Two long days he had been gone. She began to think he wouldn't return, that he had passed over without her. She had sat on the fallen log beneath the willow tree waiting, hoping, praying for him to rejoin her. And then, just as dusk was falling on what would have been her third lonely night, the fronds of the tree parted and he was there, his dear face set with anguish. For a moment they had faced each other. She had vowed that she wouldn't make the first move yet was it not nearly always the women who swallowed their pride and instigated forgiveness? So, she'd lifted her arms, the lace around her wrists fluttering like the beating of her heart, and stepped towards him.

'I'm sorry,' she'd whispered, even though she felt it was not her place to apologise. 'I do not know why I made you angry, but I'm sorry.'

He'd held her tightly and briefly she'd felt safe again, but something had changed between them. He was still her beloved protector, but there was a suppressed nervousness which rippled from him, a restlessness, even more of an imperative to move on. He thought that he hid it, but she knew him too well. In addition, he was keeping something else from her, but she couldn't work out what that was. Her memory was so tiresome! She was sure there were things from long ago which, however hard she tried, eluded her; strands of their life floated like distant shapes within the mist that rolled in from The Solent some days. She grasped for those memories, but as soon as they seemed to be within reach they would fade away. She was left bereft and with a feeling of failure that she did her best to suppress. If Isaac thought she was unhappy, there was a danger he would accelerate their plans to depart and that could not happen. He himself said that she knew what others needed in advance of their own awareness – that was her gift. Instinctively Eliza knew that she would not get the answers she needed by leaving. She had always devoted herself to Isaac and to others. Now it was time to be aware of her own needs, too, and if they involved her remaining and Isaac departing, she would have to steel herself and find a way to endure without him.

'Do you have an inkling as to when our next guest is due to arrive?' he asked, jolting her from her reverie.

Eliza looked up at him, his dear face now smiling tenderly

down at her. She transferred her gaze across the garden towards
the horizon where the silver sliver of water merged with an
expanse of summer sky.

'Soon,' she murmured. 'Very soon.'

ONE

Jules stretched out her arm. It met empty space. In truth, she hadn't needed to reach out to know that the other side of the bed was empty. She lifted her head to look at the clock: 5.23 a.m., although you wouldn't know it from the light filtering through the curtains. It was so bright it could have been midday. She lay there for a moment, listening. Through the briefest of pauses in the birdsong, she could hear the tap, tap of fingers on a keyboard. Dread gripped at her stomach and she tried to calm herself. She was being ridiculous. The feeling was totally illogical. There was bound to be a good reason why Gavin kept getting up in the early hours to look at his laptop, but up until now she hadn't managed to find out what it was. Just sending a few emails, he said when she asked. She wanted to believe him, but... Throwing back the duvet she swung her legs over the side of the bed and padded, barefooted, across the varnished floorboards towards the sitting room. If she could just get a look at that screen... It wasn't that she didn't trust him, she just needed to reassure herself.

Gavin was perched on the edge of the sofa, his hair tousled from another restless night, and seemed oblivious to her presence. She was almost there, almost close enough to read the words when he sensed her and in one sharp, practised movement slammed the laptop closed.

'What are you doing?' she asked, keeping her tone light as she leaned forwards to drape her arms over his shoulders, and nuzzle his neck.

'Nothing.'

He jerked away, Jules's teeth snagging hard against her bottom lip with the suddenness of it.

'Ouch!' she said, tasting blood, hand flying to her mouth.

'Sorry, baby,' he said, twisting to look at her, 'but you really shouldn't creep up on me like that. Made me jump. You okay?'

She nodded half-heartedly, but in reality, she wanted to cry.

He reached up and pressed his index finger against her lip which felt as if it was beginning to swell.

'Poor angel. Come and sit here.' He patted the cushion next to him. 'I'll get some ice.'

He pressed her down gently and dropped a kiss on the top of her head. He was like that, so caring, so kind. If only he could trust her with whatever was worrying him. They may not have known each other long, but it was for keeps. She'd known that from the beginning and so had he. Surely that meant they should share everything?

'Your colleagues will think I've been beating you up,' he joked from the kitchen as he rummaged in the fridge.

Perhaps she could open the laptop and sneak a look at the screen now, but no, he was back already, ice wrapped in a clean tea towel.

'Anything interesting?' she asked, nodding towards the computer.

'Oh, not really. Just looking for another development opportunity for when I've finished Beech House. Not much out there though.'

He sounded convincing.

'Want me to take a look?' she asked. 'I mean, if we're to be business partners as well as... well, you know.'

Please say yes, she thought. Please, please say yes and then it will all be all right.

He smiled, leaned forwards and kissed the side of her mouth.

'Of course you can look.'

And she felt a shiver of relief run through her. He arched his back slightly and yawned.

'But not now. Let's go back to bed.'

No, she thought. Let's not. Let's sit here and talk and tell each other everything, but in truth there was little more to tell from her side. She had spent the last twelve weeks telling him about her life.

Maybe that was the problem. Maybe she just hadn't given him time to tell her about his. She wasn't really worried – not like Carrie was, but Carrie didn't really know him. She'd moved out of the flat to go and live in the South of England and Gavin had moved in. Jules had never thought when she suggested a much-needed two-week break at a picture-perfect cottage on the Isle of Wight that Carrie would meet the love of her life and decide to embrace island life. She bit her lip. She was really happy for Carrie, but she still missed their late-night chats and the sprigs of wildflowers in a little glass bottle on the windowsill. Gavin bought her flowers all of the time but somehow his extravagant bouquets didn't touch her soul quite like Carrie's 'weeds', as she used to call them.

'It's early days,' Jules said on one of their frequent phone calls, 'we haven't got around to talking about his background much. We've been busy with other things.'

'It's been three months,' Carrie replied. 'You must have had time to talk as well as have sex.'

'We talk about the theatre and books and football,' Jules said defensively.

'Football? You?' Carrie snorted.

'Okay. Gavin talks and I listen.'

'Do you listen to what he's not saying, too?'

'I have no idea what you mean,' Jules replied, holding her phone slightly further away from her ear.

'Yes, you do,' Carrie persisted. 'Like where he grew up, why he doesn't see his parents, who his friends are? Don't you think it's weird that you haven't met any of his friends?'

'Not really. He's not been in Manchester that long.'

'But long enough to have a house. Have you been there yet?'

'Yes, I have actually. He took me last week and it's amazing. At least, it's going to be. It's Grade II listed so everything's taking a bit longer than usual. He's waiting for new windows at the moment. They're having to be individually made and are hugely expensive.'

Carrie was silent for a few seconds. Jules bit her lip. She shouldn't have said that. She and Carrie may have only shared a home for a few months, but they'd hit it off straight away and Jules knew that the next question was inevitable.

'You haven't lent him any more money, have you, Jules?'

There was a lump in her chest. Why did Carrie make her feel like this? It was her money. She was free to do what she liked with it.

'Just a bit. To tide him over.'

At the end of the line Carrie couldn't suppress her groan.

'It's fine. Honestly. He's going to pay me back as soon as he can. It's a cash flow problem. That's all. Loads of businesses have those. It's not unusual.'

'And the rent on your place to cover the mortgage? Is he contributing to that? Because he wasn't planning to move in permanently, was he? Not at the beginning.' She paused. 'Or perhaps he was.'

It took all of Jules's self-control to ignore that last comment.

'Of course he wasn't. You know it was only meant to be temporary. I didn't realise that you wouldn't be coming back.'

She sounded peeved. She couldn't help herself. Carrie was quiet at the end of the line.

'He's paying for some food and a bit of other stuff.'

'But not rent?'

'I can manage for now,' she said snappily.

'Are you doing loads of overtime?'

'Only the odd shift here and there.'

Another silence. Even without FaceTime Carrie could probably tell how dog-tired she was. She'd always said that you could tell a lot about people from their voice on the telephone.

'I'm really worried about you, Jules. I wish I was closer.'

Jules felt a lump in her throat.

I wish you were closer, too, she thought, but managed to stop herself from saying it. One hint of worry or weakness and Carrie would drop everything and head back to the mainland. That was the sort of person she was.

'I'm fine. We're fine,' Jules said brightly. 'I worry about you, too, you know. In a new place, starting up a new business, in a new relationship as well. How is gorgeous Guy the gardener?'

'Still gorgeous! I can't believe we've only known each other for a few months or that I came here back in the spring in such a state and something so wonderful was waiting for me. It just feels so... right. When you know, you know, don't you?'

Carrie was silent and Jules knew exactly what she was thinking – that Jules 'knew' with almost every person she went out with that he was 'the one' until suddenly he wasn't.

She took a deep breath.

'Look, I know that I've got a chequered romantic history, that normally I'd be thinking of ditching him by now, but I've finally realised that no one is going to match up to my dad. He was a saint to put up with my mum...'

'Your mum is sweet,' Carrie said. 'She just wants to protect you.'

'Suffocate me, more like,' Jules replied.

'You can't blame her for worrying after what happened. From what you've told me, she and your dad adored each other.'

'Dad devoted himself to her. He was so patient. Mum's acting career always came first and Dad was very open about that, but for me to expect to find someone just like him... I've finally realised that's totally unrealistic.'

'So you're prepared to settle for someone who isn't very patient, from what you've told me, definitely isn't open and...'

'*Does* care about me,' Jules protested. 'When you came back to pick up your things you saw how he was with me. He treats me like a princess. You said yourself that he was charming.'

'Yes, I did, didn't I?' Carrie replied. 'The trouble is, Jules, charmers aren't always to be trusted.'

Jules felt the beginnings of a headache. Why did Carrie have to be like this? Why couldn't she be more supportive? She was thrilled that Carrie had met Guy and found real happiness after that nightmare of an ex-fiancé and the trauma over her job. Surely the least Carrie could do would be to feel the same way about her relationship with Gavin.

'I don't want to argue about this anymore,' Jules said, beginning to feel as frayed as the edge of the old sofa in the living room. 'He's the one, Carrie. I know it and if you can't accept that, then...'

She shrugged even though she knew Carrie couldn't see. Tears were pricking at her eyes and she never cried. Never. Ever. Prided herself on her stoicism. The other midwives shed tears when a birth went wrong, as it sometimes did, but not her. She was the one who held them all together.

'...it's not exactly as if we're going to be seeing a lot of each other going forwards with you on the Isle of Wight and me in Manchester.'

Carrie was quiet for a second or two and Jules inwardly cursed herself.

'What are you trying to say, Jules?"

'Maybe we ought to stop speaking as often.'

'If that's what you want.'

There was a tightness in her chest. She put her palm against her heart, which was beating faster than usual.

'It is. I'm really busy with work for the next couple of weeks anyway.'

'Okay,' Carrie said, her hurt travelling across the miles to Manchester.

And the call had ended there with the most cursory of good-byes. It felt like the end of something, and Carrie hadn't really put up much of a fight, had she? Some friend she was.

Jules stood still for a minute, the phone still clutched in her hand. The brief euphoria she'd felt at making such a positive decision was disappointingly short-lived. Then she'd felt sick and shaky and angry. She lifted her arm and hurled the phone through the air. She was aiming for a cushion on the sofa, but it had bounced off and hit the metal edge of the hateful coffee table, which always scraped your shins if you misjudged the amount of space you needed to edge around it. Jules winced as she heard the screen crack a split second before the phone landed face down on the floor. When she tried to pick it up, little shards of glass dropped out onto the beige twist pile carpet and finally she burst into tears.

That was two weeks ago, and she hadn't heard from Carrie since, not an apologetic text or a conciliatory email. She could have initiated contact herself, of course, could have been the one to make amends, but why should she? Did Carrie feel the gaping hole that was left, the grief? Obviously not. If only Carrie had kept her thoughts to herself. Then, when she had got to know Gavin better, she would have realised that she didn't have anything to worry about. Gavin was solid. And Jules needed to concentrate on him now. Think about the future. A future with Gavin. He was what mattered more than anything else.

Gavin stood up and pulled her into his arms.

'I love you,' she murmured into his chest, feeling the beating of his heart, the heart that was entwined with hers.

'And I lo... Ouch!' he said, wriggling from her grasp and hopping about on one foot.

'What? What is it?' she said.

He flumped back onto the sofa and examined his sole.

'There's still glass down here,' he said, picking out a shard from the fleshy base of his big toe. Jules blinked. She loved everything about Gavin, but his toes really weren't his best feature.

'You haven't cleared it up properly.'

'Sorry, sorry, I thought I had. A piece must have got embedded in the carpet.'

'More than one,' he said, picking at his heel which really needed some cream on it. She must offer to massage his feet later. He liked that.

'You really should have been more careful, Jules.'

Jules flinched and closed her eyes for a moment. Her lip was beginning to throb.

'I tried. It really needs the vacuum cleaner on it, but, well... you know the issue with that.'

'Why don't you just order a new one and put it on the credit card?'

'I've told you I don't want to do that. Perhaps I'll go and ask next door if I can borrow theirs. They're not very friendly, but...'

'We could get a new sofa while we're about it,' Gavin said. 'It looks as if some wild animal has been shredding it for a nest.'

'My aunt gave it to me. She had a rescue cat.'

'And while we're about it we really need to get rid of this carpet. I'll sand the boards so they match the ones in the bedroom, and we can buy a nice rug.'

'If we just took up the carpet we wouldn't need a new vacuum cleaner so urgently,' Jules said with a weak smile. She fell on to her hands and knees and began to pull apart the carpet pile with slightly shaky fingers.

'I can't see any more glass,' she said, straightening up, 'but perhaps we ought to get you some slippers anyway.'

She took the two miniscule shards of glass from his hand and moved through to the kitchen.

Opening the cupboard under the sink to drop them carefully into the bin, a cloud of damp rose to meet her. There was definitely a leak somewhere. Gavin kept saying that he'd get his plumber to look at it but she couldn't afford to shell out for anything extra until her next pay cheque came in, not if she and Gavin wanted to eat, and he did like his smoked salmon breakfasts at the weekend with those muffins which came from the corner deli and were delicious, but two cost more than a pack of four from the supermarket. She liked to indulge him though, and he deserved it, especially at the moment when he was obviously under stress. He more than made up for her treats with his own; the flowers, the bottle of Barolo which they'd consumed with dinner the previous night and the chocolates, seventy percent cocoa salted caramel deliciousness from a local chocolatier nestled in the most gorgeous gift box with Florentine style decoration and an extravagant cream satin ribbon tied in a bow. She would keep that box for ever. One day she would fill it with their children's tiny name tags and other precious mementoes of the life they were building together. The cost of the muffins was nothing in comparison to what he gave her. And then there were the promises; to take her to the Caribbean after Christmas and skiing at Easter and next summer they could tour the Loire valley, staying in some of the stunning chateaux which he'd been to before. He was so appreciative of nice things. It wasn't surprising that he found living in this poky, slightly shabby little place a bit challenging. Funny, she'd never thought of it as shabby when Carrie was here. They'd covered the sofa with a teal velour throw and Jules's Gran had run up some pretty cushions in a retro fabric.

Carrie had draped fairy lights from the picture rail and in the evening she always lit a candle or two. It had all felt cosy and relaxing, lived in and full of laughter. When they had people around, no one had to worry about spilling anything and everyone said how homely it was. They hadn't needed expensive new things to give them happiness, but some people did. Gavin was one of those people and there was absolutely nothing wrong with that, was there?

Back in the living room Gavin was still suspiciously inspecting both his feet and the carpet.

'You're right,' she said, sitting down next to him. 'We should roll up this carpet and get rid of it – and the sofa, too. I've hardly got anything on my credit card. We'll go and choose something at the weekend.'

He leaned forwards and ran a finger around her lips. She shivered with pleasure at his touch and pushed to the back of her mind how many extra shifts she would have to take on in order to pay for a new sofa.

'Gavin,' she said, gazing into his incredibly blue eyes, 'you would tell me if there was anything really wrong, wouldn't you?'

'With us?' he asked. 'How could there be anything wrong with us? You're perfect.'

She snuggled into him, resting her head on his shoulder.

'And you're perfect, too. We're so lucky, aren't we, to have found each other?'

'The luckiest,' he said, kissing her hair even though she hadn't washed it for three days.

'I want you to feel that you can tell me if there's anything worrying you. I know that you think I have a stressful job and don't want to bother me, but...'

He twisted and took her face in his hands.

'There's absolutely nothing to fret about, babe. We're fine. Everything's absolutely fine.'

'But you'd tell me if it wasn't?'

'Of course I would. I tell you everything, you know that.'

Except he didn't. At least, not yet. But she was sure he would, given time. Besides, she liked a bit of mystery in a man. It gave him gravitas. A lot of her previous boyfriends – could she really call them that when they'd barely been together for more than a few weeks? – male acquaintances then, had been only too eager to offload about previous relationships, childhood traumas and workplace jealousies. No, it was nice to have someone who protected her from all that.

He wanted to make her life better, and she loved him for that. If he got grumpy and impatient from time to time, who could blame him? Besides, he was right, she should have taken more care removing the bits of glass.

TWO

Jules had only been asleep for about an hour after a gruelling night shift when she was woken by someone hammering on the front door. Next to her the bed was empty and cold. She stretched out her fingers for the little lovingly scribbled note Gavin always left for her to find when she woke up. Instead of the piece of paper she was expecting, there was just a dent in the pillow where his head had been.

'Yes?' she snapped, swinging the front door open to confront two burly looking men in ill-fitting suits.

'We're looking for Gavin Stone. Is he in?'

Jules pulled her dressing gown more tightly around her.

'No. Why?'

'We want a chat, darling, about some money he owes us. So, if you'd be good enough to tell us where he is...'

The larger of the two men peered over her shoulder. Jules felt her legs begin to tremble slightly.

'You must have made a mistake and I'm definitely not your darling.'

'No mistake,' said the other man, stretching out an arm and placing his hand on the doorframe.

Jules lifted her chin a little.

'He's gone to work.'

'Work!' Bushy Eyebrows chuckled. 'And what work would that be?'

She summoned up all her courage, reminded herself that she was used to dealing with difficult people. Sometimes some of the families in the maternity unit could get a bit tricky if they couldn't visit the new baby.

'Look, why don't I give him a call and we can sort this out? You wait there. I'll be back in a couple of minutes.'

Slowly the man retracted his hand, allowing Jules to close the door.

'Come on, Gavin. Pick up. Please, please, pick up,' she muttered as she sat on the bed and listened to the phone ringing out.

After a few rings it went to answerphone. Jules could have wept.

'We're still waiting,' one of the men called.

She moved towards the front door but didn't open it.

'He's not answering.'

There was silence apart from heavy breathing.

'Give me your number and I'll get him to call.'

'No need,' came the reply. 'Just tell him we'll be back.'

As Jules listened to their heavy tread getting further away, she sank to the floor, the coir from the doormat prickling her calves. She couldn't stop shaking. It was all she could do to press redial, but it didn't matter how many times she rang, Gavin wasn't picking up.

No way could she sleep so she made herself a cup of sweet tea from which she took little revitalising sips as she pulled on jeans and a jumper. There was no point sitting around torturing herself with possibilities. She had to sort this out. Creeping down the stairs and out of the front door she checked up and down the road just in case her unwelcome visitors were loitering outside, but presumably they had moved on to their next victim. She walked the surrounding streets checking that Gavin's BMW wasn't parked a bit further away and he hadn't just gone to the shops for provisions or fancied a walk in the park. Actually, that last thought was ridiculous – he really wasn't into walking. Heading back towards home she stopped on the corner and rang for an Uber. A small tabby cat came and rubbed around her ankles as she waited, its identity disc flashing in the sunlight.

'Where is he?' she murmured, bending down to rub the cat's chin. 'I bet he's at the house renovation. I bet he's got his phone on silent. All of this is just a horrible mistake.'

But in the pit of her stomach something told her that there was more to it than that.

The journey to Beech House took about twenty minutes through the city centre traffic. The road was tree-lined and wide, the expensive houses set well back.

'Posh area this,' the driver said as he dropped her off.

'My boyfriend is doing up a house here,' she said, pointing down the grass-tufted driveway towards an impressive three-storey redbrick Arts and Crafts house.

'Be nice when it's done,' he said. 'You take care.'

He was looking at her keenly and she realised that her anxiety must have permeated the car.

'Yes, I will. Thank you.'

She stepped back and waved as he pulled away and suddenly, without him there, without a soul on the street, and only the rustling of the trees for company, she felt very alone.

The driveway looped around the back of the house and Jules was convinced that Gavin's car would be there alongside a couple of workmen's vans. She skirted the overgrown circular bed at the front, containing some poor straggly roses which were doing their best to flower. Perhaps she would offer to prune them and try to give them a new lease of life, although Gavin would probably want to pull them out and replant with something new. He wasn't a rescuer like her; she got an immense feeling of satisfaction from giving things a new lease of life. Old roses had such a beautiful scent as well.

'Don't you worry,' she whispered to them. 'I'm in your corner. Even if you end up being uprooted, I'll make sure you get a second chance.'

She stood up straighter, slowed her breathing and began to feel more in control, except the house looked empty and there was no sound of the electrician's radio or the plumber's cheerful whistling.

There was no sign of Gavin's car either. No sign of anyone. The windows were still boarded up, although she was sure he'd said the new custom-made ones were arriving a couple of days ago and were about to be installed. She sank on to the shady back steps, pulling her cardigan closer. If only she could talk to Carrie; just hear her voice saying that everything would be fine. She took her phone out of her back pocket, her finger hovering over Carrie's name. It should be the easiest thing in the world to press that brand new shiny screen. Instead, she stood up and, without a backwards glance, walked away from the house, heading towards the centre of town where she could pick up a bus back home to wait.

Jules made a cup of tea and picked up a magazine, but she couldn't concentrate. Her muscles were solid with tension. Maybe a bath would help, with that nice neroli oil which her mother had sent and she'd been saving for a special moment. She turned on the taps, opened the bathroom cabinet and paused, arms raised. The two shelves that Gavin had commandeered for all of his lotions and potions were empty. Behind her the water gushed into the bath. Despite the steam filling the small room, Jules went cold. Turning off the taps, she walked as steadily as possible through to Carrie's old bedroom, pausing before the wardrobe where Gavin kept his immaculately presented clothes. She stood for a whole minute, afraid to open the door. Bile rose in her throat. She reached out, took hold of the metal teardrop handle, placed her palm flat against the opposing door. She was always afraid that the wardrobe would topple over because you had to yank the door open. A sob shuddered up through her. The wardrobe was empty. All of his clothes had gone, too.

It was a week later when Jules heard a key in the lock. She had been off work, unable to eat, barely able to sleep although that was all she wanted to do – to sleep and wake up to find that it had all been a terrible nightmare. The burly men had been back, but she had hidden in a corner, crouched between her dressing table and the wall, pretended that she wasn't there, listening to them telling her how she wasn't the only one, how they didn't want to harass her, but they had a job to do.

She felt as if she was existing in a parallel world, one which she'd never have been able to conjure up. It had been one of the worst weeks of her life, almost as bad as when her father had died. At least her father hadn't meant to leave her, but Gavin obviously had. He'd conned her, strolling away without a word, taking the money she'd lent him, leaving God knows how many debts and maybe other broken-hearted women behind. She couldn't believe she'd been so stupid as to believe in him.

And then late that afternoon, sitting on the sofa in the rabbit pyjamas which she'd been wearing all week and barely watching some film which she'd hoped would be distracting, she'd heard the door open. He was back. She spilt her hot chocolate all over herself as she leapt up. She looked terrible but what did that matter? He was here to explain and apologise and tell her that he still loved her. The door from the hallway opened and at the sight of the person gazing back at her Jules promptly burst into tears all over again.

'Shh,' Carrie said, dropping her bag on the floor and moving swiftly towards her.

Gently she took the mug from Jules's hands and put it on the table before stroking her disgustingly manky and matted hair back from her unwashed face.

'Please don't cry,' Carrie soothed, wrapping gentle arms around her. 'It's going to be all right. I promise.'

Jules allowed herself to be held until the sobs began to subside and Carrie eased her back down onto the sofa.

'W-what are you doing here?' she snuffled.

'I'm here,' Carrie said, softly, but in a voice that didn't brook any opposition, 'to take care of you.'

'H-how did you know?'

'Your mum rang me. Said she didn't know what to do. She'd called the hospital because you weren't answering your phone and they told her you weren't at work and had been signed off with stress. She said she came to see you, to take you home with her, but you wouldn't open the door to her or to your sister.'

Jules grabbed a tissue from the almost empty box on the coffee table and wiped her eyes. She shook her head, stared at her lap, couldn't look Carrie in the eye.

'I couldn't face them. I couldn't face anyone. What is there to say except I've been an idiot.'

Carrie reached for one of her hands and held it firmly.

'You're far from alone in that. We've all been there at one time or another. You were there for me when I needed it and I'm here for you now.'

'I went into work when I shouldn't have done, the evening after Gavin left. I was too upset, not concentrating and...'

She could hardly bear to think about it.

'We were short-staffed and it was a busy night and I was distracted and...'

Her voice dropped to a whisper.

'I nearly made a mistake. I nearly left it too long before calling for back-up. I've never done that before. It could have all gone so wrong. I could have cost that baby his life.'

Carrie took her hands.

'But you didn't, did you?'

Jules shook her head.

'Afterwards I went to pieces. They sent me home. I'm not to be trusted, Carrie.'

'Of course you are,' Carrie said, leaning closer. 'I would absolutely trust you if I was giving birth.'

'But I don't trust myself – with anything.'

'Have you seen your doctor?'

Jules nodded.

'She's the only person I've seen in the last few days. She's signed me off for six weeks. Part of me is relieved and part of me feels really guilty and part of me thinks six weeks isn't nearly long enough and another part thinks it's far too long because I just don't know how to stop thinking about everything.'

'Which is why I'm taking you back with me, back to the Isle of Wight for as long as you need, where I can look after you and you can learn to believe that one day life will be good again. I don't want any arguing. Tomorrow the car is booked on the return journey and I'm not getting back on that ferry without you.'

Jules knew that if she was to survive in any way at all, she had to give in. So she leaned her head on Carrie's shoulder and just whispered, 'Thank you.'

THREE

'Almost there,' Carrie said, as they pulled off the main road and the car meandered past a low redbrick building with a sign outside which read 'Local Pottery'.

'That's an interesting place,' she continued, 'and it has a brilliant tearoom with fabulous cakes. One of my favourite beaches isn't far from here and there's a track just past that field with the horses in which leads to Tennyson Down. The great poet used to stride along it in his cloak whatever the weather. I never really appreciated Tennyson until I came here. We can take a walk along there when you're feeling up to it. You won't have to talk to anyone up there, not even me if you don't want to. And there's a great pub which we'll pass in a minute. We can finish up there for a glass of fizz overlooking the water.'

Jules let Carrie's enthusiasm wash over her in the hope that it would help her to feel less battered.

'And here's the village,' Carrie said, slowing down for some hens that were drifting from the grass verge into the road. 'They're Cressie's hens. She's away at the moment so Rita and I are looking after them. Rita, who helps to look after the cottage, lives down there.'

She pointed to a sign which said Orchard Farm in bold letters, a tractor rumbling up the rutted, sun-baked track.

'That's Alastair, Rita's son,' she said, allowing the large vehicle to pull out into the road. 'Their farmyard backs on to the cottage garden so there's a bit of disturbance from the cows and machinery. It's not all total peace and quiet.'

Jules felt a void of panic open up inside of her.

'I didn't realise I'd be staying at the cottage. I thought I'd be staying with you and Guy.'

'No, and it's not because we don't want you so don't think that. It's because I think you need some space.'

'I had that at home.'

'That was different. This is somewhere new, somewhere special.'

Jules felt her breath starting to stall.

'I'm not sure I want to be completely on my own, not in a strange place and...'

She swallowed hard. It felt as if there had been a lump in her throat ever since Gavin had left.

'You haven't even seen Hideaway Cottage yet. Wait until you see it and then you might change your mind.'

'I'm sorry, but I can't afford to pay. Gavin...'

'Guy doesn't expect you to pay, Jules, so don't worry. In fact, if you offered, he'd probably be offended.'

She placed a hand on Jules's shoulder.

'You're family, sweetheart, better than some family,' she said with a smile. 'Guy knows that. And if you don't want to be on your own, I'll stay with you at the cottage for as long as you like.'

Jules sank back into the seat. She was so lucky. How stupid of her to have nearly blown this friendship. Stupid, stupid, stupid.

They passed the church and The Manor, which Carrie had talked about so much and where Guy worked. Then she turned the car down a single-track lane, protected by high hedges. As the road descended Jules could see the sea in the distance and then the cottage straight ahead. With its deeply sloping thatched roof, a small reed sculpture of a border terrier scampering along its ridge, the pale turquoise paintwork and the flower-filled front garden Jules had to admit it was enchanting.

'Well?' Carrie asked, grinning as she pulled the car on to a gravel area reserved for parking. 'Isn't it better than I described?'

'It's stunning,' Jules murmured.

And it really was the prettiest house she'd ever seen.

'It's all yours,' Carrie said, 'for as long as you need it.'

Jules went and stood beneath the honeysuckle archway that framed the front gate. Lavender formed a low hedge bordering the path to the front door, its scent and the buzz of the bees filling the air. Marigolds intermingled with vibrant blue cornflowers crowded against the picket fence at the front, and above the front door a milky white rose was heavy with blooms. For the last week she'd felt almost numb with despair and disbelief, had no hope that she'd be able to feel anything approaching happiness ever again, but standing here with the sun on her head and a couple of swallows swooping in and out of the eaves, there was the pinprick of a feeling that maybe, just maybe, she would eventually be able to rebuild some sort of life; not the one she had imagined, not even one to savour, but something at least which would enable her to move through the days.

'Come on,' Carrie said, leaning around her and lifting the latch. 'Let's get inside and start to settle you in. We can sit down on the patio with a cup of tea and a slice of one of Rita's amazing cakes.'

She handed Jules the key.

'You go first.'

Jules walked unsteadily up the path and paused beneath the little wooden porch. Carrie had talked about this house as if it had special healing properties, which she'd honestly thought was ridiculous. But look at Carrie. She exuded happiness, yet more than that, she seemed at peace with herself. Could a house really do that or was it just the fact that she had met Guy? Would she feel anything as she crossed the threshold, or would it be like entering any other pretty holiday cottage? She really couldn't cope with any more disappointment so there was no point building her hopes up. All the same, she took a deep breath before turning the key in the lock.

Jules had to admit that the hall was charming. A blue jug overflowing with some of the same white roses that surrounded the front door stood on the central octagonal table. Beside it was a welcome note from Rita in generous looped writing with a single kiss at the end.

Carrie placed Jules's case at the bottom of the stairs.

'You have a wander around while I put the kettle on,' she said, heading through a door to the right.

Jules glanced at the case, but didn't really feel as if she had the strength to haul that upstairs as well as herself. The window was slightly open in the main bedroom, letting in a delicious breeze. She pushed back the fluttering curtains to sit on the built-in seat. The sun had warmed the padded cushion and was throwing flickering beams on to the carpet. She twisted and looked out over the rear garden to the fields beyond and then to the sea. Gavin was out there somewhere, across the water. For all she knew, he might not even be in Britain anymore. She didn't expect to ever see him again and she'd probably never find out whether he'd meant any of the things he'd said to her. Perhaps it had all been lies. Perhaps he'd just been a conman and he hadn't loved her at all. Perhaps her mother, sister and Carrie were right and she should report him to the police, or perhaps, and she really wanted to believe this, he had loved her but had got himself so deeply in debt that he couldn't think of another way out. Perhaps he was so ashamed of the way he'd treated her that he just couldn't face her. Perhaps he wasn't actually out there after all. Perhaps he had felt such despair that he'd decided to end things, and his body was lying undiscovered. She didn't know whether that made her feel better or worse. For the first couple of days, she'd clung to the thought he'd call or just turn up and explain, apologise, get down on bended knee and beg forgiveness, but she'd always known deep down that wasn't going to happen. She'd been a fool. A stupid fool.

Gavin wouldn't commit suicide. She might not know much about him, but she knew him well enough to be pretty sure of that. Out in the garden Carrie was carrying a tray laden with cups and saucers and a large, fluted teapot with a little domed lid topped with a gold acorn. She placed the tray on a wooden table and looked up towards the open window.

'That's one of my favourite places. Do you want your tea up there or are you coming down? Rita's left chocolate and orange cake. I said you were partial to it.'

Jules felt a familiar tightness in her chest, the one that preceded floods of tears. She tried to massage it away with the palm of her hand. Kindness and chocolate cake; not so long ago she'd have thought that would have been the solution to almost anything. Now eating was an effort and kindness just left her in a thousand pieces, but she had to try, for Carrie's sake, for the sake of their friendship.

'I'll come down,' she said.

She paused as she made her way through the sitting room, trying to take in the squashy sofas, the carefully arranged ornaments on the mantelpiece and the higgledy-piggledy bookshelves to one side of the fireplace, but feeling as if she was seeing everything from a distance. Her feet on the carpet told her that she was really here, but the rest of her felt absent as if she had left the part of her that engaged with the world somewhere else entirely. Carrie met up with her in the kitchen.

'Forgot the milk,' she said, wielding a small blue pottery jug.

She draped an arm around Jules's shoulder.

'Come and sit down in the sun. You look shattered.'

Jules allowed herself to be led. She didn't think she'd ever be able to make another decision for herself ever again. How on earth she was ever going to go back to work she had no idea. Carrie cut her a large slice of cake and placed it in front of her. She wanted to eat it, but...

'It looks delicious, but I'm sorry, I can't. I'm just not hungry.'

Carrie poured the tea and passed Jules the milk jug. She stared at it as if she didn't know what to do.

Did she even want milk in her tea? She had this urge to change everything, the way she looked, what she ate, what she read, the way she felt, especially the way she felt.

'I've got lemon, if you'd rather.'

Jules blinked. Carrie understood. Of course she did. She'd been here. Well, not quite here, nobody else could be as stupid as that, to be duped by a man like Gavin. But she'd been at rock bottom and look at her now, brown hair bouncy and loosely curled, skin clear and lightly tanned, but above all happy. No, it was more than that. Content. It radiated from her, a sort of groundedness, a belonging, a knowledge of who she was and what she wanted for herself.

'What?' Carrie asked, leaning forwards slightly.

'I just...' Jules looked around, at the garden with its butterfly-laden summer flowers, neatly mown lawn and the soft borders of the fields beyond leading the eye towards the silver sliver of sea. 'I just don't know how I got here. It's like a dream.'

'I told you. You have your mum to thank. She was frantically worried. She said she'd peered through the keyhole and you looked really thin. She thought you'd barely eaten for a week.'

'Toast,' Jules murmured. 'I had toast. And tea.'

'Better than nothing, I suppose,' Carrie said, 'but not exactly nutritious.'

'I suppose I should let her know that I'm okay,' Jules said.

'I phoned her from the service station and said that I was bringing you back here,' Carrie replied. 'She knows that you're safe.'

Safe... the very word made Jules want to burst into tears.

'But she'd love to speak to you. They both would. Your sister, too.'

'I don't think so,' Jules muttered.

'You'll have to use the landline though,' Carrie said, as if Jules hadn't spoken. 'Phone signal here is awful and, as you know very well, there's no internet.'

Jules pressed her lips together. Carrie had been so cross when she'd first arrived at the cottage to find that she was without the internet, but Jules had thought it would be good for her. She threw her head back and let the sun warm her face. She just felt cold all the time.

'I don't think I can face speaking to either of them just yet.'

Carrie stood up and placed a hand lightly on Jules's shoulder.

'They'll be there for you, Jules, whenever you're ready. And your mum knows not to fuss.'

Jules wanted to raise an eyebrow, but the effort was too much.

'I know she can be a bit suffocating, but she does love you. Remember that. I'm going to get some lemon for your tea and you're right, that is a pretty big piece of cake. I'll cut it in half and we'll share it. It's made with the best butter from the island and the sugar will do you good.'

'Sugar's bad for you, didn't you know that?' Jules murmured.

'Sometimes,' Carrie replied, 'you need sugar. And this is one of those times. Besides, the chocolate and eggs contain iron and the orange has Vitamin C, so we can also pretend that it's one of your five a day!'

'Like the toast with a scraping of jam,' she said, with the ghost of a smile.

'Exactly!'

Jules sat back and listened as Carrie's flip-flops slapped across the patio and back into the kitchen. Who would have thought that the tables would have turned like this? Back in Manchester, she had been the one to reassure Carrie, persuading her to eat properly when she was stressed, boosting her confidence when she got down. She'd always thought of herself as the dependable one, the person who everyone could come to when they were depressed or in trouble and now look at her, in total pieces and no good to anyone at all.

· · ·

'Will you be all right?' Carrie asked a little later. 'I'll only be half an hour, forty-five minutes at the most. You can come with me if you like?'

Jules shook her head. Now was not the time to meet Guy for the first time. In fact, now was not the time to meet anyone.

'No, you go. I'll be fine.'

But watching Carrie's car pull out of the drive, she'd felt a rising panic. Once again, she was alone, totally alone with her own thoughts. She walked back through the house and out into the garden, the sun already dropping slightly and changing hue. Jules slipped out of her green suede sandals and walked barefoot across the soft, springy grass towards the boundary. Off to the right was an old barn and seated on the ground, hidden from the rest of the farmyard, was a girl, her back leaning against the shaling brick wall, her hand moving quickly across the pages of a notebook resting on her lap. She looked up as if suddenly aware she was being watched and hesitated before sending a small wave. Jules raised her hand to wave back, but just at that moment, a woman in white linen trousers and a pale lemon shirt strode into the yard. Instinctively Jules's hand moved to her hair, as if her intention all along had been to brush it back from her face.

'Tasha! Where are you?'

The woman's voice was serrated with irritation. The girl shrank back, almost turning herself into a small ball, her forehead pressed tightly against her bent knees. Jules twisted away towards the house.

'Excuse me,' the woman called in a sharp, don't-ignore-me kind of voice, 'you there.'

Even in her stupor Jules felt a stab of objection to the 'you there', but deeply ingrained politeness got the better of her. She swivelled somewhat stiffly towards the angular woman who was now striding towards her. Thank goodness there was a prickly hawthorn hedge, a well-worn farm track and then a rusty five-bar metal gate between them. Maybe she was a bit more present than she thought after all.

'You haven't seen my daughter, have you? She came out to collect the eggs, but she's been a long time. Scruffy-looking fourteen-year-old with tousled hair which needs a good brush. She's probably red-eyed from crying. She's always crying.'

Jules avoided eye contact with the woman who even from this distance was obviously immaculately made up. Do not look towards the barn, she instructed herself.

'Did you hear me?'

The woman was craning over the gate now, miraculously managing to avoid touching it with her pristine clothing.

'Yes,' Jules replied. 'I heard you and no, sorry, I haven't seen your daughter.'

The woman stared at her for a moment, and Jules felt herself begin to flush. Out of the corner of her eye she saw the girl shuffle along the side of the barn. The woman took a step forward as if to venture further into the yard and peer around the corner of the old building. Jules took a couple of steps forward herself, almost falling into the hedge.

'If I do see her, I'll tell her you were looking for her.'

Without so much as a brief thank you the woman swivelled and wove her way carefully back across the farmyard. When Jules looked back towards the barn, the girl had gone.

Tasha reached up and unlatched the heavy old door to the barn. She slipped inside and closed it behind her, pausing for a moment to lean against an upright timber beam and regulate her breath.

Her eyes quickly adjusting to the gloaming, she tucked her diary under one arm and, sticking her pen between her teeth, scooted up the ladder to the hayloft. She'd done this so many times she could do it blindfold; knew exactly the amount of space between each rung, where to place her feet, which part of the handrail was rough with splinters. Once on the first floor she padded across the boards and squeezed herself between the bales of hay to where she had formed a hiding place.

There was just enough light coming through from the gap in the upper doors for her to see, but she kept a torch up here as well for dull, wintery days or when it was getting dark. It was one of her favourite places, warm, scented with the sweet smell of the hay and quiet; away from the complications of life. She had Granny to thank for it still being used to store the bales. She insisted upon it for 'old times' sake'.

'Used to love going up there when I was younger,' Rita said when it came up in a family discussion, as it did with increasing regularity. 'Would settle myself in with a book and a packet of pear drops and time would fly by.'

'Well, you're not going to do that now, Mum, are you?' Alastair had snapped.

It was always a statement rather than a question, which Tasha thought was presumptuous. She'd felt that familiar thudding in her chest when a row was brewing. Often Dad had the knack of saying just the wrong thing at the wrong time. She'd been sitting in the big, worn leather chair in Granny's kitchen, another of her favourite places. She'd squirmed and dug her nails into the seams, which were starting to come apart a little. It had been Grandpa George's chair and Tasha tried to take herself back to when she was little and sitting on his knee as he read her a story. When she was older, she would sit at his feet as he talked to her about the birds and the wildflowers and cricket.

Sometimes he produced a sketchbook and a pencil sharpened to a point with the penknife he always carried and they would draw together. In spite of the pressures of the farm he always had so much time for her and Will. She wished he was here now. Dad wouldn't dare speak to Granny the way he did if Grandpa George was around.

'I might go up to the hayloft,' Granny replied defiantly to Dad.

She sent Tasha a wink as if to reassure her.

'Your father and I had some fun times up there when we were courting.'

'Mum!'

Dad had looked so shocked Tasha almost laughed. Will put his hand over his mouth to unsuccessfully stifle a giggle.

'Oh, don't be such a prude!' Granny snorted. 'They both know all about the birds and the bees.'

'What Alastair means,' Mum had weighed in, brushing some imaginary crumbs from the kitchen table before leaning across it just enough to indicate earnestness, but not far enough to make Hercules growl properly, 'is that he doesn't think it appropriate for you to be climbing that ladder.'

She had paused and splayed her fingers so that light bounced off her scarlet nails.

'Particularly at your age, Rita.'

That's Mum, Tasha thought, wincing, always one for the killer blow.

Rita had pushed her chair back and stood up, Hercules in her arms. For one moment Tasha thought Granny was going to march straight to the barn and climb the ladder there and then to prove to them all that she still could. Not that she needed to prove anything to Tasha. Often, when she was in hiding, Granny's head would appear through the hatch. Sometimes she would call softly, 'Are you there, sweetheart? Are you all right?'

Sometimes Tasha would answer and sometimes not. Granny would never give her away, but more speaking could feel like too much effort, especially if she'd been shouting at Mum. There would be the soft thud of a tray being placed on the floor and she'd wait until the clunk of the latch downstairs told her that Granny was heading back across the yard again. There was always a glass of homemade lemon barley water or a mug of tea on that tray and of course a chewy cookie or good wedge of cake.

'I may have a slightly dodgy ankle, and I may not be as fast as I used to be, but I'm not in my dotage yet, Christabel.'

Granny's eyes had flashed challengingly. She always used Mum's full name, never the shortened version which Dad used and she preferred.

'I'm not quite ready for the care home.'

Or the bungalow, Tasha knew she was thinking. But thank goodness she didn't say that.

'Of course, I wasn't...'

Mum had done that thing she did with her hands, as if to wrap Granny in a large virtual embrace which Tasha was sure was the last thing she wanted to do and absolutely the last thing Granny desired. She wouldn't be at all surprised if Granny hadn't included in her statement of wishes attached to her will 'no hugs from my daughter-in-law'. Granny had thrown Mum an impressively disparaging look before turning her attention back to Dad.

'Your father was stacking bales in that loft even after he was diagnosed with the cancer.'

'And maybe it's stacking the bales that...'

Tasha felt her breath stall.

'What?' Granny had said, shifting Hercules closer to her. 'You think stacking a few bales of hay hastened his demise?'

'No, no, of course not.'

Dad had gone white. Will was studying his astronomy book with such intensity that Tasha was sure he wasn't really reading it.

'It was doing things around the farm that kept him going. It was making sure that things were done properly, the way they always had been, which gave him a purpose. You mark my words, we'd have lost him long before if he hadn't had that.'

Tasha watched under lowered lashes as Granny ferreted in her cardigan pocket for a handkerchief.

'It's not as if you have to haul the bales up there by hand like we used to when I was a girl,' Rita huffed. 'You've got that all-singing, all-dancing tractor now although goodness knows how we're going to afford the payments.'

'Well, maybe if Dad had invested more money in the machinery over the years, I wouldn't have had to...'

Rita stood stock still. Tasha was sure all of the air had been sucked out of the room.

'Don't you dare criticise your father like that,' she roared. 'If it wasn't for him, you wouldn't have a farm to run or a house to live in.'

'A rather small house,' Christabel muttered, 'for a family of four.'

Granny looked as if she was about to spontaneously combust. Tasha stood up, her legs as wobbly as a newborn calf's.

'Stop it!' she shouted at her parents. 'Stop it. Leave Granny alone. This is her house, her farm.'

'You would take her side,' Christabel scolded.

She turned to Rita.

'You have turned my daughter against me. I should stop her coming here. I should make her stay in our poky little bungalow which you and George actually built for yourselves, not that there's any sign of you wanting to move in,' Christabel said cuttingly. 'Then you'd only be able to see Tasha through the window when she crosses the farmyard to do her chores.'

Rita sank heavily onto one of the chairs. Instantly Tasha had gone and draped her arms around Granny's shoulders.

'She will not do that, Granny. I won't let her,' she whispered.

Tasha stared directly over the top of Granny's head towards her mother.

'You will never, ever do that,' she said. 'And if you try, I'll leave home.'

Now she sat in the loft and leaned her head back against a pillow of hay thankful for a few more moments of calm. People thought happiness was found in shiny new things or excitement. For Tasha the closest thing to happiness, apart from spending time with Erin at The Pottery or being wrapped in one of Granny's loving hugs, was the peace she found up here. The woman in the cottage looked frail and drawn, but she hadn't given her away. She could have. Most people would have done. Tasha couldn't thank her enough.

FOUR

'I've picked up some extra provisions,' Carrie said, when she returned. 'I'd done a food shop, but it was mainly enough for just you to start with.'

Jules sat at the kitchen table and watched Carrie unpack.

'I'm sorry. I'm being such a nuisance.'

'Of course you're not,' Carrie replied, placing a packet of risotto rice on the counter.

'I bet Guy thinks that I am. You've only just moved in together and I'm here being pathetic and not wanting to spend a night on my own.'

'You are not being pathetic, and he doesn't mind. He's going to have supper with his gran. They're very close. She virtually brought him up.'

'I remember you saying.'

'I'll introduce you to her while you're here. She's a lovely lady.'

Jules felt herself flooded with anxiety again. She really didn't know what was happening to her. She wasn't a nervous person. The opposite, in fact.

'Please don't.'

Carrie looked up.

'Not yet, so you don't have to worry. I know you need some quiet time.'

Jules nodded. She wanted to be alone, but not be alone. Quiet time meant time for thoughts. Did Gavin feel guilty or had he just seen her as a way to get some more money and a bit of sex, actually a lot of sex, and now he was satisfied in more ways than one?

'Jules!'

Carrie clicked her fingers in front of Jules's face.

'I'm going to make a tomato risotto and I picked up a couple of pieces of sea bass to go with it. Is that okay?'

'Yes, fine. Nothing tastes right at the moment though.'

'I could cook you something really rank then and it wouldn't matter,' Carrie joked. 'Like that cold cucumber soup I made when I first moved in with you. Remember that?'

'How could I forget it!'

'Or the curried eggs. God, they made us fart!'

'They were disgusting, too.'

Carrie pulled a bottle of wine out of the fridge.

'I don't know about you, but I could do with a glass of something. I'm whacked.'

'I'm sorry. It's such a long way from here to Manchester and you've done the journey twice in two days. You really shouldn't have.'

'Yes, I should, but I wouldn't say no if you're up to chopping a couple of shallots and then taking a turn stirring the risotto.'

Carrie took out two tall wine glasses from the glass-fronted cupboard and half-filled them with a grassy-scented wine.

'To you,' she said, handing one to Jules.

'To friendship,' Jules replied, clinking her glass against Carrie's.

'I'll drink to that as well,' Carrie said, taking a double gulp.

Twenty minutes later, as Carrie carefully added more stock to the risotto and Jules gently stirred, it occurred to her that at this particular point in time there couldn't have been a better dish. There was something about the process that was meditative and soothing.

'I saw a girl earlier,' she said, 'by the barn. About fourteen. Very pretty.'

'That'll be Tasha,' Carrie said. 'Rita's granddaughter.'

'Her mother was looking for her.'

'Christabel. She's always looking for Tasha and Tasha is always trying to escape.'

'She did look as if she was hiding.'

Carrie stooped to extricate a large hunk of parmesan from the fridge.

'Don't blame her.'

'I didn't give her away.'

Carrie threw her a smile.

'Good for you.'

Jules briefly felt proud of herself, as if she, too, had bestowed some breathing space to someone in need.

'I felt as if she needed protecting. Maybe it's because I used to hide at her age as well. I wasn't very good at it though. Mum always found me.'

'You didn't have a hundred-acre farm to take advantage of. A three-bedroomed semi in Sidcup doesn't offer the same scope and your mum does have that famous sixth sense of hers.'

Jules pulled a wry face and stirred the rice. The fragrance of tomatoes and fresh thyme from the garden, mixed with the saltiness of the fish in the frying pan, wafted up to her. She had to admit that even for her grief-compromised taste buds it smelled good.

'I suppose I'm sort of hiding now,' she said.

'Not hiding, incubating,' Carrie said, removing the pasta bowls from the bottom oven of the range. 'There's a distinct difference.'

Jules bit into a grain of rice. Incubating. She liked that. It made her feel less like a victim.

'This is ready,' she said, lifting the pan on to a hen-shaped metal trivet.

'Fish, too,' Carrie said. 'Perfect timing. We make a good team.'

Carrie began to serve.

I'm going to make an effort to eat this, Jules thought, not just for Carrie, but for myself.

Jules lay in bed. Wow, it was dark. The clouds had gathered during the evening and now rain pitter-pattered against the window. Her sleep patterns were all over the place, partly due to the night shifts at work and partly due to Gavin. She got up and sat on the little window seat, peering out into the night. Everything always seemed so much worse in the small hours. It was beautiful and comfortable here and Carrie was being so kind, but she couldn't stay long. She needed to do something, to keep busy, to earn some money.

'I don't want to mention the elephant in the room,' Carrie had said as they cleared the table after supper, 'but he hasn't got access to your bank accounts, has he?'

'No!'

'You're sure? He hasn't looked over your shoulder and seen you type your pin number into the machine or ever ordered anything on your card.'

'Once or twice, but he wouldn't...'

'Maybe not, but better to be safe than sorry.'

So she'd made Jules call the bank there and then to put a stop on her account. She should have done it before, of course, and Carrie said it was lucky that he hadn't used her credit card details.

Funny that she couldn't even feel fortunate for that. Funny that as soon as you got away from somewhere you realised what you really should be doing, should have done or not done. But she was too tired to think about anything to do with her old life. She yawned and padded back to bed. Give in, a voice whispered as she sank back against the soft pillow, allow yourself to be looked after for a change. That's really not so hard. Is it? Actually, Jules thought, yes, it is, but she closed her eyes and finally drifted off to sleep.

PURPOSE

'Oh my,' Eliza whispered. 'She's in such a bad way, poor lamb. Couldn't even eat all of her supper.'

'Come away,' Isaac whispered from the doorway. 'You'll wake her, and she might see you.'

Eliza ignored him. She stood by the bed and reached out to touch the girl's dark blonde hair spread across the pillow like strands of seaweed. Looked as if it was some time since she had washed it properly. Hair was so important, Eliza thought. If your hair didn't feel right, you didn't feel right. Their guest may have been a fully grown woman, but curled up on her side, her pale face full of sorrow even in sleep, she looked young and vulnerable.

Eliza allowed her hand to float away.

'That's not likely,' she said. 'The majority of people are completely unaware of our existence.'

'But some are,' Isaac said, 'and as I keep trying to remind you, not all are amenable.'

Eliza looked back towards Jules.

'If she is a friend of Carrie's I can't believe she would do us harm.'

'Maybe not,' Isaac mused, 'but we would not want to alarm her. When people are afraid, they become unpredictable.'

'She is so in need of comfort though, Isaac. It is worth the risk, isn't it, to give her a little of that?'

Her husband stared at her for a moment in a way which she didn't recognise. Then he shook his head.

'Do as you will, Eliza,' he huffed.

She stifled her indignation and summoned up her previous feelings of compassion before turning back towards the bed. Reaching for the duvet she pulled it up softly to cover Jules's bare shoulder before blowing a kiss to settle on one of those pallid cheeks.

'You do not have to worry, Isaac,' she said, following him down the stairs and into the sitting room. 'She didn't stir, and she'll sleep until morning now.'

Isaac settled himself into his favourite tall-backed chair by the old stone fireplace.

'I had forgotten,' he said, 'how nerve-wracking it is to have a new visitor.'

Eliza wanted to go and perch on his lap as usual, but he was still out of sorts. His form was jagged.

Looking at him reminded her of the hedgehogs which resided at the bottom of the garden. Instead, she sank onto the sofa and tucked her legs beneath her.

'We got used to Carrie,' she said, fiddling with the frill on the hem of her dress. She did so love the way it ruffled against her ankles as she walked. 'We shall become used to Jules, too.'

'Unless she leaves,' Isaac replied.

'Why would you say that?' Eliza gasped. 'She has only just arrived.'

'Something I discerned.'

'How did you discern it? Did she say something to Carrie?'

'You are not the only one with intuition, Eliza. Sometimes I, too, pick up on thoughts which escape into the ether.'

'Oh!'

'So all the more reason not to alarm her in any way.'

'Absolutely not,' Eliza said, shaking her head and allowing her hair to tumble over her shoulders. 'If she leaves too soon the cottage won't have the time required to work its magic.'

'I believe Carrie knows that. She'll try her best to keep her here.'

'And if she can't?' Eliza fretted. 'Oh, Isaac, is this my fault?'

'Why would it be your fault, my love?'

'I don't know. Have I done something wrong? Has our brief marital disagreement tarnished the atmosphere in some way so that she can't recognise the healing that she'll find here?'

Isaac moved from the sofa and settled himself next to her. He kissed her softly on the lips.

'There are some things, my love, even you can't control.'

'But I can't bear all the pain in the world, Isaac. I can't bear the way people treat one another with such, such...'

'Heartlessness.'

'Yes! I couldn't believe what I was hearing earlier. The way that man treated Jules, duped her.'

'But she is lucky because she has a friend like Carrie to help her. Some people do not even have that.'

'And she has this house,' Eliza added. 'And us. We're her friends, too, even if she doesn't know it. And we will do whatever it takes to restore her faith in humankind.'

Isaac wrapped his arms around his wife and buried his face in her neck.

'You,' he whispered, 'are the best of women.'

'And you,' she replied, 'are the best of husbands and we're stronger together.'

Isaac nodded.

'Together,' he repeated. 'I'm sorry I left you, Eliza. I promise that it won't happen again.'

She nodded. Of course he meant it, just as she meant it when she declared that she would refrain from meddling, but sometimes one just couldn't help oneself. Sometimes promises had to be broken.

When Jules woke up it was after eleven o'clock. She wandered downstairs in a clean lilac dressing gown, which she found on the end of her bed, to discover Carrie sitting at the kitchen table with a smiley-faced woman in a spotted, rose-pink, crisp cotton dress.

'Oh, sorry,' she said, 'I didn't realise there was anyone else here. I thought the voices were coming from the radio. I haven't showered or washed my hair properly and I'd have got dressed.'

The woman rose from her chair in a surprisingly sprightly fashion and extended a hand.

'I'm Rita. I look after things here and no need at all to apologise for anything. Between you and me, a dressing gown is my favourite item of clothing. Would wear mine all day every day if I could. Might look a bit odd at the farmer's market though. Having said that there are some pretty odd people there, so I'd probably just fit right in.'

She threw back her head, stuck out her chest and let out a throaty laugh which reverberated around the whole kitchen. So this was Saint Rita, Jules thought, the solver of all problems and bringer of smiles and cake.

'I'm very pleased to meet you,' she said, shaking the warm, soft hand. 'And it's lovely to be able to tell you in person how much I appreciate the way you looked after Carrie when she first moved here.'

'Oh, it was nothing,' Rita protested. 'I would do the same for anyone.'

She threw a glance towards Carrie who was leaning back in her chair and beaming from behind her mug of coffee.

'Mind you,' Rita said, conspiratorially to Jules, 'I've got a bit of a soft spot for this one.'

'Me too,' Jules replied.

'Stop it, you two,' Carrie said, 'you're embarrassing me.'

'Anyway,' Rita said, 'I must be on my way. I've got some deliveries to make on the other side of the island. I just wanted to make sure that you were all settled, Jules. You don't mind if I call you that, do you? I had no idea Carrie was here until I saw the car, but I needed to talk to her anyway.'

'I'm so sorry I can't help you out,' Carrie said. 'But I've had this meeting planned in Bembridge forever and it's had to be rearranged twice already.'

'No worries,' Rita replied. 'I'm sure I can find someone else to collect Tasha. If necessary, she can just wait at The Pottery until I've finished my deliveries. Lance won't mind and Erin will be pleased.'

She turned to Jules.

'You must have passed The Pottery on your way here yesterday. It's a wonderful place and my granddaughter is doing a summer course there and needs picking up at four.'

'Remember, Jules?' Carrie said. 'I pointed it out to you.'

Jules nodded.

'Lance has worked hard to make a go of it,' Rita mused, 'and it hasn't been easy, bless him. With losing his wife and bringing up two children. Mind you, we all seem to be snowed under these days, one way or another, don't we? All of these gadgets and inventions, which are meant to make life easier but just seem to me to create a lot of stress and complications. The Lord is my shepherd, I remind myself when it all gets too much. He leads me beside quiet waters, He refreshes my soul. Except the waters are sometimes whipped up into a frenzy and my soul is parched like too many other people's.' She burst into a peal of laughter. 'Listen to me, feeling sorry for myself. I don't have anything to complain about really. I live on the perfect island, have a comfortable home, clean water, good neighbours and the most wonderful grandchildren, two of them living right next door to me. How lucky is that!'

'I think I saw Tasha yesterday,' Jules said, 'sitting at the side of the barn.'

'Hiding no doubt,' Rita said. 'Feel like doing that myself sometimes, I can tell you.'

'We waved to each other,' Jules said.

'I'd forgotten that you've already met!' Carrie interjected.

'Well, no, not exactly.'

'You wouldn't mind picking her up, would you?'

Yes, yes, I would. I'd mind a lot. Was Carrie deliberately ignoring her signals?

'Rita has an old jalopy you can use. It's fine for short trips and you're still insured, aren't you?'

'Tasha wouldn't want a complete stranger collecting her and...'

Jules felt her breath coming in little gasps. Panic gripped at her chest. She couldn't do this. It was such a simple request, but she just couldn't do it.

'Don't you worry, my love,' Rita said. 'I wouldn't dream of imposing. You're here on a break, not to run around after other folks.'

The pressure behind her breastbone eased a little.

'I'm sorry,' Jules said, aware that she sounded slightly out of breath and as if she was about to burst into tears. 'Normally it would be fine, but I'm a bit useless at the moment.'

'Oh, dearie,' Rita said. 'We all feel useless from time to time. It's part of the human condition. But as it says in the Bible, 'even the hairs of your head are all numbered. Fear not, therefore; you are of more value than many sparrows.' Matthew: Ten, I think. And there are a lot of sparrows, aren't there? Now they *are* busy little birds and such lovely tuneful voices. Anyway, I digress and I must get on. Remember, if there's anything you need, I'm just around the corner. You're always welcome at the farmhouse and the kettle's always at the ready. Carrie can attest to that.'

Jules and Carrie sat in silence for a moment after Rita had whirled out.

'Why did you do that?' Jules said at last, when the air had settled. 'I thought you were the one who wanted me to veg out and do absolutely nothing.'

'And you were the one saying that you might need some distractions. You're always saying that you like to help.'

'That was the old me.'

'I don't think the new you will be that much different,' Carrie said gently.

Jules's eyes widened.

'I hope she will be. I hope she'll be completely different.'

'I'm sure Rita would have some biblical quote which says that helping others is a way of helping yourself,' Carrie murmured.

'Tasha did look like a child with the weight of the world on her shoulders and she *was* hiding.'

'She has a difficult mother.'

'Who doesn't?' Jules quipped.

'Your mother isn't anything like Christabel. She's gone to the mainland, apparently, on one of her spur of the moment jaunts, but she'll be back later, and Rita wants Tasha home before that to avoid any trouble.'

'Why would there be trouble with Tasha going to The Pottery?'

'I think,' Carrie said slowly, 'that Christabel has tried out her charms on Lance over the years without much success. You will soon learn if you stay here for a while that Christabel doesn't react well to not getting her own way. Sometimes she's eager for Tasha to go to The Pottery and presumably thinks of it as another opportunity to enchant Lance and other times she goes into a major sulk and resolves never to let Tash see Erin again out of school. Erin is Lance's daughter and Tasha's best friend.'

'What about Tasha's father? Can't he collect her?'

'Up to his eyes with the harvest and Rita wouldn't want to drag him away. Her whole life is devoted to making Alastair, Tasha and Will's lives as smooth as possible, which I can tell you, with a daughter-in-law like Christabel is no mean feat.'

Jules was quiet for a moment.

'So if Tasha isn't home before her mother returns, she'll be in trouble?'

'Maybe, depending upon what sort of mood Christabel is in, but don't worry. I'm sure we can sort it out.'

At five to four Jules pulled the boneshaker of a jeep into the little car park at the front of Island Pottery. Her shoulder ached from yanking at the gearstick, and she massaged the side of her neck after pulling up the hand brake. It was only a couple of months since she'd driven, but she felt completely traumatised by the car, the country roads and the feeling that she didn't trust herself.

Before Carrie had headed off to her appointment they'd spent most of the day sitting in the garden talking about everything except Gavin. Actually, Carrie had talked and she had listened, the calm and steady tone of her friend's voice and the warmth of the sun actually helping her to doze at one point.

'Jules,' Carrie had said, lightly touching her hand and bringing her back to the real world from a distressing dream where she crashed the jeep into a ditch. 'I've got to go. I'm really sorry. Rita's left the car at the front of the cottage. Keys are on the kitchen table. Will you be all right?'

'Mmm,' she replied with not much conviction.

'It's a bit of a tank, that vehicle. Don't be afraid to use brute force.'

'What time is it?'

'Just after three. You've got nearly an hour. The Pottery's less than ten minutes down the road. Just keep going. You can't miss it.'

But she almost had missed it. She'd nearly gone shooting past because she was thinking about Gavin. It was as if the beauty of the island emphasised her feelings of hopelessness. Another car pulled up next to her and a woman with a flowing scarf, flowing skirt and flowing hair got out.

'What a glorious day,' she said, smiling at Jules through the open window. 'And I absolutely love this place. It has such a wonderful energy. Are you waiting here or walking through?'

She tilted her head towards the brick archway in the corner of the car park.

'Oh, I'm not sure,' Jules replied. 'I've not been here before. In fact, I've only just arrived on the island.'

The woman looked as if she knew that already and Jules felt something curl up inside her. She obviously looked like a newcomer, as if she didn't fit in. She'd felt like that at school with all of those cool girls making fun of her for her braces and plaits and homemade clothes.

'You're in for a treat. This island is the best place in the world. You can take the Caribbean or the Mediterranean any day. This beats them all, as far as I'm concerned.'

The woman smiled and gestured to Jules.

'Shall we? Are you on pick-up duty or going to the tearoom?'

Jules felt trapped. She turned to lock the car, even though the other woman didn't bother to do the same, and reluctantly fell into step beside her.

'I'm collecting for a friend.'

They walked through to an area bordered on three sides with low buildings; converted stables or cow sheds, Jules guessed. The windows were all flung open and inside the far building Jules could see young heads bobbing about.

'I bet they're running late. Lance has no concept of time. Just gets carried away with what he's doing.'

She wandered over and stuck her head through a window and

following a brief chat with a man with curly brown hair and an intense, worried looking face, she returned.

'They'll be a while yet. Time for a cup of tea,' she said to Jules. 'My treat. What do you fancy?'

She had an overwhelming desire to run away. This wasn't meant to happen. She was meant to come, collect Tasha and go, drop her at home and retreat to the safety of the cottage.

'Oh, I'm not sure... perhaps I'll wait in the car.'

'It's a bit hot for that, isn't it?'

'Well, yes, I suppose so.'

'We can get a table in the shade over there under the sweet chestnut. Such an interesting tree. It's often mentioned in folk tales concerned with sustenance and survival.'

She twirled around and held out her arms, her hair rippling, her hands presented as if in the process of accepting something.

'The creative vibes here are just amazing,' she said, coming to a stop and smiling beatifically. 'You don't have to sit with me if you'd rather be on your own, I won't be offended, but please let me buy you a welcome drink. They do great smoothies here if you're not a fan of tea.'

Jules didn't mean to frown, to give an impression of unfriendliness, and she didn't want to give away the fact that she'd normally run a mile from someone who reminded her so much of her mother.

'I'm sorry if I appear rude. I'm not great at conversation at the moment.'

You're good with people, Jules, she said to herself. You work as part of a team, deal with parents and grandparents, doctors, hospital porters, all sorts of different people, every day. This social phobia is getting out of hand. You don't want to go back to the time after Dad died when you totally withdrew into yourself. You've worked hard to overcome that.

'Then let's just sit together,' the woman said. 'Talking can be very over-rated at times and not everyone wants an over-enthusiastic welcome to a new place.'

She smiled in such an understanding way that Jules felt flooded with guilt.

'I'm Jo, by the way.'

'Jules, and...'

Jo's eyes flickered briefly as if she knew something that Jules didn't, which was completely ridiculous.

'...I'd love to have a cup of tea with you, Jo. Just normal tea. Thank you.'

Jules took a seat at one of the outside tables and listened to the happy chatter of the other people waiting to pick up their sons or daughters or grandchildren. There were little jam jars of flowers in the centre of each table and a bee landed on a pale pink dahlia. Jules sat back and watched as it gathered pollen.

'Here we are,' Jo said, placing a tray on the table. 'I picked up some cake as well. It's a sin to have tea at this time of day without a slice of something sweet. Raspberry Bakewell and a pistachio slice. Take your pick or I can cut them in half and we can both have a bit of each. If you don't want any, I can take it back for my son, Dan. He never says no to any sort of food.'

'They do look good,' Jules said. 'I'll try a tiny piece of the Bakewell tart, please.'

Jo passed her a vintage flowered plate and cut up the cakes before pouring the tea. Jules waved away the offer of milk.

'I really don't know why you don't drink it black,' Gavin used to say as he measured a teaspoon full of milk into her drinks. Any more and she'd have to risk upsetting him and chuck the tea away.

Her worrying about upsetting him. That was rich! She nibbled at the shortcrust pastry and settled back in her chair. Through the window she could hear children's laughter and a man's rich voice telling them all how well they had done. She glanced at Jo, who had her head thrown back and eyes closed.

'Are you Isle of Wight born and bred?' Jules asked.

'Goodness, no,' Jo said, placing her cup back in its saucer and breaking off a small piece of pistachio cake. 'We've only been here a few years.'

Suddenly Jules sensed that she was more guarded. Her body language had changed. Only slightly, but Jules was used to noticing things like that.

'It feels like a good place to move to. My friend settled here in the spring. I'm visiting her, sort of.'

'That's nice. Good friends are very important.'

'Carrie's the best.'

Jo nodded slowly.

'You know her? Does everyone know everyone else on this island?'

'It feels like that sometimes,' Jo said, half laughing, but her green eyes were wary, and she looked vaguely familiar.

'I'm staying at Hideaway Cottage. Do we, I mean, this sounds ridiculous,' Jules stuttered, 'but do we know each other? You seem familiar. You didn't have your son at the maternity unit in Manchester, did you? I remember a lot of my mums, but sometimes I bump into someone, and they tell me I looked after them when they had their baby.'

The woman hesitated. Her eyes studied Jules very carefully.

'I'm from somewhere near London so no is the answer to your last question.'

She leaned closer and wrapped her hands completely around her teacup, holding it steady in the saucer.

'We've met before though, but not for a very long time. I think you were about eight. I'm a friend of your mother's. She still refers to me as Claudia from time to time, although I wish she wouldn't. My name is Jo now.'

Jules gasped.

'You are the person who sent Mum the details about Hideaway Cottage, which became a sanctuary for Carrie and caused her to meet Guy and...'

'...and now you're here,' Jo whispered. 'I thought I recognised you, but...'

'...but I look more like my dad so not surprising you didn't.'

'You look like both of your parents,' Jo replied.

Except I want to look more like Dad, Jules thought. I don't want to look like Mum. She studied the woman opposite. She did remember her vaguely.

'You look different to how I remember, too.'

'Well, I am older,' Jo said, biting into a pistachio.

'And your hair is different. Nice, but different.'

Jo put a hand to her mahogany-coloured hair.

'Thank you. I do miss your mum. We were good friends.'

'I remember now. You left quite suddenly. I can't believe the coincidence of us meeting up like this.'

'Some believe there are no such things as coincidences, more inevitabilities. You don't know why I moved away?'

Jules shook her head.

'Mum never said.'

'My husband mistreated me. Badly. I had to get away with Daniel. I left my daughters behind, changed my name, grew my hair and made a new life for myself. I pray every day that he'll never find us.'

'I'm so sorry.'

Jo shrugged.

'Life can test us to our limits, Jules. No one is immune.'

'No. I suppose not.'

'What do you think about Hideaway Cottage? Just walking past it gives me goosebumps.'

'I only arrived yesterday, but it's very cocooning.'

'I expect it was difficult to drag yourself away so soon after getting there.'

'It was a bit spur of the moment,' Jules mumbled. 'I'm doing a favour for Rita – collecting Tasha. I don't even know her. All we've done is wave at each other from a distance. She probably won't want to come with me.'

'Now's the time to find out.'

Jules stood up as Tasha paused outside the studio door. A tall man appeared behind her and put his hand on her shoulder, whispering something in her ear. She nodded, glanced around the courtyard and then pointed towards Jules.

'Hello,' the man said, approaching with long, loping strides, his hand still firmly attached to Tasha's shoulder, part propelling her along, part preventing her from running away, Jules suspected. Tasha looked as apprehensive as she felt.

The man held out his free hand, smiling at Jo and leaning across the table towards Jules at the same time. Just as quickly as he extended his hand, he withdrew it and wiped it on his grey jeans, which looked as if they had seen better days.

'Sorry, still a bit covered in clay,' he said. 'As usual. Probably better stick to hello. I'm Lance.' He smiled, making his eyes crinkle at the corners. 'I understand you've kindly offered to give Tash a ride home.'

'Yes.'

'I could have walked,' Tasha said, seemingly fascinated by the gravel at her feet. 'I'm not a baby.'

Lance's cool grey eyes travelled from Jules back towards the girl at his side.

'No one is suggesting you are,' he said, 'but it's a narrow lane in parts and sometimes cars go along it too fast. Your granny worries about you when you walk. We all worry about you.'

'I could have stayed with Erin, and you could have run me home later,' Tasha persisted.

Jules's heart felt as if it was sinking into her boots. She didn't blame the girl at all. She didn't want to spend time with a complete stranger either at the moment.

'You could, but this lady here...'

His eyes met hers.

'Jules,' she whispered.

'That's right. Sorry, brain's a bit frazzled at this time of the day.'

Jules noticed his finger pressure increase very slightly on Tasha's baby blue sweatshirt.

'Jules has kindly offered to do your granny a favour because you don't want to be too late back, do you?'

Tasha's eyelashes fluttered.

'Suppose not.'

Lance's hand moved and he rubbed Tasha's back briefly.

'We'll see you tomorrow,' said an elfin-faced girl of about the same age who had wandered over to stand next to Tasha. 'And you can stay for supper another time.'

'If I'm allowed.'

'More chance of that if you get home when you're supposed to,' Lance persisted.

'Mum says I'm a nuisance.'

'You're not. I promise you,' Lance reassured her.

'Here's a nuisance,' Jo said, obviously trying to lighten the mood.

A boy with an impish face bounded towards them.

'Jules, meet Daniel. What have you made today, monkey?'

'A spaceship sugar bowl,' Daniel said with a grin.

'Cool,' she said. 'For me to take with me on my journey to another planet.'

'So you don't forget me,' Daniel said as he high-fived his mother.

'As if!'

'And what did you make, Tasha?' Jules asked.

'A jug.'

'And very beautiful it is, too,' Lance said.

'Come on, Tash,' Erin said, 'let's go and get your bag.'

'No dawdling,' Lance said, as both girls disappeared through a clematis-clad gate with a private notice on the front.

'It's where we live,' Lance explained.

Jules glanced over to where Jo had gravitated towards other parents, and wished she'd come back over and keep her company.

'Handy for work,' he continued with a smile.

Jules felt ridiculously tongue-tied.

'Rita said you're staying at Hideaway Cottage. That's a lovely spot.'

'Yes.'

'Are you here for long?'

'No.'

'Shame. There's a lot to see and do on the island; lovely walks, beautiful beaches, the Roman villa is amazing if that's your thing. Or maybe you don't want to do anything,' he added.

'Not really.'

Suddenly he frowned and turned on his toes, flattening the grass into a little whirlpool swirl.

'I'll go and see where those girls are and send Tasha out to you.'

'Tell her I'll wait in the car,' Jules called after him.

<h1 style="text-align:center">SIX</h1>

Jules banged her head against the steering wheel. That had been so rude. He was just trying to make polite conversation. But what did it matter? She'd never have to see him again. Except here he was accompanying Tasha across the car park. Maybe he thought the girl would make a bolt for it if he didn't deliver her personally. As he opened the passenger door and leaned in a little, she got a waft of clay mixed with something fresh and green.

'Just a thought,' he said, looking decidedly awkward and holding out a leaflet. 'If you're at a bit of a loose end one day. Not that you will be probably. There's a lot to see and do here. It's just... well... I thought if you get fed up with beaches' – he half laughed – 'which is a stupid thing to say because no one ever gets fed up with beaches, do they?'

Jules's eyes widened.

'Anyway, if you want something to take your mind off things – which we all do sometimes, don't we – throwing a pot or clay modelling is very good for that.'

She kept her palms, which were beginning to sweat, fixed to the steering wheel.

'I really don't think...'

'No,' he said, his cheeks turning pink. 'Stupid of me. Of course.

Not your thing. I'll leave it with you anyway. Perhaps you could put it in the cottage for future guests.'

He rested the leaflet on the dashboard. Jules felt relieved when he stood back to allow Tasha to climb in even though the girl still oozed resentment.

'See you tomorrow, Tash,' he said through the open window.

She didn't reply, but Jules noticed that, half hidden by the bag on her lap, she crossed both of her fingers.

'And enjoy your hol... enjoy your stay on the island,' he said to Jules without really looking at her.

She gave him a cursory nod and turned the ignition key. The Land Rover made a horrible coughing sound followed by silence. Jules felt her heart begin to race. Please, please don't break down here, she silently begged. Sweat was gathering at the nape of her neck.

'We may have to walk after all,' she muttered.

'It always does that,' Tasha replied. 'You need to give it more gas.'

She was acutely aware of Lance watching. At the second turn of the key, she pressed her foot down hard on the accelerator and the engine roared into life. She heaved the gearstick into reverse and the car shot backwards, peppering stones at Lance's legs. He jumped out of the way and she knew she should apologise, but all she could think about was getting out of there and back to the sanctuary of Hideaway Cottage.

Tasha kept her face turned to the window for the whole ten-minute drive. The silence was a relief as was the air from the open windows rushing across her face and lifting her hair to cool the back of her neck.

'Here you are,' she said, pulling into the entrance to Orchard Farm.

'You can drop me here,' Tasha said. 'I think I can be trusted to walk the rest of the way without getting squashed.'

Jules slowed down and swerved to avoid a particularly bad pothole.

'I'm sure you can, but Rita asked me to leave the car at the farm.'

Tasha shrugged. The redbrick farm with tall sash windows and a yellow rose growing up the front of the house appeared on the left.

'Any idea where I should put it?' Jules asked.

Tasha's hand was already on the handle ready to leap out, even though they were still moving.

'We usually park the cars in the yard at the back.'

She pointed further down the track, past the house.

'Can you give these keys to Rita?' Jules asked, when she'd positioned the jeep in what seemed to be a sensible place out of the way.

Tasha took them and slid out, striding towards a back door flanked by tubs of brightly coloured geraniums. Jules stood by the side of the car for a moment and watched her before turning to head back up the track.

'Thanks for the ride,' Tasha called.

'It's okay,' Jules called back, barely turning her head as she carried on walking.

'And for not snitching on me yesterday.'

She slowed. A tribe of sparrows flew out of the hedge to her right. She could feel their wings stirring the warm air.

'Do you want a cup of tea?'

'Not rea...'

'Everybody's out. It feels a bit weird when there's nobody here.'

Jules stopped and looked back. In the half shadow of the house Tasha looked vulnerable and unsure of herself. She sighed and unclenched her hands, which she realised had been balled into tight little fists, before retracing her steps.

'A cold drink would be good.'

Tasha's whole demeanour softened.

'Granny's usually got some homemade lemon barley in the fridge.'

'That sounds delicious.'

The kitchen was large and square with a dresser in the centre of one wall crammed with random pieces of pottery. The kitchen cupboards were painted sunshine yellow, a pile of magazines formed a tower next to one of the large leather chairs in the big bay window, and gleaming copper pans created a higgledy-piggledy line on a shelf above the range. Tasha took a couple of tall glasses from a glass-fronted cupboard and placed them on the table.

'You can sit down if you like,' she said.

Jules pulled out a chair as Tasha lifted a large glass jug from the fridge. She took a long spoon from a drawer and gave the cloudy liquid a good stir before carefully filling the glasses, making sure they each got a slice of lemon.

'That's very good,' Jules said, taking a sip.

'There'll be cake if you want a piece.'

Jules put up her hand.

'Not for me. I've already had some.'

Tasha sat down opposite her.

'Sorry I was rude. I'm sure you didn't want to break into your holiday to pick me up.'

'It's not really a holiday.'

Tasha gazed at her from over the rim of her glass.

'I suppose you'd describe it as an escape,' Jules said.

'Escaping is good,' Tasha replied, 'isn't it?'

'Depends what you're escaping from,' Jules said, with a shrug. 'Must be lots of places to escape to around a farm.'

'The barn's my favourite,' Tasha said, 'and The Pottery. I like going there. That feels like an escape.'

'You're making a jug?'

'I like making jugs, different shapes and sizes, different types of handles or no handles at all. Lance says I'm good at it.'

'I think that I was a bit rude to Lance.'

'He won't mind.' She looked directly at Jules, her eyes a mixture of greys, greens and hazel. 'He's right about pottery being therapeutic. You forget everything when you're throwing a pot. You should give it a try.'

'I've done a bit in the past, at school.'

'You're an expert then,' Tasha said, a broad smile suddenly lighting up her face. 'Erin's my best friend. Is Carrie your best friend?'

'Yes.'

'I like Carrie. Have you been friends since school?'

'No. I haven't known her that long actually. She moved in with me when her relationship broke up. She had to move out of her place, and I'd put an advert in a local newsagent's window looking for someone to share because my previous lodger had moved out. We hit it off straight away. Sometimes that happens.'

Jules felt breathless. Apart from Carrie that was the longest communication she'd had with anyone for over a week.

'I haven't got lots of friends.'

'That doesn't matter. It's the quality of your friendships that's important.'

'That's what Granny says. Mum thinks I'm a bit of a billy-no-mates. She wants me to be one of the cool crowd.' She pulled at her sweatshirt. 'She thinks I'm scruffy.'

'Well, there's no point wearing anything special when you're working with clay.'

'Mum's got big plans for Will and me. Will's my brother.'

'Where's he today?'

'On the farm with Dad. That's all he wants to do, all day, every day. He wants to take over the farm when he's older.'

'What about you?'

'I'd love to be a potter, but Lance says there's no money in it and I need to get other qualifications.'

'He's probably right.'

'What do you do?'

'I'm a midwife.'

'Cool.'

'Yes, it is. Stressful, though. Quite a lot of responsibility.'

'Writing things down helps with stress,' Tasha said. 'I keep a diary, and it helps me sort my head out.'

Jules nodded.

'I know. I used to write a diary. Got me through some tough times, especially when my dad died.'

She felt the tears begin to well up. She must not cry, not in front of Tasha who would be so embarrassed.

'How old were you?'

'Fourteen.'

'I'm fourteen. The only person I've lost is my grandpa. It's four years now and I still miss him a lot. Granny talks about him all of the time, sometimes as if he's still here. I'm not sure if that makes it better or worse. Perhaps you ought to write a diary again now,' Tasha suggested.

'Maybe you're right. I filled hundreds of pages after my dad died. I sort of stopped speaking and wrote everything down instead. I used to reply to my mum with notes, if I replied at all.'

'My mum would be apoplectic if I did that. Did you get in trouble?'

'No. She was extraordinarily patient. I've only just realised that. It must have been very difficult for her.'

Jules gulped and a tear escaped and rolled down her cheek.

Tasha went to the dresser and brought back a box of tissues.

'Sorry I upset you,' she said.

'Sorry I'm crying in your kitchen.'

'It's not my kitchen. It's Granny's and it's okay. She won't mind. I've cried a lot in this kitchen. She understands. Mum says I need to get a grip. Says crying won't get me anywhere. She just shouts.'

'Everyone has their thing.' Jules sniffed.

'Means her mascara doesn't run and her nose doesn't go red. She's got this vertical line between her eyebrows though. It's like an anger line. She uses these things called Frownies at night to try and make it go away, smooth it out. If she just stopped shouting, it would probably soften all on its own.'

She paused. 'Or maybe not.' She looked up at the clock above the back door. 'She might be back soon. I'd better go home. There'll be hell to pay if she finds me here again.'

'Where's home?'

'The bungalow behind that building over there. You can just see the edge of the roof. Granny and Grandpa built it to move into when they retired, but then Grandpa got ill and died and we're still there and she's still here.'

She placed the jug back in the fridge and took both glasses over to the sink.

Jules stood up.

'Won't that house be empty, too?'

Tasha nodded.

'Yes, but I'll be all right now.' She cast a sidelong glance at Jules. 'I get a bit anxious sometimes.'

'Were you anxious about me picking you up from The Pottery?'

Tasha nodded.

'Although I thought you'd be all right if you were a friend of Carrie's.'

Jules bit her bottom lip.

'I'll let you into a secret. I was nervous about it, too. I'm not very good at talking to new people at the moment.'

'You could always have written me a note,' Tasha quipped.

Jules smiled.

'I could have done, but then you'd have thought I was really weird.'

'I wouldn't now though.'

'I'll remember that when I don't feel up to talking.'

'That's what I like about throwing a pot. You don't have to talk. You just concentrate on breathing and the rhythm of the wheel and the feel of the clay. It's magical. You should try it, you know.'

She placed the washed glasses on the draining board and ushered Jules out of the door.

'Thanks for the chat,' she said.

'Thanks for the drink and the tissues,' Jules said, still clutching a clump in her hand.

'We criers need Kleenex,' Tasha said with a smile. 'See you around, Jules.'

'Maybe – or if you don't see me, you might hear me blubbing.'

'Gotta get those tears out,' Tasha joked, leaning forward to give Jules a quick, shy hug and then almost running away, but turning to wave at the corner of the old cowshed before disappearing out of sight.

Jules kicked at a loose stone and strolled back up the driveway towards Hideaway Cottage, remembering how difficult it was to be fourteen. Peoples' lives were so complicated. You could never really know what was going on even if you knew that person well, let alone if you'd only just met them.

'What's this?' Carrie asked, plucking something from the back pocket of Jules's jeans. 'Are you thinking about doing a course at The Pottery?'

'What? No! Certainly not!'

Jules stared at the leaflet Carrie was studying intently.

'I've got no idea how that got in there. I'm sure I left it in the front of the Land Rover.'

'Didn't you pick it up then?'

'He gave it to me. The chap who runs the place.'

'Lance. He's a sweetie, isn't he?'

'A bit pushy.'

'He worked really hard to get the business back on an even keel after his wife died. He had to close it for a few months and then Covid struck and now people are being really careful how they spend their money. He's not exactly had an easy time.'

Jules took her tea out into the garden and sat on the bench at the back of the house. She gazed across the lawn towards the sea, a silver ribbon in the distance. Sunshine, tea, friendship. It was amazing how such things could make life seem a tiny bit more bearable.

'The pottery seemed to be doing well enough today,' she said as Carrie sat beside her. 'Must have been twenty kids on that course.'

'That's good. How was Tasha?'

'She warmed up.'

'She can be introverted. It's good that she's got Erin. She makes sure Tasha doesn't wallow too much.'

'Is there just the one child?'

'No, there's Fitz. He's a bit younger and a bit of a handful, I gather. I've only met him a couple of times. Sarah, Lance's wife, was pregnant with Fitz when she discovered she'd got cancer. She delayed treatment until after he was born. They thought it had been successful, but less than a year later it came back.'

'That's tough. How old was she?'

'Not sure. Not that much older than us, I think. They're not from the island either so they haven't got the usual support network, although everyone here tries to help out when and where they can, as you may have gathered.'

'It's a proper little utopia,' Jules said.

'Don't knock it.'

Carrie's tone was definitely defensive.

'I'm not. It just seems a bit too good to be true. Not everyone can be lovely. There must be simmering jealousies and resentments beneath the surface.'

Carrie was quiet for a moment.

'Of course there are. And sadnesses, too. But if you have a strong community where the whole is treasured and seen as not just a benefit to the individual, but an enrichment for everyone who wants to be part of it, you try hard to overcome those.'

'Doesn't it get a bit claustrophobic?' Jules asked. 'Doesn't it just add extra responsibility to lives that are already busy, maybe even stretched to their limits?'

'It depends how you approach it. You can give as much or as little as you like. No one is going to challenge you. Some people like to be involved and others don't. But that doesn't mean that the ones who don't won't be welcomed with open arms if at some time they need the support of a wider network.'

Jules screwed up her face.

'I'm not sure that it's workable long term. Someone or something is bound to throw a spanner in the works.'

Carrie got up and gathered the plates.

'You have to be here to experience it, the benefits, the sense of acceptance.' She shot Jules a knowing glance. 'You have to give it time.'

Jules turned and looked out of the window as Carrie walked through to the kitchen. Had she really been that obvious? Could Carrie sense that she wasn't planning on staying that long?

She popped her head around the doorframe.

'Why don't you book in for a session at The Pottery? It might be good for you.'

'Absolutely not.'

'I'll come with you. I've never worked with clay. It looks like fun.'

Jules leant back and closed her eyes. She didn't like the way this conversation was going. Maybe if she pretended to be asleep Carrie would let it drop. Quietly Carrie got up and went inside. Surreptitiously, Jules opened one eye. Crisis averted. For the next few days, at least, she could go back to concentrating on being a hermit.

SEVEN

Jules was sitting at the kitchen table with a glass of wine when a man in a blue shirt walked past the window.

'Hello,' he said, leaning over the half-open stable door to the kitchen. 'You must be Jules. I'm Guy. How are you doing?'

Jules scraped her chair back and wished she didn't look so unkempt for her first meeting with Carrie's boyfriend.

'Um, I'm okay, thanks, not too bad. Please come in.'

He opened the lower part of the door and allowed a brown Labrador to precede him into the cottage.

'Sorry,' he said as the dog came over and sniffed the side of her knee. 'I should have checked. Are you okay with dogs?'

'Fine,' Jules replied, stretching her arm to fondle a soft doggy ear.

'That rude mutt is Wilbur.' Guy chuckled. 'Come here, Wilbur. Where are your manners?'

Wilbur plonked himself down by the range, made a disgruntled huffing sound and put his head on his paws.

'Thank you for letting me stay here,' Jules said, standing awkwardly and wondering what to do with her arms now the dog had left her side.

'You're very welcome. It's nice to meet you at last. Carrie talks about you such a lot. Just sorry that it's not under happier circumstances.'

Jules swallowed and nodded.

'Anyway,' he continued, 'I hope everything's okay for you. Rita's fantastic, of course, and now Carrie's on board, too. Well, the place should be perfect, but everyone's different and there's bound to be the odd thing you need that we've forgotten to cater for or something that goes a bit awry.'

'No, everything *is* perfect. It's just so welcoming and peaceful and having Carrie here last night was an extra comfort. I'm sorry to drag her away from you.'

'Don't apologise. I wouldn't have expected her to do any differently.' He glanced through the sitting room door. 'Is she around?'

'Oh, she's just wandered up to the gardens to find you.'

'We must have missed each other. I came the back way because I was working in the woods over to the right.' He checked his watch. 'Do you mind if I wait until she gets back? There's no point sending a message. It probably won't come through until much later, if at all.'

Jules wondered if he registered the ridiculous alarm she felt because he then slapped his thigh and called Wilbur to his side.

'I've got a few things to do in the garden in the meantime. Carrie won't be long and then I'll leave you in peace.'

And with a reassuring smile he strode outside and headed towards the little shed to the right of the weeping willow. Jules watched from the window as he extricated a few tools and strolled over to the rockery, dropping on to his hands and knees in order to fork through the soil. She should have at least offered him a tea. This was his house, for goodness' sake, and she was staying in it for free when he could be getting a good income in peak season. What on earth must he think of her? She was just pouring some milk into a small jug and setting it on a tray next to a steaming mug when Carrie burst back into the kitchen.

'Is Guy here?' she asked.

'In the garden,' Jules replied. 'I'm just making him a drink.'

'Oh, that's nice. I bumped into The Major who said that Guy was heading here to find me and then we got chatting or I'd have been back sooner. Thought I might have missed him again.'

'Nope, he's still here, waiting for you.'

Jules watched enviously as Carrie's eyes lit up when she looked out of the window towards where Guy was carefully pruning a small plant.

'What do you think?' she asked. 'Do you like him?'

She placed her palms together as if in prayer.

'Please say you like him!'

'We've barely met,' Jules said and then, seeing the disappointment cloud Carrie's features, 'but yes, he seems lovely.'

'Is there enough tea in that pot for me?' Carrie asked. 'We can take it into the garden and you can get to know him better.'

'It's you he wants to see, not me,' Jules said, pouring an extra mug and handing the tray to Carrie. 'Besides, I'm not up to small talk at the moment. There'll be plenty of time for us to bond, I'm sure.'

She didn't like to add that she really couldn't bear to be around other people's happiness right now.

People said that happiness was infectious, but that wasn't always true. If you were feeling in the depths of despair, seeing other people's joy could make you feel even worse. She felt churlish and small-minded and while deep down she really was pleased for Carrie she just didn't need happiness shoved in her face, however unintentionally. She hoped to God that Carrie didn't ask him to stay for supper.

'I've booked us in,' Carrie said, later, after Guy had finally gone.

'To what?' Jules asked, panic immediately forming a clenched ball in her stomach.

'A day course at The Pottery.'

Jules stared at her in disbelief. How could she have done this? 'Why?'

Carrie came over and placed her hands on Jules's shoulders.

'Because I think it will do you good. Take you out of yourself as my grandma used to say.'

'I'm not sure that I can.'

'Why? Have you got something else planned?'

'No, it's just that... I-I don't want to be taken out of myself. I don't want to be taken out anywhere. I want to stay here.'

She felt like a little girl begging not to go to the drama classes her mother had booked her into 'because it would be good for her confidence' even though she didn't know anyone.

'It's just for a few hours. It will be fun.'

Carrie went to the fridge and poured two glasses of water while Jules sank on to a kitchen chair before her legs collapsed beneath her.

'I'm sorry, Carrie. I really don't think I can. Not at the moment.'

Carrie placed the glasses on the table next to her and pulled out a chair. She took Jules's hands between hers.

'You, above and beyond anyone I've ever met, are the woman who can do anything she sets her mind to,' she said softly.

Jules shook her head.

'No,' she whispered. 'Not anymore. That was the old me, before...'

Carrie's grip tightened.

'I know that life can kick you in the stomach, Jules, and I know how hard it is to pick yourself up from that, but trust me with this... like I trusted you, when you sent me here to a place without Wi-Fi, a barely functioning phone signal and not knowing a soul within a hundred-mile radius.'

'I'm just not ready to meet people and have to explain things.'

'It's a pottery course, not a confessional. You won't have to explain anything.'

'Can I at least think about it?' she asked.

'Of course you can. As long as you talk yourself into it and not out of it because I really don't want to let Lance down. He might have been able to fill those two spaces with other people at the last minute.'

'You're putting pressure on me. That's not fair.'

'Life, my sweet,' Carrie said, 'is far from fair. You don't get to our age without finding that out several times over.'

Jules woke early, made herself a cup of green tea and took it into the garden. She walked barefoot across the bejewelled grass towards the view of the sea. There was a haze in the distance, a sign that the day was going to be hot. She was just about to sit down on the strategically placed bench when she spotted an egg balancing between the slats. She picked it up, expecting it to be cold, but it was still warm.

'Hi!' a voice called. 'Jules, you haven't seen a hen in your garden, have you? Mainly white like all of the others, but with a particularly pretty lacy black hackle.'

'Sorry to be ignorant, but what's a hackle?'

'It's those markings around the neck. I think it looks a bit like one of those Flemish collars from the seventeenth century.'

Tasha was standing on tiptoes and looking up over the hedge towards her. Jules held up the egg.

'No sign of a hen, but I've found this and it's still warm.'

'Evidence!' Tasha said with a grin. 'Was it on the bench? She hasn't done that in forever. She's a pretty intelligent bird except when it comes to where she lays her eggs. It could easily have rolled off.'

'Shall I bring it around?' Jules asked. 'I can't exactly throw it to you!'

'No, keep it. We've got quite a few already. Dad lets the girls out really early at this time of year and they usually lay within the first hour.'

She held up a wicker basket carefully stacked with light brown and cream eggs.

'Is that your job, collecting the eggs?' Jules asked.

'I don't think of it as a job,' Tasha said. 'I think of it as a bit of time to myself and I do love the chickens. People think they're dense, but they're not. This breed, the Light Sussex, are really sociable and clever. Did you know that they have been here for nearly two thousand years? Isn't that amazing? Granny says they could even have been here when Jesus was alive although people think they might have been first bred in Britain around the time of the Roman invasion in AD43. There's a cool Roman villa at Brading. You must go if you've got time. The mosaics are amazing.'

She hesitated and tugged at a bit of hair.

'That's if you're interested in that sort of thing. Some people aren't. Sorry, if I'm boring you.'

'You're not boring me.'

Jules thought that no fourteen-year-old could ever be boring. You just had to draw them out, listen to them, find out what they were interested in.

'And I'll keep my eyes peeled for your hen.'

'Thanks. Sussexes are a curious breed and Scattihen, that's the one I'm looking for, she's a bit too nosy for her own good. Granny says the fox is bound to get her one day.'

'Oh no! That would be awful. We must find her.'

'She's probably found somewhere shady to rest or some good bugs and worms to eat. If she's not back later, do you mind if I stop by and look around the garden?'

'No. Come around now if you like.'

'I can't. Jo's picking me up to go to the pottery. Scatti's obviously okay because that egg's fresh. I bet she came to meet you and left that as a present.'

'Well, I must thank Scattihen when I see her. There are some hens at that house as you come into the village. Could she have gone up there?'

'They're Cressie's hens and yes, anything's possible. I'll get Granny to check when she goes up. I'd better scoot or I'm going to be late.'

'Have a good time,' Jules said and watched as Tasha bounded back towards the house, swinging the basket of eggs as she went.

'So,' Carrie said, tapping into her boiled egg, 'what do you fancy doing today?'

Jules didn't actually feel like doing anything. What she really wanted was to go back to bed, close her eyes and never wake up. But from the determined set of Carrie's mouth, that wasn't going to happen.

'Beach?' Carrie asked. 'It's going to be a nice day. I could show you the dinosaur foot casts. They're amazing. Or we could take a trip to Carisbrooke Castle. That's pretty impressive.'

Jules dipped a toast soldier into the top of her egg and half shook her head at the same time.

'I'm happy to just mooch around here today if you don't mind.'

Carrie wrinkled up her nose.

'Mooching is not good.'

'Sometimes it's all you're capable of.'

'Why don't we wander up to the gardens then? It's closed to the public today, but we can still have a mooch around there for an hour and then you can carry on your mooching back here.'

Jules really didn't have the energy to protest, which is how she found herself following Carrie into The Manor gardens and closing the solid side gate behind them. Carrie had brought a flask of coffee, and she led the way down some steps into what was called the tropical garden. There was a grass maze in the middle of the lawn, borders all around the edge and a choice of four wooden benches to sit on.

'We can have two each,' Carrie said, 'and then you don't have to talk to me. Take your pick.'

Jules settled herself on a bench at the far side with a tall stone wall to the back of her and the sun slanting in from the side. She was glad that Carrie had suggested taking a hat and sunglasses. She couldn't think of anything practical at the moment and she was normally such a practical person.

Carrie poured the coffee and produced a couple of ginger biscuits from her pocket.

'Where are you going?' Jules asked, as she began to walk away.

'Over there,' she said, pointing to a bench on the far side of the lawn.

'Now I feel guilty.'

'No need to. I'm going to meditate, and you can sit here and soak up the beauty of this place. It's very healing.'

'You said that about the cottage.'

'Because it's true.'

'I haven't felt it yet.'

'You think you haven't felt it yet.'

Jules looked up at her.

'What does that mean?'

'You don't want to know.'

'Yes, I do.'

Carrie twisted her lips and came and sat cross-legged on the grass in front of Jules.

'Okay,' she said, slowly. 'Stop feeling sorry for yourself for a moment and listen. Really listen.'

'I think I'm entitled to feel sorry for myself.'

'Yes, you are, but there comes a time when you have to move forwards.'

'Maybe I'm not ready for that yet.'

Carrie swivelled on to her knees, wincing as coffee slopped over her ankle.

'No,' she said, 'maybe you're not.'

'But you might as well spit it out anyway,' Jules said, 'instead of keeping it bottled up. I know what you thought of Gavin and, let's face it, you were right.'

'I didn't want to be proved right,' Carrie said, softly. 'God,

Jules, I care about you. I didn't want to see him making you unhappy.'

'I don't think I'm destined for happiness. Not romantically anyway.'

A tear dropped into her coffee.

Carrie took the cup from her hands and put it down on the grass before sitting next to her.

'Jules, give yourself a break, will you? I can't bear to see you like this. You *are* a strong person.'

'No, no, I'm not. Everyone thinks that, but I've just been pretending all this time.'

'Actually, I don't think that's true. It's just what your brain is telling you at the moment because it's scrambled.'

Carrie handed Jules a tissue.

'I've got one. Tasha says to never go anywhere without a tissue.'

'Well, she's right.'

Carrie clasped Jules's hands.

'Just tell me, why are you crying?'

'What sort of a stupid question is that?' Jules sniffed.

'One that at least has got your attention. I know that you desperately wanted Gavin to be "the one", but did he really make you happy, in a spending the rest of your lives together way?'

'I was happy when I was with him.'

'But you were also worried. I know you were.'

Jules nodded.

'Maybe.'

'More than maybe.'

'I miss him.'

Carrie clasped her hands tighter, despite the fact that Jules's tears were falling on to them.

'I wonder if you're crying for the relationship that you thought you were going to have, rather than the one you actually did.'

Jules took a gulp of air.

'I thought...' she gasped. 'I really thought...'

'I know you did and, believe me, I wanted it almost as much as you did, but it's not the end of the world. I know it feels like it right now, but it's not. I'm testament to that. Coming here is the best thing you could have done. I promise you. This place will make the world seem a better place and one day you will meet someone who is wonderful and loyal and funny and makes you realise that true love is worth waiting for. But you need to start trusting yourself, caring for yourself, honouring yourself.'

'I don't know how to do that.'

'Which is why I'm here. To help you.'

'To boss me about, you mean,' Jules said, wiping her eyes.

'That, too.'

'Okay, Miss Bossy Boots. Where do I start on this journey into my newfound self.'

Carrie smiled.

'By drinking your coffee which now has a nice bug floating in it and then we're going to walk the maze.'

'Apt,' Jules said.

'I think so,' said Carrie.

And Jules fished the bug out of her drink and thought that Carrie made it all sound so simple, even though love and guilt and shame and the human mind were far from that. But she'd go through the motions just to please her friend. Who knew, they might even have the teeniest tiniest beneficial effect?

'Are you an interloper?'

The voice came from behind a camellia bush and made her jump.

'I don't think so. Are you The Major?'

The man stepped into full view wearing a navy blazer, blue shirt and striped tie in spite of the heat of the day. Jules felt warm just looking at him.

'I might be. Who's asking?'

'Jules.'

He tilted his head to one side and studied her.

'That rings a bell.'

'I'm a friend of Carrie's who's now with Guy who...'

'Yes, yes, yes, I know who Carrie is and what Guy does. I may look old, but I'm not completely senile. Is she here, Carrie?'

'Gone to look for you, I think.'

He looked vaguely pleased and then adopted a sterner expression.

'Checking up on me, seeing whether I've eaten my lunch or fallen flat on my face again.'

He pointed to a bruise on the side of his head.

'Fell down the steps. You'd think after living here all these years I'd know better.'

'It happens to the best of us.'

'Can't let my son know. He'll have me out of here.'

'I won't tell.'

Jules crossed her arms over her chest.

'Anyway, I'm a nurse and you look pretty hale and hearty to me.'

He glanced behind her and then back at his stick.

'Can't climb that tree any more though. Used to scramble up it years ago.'

Jules glanced up at the large oak tree.

'Really? I don't think I'd ever have been able to climb it.'

'Used to have a treehouse halfway up. Just squirrels living there now.'

'Red ones?'

'Of course.'

'I'd love to see a red squirrel.'

'You have to keep your eyes peeled and stop talking. They're very shy. If you sit there for long enough you might spot one.'

'I will, if you don't mind. You have a very beautiful garden for sitting in.'

'My wife's work. We're making a few changes but nothing major. I wanted it to stay exactly the same, but Carrie and Guy have made me realise that gardens need to evolve.

'Carrie's certainly evolved since she came here.'

'I'll venture to find her,' he said, turning on his heel, 'and reassure her that I'm still breathing.'

'She'll be very pleased,' Jules said.

'Huh! One of the few who is! Are you staying at the cottage?'

She nodded.

'That has a pretty garden, but if you need more space, you're welcome to come over here at any time. If the main gates are closed, you can walk up the holloway into the woods and come through a small gate at the back. Don't mind bats, do you?'

'Um, no, I don't think so.'

'Good, plenty of bats if you come at dusk. Some people find them disturbing. Rita doesn't like them. Something to do with her mother being frightened by one when she was expecting. Not sure I believe it, but Rita's not a person to make things up. She'll look after you, and Carrie too. They look after me even though I'm a grumpy old so and so. You'll be all right with those two around.'

He tipped his hat and set off down the lawn back towards the house and Jules smiled. The irascible old man who Carrie had described when she first came to the island certainly seemed to have mellowed in the last three months. Underneath that gruff exterior, Jules sensed there was a very kind heart.

'You sure you'll be okay?' Carrie asked later.

'Absolutely,' Jules replied. 'As long as those ghosts you mentioned don't make an appearance and things don't start flying through the air.'

'If there are ghosts,' Carrie said, 'they're very benign. Definitely not poltergeists. I think the spirits here want the best for the house and everyone who visits.'

'Hmm,' Jules replied.

'I know you're a sceptic, so I don't know why you're worried.'

'I wouldn't be normally. I suppose I'm just a bit on edge.'

'And that's perfectly understandable,' Carrie soothed.

'You've got to admit,' Jules said, glancing all around the room, 'it's a bit creepy to think of some entities wafting around the house while you're asleep and whatever you say, you were spooked by that blanket being moved when you first stayed here. Then when you lost your ring and found the little box under the floorboards containing the teething ring and the baby's bonnet and—'

'And the little auburn curl in an envelope with the name Philly on it in the most beautiful copperplate writing,' Carrie added.

'You said it was as if someone tried to push you away, to stop you taking up the floor and discovering what lay beneath it.'

'I admit it was a bit strange.'

'Don't you mean scary?'

'Maybe a little. I'll stay and make sure they don't disturb you.'

Jules felt an unexpected flood of relief. How ridiculous. She wasn't afraid of ghosts. She didn't even believe in ghosts. She'd spent years waiting for her father to make an appearance or even send her a sign and she hadn't felt his presence once.

'You're trying too hard,' her mother had said.

'Of course I'm trying,' she'd yelled. 'I want to believe that he's there, just the other side of some great divide, that he's watching over me, protecting me, loving me, but he's not, is he? He's dead, buried in the ground, gone for good, and there isn't anything else.'

She'd stormed off, up to her room, and slammed the door so hard a little Beswick china dog had fallen from her shelves and smashed on the wooden floor. She had knelt amongst the pieces and wept, shaking her mother away when she'd come to comfort her. Now, she turned to Carrie with conviction.

'I'm being completely fanciful. You know I don't believe in all that stuff. I'll be fine. You go back to your beloved.'

Carrie looked doubtful.

'Go on,' Jules said with as much of a smile as she could muster. 'It will be good for me to have some time on my own and I'm really tired. Everything must be catching up with me. I'm going to get myself a simple supper, watch some TV and go to bed early so that I'm ready for tomorrow.'

'And you'll call if you want anything?'

Jules nodded, trying to usher Carrie towards the door without looking too much as if she wanted to get rid of her. Carrie's shoulders visibly dropped. She seemed appeased.

After she had gone, Jules made herself a cheese and tomato sandwich and took it out into the garden. There was a cool breeze rustling the branches of the willow tree. Tomorrow the weather might change. She'd thought that once Carrie had gone, she'd sit down and have a good cry, but surprisingly enough the urge passed. Was Carrie right? Was she mourning the life she'd thought she was going to have with Gavin as much as their time together? She'd certainly done her best to dream of living in the house he was doing up, having children there, growing old together in some pink-hazed utopia. She'd really got ahead of herself, hadn't she? She stood up and stretched, walked around the garden, looked for Tasha, but was disappointed when there wasn't any sign of her.

Instead, she saw Rita in the distance and waved before turning with indecent haste to retreat inside.

She ran a bath, pouring in some essential oil, swirling it through the warm water so the small bathroom was filled with the scent of patchouli. Afterwards she found a programme to watch about going on a pilgrimage, which was surprisingly soothing. Tomorrow she was going to be surrounded by strangers and she felt irrationally nervous about it. At work she was surrounded by people all the time and she loved it. What had happened to her? And the thought of actually having to make something, to mould a lump of clay into a presentable offering made her feel all clammy. Her brain was barely able to decide whether to drink tea or coffee or to spread her breakfast toast with marmalade or strawberry jam, let alone create a mug or pot.

'It doesn't matter if you make a fool of yourself,' she murmured. 'There will be other people there who have never thrown a pot before. If you don't get it right first time, it's okay and Carrie won't judge, and you'll never have to see any of those other people ever again.'

She took herself to bed and snuggled down. The wind rattled at the window. Maybe there was a storm coming. Maybe she wouldn't be able to get to The Pottery after all. Perhaps the road would be flooded, or a tree would come down, and she could just stay here curled up, eyes closed until she felt better.

TRUST

'Poor lamb,' Eliza whispered, hovering in the doorway. 'She's had all of the confidence taken from her. You could feel her sadness and bewilderment from the moment she walked in through the door. She doesn't know who she is anymore.'

Isaac gently pulled at her sleeve.

'Don't get any closer, Eliza. You might wake her, and she needs her sleep.'

'I want to give her a blessing,' Eliza said, firmly removing his hand and drifting forwards into the room. 'A blessing will help her to sleep more sweetly.'

Ignoring the protest which she knew was about to emerge from Isaac's lips, she tiptoed across the carpet and stood by the bed, looking down at Jules.

'Everything is going to be all right, my dear,' she whispered. 'Don't give up hope. You are here for a reason. We're watching over you, protecting you. The house is helping you to heal, and sleep is one of the best healers of all.'

Eliza reached out her hand.

'Eliza, no!' Isaac called.

In an instant he was by her side, his arm around her waist, guiding her back out of the room.

'You were going to touch her, weren't you?'

'Only her hair,' Eliza said, resisting him as he began to lead her down the stairs, 'and only very gently. She wouldn't have felt anything.'

She gazed back over her shoulder.

'Her hair is dark blonde, but have you noticed, Isaac, that in some lights it contains some strands of auburn?'

She hesitated, wondered whether to continue. She had never felt like this before that she could remember, never had to hold her words or feelings back from him. It made her feel unlike herself.

'It reminds me of...'

Isaac propelled her towards the stairs. Halfway down she turned to place her hands against his chest. She *would* say what was needed.

'You didn't let me finish my sentence, Isaac. It's almost the same colour as the lock of hair in that little box.'

'The box?' Isaac asked.

Eliza felt a frisson of irritation. He couldn't possibly have forgotten so why would he pretend to have done so?

'The wooden box beneath the floorboards. The tea caddy that Carrie found.'

'Oh, that box.'

She tried to look at him directly, but he had turned his head away so that she could only see the strong, determined line of his jaw, his aquiline nose and high forehead. Eliza felt her resolve deepen. She took Isaac's face between her hands and twisted it towards her.

'I feel as if that box means something, Isaac.'

An obstinate silence. He couldn't have made his unwillingness to participate in this line of conversation more obvious, Eliza thought.

'Is there something you're not telling me? Something that I need to know?'

He removed her hands from his face and took hold of one firmly. He tugged her down the remaining steps with rather more force than she thought necessary before halting at the bottom. The scent of roses from the vase on the table filled the hall. She had planted many roses in the garden when they lived here. When she was not well Isaac would pick one and place it in a little cut-glass vase on her breakfast tray. The vase had been a wedding present from one of her brothers, the only gift they had received from either of their families. Isaac would position it on her bedside table, and its beauty would sustain her during the long weeks of her recovery. Consumption, he had said, and he had nearly lost her, but she had little memory of that time or indeed the months that followed.

'How many times do I have to tell you? There's nothing, absolutely nothing, Eliza, that you need to know.'

She should believe him. That's what a good, loyal, trusting wife did. She had never had cause to doubt him before, but now... He was still full of love for her. She could see that.

'There are no secrets between us?'

'Oh, Eliza,' he sighed and leaned forwards to kiss her softly on the lips. 'You know that you mean everything to me. We are as one. Always have been and always will be.'

Eliza gazed up the stairs.

'It must be distressing to discover that someone you love has withheld things from you.' She glanced back at Isaac. 'It must feel like a betrayal of trust, and trust once lost is hard to regain.'

'Our guest will, in time, learn to trust again, I'm sure,' Isaac replied.

'Perhaps,' Eliza said, but she hadn't just been referring to Jules and she was acutely aware that he hadn't answered her question.

EIGHT

Jules was pacing up and down in the kitchen when Carrie arrived.

'You're not dressed.'

'I really don't think this is a good idea. You go. I'll pay you back for my place.'

Carrie led her to the table and sat her down.

'I'm not going without you.'

Jules put her head in her hands.

'I know it's stupid, but I just can't do it.'

'There are only five in the class,' Carrie said. 'Three other people and us. It's a beginner's class and none of us have any experience at all, except for you.'

'Not for a long time. Anyway, how do you know this?'

'Because I knew you felt anxious about it, so I rang Lance and asked him.'

Jules groaned.

'Oh my God! Did you tell him that?'

'No, of course not. He probably thought that it was me who was worried. He sounded as if he was used to people getting cold feet at the last minute. He said most people feel a bit intimidated because we all want to be good at something instantly. We don't want to fail.'

'I want to be good at relationships, but I fail all the time.'

'That's actually not true. Usually, you're the one to end them. This time your pride is hurt as well as everything else.'

'That's a bit harsh.'

'Sometimes,' Carrie said, 'you have to be cruel to be kind.'

She took Jules firmly by the elbow.

'Come on, let's get you dressed and go and play with some clay.'

Jules' legs were shaking as she walked under the archway to the pottery. They were late and were going to have to walk into a room full of other people who would turn and stare. Even worse, Lance was standing and waiting for them outside the tearoom.

'Carrie,' he said, throwing her a smile which lit up his whole face, and then leaned forwards to embrace her warmly. 'And Jules.' He glanced more warily at her, she thought. As if she might bite. 'Lovely to have you here.'

Give him his due, Jules thought, he sounded as if he really meant it in spite of her frozen expression and rooted-to-the-spot pose.

'Sorry we're a bit late,' Carrie said, turning and linking her arm through Jules's as if sensing her desire to run away.

'You're fine,' Lance replied, holding the tearoom door open for them. 'A bit less time for victuals, that's all. Come and meet the others.'

Jules's heartbeat ramped up several notches as her jaw clenched and an iron band felt as if it was compressing her sternum.

'I've been wanting to have a go at this ever since I moved here,' Carrie said, weaving amongst wooden tables and chairs and still miraculously managing to keep hold of Jules as if she was a small, recalcitrant child. The tearoom was already half full and despite the roof being open to the rafters the noise seemed concentrated at ground level. It felt like an assault, the chatter, the chairs scraping, the hiss of the coffee machine, cups clattering. She wanted to put her hands over her ears.

A week at home with the windows closed had hermetically sealed her from real life and she wasn't ready to go back to it just yet. A sweetness hung in the air from the cakes and pastries. She felt sick.

She'd not had a panic attack since her teens, but she recognised the early warning signs as if it was yesterday.

'Carrie...'

But Carrie wasn't listening and now Lance was introducing them to three people whose attention was fully directed towards her. Her eyes darted around the room for the safety of the toilets, but she couldn't see them. They must be behind her like Lance, who had moved around and was now blocking her escape. Her breath felt as if it was coming in short gasps, but no one seemed to notice her distress. She didn't hear anyone's names, barely registered their faces. Little black dots danced in front of her eyes. She swayed and then someone was saying something and leading her, half supporting her towards a door in the corner. Sunlight shone through the open margin, and she focused on that gleam as if her life depended upon it. She was pressed down on to a wooden chair near an open window.

'Breathe,' someone said, 'into your back and the sides of your ribs. Breathe into your shoulders.'

She heard the rush of water as a tap was turned on.

'Drink this,' Lance said, pulling up a chair beside her and holding a glass to her lips.

Jules took a sip.

The water was cold and delicious, as if it had come straight from a mountain stream. She took the glass between her clammy palms and let the coolness calm her skin.

'Better?' he asked.

She nodded and he got up to open the window a little more.

'Sorry,' she murmured. 'Not usually like this.'

'No need to apologise.'

He was making a pretence of arranging things on a workbench, but she knew he was studying her from a safe distance.

'I'd better rejoin the others,' he said.

She put the glass on the windowsill and summoned up the strength to stand.

'Why don't you stay here for a bit longer?' he said. 'We'll be through in ten minutes or so. If you need more fresh air, that door goes into our house. There's a little hall which leads into the private garden you can see from this window. You're welcome to sit in it although you'll probably be accosted by the cat.'

'I like cats,' she whispered.

'Or,' he said, 'that other door over there leads back out to the front, the tearoom garden where you were yesterday.'

And the exit, she thought. He's offering me a way out.

'You're sure you're okay if I go back through? I can send Carrie if you like.'

She shook her head.

'No. I'm fine. Really.'

Now, Jules. Make your escape now, she said to herself when Lance had headed back to the tearoom.

She placed her palms on her thighs as if to calm her jittery legs. A cat wound its way through the window behind her, brushed some red petals from a trailing geranium in a terracotta pot and jumped down to come and rub at her legs.

'Hello, you,' she said, stooping momentarily to run her fingers along its back.

For the first time she looked around her surroundings. The studio was light and bright with four large windows along one wall overlooking a cottage garden containing a small pond with a delicate fountain in the middle. Around the room the shelves jostled with expertly thrown and decorated pots, together with a fascinating selection of books on art, photography, sculpture and philosophy. There was an old washstand holding vintage jars full of brushes and pencils plus a neat pile of paper. Plants crowded on the windowsills, ferns, tradescantia and a plethora of geraniums, some upright and others trailing, their red, pink and orange flowers glowing like medieval illuminations against the brilliant white walls. And in the air the scent of clay and paint and creativity. She sat down again to soak it all in and immediately the cat jumped on to her lap.

'Well,' she said, scratching the cat behind its ears, 'this isn't a bad place to live, is it? Lucky you.'

And as if she had understood every world her feline companion began to purr with pleasure.

'You're still here,' Lance said, looking slightly surprised. 'Pinned to the spot by Morwenna.'

'Oh no, I wasn't thinking, really...'

Her voice tapered away as Carrie and the three other people she vaguely remembered sitting around the table in the café filed into the room.

'Are you okay?' Carrie said, rushing over to her. 'I bought you cake and a warm drink.'

'Fine. I just went a bit dizzy, that's all.'

'Happens to me all the time,' said a tall slim lady with a sympathetic coral-lipsticked smile and long grey hair tied back in a loose ponytail with a velvet ribbon. She could have been anywhere between late fifties and mid-seventies and looked artfully elegant in her loose putty-coloured dungarees and what looked like a Liberty print shirt in oranges and yellows.

'Always carry some rescue remedy in my bag if you need it,' she said softly to Jules, her multi-stranded drop pearl earrings swinging gently as she leaned to touch her briefly on the shoulder. 'I'm Daphne, by the way.'

'Thank you, Daphne. That's very kind.'

'And I'm John,' said a man in his fifties, with an immaculately trimmed beard and wearing a statement leather waistcoat. 'Good to meet you, Jules.'

He sent her a small wave and she raised her hand in return.

'And last, but not least, this is Iris,' Lance said, introducing a woman of about her age with an asymmetric haircut and intense eyes.

'I do hope you're all right,' she said. 'I used to get dizzy when I was pregnant. It's a horrible feeling.'

'Oh, I'm not pregnant,' she protested as a feeling of utter shock threaded through her.

She sat stock still, trying to work out her dates.

'Just too much rushing around, I expect,' Carrie added, but Jules looked up to see the question in her eyes.

'This is going to be a very relaxed day,' Lance said. 'Rushing around is not permitted in this place. In fact, all you have to do to begin with is to watch. I'll give you a short demonstration for a simple bowl and then you can have a go yourselves. I hope today begins a lifelong love affair with pots, but at the very least I hope it makes you happy. Pull up a chair and let's make some magic.'

Jules lifted Morwenna on to the floor and picked up the hot chocolate which Carrie had brought her.

She watched as Lance made himself comfortable in front of the wheel. Her shoulders twitched as she lifted the mug to her lips. This was ridiculous. How on earth was she going to be able to mould a pot when she couldn't keep her body steady? She tried to concentrate on what Lance was saying and the delicious sweetness of the chocolate. Soon she became mesmerised by the turn of the wheel, the way Lance drew up the edges of a ball of clay with his fingertips explaining as he worked. She settled back into her seat and listened to his voice. It was deep, smooth and brimming with enthusiasm. Enthusiasm, the Greek word for the god within, divinely inspired. She could see how he would inspire people, even those who probably had little aptitude for throwing a pot. As he made eye contact with them all in turn, she found it difficult to believe that he would ever say a bad word about anyone.

'First and foremost, I want you to be kind to yourselves. When we start something new it's best not to rush headlong into it, and keep your expectations... not low exactly, but manageable. If you aim too high from the outset you risk frustration and disappointment. By expecting too much, too soon, we may put ourselves and our projects at risk of being less than they could be if we allowed ourselves to be present and free of judgement. I know that you are only here for a few hours and that you will want to go away with something to be proud of, which I hope will be the case. But I'd like you to think of this as the beginning of a journey. For some of you, you may return to develop your skills, for others, maybe all, this may be the gateway to another creative endeavour. Whatever the outcome this day, what you produce won't be wasted. Nothing is ever wasted. Every experience has something to teach us, about ourselves and others. Throwing pots is a way of slowing down. That is why my wife and I came here, to reclaim our lives after we both became burnt out by city living. Unfortunately, she became ill soon after we moved to the island, but I knew that she wouldn't want me to give up on our dream, and all creative endeavours begin with a dream.'

As he worked the wheel, something stirred in Jules's memory – a feeling of being at one with what she was doing. She felt her shoulders drop a little and a loosening in that place at the base of her neck which had become so persistently tight and sore.

'The speed of the wheel is really important,' he said. 'Not too fast and not too slow. Nice and steady. Remember that the clay wants to be formed into something.'

A smooth bowl was taking shape, his hands firm, but gentle. He had very nice hands, Jules thought, with long, slender fingers and tactile thumbs expertly working the clay until he was satisfied with what he had created. He made it look so easy, but Jules knew from past experience that it wasn't. She thought back to her school days, when elbow deep in clay she had got so frustrated with the medium that wouldn't do what she wanted, and how she had nearly given up. Then one day she had stopped trying so hard and given herself the freedom to follow what wanted to be born from this unpromising piece of earth, not expecting it to be perfect or to fulfil all her expectations, just allowing it to be something. She remembered the euphoria that followed, and how after that revelation she looked forward to those lessons, which would always be over far too quickly. But that was then and this was now, and so much had happened. She wasn't the same person. She would never be the same again after what Gavin had done. Lance moved around the room, sitting with each person in turn, talking to them about the best way for them to sit, how to hold the clay, how to use their arms, their wrists, their hands, their fingers. First Daphne, then Iris, then John, then Carrie and next it was to be her turn. She felt the panic rise inside her and that part of her spine at the base of her neck was jammed solid again, a dull ache radiating out across her shoulder blades and up behind her right ear.

'Jules, you okay?'

She was suddenly aware of him bending over her. He was close, too close. She could smell the fabric conditioner on his creased navy linen shirt, see the hairs glistening gold on his forearms. He pulled up a stool and sat next to her. She sat stock still, unable to move, barely able to breathe. She couldn't do this. She really couldn't.

'There's absolutely no pressure here,' he murmured. 'The only pressure is from yourself.'

She managed the smallest of nods, so small she thought he wouldn't notice, but he did because he dipped his head in acknowledgement, a loose curl falling forwards on his forehead.

'It's clay,' he whispered. 'You can't not touch it. It's one of the most tactile substances around. May I?' His hand hovered above hers.

She nodded and he lifted her wrist, placing her palm upon the wedge of clay in front of her. If he was aware of her flinching, he didn't let on. Instead, he placed his own palm over the back of her hand and held it in place.

'There,' he said, the corners of his eyes crinkling with his smile. 'That's not too terrible, is it?'

'No,' she whispered, feeling the warmth of his skin and the

coolness of the clay and veering between wanting to run as far and fast as she could and staying right there for ever.

'You're the expert,' he whispered. 'No one else has done anything like this before.'

'It's a long time ago.'

'You won't have forgotten what to do,' he said. 'That learning process will still be there inside. You just have to let it out. I'm sure you could make something more complicated, but a bowl will give you confidence.'

He leaned back, but kept his hand connected to hers.

'We take bowls for granted,' he said to them all, 'but they are full of symbolism. They represent the Divine Feminine, creative fulfilment, abundance and nourishment. Bowls are used for sharing food, but also for sustaining ourselves. They have been used in rituals and celebrations for thousands of years. A circular bowl can remind us of unity and wholeness, of giving to ourselves and to others, and it doesn't have to be perfect.'

An imperfect bowl. She could do that. She'd never been a fan of perfection. Gavin had been the one chasing that and she'd got caught up in his quest. She'd tried to make herself perfect for him, bought new make-up, new clothes which were completely impractical and not really her, some ridiculously expensive shoes, and spent a fortune which she couldn't afford on her hair trying to obliterate those coppery strands that he didn't like. And look where all of that had got her. Her bowl could even have a wavy rim. She liked waves and ripples and quirky things. It could be perfectly imperfect. It could be a symbol of the new her.

'Remember to breathe,' he said softly.

She was acutely aware that his hand was still on hers, holding it gently, but firmly against the clay.

'Remember to connect with your breath, everyone,' he said to the others. 'Making pots is about many things: patience, trust, strength, posture and breath. Everything is connected. We're all connected, to each other and to the clay. It's our oldest handicraft. It's in our DNA.'

For a moment his eyes met hers and illogically she felt pure terror.

'Ready?' he asked.

She nodded. Anything to get him to remove skin to skin contact, to stop him being so kind. It was more than she could bear.

'Off you go then,' he said, moving away and turning back to Carrie whose beginnings of a bowl had collapsed, resulting in part laughter, part frustrated expletives.

Jules dipped her hand in the bowl of water, pressed her foot to the treadle and the wheel began to turn. After a few false starts and some staring out of the window, she began to feel remnants of memory returning; memory which wasn't just in her head, but in her entire body. Maybe if she just let her body take the lead, she thought. The wheel was immersive. Jules couldn't think about anything except the water, the clay, her feet, her hands, the form in front of her which grew and shrank and collapsed and grew again, keeping her totally in the moment. And suddenly she realised that this was good, that it made her forget for a while, that it was just what she needed.

At lunchtime they were directed to a long pine table outside under the trees. John pulled out a chair for her. Gavin used to do that. Always a gentleman on the surface. Lance fetched a cushion for Daphne, whose back was aching, and Carrie cut slices from a crusty loaf while Iris poured them all a tall glass of summer fruit cordial, making sure everyone had a piece of strawberry, a raspberry and a sprig of mint. They were nice, these people, she thought as she listened to them chatter about their morning's attempts and the feast of food laid out in front of them; a delicious selection of salads, cold fish and meats arranged on vintage crockery. Kind people. If they knew how stupid she had been, how ashamed she was of her gullibility, they would wrap her in understanding. Besides, who knew what they themselves had been through, what mistakes they had made, failures they'd had to overcome?

John, she had gleaned, was trying to find a new purpose in retirement and Iris had been given the day as a gift by her grand-mother, but Jules sensed that it wasn't a birthday gift, it was for some other reason. Beneath the serene features there was a battle going on. She used to be good at sensing things. You had to be as a midwife.

Daphne was talking about her children and grandchildren, her husband of over fifty years and Jules wondered if she was putting a gloss on her life or maybe she was one of those people who deliber-ately made everything and everyone sound adorable not to impress others, but to reassure herself. Jules wasn't convinced she was giving much of her real self away. Lance, on the other hand, seemed refreshingly uncomplicated. As she listened to the chatter around the table, ankles tightly crossed beneath the chair, she picked at a piece of mushroom and thyme quiche and gradually began to relax. Food always tasted so much better in the open air, she thought; the tomatoes were perfectly ripe, the quinoa salad tangy with mint and lemon, the salmon melt in the mouth soft, the bread pillowy on the inside with a satisfyingly chewy contrasting crust. For the first time in a couple of weeks she actually felt hungry.

'After Sarah died I could have gone back to London, returned to my job in finance and got a nanny for the children,' Lance was saying, 'which was what my parents thought was for the best.'

He paused and glanced across the lawn towards the studio.

'But this place had a hold on me and being a potter is in my veins. I think you said you're a midwife, Jules?'

'Oh! Yes!'

She was aware that she sounded like a startled bird. Did she tell him that? She didn't remember. He was looking at her directly across the table.

'That's meant to be a calling, isn't it?'

'Um, I suppose so.'

That probably wasn't what he wanted, she thought. He probably wanted her to sound more definite, more glowing. Everyone was looking at her, waiting for her to say more.

'I never really wanted to do anything else,' she added, her voice quavering beneath the attention.

She really, really couldn't do this, sit here for the rest of the day with a group of strangers. It was too much. She had to say something, but Carrie didn't appear to notice her distress and Lance was still talking.

'I felt like that about potting,' he said, 'ever since I first squidged some clay into a Christmas angel at primary school. But pottery isn't really seen as a 'proper' job, at least not in my family, so I went down the conventional route until I couldn't do that any longer without suffering long term damage to my mental and physical health. Which is how I came to be here and why I decided, after we lost Sarah, that there were more important things than money. As long as I could earn enough to support myself and my family, to run this place, to give something back, pass on my passion, then I would be happy.'

A passion for pots, she thought. That sounded safe. That's what she needed to do, find a passion for something which would be all consuming. Something she would be able to turn to if she was ever tempted to get into a romantic relationship ever again.

Halfway through the afternoon Erin and Tasha arrived in the studio with a tray of cakes and mugs of tea.

'Wow!' Erin said to Carrie. 'For a first attempt, that's really good.'

'You're too kind, but I don't think I'm a natural,' Carrie replied, her laughter reverberating around the room. She stretched. 'It's tiring though, learning something new. All of that concentrating, I suppose.'

'Concentrating is good,' Jules said, working some sgraffito decoration around the edge of her bowl.

'And that,' said Erin, 'is really, really good.'

Jules felt herself beginning to blush.

'Look at this, Dad,' Erin said, handing her father a large mug with the words Keep Calm and Carry On emblazoned on it in scarlet font.

'I've seen it,' he said, looking up from where he was chatting to John.

'I've done this a bit before,' Jules murmured.

'Not since you were twelve,' Carrie protested, 'and that's ages ago.'

'Thanks!' Jules replied, and everyone laughed.

'You ought to keep going,' Erin said, 'shouldn't she, Dad?'

Jules glanced over at Lance who was now busy clearing a few things away.

'I think so,' he replied, 'but Jules might not want to. It might not be for her.'

'You must come back,' Erin said, earnestly. 'We do a discount for returning customers.'

'Erin,' Lance said, moving over and putting an arm around her shoulders, 'give Jules a bit of space. She's here on holiday. She might not want to spend another day wrapped in a massive apron and getting clay all over her face.'

'Oh,' Jules exclaimed, blushing even more. 'I haven't, have I?'

She put her hand up to her cheek and then realised that she'd be putting even more clay on herself.

'Does it make a good facemask?' she asked.

'Not if my wrinkles are anything to go by,' Lance replied, passing her a box of tissues.

'My granny says that we earn our wrinkles and we shouldn't wish them away. They tell the story of our lives,' Tasha said, perching on the windowsill, fingering some geranium petals.

'Your granny is a very wise woman,' Lance said.

As Erin went to talk to Daphne and Tasha joined her, Lance sidled over to Jules.

'I'm sorry about Erin being a bit pushy,' he said, his voice dropping to a whisper. 'She's always been involved in the business and she's so eager to keep it going, expand it even. She thinks I'm not commercially minded enough. But...'

He shrugged and glanced out of the window for a brief second before allowing his gaze to rest on her bowl.

'She's right about your bowl though. That's pretty good.'

Jules blushed as everyone looked over and murmured their agreement. They were such a nice group, so supportive. She felt silly for being so worried about coming.

'It's not totally symmetrical.'

'Neither is life, Jules,' Lance said. 'We're all works in progress.' He was about to move away and then turned back, dropping his voice. 'If you do want to carry on while you're here, but don't want to join a class, you can always come back later in the day. You could have the place to yourself then. No charge.'

She blinked up at him. That was so kind. She dropped her head low so he wouldn't see the tears pooling.

'Thanks,' she muttered, 'but I couldn't possibly.'

'Why on earth did you rebuff him like that?' Carrie chastised on the way home. 'He was just being nice.'

'I know, but I'm allowed to say no to things.'

'There are ways of saying it.'

'Was I offhand?'

Carrie pressed her lips together.

'I didn't mean to be. Anyway, what does it matter? I'm not going to see him again.'

'Except when you go to collect your bowl after it's been in the drying room.'

'You could do that for me, couldn't you?'

'Maybe,' Carrie said, 'if you're nice to me.'

'I'm always nice to you. Well, almost always.'

'And wasn't I right to book us in there today?'

'Don't crow.'

'I'm not.'

'Yes, you are.'

Carrie punched her lightly on the arm.

'Admit it, you enjoyed yourself once you got over the initial nerves and your bowl is brilliant.'

'Lance is right,' Jules said, winding down the window and allowing her fingertips to brush the hedges as Carrie pulled the car into the lane leading down to the cottage. 'It is like riding a bicycle. Once you've done it, you don't completely forget.'

Jules smiled at Carrie and for the first time in several weeks it felt like a proper smile, from behind her eyes, from her heart space. How on earth could she have been stupid enough to risk this friendship for someone like Gavin? The friendship between women was more enduring, more sustaining, more precious than any man. She was never going to let a man steal her heart ever again.

Carrie dropped her outside the cottage.

'You're sure you don't want me to come in?'

Jules shook her head.

'No, you get back to your beloved. He'll be pining for you.'

She stood beneath the archway and watched as Carrie turned the car around and headed back up the lane. A tendril of honeysuckle caressed her skin, its thick sweet scent filling her nostrils. She lifted her arm for one last wave and turned towards the cottage.

'Hello, house,' she said. 'Just you and me again tonight.'

The air in the hall was still and warm, draping itself over her like the softest cashmere. The windows in this room faced east so it was in shadow in the afternoon, but the subdued light was calming after such an intense day. Jules put her bag down at the bottom of the stairs and lifted her hair to rub the back of her neck. She was beginning to stiffen up after the time spent hunched over at the wheel.

'A bath is definitely needed,' she said, catching sight of herself in the mirror above the fireplace.

First, she made a pot of tea, placing the little silver pot on a circular tray alongside a china cup and saucer and a plate with a couple of freshly made ginger biscuits which she had found on the doorstep with a note from Rita.

I know you won't have finished the cake yet, but I've been baking and thought you might like to try some of these.

Rita

X

Rita, Jules thought, was one of those people who had kindness running through her like a seam of gold. She probably couldn't be mean if she tried.

She headed upstairs and turned on the taps. There was a small velvet, button-backed chair in a corner of the bathroom and whilst the room filled with the scent of rose and patchouli and the bath frothed with bubbles, she sat in it and poured herself a cup of amber liquid. Even though it was still light she lit a couple of candles, one called Peace, which had a snow-white quartz embedded in the wax, and another that was prettily pink and glowing. Taking off her clothes she sank into the water, closed her eyes and gave thanks for her day.

CHOICES

'That worked well,' Isaac said, as he and Eliza sat on the bench enjoying the last of the evening sun. 'Our guest definitely had a different demeanour when she returned.'

'Tired,' Eliza said, 'but you are right, Isaac, there was a change.'

'Did you put that idea into Carrie's head?' Isaac asked, his eyes twinkling as he studied his wife.

'I might have floated the suggestion around her,' Eliza replied, with a mischievous smile, 'but I believe that our lovely Carrie would have got there on her own, without my help.'

Isaac shook his head.

'How did you know that was what our guest needed?'

Eliza shrugged.

'When Carrie arrived, I could see that she needed to sleep, to do nothing for the first few days, but Jules is different. She has already had a week on her own and although she needs rest, she will also benefit from activities which take her mind off her troubles. Carrie recognises that, too.'

'But pottery?' Isaac said with a frown. 'It could have been a disaster. Sent her self-esteem plummeting even further.'

'Possibly, but we didn't think so. Our guest delivers babies, she helps to give birth. Creating something with your hands is another form of that.'

They sat for a moment quietly, watching the sun go down.

'Modern medicine is a marvellous thing,' Eliza reflected. 'Perhaps if we had been granted a different time in which to live…'

Isaac took her hand and lifted it to his lips. She pulled herself up a little from her waist, shuffled her shoulders.

'We made the best of our situation, didn't we, Isaac? We've been happy, just the two of us, have we not?'

He rested his forehead against hers.

'Of course, my love. You know that you are my world.'

She closed her eyes for a moment.

'And of course we may not have met each other if the timing of our lives had been altered,' she said.

'What is meant to be is meant to be, isn't it?'

He nodded.

'And you don't have to give birth to be maternal, do you? You can fulfil that instinct, that purpose in other ways.'

'And you have, my love,' he said, kissing her on the cheek. 'You still are.'

She leaned her head against his shoulder.

'I couldn't have borne an existence without you, Isaac.'

'But you would not have known,' Isaac said, smiling.

Eliza felt his chin drop to nuzzle her forehead.

'I would have known that something, someone was missing. I'm sure of it.'

Just like I feel that something is missing now, she thought.

'Isaac,' she asked tentatively. 'Why did I lose my memory? Why is there a period of my life that I can't remember?'

He was quiet for a moment.

'I've told you, Eliza, you were ill, very ill. I feared that I might lose you.'

'Consumption, you said?'

'Yes.'

'I was lucky to survive.'

'Very lucky. Most didn't. Your life hung in the balance for several weeks, my love, and your recuperation was long.'

'I'm sorry to keep asking, but I remember little of this time.'

She turned to him.

'And you planted this willow tree to celebrate my return to health. That was such a lovely thing to do, Isaac. I feel at peace when I sit beneath its canopy.'

'Willow is a symbol of resilience and healing. It felt appropriate.'

'It is, and resilience is such an essential characteristic. I wonder if it is the result of nature or nurture.'

'A combination of both, I believe. You were born with resilience, Eliza, but you had the courage to disregard your family's wishes for your future. Having the courage to face up to challenges in itself breeds resilience.'

'I knew that we were meant to be together,' she said, lifting her face slightly to his, 'so my choice didn't take too much courage.'

'I think you are doing yourself a disservice, my love.'

'And I believe that we were always meant to come to this place,' Eliza said, looking out towards the horizon. 'Do you believe that some places choose you?'

She didn't wait for him to reply.

'I think that being here made it easier for me to bear my barrenness. I hope it did for you, too.'

'You know that I do not like that word, Eliza. It is so misleading.'

'Sterile, unproductive then.'

Isaac took her gently by the shoulders.

'I wish you would not still punish yourself this way. You were and are far from unproductive. Look at what we achieved here. The layout of this garden still adheres to your original creation. The cottage still resonates with your love. Our little dogs, buried beneath our feet, knew your tenderness, as have I. All I ever wanted was you,' he whispered, burying his face in her hair. 'You have been more than enough.'

'Oh, Isaac.'

She put her hand upon his dear head. She wished she could say the same, but she had wanted more.

She had wanted a child and the emptiness of not being blessed with that never left her. Perhaps that was what she was looking for – acceptance, peace. She felt a weight lift from her form. That was it!

She would begin to work on bringing herself peace of mind. Then, when she had attained that, maybe she would be ready to leave.

NINE

The following morning, Jules was sitting on the sofa reading a magazine when she saw Tasha walking up the path. She waved through the window and went to the front door.

'Hello. What can I do for you?'

'Carrie rang. Said you were short of eggs, so I've brought some.' She held out a brown cardboard box. 'Laid this morning.'

'Thank you. Did you find Scattihen?'

Tasha lifted the lid and pointed to a creamy pink egg.

'That's hers. She reappeared last night. We've no idea where she's been, but she still had all of her feathers.'

'That's a relief.'

Jules took the box and Tasha hovered on the doorstep.

'Do you want to come in?' she asked. 'I was just about to make a coffee.'

Tasha bit her lip.

'Mum says not to bother you.'

'You're not bothering me. I wouldn't have asked otherwise. I don't want to get you into trouble though.'

'I'm always in trouble. Coffee sounds nice, although Mum says it's bad for my skin.'

'But good for you in other ways. I won't tell her if you don't.'

Tasha smiled and Jules stepped back to let her pass. She wandered around the kitchen, trailing her fingers across the worktops as Jules scooped mahogany grains into the cafetiere.

'When Mum goes away, I hope that she won't come back. That's wrong, isn't it? Abnormal?'

Jules looked back over her shoulder.

'Not necessarily.'

Tasha screwed up her nose a little.

'Two days is the average time she's gone. I wish she'd stay away longer.'

'We all need to get away sometimes and this is quite a small island.'

'Dad doesn't,' Tasha said. 'He says that there's nowhere better than here.'

'That must be nice. To feel so settled.'

'Mum thinks it's boring here. She thinks Dad's boring.'

Jules placed the cafetiere and mugs on the table.

'And what about you? What do you think?'

Tasha carefully poured the tiniest bit of milk into her coffee.

'I want to see the world.'

She looked at the ginger biscuits as if she really wanted one, but was trying to resist, then turned sideways on the chair and stretched herself upwards.

'Do you think I'm fat?'

Jules looked at the chiselled cheekbones, the slim hips, the delicate wrists. A blast of wind from the Solent and Tasha looked as if she could be carried on the air currents to the mainland.

'No, of course not...'

'Mum does. She's always telling me to hold my stomach in, not to slouch, that sugar's bad for me. She never allows me syrup in my coffee when we go out. She only lets me have coffee if I insist.'

'Your mother is very elegant.'

'She used to do a bit of modelling, but she wasn't good enough to make the big time.'

'Is that where she goes,' Jules asked, 'when she goes to the mainland, to do some modelling?'

Tasha laughed out loud. It was short and sharp.

'Oh no! She goes to see an old boyfriend. They're just friends now – or so she says.'

'Well, perhaps they are. It is possible to be friends with old boyfriends.'

Tasha raised an eyebrow and immediately Jules thought of Gavin. She could never be friends with him.

'Mum prefers male friends to female ones.'

Tasha said 'friends' in a specific way.

'Some women do.'

'She wanted to be friends with Guy, but until Carrie came, he wasn't interested in anyone, least of all Mum. She's not his type. So she turned her attention to Lance. Even did a course at the pottery.'

Jules took a biscuit. They were very moreish.

'But she was too impatient.'

'It can take time to get the hang of it,' Jules said.

Tasha threw her a withering look.

'Not with the pots, with Lance.'

'Oh!'

'You know his wife died?'

'Yes.'

'He puts Erin and Fitz first, above everything. Did your dad do that, put you first?'

Jules thought for a moment.

'He tried to, but my mother was, *is* quite needy.'

Tasha nodded.

'I get that. Dad's always trying to keep the peace. He thinks I wind Mum up on purpose.'

'Do you?'

Tasha stared at her and clasped her cup so tightly her knuckles turned white.

'Mum only has to look at me to get wound up. She says I have a surly face.' Tasha lifted her chin and tilted her head to one side. 'Do you think I have a surly face?'

'No, I don't.'

She smiled and reached for a biscuit, taking a mouse bite from the edge.

'I have a theory that she resents me because I ruined her figure. I know that I wasn't an easy baby because she's always telling me. Apparently, the birth was horrendous. She thinks she should have had a caesarean, but in the end, she gave birth naturally. She lost a lot of blood and had to have a transfusion. We've never bonded. That happens, doesn't it?'

'Sometimes, but you mustn't blame yourself.'

'Do you think that deep down we can remember our birth and being inside the womb and whether we were wanted? Do you think that affects us and our relationships with people, with ourselves?'

'Wow, um... those are big questions. I don't know. They do say that we never forget anything and there's so much we still don't know about memory and how the body and brain work. It must have been hard for your mum to go through that experience though.'

'She bonded with Will straight away. He was an easy baby apparently. Erin was really wanted, too. Her mum had had a couple of miscarriages. She and Lance didn't think they could have children so when she came along it was like a miracle. She was adored from the get-go. You can tell, can't you?'

Jules thought back to the girl she'd briefly seen at the pottery; her lovely heart-shaped face, smiling eyes and upturned lips. In spite of the sadness she'd suffered, she looked balanced and secure.

'Yes, I think you can.'

'And Fitz, too. They really wanted him. So much that Erin's mum delayed having chemo rather than risk losing the baby. Erin says that probably cost her life.'

'That's very sad.'

'Lance talks about her a lot and there are photos everywhere in the house. Erin says that her dad does his best to make up for them not having a mum. He always says the three of them are a team. He doesn't do anything without asking them. I think Mum's jealous of how close they are. She doesn't like me going to the pottery much, but Erin's my best friend and Granny stands up for me. I love it there. It's so chilled.'

'What are you making?'

'Another jug. I'm getting quite good at them now.'

Suddenly she sat up straighter.

'When I'm sitting at that wheel, I forget about everything else, about Mum and Dad and problems at school, and being fat and what I'm going to do with my life that will make everyone happy.'

Jules stared at her for a moment, at her beautiful translucent skin with its smattering of freckles, at her long, wavy hair, at her blonde-tipped eyelashes.

'I felt the same when I was there,' Jules said. 'Totally absorbed. I've had a bad time. Someone, a man who I thought I loved, has let me down very badly. Taken money from me.'

'Taken your trust,' Tasha said, softly.

'Yes.'

'In everything?'

'I thought so, until I came here. Of course, I had Carrie. She is one of the best friends anyone could have.'

'Like Erin.'

Jules nodded.

'We all need a friend like that. I nearly lost Carrie. Don't you let that happen with Erin. Don't let some silly argument jeopardise your friendship.'

'But when you sat at the wheel,' Tasha said, 'you felt better?'

Jules gazed out of the window towards the side garden where birds were pecking seed from the feeder which Guy had filled yesterday while they were out.

'It was like – like the aftermath of delivering my first baby. A feeling of contentment, of knowing that this was something I could do, was meant to do, does that sound weird?'

Tasha shook her head.

'Do you believe in reincarnation?'

'Oh, my goodness, that's another big question, especially for a midwife. I'm not sure. I've noticed how uncanny it is that after one person passes on from a family, a new baby arrives as if to fill the space.'

Tasha started to blush.

'You'll think I'm stupid if I tell you this. I haven't even told Erin.'

'I won't think you're stupid at all, but if it's something that you'll regret telling me afterwards, then don't. Some things are best kept to yourself.'

She thought of Gavin. She couldn't imagine ever telling anyone how he had treated her, how she had allowed herself to be duped.

Tasha paused.

'It's just that I feel as if I've thrown pots before, in a previous life maybe.'

'And maybe you have.'

'Do you believe in ghosts?'

'No, I don't think so. Carrie's the person you should be talking to about all of this. I'm more of a black and white person, or I was.'

She thought how mixed up she must sound. Was this the sort of person she had thought she'd become when she was fourteen?

Tasha glanced around the kitchen.

'This house has a nice atmosphere, doesn't it?'

'Yes, very.'

'Whoever lived here before must have been happy and kind. Houses absorb the atmosphere of their occupants, I think.'

'That's a nice thought.'

'Mum wanted this house, you know.'

'No, I didn't.'

'Guy's gran, Irene, is related to my gran, Rita, and their great-aunt lived here – Agnes, she was called. She never married, but because Gran had inherited the farm, and Irene had had a difficult time with her husband leaving, Agnes left the cottage to Irene who then made it over to Guy. Mum was spitting.'

'I'm sorry.'

'I'm not. Mum would have ruined it. She'd have put a whacking great extension on the side and taken the heart out of it. When Guy was doing it up, I used to come and sit in the garden. Sometimes I'd hide under the willow' – she paused – 'but I'd always check before I went into the space in case someone else was there, not physical people, but spirits. It's one of their favourite places.'

'Oh?'

'Not that I've seen them. Just a wispy shape here and there. Gran's seen them, too, when she's been in the cottage cleaning and she's heard them whispering. Have I scared you?'

Jules shook her head.

'No, not at all.'

'Because you don't believe in them,' Tasha said. 'They won't bother you if you don't think they exist.'

'Hopefully not. Unless they want to convince me of their presence.'

Tasha glanced at the kitchen clock.

'I'd better go or I'll be in even more trouble than usual, and I'll get you into trouble, too.' She leapt up and headed for the back door. 'Thanks for the coffee.'

'Thank you for the eggs, and Tasha, if you want to stop by anytime, just for a chat or to sit in the garden under the willow tree, you don't have to ask.'

'How was your morning?' Carrie asked.

'Fine,' Jules replied. Then she smiled down the phone. 'Actually, no, it was better than fine.'

'Good. I was worried about you on your own. Sorry I couldn't get out of this appointment.'

'Actually, it turns out I'm okay on my own here. It's different to being back home. No memories of you know who and although Tasha and you and Rita think it's haunted, there's a real sense of peace here.'

'We're all ultra-sensitive girls!'

'Did you know that Tasha senses figures under the willow tree sometimes?'

'No, I didn't. She's obviously bonded with you.'

'Wouldn't it be nice to feel that you're being watched over and protected?'

She paused and closed her eyes for a second.

'I've never believed in all that stuff, but here it almost feels possible. My Mum would be thrilled. She's adamant that Dad's watching over us all. I've always thought she was deluding herself because she wanted it so badly, but here – and don't laugh because I know this sounds weird – but here it feels as if someone has put an arm around my shoulders and is whispering to me that everything is going to be all right. I sound completely flaky, don't I?'

Carrie laughed.

'No! I'm the flaky one, remember.'

'And I'm really worried that I might be turning into my mother! I was even thinking of going for a walk this afternoon, up to the Longstone, which is exactly what she'd be doing.'

'Jules, she'd have done that the moment she arrived here, so you've still got some catching up to do on that front.'

Jules wrinkled up her nose and felt a small smile tease the corners of her lips.

'Don't suppose you're free, are you?'

'Blissfully, which is one of the reasons I was ringing, to suggest the same thing, a walk of some sort and the Longstone is the perfect place because I can bring you back through the woods into The Manor gardens and we can have tea on the lawn like two ladies of leisure.'

Carrie stopped talking suddenly.

'Or we can go back to the cottage if you don't want to mingle.'

Jules leaned her head back against the chair and studied the beams on the ceiling with all of their knots and chips, bits shaved off here, other strengthening pieces added there. The main beam across the centre of the room had probably once been part of a ship, Guy had said. Maybe the mast, Jules thought, with beautiful linen sails unfurling from it and a fair wind blowing the boat in the right direction. Was that what was happening to her? By some quirk of fate, was her misfortune actually blowing her in the right direction, not one she would have chosen, but one which had been chosen for her by something or someone with more knowledge of what she needed. Goodness me, she *was* turning into her mother. Outside the window a robin landed on the sill and looked her in the eye. The day after her father died there had been three robins on the rockery at home.

'I've never seen that before,' Beulah had said. 'It must be a sign.'

'A sign of what, Mum?' Jules had snapped back. 'A sign that there's a robin's nest in the hedge?'

Her mother had looked hurt.

'I know you want to lash out, Jules, and I understand that, but I believe that your father is still here with us. It might help if you could open yourself up to that possibility, too.'

And Jules had pushed Beulah away, so hard that she'd staggered back against the table and cut the back of her head. They had both stood there, Beulah's hand smeared with blood from where she'd put her hand up to her crown. Jules hadn't even said sorry. She'd just run out and up to her room and thrown herself on to the bed in a torrent of desperate tears, leaving her sister to sort out the wound. On the day of her father's funeral a robin had swooped down and landed on his coffin just before it entered the crematorium.

'Jules, look,' her mother had said. 'Didn't I tell you he was still with us?'

Jules had shaken her head in disbelief, and the robin had flown away.

'Jules, are you still there?' Carrie asked.

'Yes, sorry. Just thinking. I think mingling might do me good as long as I don't have to talk to anyone for too long.'

'I'll have a bite to eat at home, nip in to see Guy's gran and take her some shopping I've picked up and then I'll be with you.'

'Whenever you're ready,' Jules said.

She was in the garden, sketching, when Carrie arrived.

'Haven't seen you do that before.'

'I found this sketch pad and the pencils in a drawer. I thought you'd put them there.'

Carrie shook her head.

'Maybe Rita then,' Jules replied. 'I used to draw all the time when I was in my teens. I just loved it. Then, when Dad died, I put my pencils and paper away and that was it.'

She held up a delicate drawing of the willow tree.

'It's beautiful.'

'I might see if I can get some watercolour paints tomorrow and then I can put a wash on it.'

'I told you that creativity can help with stress,' Carrie said.

'I'm a nurse. I knew that!'

'It's one thing knowing it and another doing it, though, isn't it?'

'Yes, it is,' Jules said. 'I wonder why we do that? We allow the things we love doing to get pushed to the sidelines when deep down we know how much they can benefit us.'

TEN

They headed up the lane and crossed the road by the church where a sign pointed towards the Longstone. The dappled shade of the holloway was welcome, the high banked sides like an embroidery of moss and roots and ferns. Underfoot the ground was pleasingly uneven, Jules thought. You had to concentrate on each step, but they paused often to study a leaf or a flower or just to absorb the atmosphere.

'Think how many people have walked up here over the years,' Jules said.

'Thousands,' Carrie replied. 'All leaving a little bit of themselves.'

'And hopefully taking something away, too, metaphorically speaking.'

As the holloway levelled out and the path snaked around between the trees, they paused to look down into The Manor gardens where, a way in the distance, Guy was moving some pots around the vegetable patch. As if sensing Carrie's presence, he looked up and waved. That's love, Jules thought. That connection which meant he knew she was there, just at that moment.

Further on, as the climb got steeper, Carrie pushed open a gate and they passed out of one part of the woods and into another.

'Nearly there,' she said as Jules trailed along behind her.

'I'm so out of shape,' Jules said, ruefully. 'And I've no one to blame by myself. Too much chocolate and terrible food.'

'You've been working pretty hard,' Carrie said. 'There hasn't been much time for home cooking and exercise between your shifts.'

'I had that stupid gym subscription and barely used it. I'm regretting that now.'

'Having it in the first place?' Carrie said with a grin. 'You were never going to get the most out of that. You're just not the gym type.'

'It was super expensive, too.'

'Have you cancelled it?'

'Can't. Not until the end of the year. There's no point worrying about that now, but I could do without that extra money going out of my account. Thank goodness I don't have a massive mortgage. If Grandad hadn't left me that bit of money and I hadn't been sensible and paid off some of it, I'd be in a right pickle.'

She squared her shoulders.

'What are we waiting for? Let's get going. I'm not going to get fitter standing here looking at the view, however beautiful it is.'

Carrie grinned and gave a mock salute.

'Fall into line then, trooper, and follow me!'

It wasn't long before Jules could see the path opening up and the sky revealed beyond the trees. Carrie stopped again.

'You go first,' she said. 'You should see this on your own. I'm going to wait here for a couple of minutes and let you have the space to yourself. Hopefully there won't be anyone else up there. It's extra special when you're alone.'

Loose stones skittered under Jules's feet as she approached the end of the path and there was the Longstone with the valley stretching away to the right. She took a deep breath, unclipped her hair and threw back her head, letting the wind stream through it. She walked over to the Longstone and touched it gently with her fingertips. The stone was surprisingly warm, and she leaned her back against it surveying the view, the weather-hewn surface feeling like a massage for her tight muscles.

She could come and draw up here, sit on the part of the stone that had fallen over and sketch.

With paper and pencils or a small tin of watercolours and a long-suppressed desire to draw, she could try to capture what she saw in front of her and perhaps that would help her escape the loneliness which still gnawed away at her. Perhaps the miracle of nature would reconnect her to life, and she'd learn to accept change. In the distance a hare bolted out of a clearing of trees, stopped, gazed at her, ears pricked, senses completely in tune with everything around it, before running free down the hill. It felt like a privilege to see a hare up close, especially for a girl born and brought up in the city like her.

'I saw a hare,' she said, unable to stop the beaming smile that spread across her face as Carrie appeared.

'Where did it go?'

Jules pointed down into the valley and Carrie squinted.

'They're protective,' Carrie said, as if reading her mind. 'A sign of a new dawn, new opportunities.'

'If you believe in that sort of thing,' Jules said, aware she probably sounded churlish.

'It's still a sign,' Carrie said, the stubborn tone that Jules recognised so well inflecting her voice, 'even if you don't believe.'

Carrie settled on the fallen piece of granite and Jules came to sit beside her.

'I'd like to believe,' she whispered.

Carrie took hold of her hand and clasped it within both of hers.

'Trust me, to see a hare up here on your first visit is very auspicious.'

'Trust is a word which has almost disappeared from my world, present company excepted.'

'I get that, really, I do. Sometimes we can close ourselves down without even realising it's happening. Stuff happens.'

'And we make terrible choices.'

'You're being too hard on yourself and it's not going to help. Choice implies options, that you're in control, but when you're in love with something or someone or allowing yourself to be driven by society's expectations, you're not totally in control. We don't always have the space or time or clarity to think about making good choices. Sometimes you're just on the travellator part of life and you have to get to the end of it before you can get off. And perhaps those parts are there to teach us something, to make us better human beings. I like to think that, because I want there to be a reason, and if there's an easy way and a hard way, a lot of people take the hard way.'

'Isn't that because we're brought up to believe that hard work equals progress and that if something's easy it's not worthwhile or we don't deserve it?' She bit her lip. 'Everything felt really easy with Gavin at the beginning. I should have known it was too good to be true.'

'I felt the same about Guy, although he wasn't too good to be true – but he's not perfect. If you're looking for perfection, you won't find it.'

'I'm not looking for anyone or anything,' Jules said. 'I'm going to try to learn to be happy on my own. I've spent too long chasing rainbows. I think because of my dad dying I've always wanted someone to look after me, to cherish me like he did my mum.'

She ran the pad of her finger over a piece of lichen on the stone next to her.

'And I'm not going to find that. I think subconsciously I've known that all along, which is why I've ended relationships after a few weeks. It wasn't that I was afraid of the commitment. It was that I realised they couldn't live up to my dreams.'

'There will be someone out there for you, Jules.'

'I can't go through this again. I have my job which I love, and in spite of what I do, and I know people think you're a bit selfish if you admit this, I've never particularly wanted children of my own. I did think about having Gavin's babies, but that was just me in some romantic stupor. I wasn't thinking about the realities and I'm a very realistic person. There's no desperate ticking of my biological clock and instead of feeling as if I'm a bit of a freak, I should allow myself to feel liberated by that. Delivering other people's babies seems to fulfil that need. It's like when you've cooked a meal for people, you often end up not being that hungry, as if all your senses have been fed by the preparing of it.'

Carrie squeezed her hand.

'I don't think you're selfish at all and I'm really proud of you, how you're handling this.'

Jules turned to look at her and blushed.

'I don't know why. I'm thoroughly ashamed of myself.' She gave herself a little shake and looked around. 'Good thing you came to get me or I'd probably still be moping around, my mum hammering on the door or calling the fire brigade to put a ladder up to the window.'

'She cares about you.'

'I know, but I can't be the daughter she wants me to be. I can't take Dad's place and be at her beck and call all the time. She needs so much support. I do feel a bit guilty that Phoebe has to shoulder most of the burden, but she was always closer to Mum anyway.'

'I'm sure your mum loves both of you equally.'

Jules shrugged and turned away slightly.

The trouble was she hadn't loved both of her parents equally. She wondered if any child did if they were honest. Wasn't there always one parent who you had a closer connection with and therefore loved more? If her mother had died, would she have felt as devastated?

'Do your parents love you and your brother equally?'

Carrie twisted her lips.

'I always thought they loved my brother more – until he dropped out of the life they had planned for him. Then it was my turn.'

'For more love?'

'I don't think they'd see it like that, but yes, that's how it felt.'

'And now?'

Carrie laughed.

'Well, now we've both disappointed them so I suppose we're equal in the love stakes again.'

'Maybe it's impossible to give all of your children the same amount of love at the same time.'

She shifted a little on the rock as a slight ache started in her right-hand side. Hopefully her period was about to start at last.

'Tell me a bit about this place, about the people who came here,' she said.

'Well,' Carrie said, twisting around and looking behind them. 'Over there, beneath those blackberry brambles is the long barrow, a burial chamber.'

'Oh!' Jules said. 'Do you think there are children buried there?'

'Probably.'

'I wonder if they felt the same as we do now. Hundreds of years ago they were struggling with the same issues or maybe they were too bothered with survival. Maybe we're too much in our heads these days and not enough in our bodies. Life and death,' she murmured, 'it's as if you can feel the two worlds mingling up here. The wind and the landscape make you feel more alive, but that barrow is a reminder of how temporary it all is.'

'Listen to you getting all philosophical,' Carrie half-joked. 'People do come here because of its spiritual significance, its energy. You'll often find flowers at the base of the stone or crystals in the weatherworn pockets.'

She stood up and Jules followed her.

'Look, here's a turquoise, and an amethyst.'

They walked around in a circle.

'And a beautiful little pink quartz shaped like a heart,' Jules said. She looked at Carrie. 'These are people's hopes and dreams.'

'And sometimes their memories. It steals a little of your soul, this place, which is why people use it as a shrine.'

Jules breathed in the fresh, slightly salty air.

'I get that, more than I've ever got churches or cathedrals. I bet you get amazing birds, too.'

'They've recently released sea eagles on the island, which is a bit controversial, but I haven't seen one yet.'

'I'd love to see a sea eagle,' Jules said. 'My dad used to take me birdwatching sometimes. It was our time together.'

'Well, we can wait up here and see if one comes by or we can go and get some cake,' Carrie said. 'My stomach's rumbling.'

'And your heart is pining for Guy,' Jules teased.

'Maybe that, too,' Carrie said, a bit sheepishly.

Jules reached out to touch the stone again before they headed back towards The Manor. She needed to create some new dreams. Maybe up here would be the place to begin.

They walked back down the path through the woods and halfway down took a slightly different direction, which led to a little wooden gate.

'It says private,' Jules said.

'But we can use it,' Carrie replied. 'The Major doesn't mind.'

'You get on well with him, don't you?'

'I do now. I'm very fond of him. He can be a bit crabby, but underneath it all he's just lonely. He and his wife were devoted to one another. She's responsible for a lot of the landscaping of the gardens.'

'What about his family? Didn't you say he had a son?'

Carrie wrinkled up her nose.

'Lives abroad. Not really interested in this place. Wants his dad to sell up and settle in a retirement bungalow. What on earth would he do with himself then? Besides, he's only in his seventies. That's not old these days. And it's this place that keeps him going.'

They walked along the top path between glossy-leaved magnolia bushes and down a little slope towards the tea garden.

'I'll get this,' Jules said, 'if you want to go and touch base with your beloved.'

'I'll just let him know we're here. You never know, he might get time to join us for a quick cuppa.'

'Which cake do you want?'

'Surprise me,' Carrie replied and headed off between a gap in the hedge in search of Guy.

Jules carefully carried her tray over to a table in the shade and pulled out a chair. She tipped her sunglasses back down over her eyes and surveyed the people at the surrounding tables.

Contentment swirled around the space, weaving in and out of the slatted tables, over and under the wooden chairs. Jules thought that if she stuck out her tongue, she'd be able to taste it, absorb it like a medicine. A dark-haired girl, deep in concentration, picked her way lightly across the grass holding a cardboard box. Jules was tempted to shrink down in her chair, hoping she wouldn't be seen. But it was too late.

Erin smiled broadly as she got closer and Jules tilted her glasses up on to her head.

'Hi!' Erin said. 'How are you?'

'I'm good, thank you,' Jules replied. 'We've been up to the Longstone.'

'That's why you looked deep in thought. It does that to you. Sorry for the disturbance, but I thought it might be rude to just walk past.'

Erin balanced the box on the edge of the table.

'And I needed to shift my grip on the box. Didn't want to drop these.'

She lifted out a small pottery vase filled with garden flowers.

'Oh, that's pretty,' Jules said, as a bee immediate landed on a spray of miniature roses.

'Carrie suggested that Dad made a few pots to go on the tables, and we're going to try and sell a few bits and pieces in the shop here, too.'

'That's a good idea.' Jules picked up the vase and turned it around to catch the light. 'It's beautiful. I love the colours.'

'Actually, I made that one.'

'It reminds me of the sea and the sky.'

Erin looked thrilled.

'You can have it if you like.'

'You can't just give it away. You've got a business to run.'

'But you're a friend. Dad always says that we don't take money from friends.'

'Would you like some tea and cake? This was for Carrie, but the tea's going cold.'

'I really like the cherry and almond cake from here and the strawberry milkshake. I can pay.'

'Then that is what you shall have,' Jules said, picking up her small satchel. 'My treat.'

While she rejoined the small queue at the little hut which served the tea, Erin placed the vases in the middle of the tables.

'Looked as if you got lots of compliments,' she said, returning with another tray.

'Hopefully they'll all stop in the shop on the way back and take a look at some of the other stuff,' Erin said. 'Dad's made some cool bowls and plates, too.'

'You must be very proud of him.'

Erin took a bite of the cake and sucked her milkshake up through the stripy straw. She touched the corners of her mouth with her index finger, wiping away a faint trace of foam.

'He's the best,' she said. 'I can't remember much about Mum before she was ill. She died when I was eight and she'd been ill for a couple of years before that.'

'I'm sorry. It must have been hard for both of you.'

'Dad says that Fitz and I kept him going. But he must have done the same for us. Being here probably helped, instead of still being in London. Even though we don't live in a village everyone rallied around. My grandparents wanted Dad to go back and I think he considered it, but I'm glad he didn't. Where do you live?'

'Manchester.'

'Do you like it?'

'Yes. I've got friends there and a good job.'

'What do you do?'

'I'm a midwife.'

'I like babies. Have you met Cressie and her twins? They're gorgeous. How many babies do you deliver each year?'

'I haven't met Cressie. She's away at the moment, I think. In the hospital where I work, believe there were about five thousand babies born last year.'

'My Mum was having Fitz when the cancer came back. The doctors advised her to have a termination so she could have chemo straight away, but she chose to wait and...'

Jules felt a tightening in her chest. She wanted to reach out and put her arms around this girl who would have to live with this loss for the rest of her life.

'I do love Fitz even though he's a pain, but sometimes when he's really winding me up, I think...'

'You think if it wasn't for him your mum might still be here.'

She nodded. Jules leant closer.

'But she might not, Erin. And then you would have lost both of them.'

Huge green eyes looked up at her.

'Dad says that, too. He says we have to respect Mum's decision. There are some people at school who are really carefree. Nothing bad has ever happened to them. Their parents are happily together, all of their grandparents are alive, the families don't have money troubles, they go on nice holidays and get what they ask for at Christmas. They have this aura of confidence. I envy them.'

'I know people like that, too, even at my age, so I know exactly what you mean. But at some time they will experience loss and hardship, that's the nature of life. You have just had to go through it when you were very young.'

'It's not fair, is it?'

'There you are!'

Jules jumped at the sound of Lance's voice.

'What's not fair is you enjoying yourself while I'm working hard!' he said teasingly, flicking Erin's plait.

'Sorry!' she mumbled through a full mouth. 'Jules bought me cake!'

'I can see that!' He smiled at Jules. 'How are you doing?'

And she immediately wondered how much he knew. What Carrie might have told him. How he might be judging her. She leaned forwards and altered the angle of the teapot slightly.

'I'm fine, thank you,' she said stiffly.

If he noticed her defensive tone, he certainly didn't give anything away.

'Your bowl is drying nicely because you made it quite thin. It might be ready for glazing in a few days. That is, if you want to glaze it. Are you still planning to be around?' He didn't wait for her to reply. 'If not, you can take it with you and maybe finish it back at home.'

'Or I could finish it for you and post it,' Erin added.

'I'm not actually sure how long I'm staying,' she murmured.

Where was Carrie? Why hadn't she come back? Suddenly Jules felt as if she needed rescuing. He was loitering, obviously not in a hurry. She was going to have to ask him to sit down and get engaged in a conversation.

'Jules has just been up to the Longstone.'

'Ah, what did you think?'

'Interesting.'

Goodness, that sounded bland. She could do better than that. He was an ordinary man. Not all men were the enemy. Not all people. She'd be hopeless back in the labour ward if she couldn't cope with meeting people.

'Amazing, I mean. Awe-inspiring.'

Now she sounded like a vacuous teenager.

'I can't really describe it properly.'

She shrugged, felt heat creeping through her body, her cheeks beginning to flare. He smiled. She'd never met anyone who smiled as much. It was disconcerting.

'The best things often can't be described. As long as it made you feel good.'

She focused on a trio of sparrows scooping up some dropped crumbs from underneath the next table.

'Some people find the burial mound to be a bit of a downer,' he said.

'Understandably.'

He gazed at her for a moment, as if trying to work something out before turning to Erin.

'Right, you. Finish that and let's get going. Jules has got better things to be doing than having us taking up her valuable time.'

She half stood up, as if to try and prevent them leaving. How ridiculous. One minute she didn't want to mingle and the next she didn't want to be left on her own. Her emotions were all over the place.

'No, really, it's fine,' she mumbled. 'It's been nice to have the company. I don't know where Carrie's gone.'

'Oh, she was helping me in the shop. Then she bumped into The Major. I'm sure she'll be here soon.' He paused as if wondering to wait with her, like a small child. 'Would you like me to drop the bowl off when I'm passing?'

Erin was standing by her father now and picked her box up from the ground.

'Or you could come by and choose the colour you want for the glaze,' she said. 'I could show you how it's done – the dipping.'

'Well...' Jules began.

'That's an excellent idea,' Carrie said, striding across the grass towards them. 'You can choose a colour for me as well.'

She beamed at Lance and Erin.

'Jules is brilliant with colour. Our home in Manchester was like something out of an interiors magazine, and she did it all on a strict budget.'

Jules felt her blush intensify and she wasn't a blusher. She didn't want to be a blusher.

'Only if you want to,' Lance added, as if sensing her hesitation. 'I tell you what, why don't you take a couple of days to think about it – providing you're not hurrying back to the mainland?'

'No, she is not!' Carrie said, proprietorially. 'She's been signed off work for six weeks so she's not scurrying back anytime soon.'

Jules cringed. She was sure the people several tables away had heard that. Now everyone would know that she wasn't just here on holiday, that there was more to it than that.

ELEVEN

'I wish you hadn't said that,' she muttered to Carrie once the others had gone.

'Sorry, it just slipped out. But it's nothing to be ashamed of, Jules. Loads of people have to take a break from work. Life is just too stressful for a lot of people these days.'

'I do love my job.'

'I know you do.'

'I don't want to give it up.'

'Whoa! Who said anything about giving it up?'

'I'm not sure I can cope with the responsibility of it going forwards.'

Carrie reached out and touched her arm.

'You're only thinking that because you need a break. Give it a bit of time and you'll be back to your mums and babies and as good a midwife as you ever were, maybe even better because you've let yourself be vulnerable.'

They sat in the sun while Carrie ate her cake and Jules had a third cup of tea. Gradually people drifted away and they were there alone, the little café shut up, and all the tables cleared.

'Imagine living in a place like this,' Jules said, throwing a glance back at the house. 'All the fun you could have as a child. Hide and seek would go on all day.'

Carrie gathered up the tray and took it to the table nearest to the closed hatch.

'Do you want a wander around? It's lovely and peaceful once all the visitors have gone.'

They walked across the gravel and up the steps at the side of the house on to a grassy area flanked by two long herbaceous borders. Catmint spilled over the edges, spires of delphiniums reached up past the top of the clipped hedge to the rear, the blue popping out against the dark green yew.

As they passed through a rose-enveloped archway at the end of the path, Wilbur came bounding up, ball in mouth. He dropped it at Jules' feet, tongue lolling out, tail wagging. She stooped to pick it up and threw it just as an elderly man emerged from behind the trees to the left. The ball knocked the Panama hat backwards on his head.

'Oh, I'm so sorry,' she called as he stopped and shielded his eyes to look at them.

'Do I need a trip to my optician or are there two interlopers now?' he asked in a gruff voice. 'And is one of them trying to kill me?'

Carrie laughed and quickly moved to his side, her arm hovering next to him as he strode across the uneven ground.

'I don't need any help,' he said, brushing her away even though she hadn't even touched him. 'I'm not senile and I'm not concussed.'

'This is my friend, Jules,' she said. 'You remember I told you about her.'

'Of course I remember,' he retorted. 'The knee might be dodgy, but the mind is still pukka, and we have already met.'

'The Major's bark is worse than his bite,' Carrie said affectionately.

'Hmph!' he said, lifting the hat from his head and examining it. 'This came from a rather special shop in Seville. My wife bought it for me before she died. Tiny little place on a corner which we discovered by chance, with tall, curved windows and fitted inside with mahogany framed glass-fronted cupboards that stretched from waist height right up to the ceiling, brimming, if you'll pardon the pun, with Panama hats of every size.'

'Oh, my goodness, I do hope I haven't damaged it,' Jules said, 'or you, sir.'

'You don't need to worry about that,' Carrie said. 'The Major is indestructible.'

Jules spotted the ghost of a smile twitching his lips.

'And the hat?'

Vivid blue eyes met hers.

'I'm pleased to report that it appears unscathed.'

She exchanged a glance with Carrie.

'Phew! That's a relief.'

'Or we'd all have had to hop on a plane to Seville,' Carrie chuckled. 'What a hardship that would have been.'

'I doubt that shop is still there,' The Major said. 'Progress has probably taken its toll.'

'Well, South America then,' Carrie added.

'You do know that Panama hats don't come from Panama, don't you?'

Jules opened her mouth to reply, but The Major continued before she could get her words out.

'They actually come from Ecuador. Toquilla straw, they're made from. Most people don't realise that. A good hat is one of life's pleasures when one gets older. The classics are often the best, don't you think?'

Again, Jules opened her mouth to reply, but...

'Like a piece of Victoria sponge cake at teatime. Most important meal of the day, tea. Have you tried the Victoria sponge? No? So many fancy cakes these days, but mark my words, a good Victoria sandwich can beat them all.'

'I'll remember that.'

'Has Carrie been showing you around?'

'We've just started.'

'Don't let me stop you. All and sundry walk around these gardens now.'

'Andrew,' Carrie said, a hint of a scold in her voice, 'remember what we agreed.'

'Hmph! Thinks I should be grateful, this one. What do you think?'

'Me?'

'Yes, you. You look like the sort of person who has opinions.'

'Andrew, Jules has come here to get away from thinking for a while.'

He threw Carrie a cursory glance.

'Nonsense! That's impossible. The brain is never still. It needs to think.'

He dug his stick into the ground and fixed his stare on Jules as if he could see right into her head, which was suddenly empty of everything except panic.

'I-I...' she stuttered, looking desperately towards Carrie who gave an almost imperceptible shrug of helplessness.

'No need to give me an answer now,' he said after what seemed like the longest pause in a conversation she had ever had to endure. 'Mull it over. I'm sure we'll meet again.'

And with a tip of his hat and a flourish of his stick he was off, striding back towards the house, Wilbur glancing apologetically back at Carrie as he followed The Major close at heel.

'Wow, I'm tired,' Jules said, rubbing her eyes.

'It's probably the stress coming out,' Carrie said. 'I slept for days when I first came here. Sleep is very healing, and I haven't let you do that. Sorry. Maybe I've been a bit selfish.'

'You haven't been selfish at all, but I could do with going back to the cottage now and putting my feet up.'

'I'll let you out of the front gate,' Carrie said, 'and I'll stop by and pick the car up later if that's okay. Although I suppose if I grab a ride back with Guy, I could leave it there until tomorrow. That's if you're okay on your own tonight?'

Jules followed Carrie back across the gravel courtyard past the front of the house with its imposing oak front door and shimmering old glass windows. Even though it was high summer there was smoke coming out of one of the chimneys and Jules guessed that the house would be dark and cold inside.

'Look at these,' Carrie said, peering through the window into the shop. 'Aren't they beautiful?'

Some of Lance's pots were arranged on the windowsill, their glaze catching the golden droplets of evening sunshine.

'You ought to go back and glaze your bowl, Jules. Finish it yourself. Erin will make a good job of it, but it won't be totally yours.'

Jules gazed at the blues and greens, silken as the sea and the island landscape. She wanted to touch them, to hold them in her hands, to feel their weight, their gloss, the love that had gone into them.

Complete what you've started, her granny used to say when she was little. Maybe this bowl, which was waiting to be finished, could be a symbol of a new approach to life, of a commitment to herself as much as to other people, to her patients, to her mother and her sister. Jules could envisage her finished bowl, deep blue and jade green glazes allowed to spill over one another, finding their own definition of beauty. She would place it on the windowsill above the sink back in the Manchester kitchen and fill it with yellow and red Isle of Wight tomatoes. She was determined that bowl would remind her not of Gavin, but of a positive turning point in her life.

Jules slept better than she had in a long time. The room was the perfect temperature, her bath had relaxed her, and she had picked up a book of poetry from the little pile on the table next to her bed. She woke briefly just before four to hear the birds begin to sing, but after that she had slept on until nine. She was just finishing her breakfast eggs when there was a knock at the door.

There was a very old Mercedes estate parked outside the

cottage. Jules paused briefly by the mirror in the hall, wiped a crumb of toast from her cheek and pulled her dressing gown more tightly around her. Through the bulls-eye glass panel she could see the back of a man's head.

'Oh!' she said, opening the door.

'Bad time?' Lance asked, turning to face her.

'I slept in.'

'You're allowed to. You're on holiday.'

'Mmm, I suppose so.'

He held out a box.

'We're on our way to collect Tasha. I thought you might like your bowl.'

'Thank you.'

She took the box from him and he turned to leave. Suddenly the passenger door of the Mercedes opened, and Erin swung her legs out.

'Hi, Jules,' she called.

'Hi, Erin.'

The girl strolled up the path, trailing her fingers over the lavender flowers and cosmos.

'This is really beautiful. Like something out of a picture book.'

'Come on, sweetheart, we'd better get going,' Lance said, placing a hand at the small of Erin's back as she peered past Jules into the hallway.

'Dad's always wanted to take a look inside,' she said. 'Guy kept telling him to come over when he was doing it up, but you never got around to it, did you, Dad?'

'No, but now isn't the time. Jules isn't even dressed.'

'She's decent. You wouldn't mind, would you, Jules?'

Erin threw her a winning smile.

'Umm...'

'We've got to go and get Tasha,' Lance protested.

'She won't be ready,' Erin said. 'You know she's always late. Tell you what, I'll wander around to the farm and chivvy her along while Jules shows you around. We'll meet you back here, then you won't have to come to the farm and can avoid you know who.'

And before either of them could say anything she had turned on her heel and was skipping back up the path and heading out on to the lane.

Lance shrugged and shook his head.

'I'm so sorry. She likes to organise me.'

'That's not always a bad thing.'

She stood to one side.

'It's fine. I can just get back in the car and wait for her and Tasha to sort themselves out.'

Let him do that, Jules. You can go and have a nice, relaxing shower and a quiet day.

'She's bound to ask you what you think of the cottage. What are you going to say?'

'Something ambiguous,' he replied with a rueful smile.

'I don't really know Erin, but I'm not sure she'll settle for that. You'd better come in and at least have a quick look around.'

It'll only take about two minutes, she thought to herself, and then I'll have the place to myself again.

'Thank you,' he said, slipping off his loafers as he crossed into the hall. 'My wife had a soft spot for this house. She liked to come and have tea at the gardens and then we'd walk around the village. When she got too weak to walk, I used to drive her in the car. She always asked me to stop outside Hideaway Cottage, said that just looking at it made her feel less afraid for the future.'

He looked around before turning back to Jules.

'If she'd come inside, I think she'd have felt that even more. It has a lovely atmosphere in here, heavy, but not in an oppressive way. It's comforting.'

His eyes fell on the flowers in the middle of the table.

'Nice vase, too,' he said, his eyes twinkling.

Of course. It was one of his. How had she not noticed that? How had she not noticed that the clock was losing time and that her dressing gown had a splodge of egg right on the front?

Suddenly she was aware of everything in sharp relief, the slight stubble on his chin, the way his hands were never still, the story of a life lived across his whole face. Embarrassed, she swivelled and headed through to the sitting room.

'Mind your...'

There was a sickening thud as Lance's head met the solid wooden lintel over the door to the sitting room.

'Ouch!' she said, as he reeled backwards slightly and swayed on the spot. 'Are you all right?'

He rubbed his forehead and looked at his hand as if expecting to see blood.

'Yes. Fine. I think.'

'I'm so sorry. I should have warned you.'

'No, no, my fault,' he protested, blinking hard as if he couldn't focus properly. 'It felt as if I tripped over something, but there isn't anything there. Must have got tangled up with my own feet. They are pretty big! You'll think this is stupid, but I sometimes forget how tall I am. My parents are both normal height so they're not sure where my giraffe-like features come from.'

'You'd better come and sit down,' Jules said. 'You could be concussed.'

She put the box containing her pot down on the coffee table, went to take his elbow and then thought better of it.

'Can you make it through to the kitchen?'

'Yes, yes, honestly, I'm fine.'

He was still holding his head as she pulled out a chair from the table. As he folded himself down it reminded her of a concertina.

'You have gone pale. The whole cottage shook.'

'I did see stars for a moment,' he said.

Jules looked at him anxiously.

'How many fingers?' she said, waving her hand in front of his face.

'Three.' He grinned. 'You really don't have to worry.'

'Except there were only two.'

'I know that. Just joking.'

'That's mean.'

'Sorry.'

'You have cut the skin slightly and I can see it's coming up in a bump. I think it ought to be bathed, and I've got a small first aid kit with some antiseptic ointment. Give me a moment.'

She filled a bowl with some warm water and pulled a piece of cotton wool from a small roll. Go into nurse mode, she instructed herself, but her hands were shaking as she approached him. He sat very still as she bathed the wound, his fingers tapping gently just above his knees almost as if he was playing the piano. She squeezed some ointment from the tube.

'This might sting a little,' she said.

He winced slightly as she applied it.

'Do I need a bandage?' he asked as she stepped away, ridiculously relieved that they no longer had to be in such close proximity.

'Not unless you're really going for the sympathy vote,' she replied. 'I could put a plaster over it, but I don't think it will stay on.'

He checked his watch and Jules thought, not for the first time, what nice wrists he had.

'Thank you for tending to my wounds. I'd better head off and get the girls.'

'I think you need to sit for a bit longer. Tea is the answer. With sugar. Erin knows where you are.'

She filled the kettle and got out two mugs.

'You look very at home here,' he said as she put the milk jug and sugar bowl on the table.

She paused and looked around and it was as if his words had connected her to something bigger than herself.

'I love this room. I love the whole house. It almost feels as if it could be mine. Carrie said she felt like that when she stayed here. It's as though the house is giving itself to you.' She shook herself and blushed. 'That sounds ridiculous and not like me at all. It does that to you as well, makes you think surreal thoughts. Tasha says it's the ghosts. Her theory is that if they like you, you're made to feel so welcome that you almost forget the house isn't yours.'

She poured him some tea and passed the milk and sugar.

'Of course, I don't believe in that sort of thing. Once you're gone, you're gone.'

She put a hand to her mouth.

'Obviously not everyone believes that. I mean, if you've lost someone it's comforting to believe that...'

She was digging herself a massive great hole. Perhaps if she was lucky, it would swallow her up.

Lance looked up from beneath thick lashes.

'Thank you for taking Tasha under your wing. She doesn't have the easiest of times at home.'

He was so gracious, she thought, changing the conversation like that.

'Growing up can be difficult at the best of times.'

He nodded, adding a splash of milk and two heaped spoonfuls of sugar to his tea, then stirred it vigorously before taking a gulp which made his cheeks turn slightly pink.

'I worry all the time whether I'm getting it right with Erin and Fitz. If Sarah would have done it differently. Not having a mother is... indescribable. I sometimes wonder if it would have been better if it had been me who died.'

He stared into his tea, and she sat down at the opposite end of the table.

'For what it's worth, losing your father is pretty indescribable, too. You can only do what you can do, as my granny says.'

He looked across at her, his eyes full of gratitude, and she threw him a very small smile.

'Dad, what on earth have you done? I only left you for a few minutes.'

Erin was looking over the top of the stable door with Tasha hovering behind her.

'It's just a small knock. You're back quickly,' Lance said.

'For the first time ever, Tasha was ready and waiting.'

'Your father bumped his head quite hard on the lintel above the sitting room door,' Jules explained.

'We didn't even get upstairs,' Lance said.

Erin and Tasha exchanged glances and stifled giggles.

Lance turned even more pink.

'Sorry, Jules, they can be a bit immature sometimes. Come on, girls, time to go and leave Jules in peace.'

He stood up and seemed to sway slightly.

'Are you sure you're all right to drive?' Jules asked. 'I can take you home and walk back.'

'We're not going home. We're going to Carisbrooke Castle for the day. It's something I do with the girls every summer and Fitz, too, if he's around. I'll be fine.'

Jules frowned.

'I'm not sure you will be.'

'Why don't you come with us, Jules?' Erin was standing right next to her. 'It's a brilliant day out.'

'Oh, that's really kind, but... I don't think... what I mean is... I'm not sure I'm ready for... maybe another time.'

'Oh, Jules, please come!'

Imperceptibly Tasha had also moved across the floor and was now standing on her other side.

'It'll be fun to have an extra person.' She wrinkled up her nose at Lance. 'No offence.'

'None taken.'

Jules felt her heart beginning to race.

'Please, please, please,' Tasha begged. 'You said you liked history and it's an amazing place. Charles I was imprisoned there, and you can walk the ramparts and there are various exhibitions. There's a lovely little chapel, too, if you like that sort of thing.'

She was being backed into a corner here.

'Tasha, I'm perfectly okay to drive and Jules has got better things to do with her day,' Lance said firmly.

He didn't want her there either, she thought. It would be awkward.

'Like brooding,' Tasha said pointedly.

Jules felt tears spring to her eyes and prayed they wouldn't pool over, or her mouth wouldn't twist into that tight little fist shape which made it so obvious that she was about to cry.

'There's nothing wrong with a bit of brooding,' Lance interjected.

'That's not what you say to me normally,' Tasha replied.

'Nor me,' Erin butted in. 'You don't have to stick with us all the time, Jules. You don't even have to be Dad's full-time carer. You can go off and explore on your own. We can just meet up for the picnic. I've made sausage rolls and Dad will tell you that I make the best sausage rolls, not just on the island or in the British Isles, but in the whole world.'

Jules glanced at Lance. He was as compromised as she was.

He lifted his hands in capitulation.

'It is true, I'm afraid. One day I'm convinced she'll be a champion sausage roll producer.'

'And Granny and I have made lavender iced cupcakes,' Tasha added.

Jules dabbed at her eyes as surreptitiously as she could.

'It seems I can't say no,' she said.

'You can always get a taxi home if we prove to be a bit too much,' Lance offered. 'There's just one thing, though, if you're going to come with us.'

'What's that?' she asked.

'You might want to get dressed!'

TWELVE

Jules had gone upstairs in an absolute panic. What a nightmare. How on earth had she allowed herself to agree to that? And how was she going to get out of it? Poor Lance. He had gone pretty quiet, too, probably worried about being lumbered with a nervous wreck of a woman for a whole day. She longed to lie down, preferably with the curtains drawn and the duvet pulled right up over her face.

From the bedroom window she watched the three of them wandering around the garden, Lance pointing out different flowers and shrubs, Erin doing a cartwheel across the lawn and Tasha saying something which made them all laugh. She pulled on jeans and a T-shirt with La Dolce Vita emblazoned across the front, washed her face, brushed her hair and applied a touch of lip gloss.

'You'd never know,' she whispered, looking at herself in the mirror, 'that on the inside you are a complete and utter quivering wreck.'

'Do you think it's going to rain?' Jules asked, standing on the back doorstep and looking up at the sky, hoping for a black cloud. Rain might force them to postpone this outing until another day and then she could be otherwise engaged.

'Twenty percent chance at twelve o'clock apparently,' Tasha called.

'Oh!'

'The weather forecast is almost as important as religion in our house,' Tasha said with a grin. 'It's a bit like a cup of tea and prayers. Granny couldn't possibly start or end the day without any of them.'

'Does twenty percent warrant an umbrella?' Jules asked.

'You're asking someone who doesn't even own an umbrella, just coats with hoods.'

'That sounds much more practical, but my coat doesn't have a hood so perhaps I'll put an umbrella in my basket just in case.'

'What *have* you got in there?' Tasha asked, peering into the wicker basket which Jules put on the garden table.

'Cardigan in case it turns cold, flip-flops in case it goes really hot, sun cream, water bottle, sun hat, book to read, small sketchpad and pencils, scarf...'

'Scarf!' Tasha scoffed. 'You don't need a scarf. This is summer on the Isle of Wight, the driest, warmest place in the British Isles.'

Jules pressed her lips together.

'Maybe you're right. I'll take the scarf out.'

'And I can see a packet of biscuits and some plasters. Oh, my goodness, there are bananas in here, too, and something wrapped in foil.'

She took out the packet and sniffed it.

'Is that cheese?'

'It's a protein snack.'

'There's a tearoom there, you know, and don't forget our picnic.'

'Going around interesting buildings makes me hungry,' Jules said. 'I get these blood sugar dips from taking in all the information...'

'Okay, the biscuits can stay,' Tasha agreed. 'Don't want you keeling over on us. Are you planning to leave some of this in the car or carry it around with you, because this basket's pretty heavy? If you take this much just for a day out, I'd hate to go on holiday with you.'

'I like to be prepared for any eventuality.'

'Like my dad,' said Erin, coming to stand next to them and rolling her eyes at Tasha. 'Flares in case we get lost between here and Carisbrooke, stretcher in case one of us falls off the battlements...'

'...hot air balloon in case we need to make a getaway from the inner courtyard,' Tasha added with a giggle. 'What is it with grown-ups?'

'I can hear what you're saying,' Lance said, strolling across the grass towards them, 'and you may mock, but remember that time Fitz fell exploring rock pools at that remote beach in Devon and I hadn't got any plasters to put over his badly cut knee. I learnt my lesson the hard way.'

'Jules has got emergency supplies, too,' Tasha piped up.

'Then we must be ready to go,' Lance said, throwing her a warm smile.

She locked the back door and took a deep breath. There was no getting out of it.

As they drove along the country roads Tasha and Erin chatted away in the back about schoolfriends and boys and things they'd watched on YouTube while Lance stared studiously at the road.

'Here we are,' he said, after about fifteen minutes, and Jules realised she had intermittently been holding her breath the whole way. He turned the car down a small lane with houses either side before it opened up suddenly into an entrance to the car park, the castle walls towering to the left. He flung open his car door as if he, too, was in a hurry to get out.

'We'll come back and get the picnic and anything else we need later,' he said to the girls. 'Why don't we meet in our usual place at one o'clock?'

Jules felt her panic levels rising. She'd thought they'd all be wandering around together. Tasha swung a neat little bag over her shoulder and made eye contact.

'We're going to look at the donkeys, Jules. Do you want to come? They're really cute.'

'Oh, thank you, that would be...'

'Dad always gets a coffee first,' Erin interrupted. 'I bet you'd rather do that, wouldn't you? Adults always need a coffee as soon as they get somewhere.'

She didn't know what to say.

'Well, I'm not desperate,' she said, but the girls had scampered ahead across the car park towards the entrance.

Lance looked at the sky.

'Don't think you'll be needing your umbrella just yet. Anything else you want to bring with you?'

She shook her head and he locked the car.

'Erin's right, I do like to get a coffee when we first arrive,' he said, as they walked beneath the gateway. 'But you're not stuck with me.'

For the first time he looked at her directly.

'Sorry if you feel as if you've been press-ganged into this. Erin and Tasha can be a pretty determined double act. You look as if you could do with a drink of something.'

She nodded and made a mental note to never let anyone talk her into anything like this again.

They sat at an outside table in the little courtyard, which was a real sun trap, and Jules began to wish she'd brought her hat, but daren't suggest going back to the car to get it.

'This was the first place I came to with my wife when we arrived on the island,' Lance said, gazing around.

OMG, Jules thought, as if it hadn't felt bad enough, now it

seemed that she was getting in the way of some pilgrimage to his wife's memory.

She spooned some of the froth from her coffee into her mouth.

'She found it so easy to settle on the island. There were plenty of times when I wondered if we'd done the right thing, but Sarah was always sure. I trusted her judgement. She was rarely wrong. She could turn her hand to anything creative, but really, she was an artist, always sketching, always stopping to examine a seed head or watch how the light changed from one moment to the next. I've got hundreds of her notebooks, all full to bursting with ideas. She was drawing right to the end. It was a part of her. Always looking to the future. She was a very positive person.'

He closed his eyes and turned his face upwards towards the sun while Jules let the statement hang between them.

'It's a wonderful quality to have,' he said softly. 'I think she was born with it.'

How lucky, Jules thought. He opened his eyes and concentrated on the sparrows pecking away at crumbs beneath their table.

'Sometimes I think we should stop coming here, but Sarah made us promise to come back at least once a year. I think it helps Erin to feel closer to her mum.'

'I'm sorry. It must have been really hard.'

'It would have been even harder without Erin and Fitz. They were the reasons I kept going. Otherwise, I'd probably have packed it all in and headed back to London. Sarah knew that. Made me commit to staying for at least a year after she'd gone. My friends and family thought I was mad. Sarah's mother was desperate for us to go back to the mainland, and I felt really guilty about that. She'd lost her daughter and wanted her grandchildren back. To be honest I couldn't see how I would make it work on my own, but I was determined not to break my word.'

He almost sounded out of breath as if he hadn't spoken so many sentences all together with such emotion for a very long time.

'And you didn't.'

'No, I didn't and that was largely due to the way people rallied around in a way I couldn't ever have imagined. Friends that Sarah had made helped out in so many ways. She made friends easily. Even when she was really ill, she could still sit at a table in the pottery café and strike up a conversation with a complete stranger and create a bond. A couple of them came back a few months later and gave me commissions.'

He paused as if to collect himself.

'That was incredibly kind. It was a lifeline and gradually I realised that it might be easier to stay than I'd thought. Then there was Rita. She was amazing, checking in, bringing food, taking Erin under her wing and Fitz for walks in his buggy. I'll never be able to thank her enough.'

Jules smiled.

'Rita *is* amazing. I knew that from the first time I met her. In fact, no, from before that. I sensed it from the first time I heard her voice over the phone when we were booking the cottage for Carrie. Although she'd hate me to say it, she's the epitome of goodness.'

'She was the one person who didn't put any pressure on me,' Lance said. 'She was just there when I needed her without expectation of anything in return. There was no suggestion of 'moving on' which is what some of my old friends started talking about after an indecently short amount of time. They were urging me to get out there, meet someone else, find a 'mother' for the children. If I'd gone back, they'd have been setting me up and I didn't want that. I also didn't want to have to summon the energy to fight their well-meaning intentions. All of that was taken up with getting through each day. The memories could, can, be difficult though. A new start might have helped with those.'

'In my experience memories do travel,' Jules said softly.

'But would they be so difficult if we were in a different location?' he asked, his blue eyes suddenly and disconcertingly locking on to hers.

'My father died when I was fourteen,' she began falteringly. It was still difficult to say those words, to accept them, to comprehend the enormity of them and the way the experience had shaped her.

'I left home at eighteen and moved away so that I wouldn't see his face every time I walked past his favourite ironmonger's shop or garden centre or the pub we used to go to for Sunday lunch sometimes. I thought that by doing that I would lessen the pain.' She shook her head. 'But then I felt guilt for running away from the places he loved.' She studied her nails which had always been disappointingly stubby. 'There are no easy answers. You have to do what's right for you.'

He drained his cup.

'Which is why I always go and have a walk around the ramparts, look at the views, try to gain some perspective. Care to join me?'

She looked at his careworn face and had the urge to stroke his cheek. He'd been through a lot.

'No, but thank you for the offer. I'm going to take a look at the chapel first.'

She glanced up at the ramparts. They looked pretty high in places and quite narrow.

'Are you sure you should be going up there when you've had a knock on the head?'

'They're not as high as they look and there are railings.'

She brushed her hair away from her face.

'The wind is getting up. I bet it's blustery up there.'

'It can be, but I like that. It blows all of your cares away.'

If only it were that simple, she thought.

'There are fantastic views, too.'

She really had wanted some time on her own, but what sort of a nurse would she be if she let him go up there on his own and then he had a dizzy spell and…? She stood up and pulled her sunglasses down over her eyes so he couldn't see her reluctance.

'Okay, you've convinced me. Lead the way.'

. . .

He was such a gentleman, she thought, when he turned to offer his hand as they climbed some steep and narrow steps. She hesitated. Get a grip, Jules, she said to herself, it's just a friendly gesture. Nothing more. Besides, it's more for his security than yours. His palm was completely unlike Gavin's, which was a relief. It felt slightly rough and his fingers were long and wrapped all the way around her hand. Gavin's hand had been small and even softer than her own. He'd gone for manicures every month, so his nails were shiny, his cuticles springy. Jules would bet her life on the fact that Lance had never had a manicure.

'Look at that,' he said, as they reached the top and he waved his free arm towards the distance. 'Isn't that beautiful? This island really gets under your skin. You can see almost all of it in every direction from up here.'

She was acutely aware of her hand still encompassed within his even though there really was no need now, not that there had been before, she thought. Although it was nice to feel that warmth and be physically connected to someone.

'The castle dates back to Anglo-Saxon times, but the Romans may have been here as well,' he said. 'In the thirteenth century it was owned by someone called Countess Isabella de Fortibus who was one of the richest women in England. On her deathbed and as all of her six children had pre-deceased her, she sold the castle to Edward I. I suppose it's most famous because Charles I was held prisoner here before his execution in 1649, and then much later Princess Beatrice, who was Queen Victoria's fifth daughter, made it her home. Sorry, I'm probably boring you to tears.'

'You're not. It's fascinating and you're a good tour guide,' she replied as they made their way around the top of the walls.

'Look, there are the girls,' he said, getting too close to the edge for Jules's comfort and waving. 'They haven't seen us.'

'They look happy.'

'At the moment,' he said with a smile. 'When you're fourteen, one minute you're happy and the next the world feels as if it's about to end.'

'And that can just be because your favourite shirt's in the wash,' Jules joked.

'Or your brother's eaten the last piece of pizza,' Lance chuckled in reply. 'Talking of food, we have our picnic right over there in that corner where the cannon is.'

Suddenly he looked down at their clasped hands and gave an embarrassed laugh.

'Thank you for keeping a hold of me.'

'I didn't want you falling off and squashing the flowers on that grassy bank,' she quipped.

'Or even worse, one of the donkeys,' he replied.

'Absolutely not.'

Slowly he unfurled his fingers.

'I think I can make my way down these steps on my own.'

He let Jules go ahead.

'You must want to have a wander,' he said when they got to the bottom. He checked his phone. 'I've got a couple of calls to make so we'll meet up at one, shall we?'

She nodded and watched as he strode off. In her back pocket her phone buzzed, and she answered.

'Where are you?' Carrie asked.

'At Carisbrooke Castle.'

'Oh, nice. I'd have come with you if I'd known.'

'I thought you were busy this morning and I sort of got rail-roaded into this.'

She explained what had happened.

'Are you all right?' Carrie asked. 'Do you need me to come and rescue you?'

'No, I'm fine,' Jules replied.

And standing there, surrounded by these ancient walls which had seen almost everything, she realised that she was fine. Almost.

At one o'clock the girls were already lying stretched out, headphones in. Erin had her eyes closed while Tasha stared at the bright blue sky. Jules took off her cardigan, spread it out on the grass and sat down. She watched people walking past, children laughing, pensioners ambling, young couples arm in arm. What were their lives like, she wondered, behind the scenes, beyond the brief respite of a day out? What joys and tragedies were they walking around with? In the distance she could see Lance walking towards them purposefully. He stopped briefly to talk to someone he obviously knew, adjusting the long strap of the cool bag on his shoulder, her basket held firmly in his other hand. He threw back his head and laughed at something the woman had said. How life enhancing, Jules thought, to bump into people you knew just on a random day out. She was so busy rushing to work and back, often in the dark, that if she did see anyone familiar, she never had time to stop and chat.

'Sorry,' he said, when he finally reached them, 'I got waylaid. Someone who did one of my courses a while back.'

Erin had opened her eyes and was sitting up.

'Dad's always being accosted by people who've been to The Pottery,' she said, rolling her eyes, but with an unmistakable air of pride.

He opened a packet of pretzels and offered Jules one before tipping them into a bowl.

'Prawn sandwich? Or ham and tomato?'

She took one of the prawn mayo ones and immediately thought it was a mistake. She was bound to spill some of the filling down her front.

'And one of Erin's sausage rolls,' Tasha said, peeling back a foil parcel.

The pastry was still warm and very flaky – another potential for making a horrible mess.

Lance leaned back on his arms and stretched out his legs. He was wearing shorts and his legs were lightly tanned. Jules bit tentatively into the most delicious cherry tomato she thought she'd ever tasted outside the Mediterranean. At least it didn't squirt all over her top. She'd forgotten how difficult picnics were to eat. It wasn't so bad if you were with people you knew, but when you were with strangers, well, the last thing you wanted was to end up splattered with food or, even worse, squirt them with food.

'My mum likes a picnic,' she said. 'She'd be impressed with this.'

Erin looked pleased.

'We saw you on the ramparts,' she said, casting a sly glance at Tasha.

She'd obviously spotted that they'd been holding hands, Jules thought. Teenagers either missed the things you desperately wanted them to notice or instantly noticed the things you didn't want them to.

'We saw you near the donkeys,' Jules said.

'Juno didn't want to turn the treadwheel today so they had to go and get Jack to show everyone how water can be brought up from the well,' Tasha said with a laugh.

'It's like a big hamster wheel,' Erin added. 'It's amazing. You ought to take a look.'

'I will. I went around the chapel earlier and into Princess Beatrice's gardens. Both are beautiful.'

'Did you see the window where Charles I tried to escape?' Tasha asked.

'No,' Jules said, impressed by the girl's enthusiasm. 'Not yet.'

'We'll show you later. He got stuck between the sill and an iron bar so had to abandon that attempt. He tried again later on even though he'd been moved to another room which was more difficult to escape from. You can see his room inside but it's been altered a bit.'

'Presumably that escape attempt failed as well?' Jules said.

'He was betrayed at the very last minute by two sentries. When he first came to the island it was meant to be a refuge, but it ended up turning into a prison, although he had a bowling green and a fair amount of freedom to begin with.'

'How long was he here for?'

'Fourteen months. You must go into the museum,' Tasha said. 'There's loads more about it in there.'

'I'm impressed,' Jules said.

'Granny says that history is important and if you don't know where you've come from, how can you work out where you want to go,' she replied, 'or something like that.'

'I can't argue with that,' Jules said, exchanging a glance with Lance.

'Wise woman,' he said, lying back on the rug and closing his eyes. 'You'll never win an argument with Rita or Tash so don't even try.'

Erin put her EarPods back in and Tasha began writing in a little notebook she had fished out of her pocket. Jules felt herself starting to relax. After a few minutes she plucked her book out of the basket, turned on to her front and began to read.

Later they dropped Tasha off at the farm and Lance drove the car around to the cottage.

'Thank you for a lovely day,' she said as he got out to open the door for her. 'I've really enjoyed it.'

'You sound surprised.'

'I am. Sorry, that sounds so ungracious. It's not the company. I mean, it's not your company.'

She was beginning to feel flustered.

'It's any company. I'm not good with strangers, not that you're a stranger...'

She glanced at Erin sitting on the back seat listening to her music. The hole she was digging felt as if it was getting deeper with every word.

'Jules, stop!'

She looked up at him, startled.

'You don't have to explain. When Sarah died, I didn't want to go anywhere or see anyone. I understand.'

'Except Gavin hasn't died. At least I don't think he has. I'm so, so sorry. Compared to what you've been through, my problems are insignificant.'

'You're still grieving, though, for someone you've lost.'

'That's true and I'm actually a bit angry too, which I suppose is a good sign.' Her eyes flashed up at him. 'People can be so disappointing, can't they?'

'It's easy to think that, but there are good people, too.'

He's a good person, she thought. That's what she needed, to spend more time around good people.

'Would you like to come in for a cup of tea?'

He shook his head.

'I won't if you don't mind. We need to get back and prepare for class tomorrow and I have to call my in-laws and check Fitz is behaving himself.'

'And you don't want to risk knocking yourself out on that lintel,' she said.

'That as well.'

'Another time, maybe.'

He nodded, but moved away slightly as if not to seem too eager.

'I'd like that. And Jules, thank you for coming. You have been perfect company. Teenage girls when they get together can be a bit...' He shrugged. 'It's like a club I don't belong to and will never have the key.'

Jules laughed. A proper laugh. Something she thought she might never be able to do again.

'I totally get that.'

And he stood there watching as she walked up the path, placed her key in the lock and went into the house with a small final wave of her hand.

POTENTIAL

Eliza was drifting around the garden, trailing her fingers over the roses. She'd always loved their velvety softness and their scent. Her homemade rosewater had been much in demand. People had often remarked on the quality of her skin, and it was Isaac who had encouraged her to start a small business. She had grown camomile and lemon balm for tea in the field at the back of the house. She'd always loved to be outside when the weather permitted, tending her flowers and plants, walking their little dogs along the beach, taking picnics up to the downs.

'You are looking very pleased with yourself,' Isaac said.

'Our guest seems to have had a very happy day,' she replied. 'There's a sparkle to her eyes which was sadly missing when she arrived.'

'And you are attributing this to what exactly?'

'Being here, of course.'

He smiled down at her. He knew her so well. Perhaps too well. A little flicker of angst flared up. Could you know anyone too well?

'And?' Isaac prompted.

'Well, getting out and about around the castle and spending time with those delightful young ladies. It's always so invigorating to spend time with younger people. They have a different perspective to impart, and Tasha is so bright. She really doesn't realise how much potential she has.'

'And our guest?'

'Of course she has potential, Isaac, potential to overcome this terrible period in her life. We're all much stronger than we give ourselves credit for, are we not?' She paused. 'But it helps if we have loved ones to support us along our sometimes precarious path in life.'

'When you say loved ones, Eliza, I trust you are not letting any romantic notions get the better of you once again? It may have worked once with Carrie and Guy, but it is unlikely to be repeatable.'

'Isaac! Would I do such a thing?'

He frowned.

'Yes, Eliza. I'm afraid to say that I think you would.'

She smiled mischievously at him.

'Sometimes, Isaac, it doesn't do any harm to throw a little magic into the air and see where it lands.'

Isaac sighed.

'Oh, Eliza, please tell me that you didn't cause Lance to hit his head on the beam above the door this morning.'

She stared at her feet.

'He may have accidentally just tripped over the point of my shoe,' she said.

'Accidentally? How? What were you even doing in such close proximity? Haven't we talked about this? You are putting yourself, putting us, at risk.'

'Oh, Isaac, he had no idea that I was there and neither did Jules. She doesn't pose any danger for she is not a believer, and the lovely potter is rather in awe of her, I think, so was not receptive to any other presence than hers.'

'But he could have really hurt himself.'

She cast him a disparaging glance.

'Isaac, you were always banging your head on that door lintel and it did no great harm. Besides, if I'd thought he was going to hit it too hard I would have made an effort to pull him back.'

Isaac paced up and down.

'I really do think that we should be making a move, Eliza. Now the cottage is to be occupied by a collection of different people, I think it will be too disquieting for us to remain.'

He looked around.

'With all of the comings and goings there will come a time when we will feel that this is no longer our home.'

'No!'

He looked startled by the vehemence of her response.

'Please do not say such a thing. It will always be our home, Isaac, even when we're no longer here.'

He took hold of her hands.

'Maybe, my dearest, maybe it is time for us to make a new home.'

'I need to stay a little longer, Isaac.'

'How much longer?'

'I wish to remain while our latest guest is here. Can you grant me that?'

Isaac sighed.

Of course he could. He could grant her anything and she knew it.

THIRTEEN

Jules was wandering around the gift shop in Yarmouth when she had the distinct feeling that someone was watching her. She skirted a rail of Indian print blouses and peered out of the two large glass windows on to the street. Across the road she could see Carrie heading into the antiques shop and a few locals standing in groups and chatting. She bought a birthday card and headed over to the deli to look for some nice chocolates or a jar of local honey.

'Shall we browse around some of the little galleries?' Carrie asked, popping her head over the top of a stand full of local bread. 'Sorry, did I make you jump?'

Jules had one hand against her breastbone. She glanced back towards the door.

'You'll think this is really stupid, but I've got the feeling that I'm being followed.'

Carrie looked around.

'There isn't anyone in here except us. Maybe it's the ghosts from the cottage.'

'Now you're being ridiculous.'

They wandered in and out of the shops and sat on a bench with an ice cream overlooking the Solent.

'This is good, isn't it?' Carrie said, licking her ice cream.

'It would be,' Jules said, 'if it wasn't for...'

Suddenly, she shoved her ice cream at Carrie and ran across the grass towards a clump of bushes. A woman in a large straw hat retreated around the far side.

'Mum!' Jules shouted. 'What on earth are you doing here?'

Beulah emerged sheepishly with some greenery stuck in the pink ribbon around the brim of her hat.

'I thought I'd drop by and check you were all right.'

'Drop by? It's not exactly next door. Why didn't you tell me you were coming and how long have you been following me for and...?' She gasped for breath. 'And where are you staying?'

'Did you know that you've got ice cream down your front?' Beulah replied. 'Pistachio by the look of it.'

Jules stared down at her top where a splodge of green was soaking into the white broderie anglaise.

'Don't change the subject,' she snapped.

'This is a marvellous place,' Beulah said, expanding her lungs and throwing back her head. 'You just know that you're heading somewhere special even before you get on the ferry. There's that lovely man at the port who ushers you up the ramp with a flourishing bow. He looks as if he enjoys his job so much.'

'I didn't notice.'

Beulah cast her a glance.

'For a nurse you're a bit short on observation sometimes, Julianna.'

Aargh, why did she insist on calling her that? Everyone else called her Jules, but Beulah insisted on that name which she hated.

'And the journey itself is delightful.' She sighed one of her well-practised sighs. 'Thank goodness the Solent was as smooth as a millpond. I've been very worried about you, darling, and it's played havoc with my digestion.' She patted her stomach tenderly. 'But everything went perfectly. I felt the cares begin to slip from my shoulders. Of course, they never completely go away when you have children, however old they are. When I disembarked, I fancied a little drive around, just to get the feel of the place, and here I am. Is that lovely Caroline over there?'

'You know perfectly well it's Carrie. Your eyesight isn't that bad. Did she know you were coming?'

Beulah shook her head vigorously. The long pink ribbon swished across Jules's face.

'Oh no, no, no. I've spoken to her once or twice and she was very reassuring, but...' Beulah put her palms together. 'I felt the need to come. It was so strong, I couldn't deny it. You're my baby, Jules. At a time like this a girl needs her mother.'

'I'm not your baby, Mum, and actually I don't...' She stared at Beulah's imploring face. '...want you to worry. I'm fine.'

Beulah looked at her disbelievingly.

'I'm sure you're not, my darling girl. You look thin. Haven't you been eating?'

'Yes, mainly cake and now ice cream.'

'It must be the stress then. Heavens above, I know what that's like.' She pressed her fingertips against her cheekbones, lifting them upwards. 'It plays havoc with one's facial muscles. If I could do anything to make you feel better, darling, I would. You know that, don't you?'

Staying away would have made me feel better, Jules thought. Not forcing yourself on me, but she hated herself for thinking it. Thoughts like that left a sour taste in your mouth despite the sweetness of the ice cream. The trouble was, the harder her mother tried to make her feel better, the worse she became.

'Are you all right for money? I haven't got much spare. Work's been a bit thin on the ground recently. I'm getting to that difficult age for an actress, but I can help a bit.'

She still hadn't let the cheekbones drop to their normal resting place, so her voice sounded a bit strained.

'Phoebe, too. She's got some savings because she's much more sensible than me. She says you only have to ask if you need any bills paying.'

And suddenly Jules felt a surge of emotion as if something had given way from the force of it, a dam bursting. She doubled over.

'Julianna. What is it? Are you ill? Oh, my giddy aunt! I must call a doctor.'

Jules shook her head and waved her hand as her mother bent beside her.

'I'm fine,' she gasped. Her vocal cords felt crushed by the sadnesses of all the years, her head spinning. She watched as ants scurried around the edge of her flip-flops and across the paving towards gaps in the big roughly hewn stones edging a border of bright red flowers, which were becoming increasingly blurred. She was vaguely aware of her mother calling Carrie and them taking her under each arm and half dragging her back to the bench. A swarm of grey clouds filled her head, pinpricks of black demanding omnipotence.

'Julianna, listen, put your head between your knees.'

No, no, that didn't work. Everyone knew that didn't work. She needed to lie down on the ground. She tilted forwards, aware of Beulah's hands holding on to her as she slid to the stone, which was warm from the sun and gritty from more ants coming and going. She did hope that she wouldn't squash any of them, but she was leaving this world, the blackness terrifyingly intense and the cold clamminess at the back of her neck spreading until...

She opened her eyes to find Beulah kneeling beside her, one hand smoothing damp hair back from her forehead. She felt so cold even though the sun was beating down on her.

'Oh, you're back. Thank goodness. Don't move. I knew you weren't well the moment I saw you.'

Jules closed her eyes again.

That was just what she wanted to hear.

'We should call a doctor.'

If only you had done that when Dad first complained of chest pains, she thought. But there was no point going there now.

She tried to sit up. There was a sandy sediment all up the side of one arm.

'I just fainted, Mum, that's all.'

'That's all! How can you be so blasé? There's a reason. Your body is telling you something. We need to get you checked out. Don't you agree, Caroline?'

'Well, maybe it would be a good...'

'I've probably got a bit too much sun. I've been sitting out.'

'You never would wear a hat. When you were little, I used to put a hat on you and ten seconds later it was off.'

She felt sick and headachey. She had to admit her mother was probably right and she should have worn a hat. Beulah studied her intently as Jules sat up and massaged her forehead with the tips of her fingers. She had no idea where that had come from. The last time she had fainted was after too much red wine on a work night out and that had been a couple of years ago.

'I'm okay, now. Honestly. I just need some water.'

Beulah foraged in her bag and produced a water bottle.

'Here,' she said, 'drink this. I've put some rescue remedy in it.'

'Thank you,' Jules said, taking a welcome sip.

'Thank goodness I'm here to keep an eye on you,' Beulah said.

Jules felt a shudder ripple through her.

'Carrie's been keeping an eye on me.'

'And a wonderful job I'm sure she's been making of it,' Beulah said.

Jules sat up straighter, trying to look better than she felt.

'You look very pale. I wonder if you're anaemic.'

'I don't think so.'

'It might be worth having a blood test.'

'When I get back to Manchester I will.'

Beulah seemed vaguely appeased.

'I know you're very independent and quite capable of coping on your own, darling. We all say those things, and we all mean them, up to a point. But there are times when it can be' – she paused, searching for the right word – 'cathartic to not be quite so independent, to let someone else look after you for a while. She left a dramatic pause. 'Which is why I'm here.'

She reached for the dripping pistachio ice cream, which Carrie was still holding.

'You don't mind if I finish it, do you? It's one of my favourites and I've hardly had a morsel all morning and it was such an early start.'

'How *did* you know where we were, Mum?' Jules asked, brushing ants from her skirt.

'Pure luck,' Beulah said, sitting down on the bench next to Carrie and biting into the waffle cone. 'I was walking through Yarmouth thinking what a beautiful little place it is and then I saw you both. What are the chances of that? I thought. My own beloved daughter in a shop all these miles from home and we just happen to bump into each other.'

'I would say the chances of that are pretty negligible,' Jules replied drily.

She used all her remaining energy to glare at Carrie, who shook her head vehemently.

'Dearie me!' Beulah chortled. 'You think that we're in cahoots, Caroline and I. Nothing could be further from the truth.'

Jules stared up at her mother.

'The only other explanation is that you've been stalking us.'

'I prefer to call it shadowing,' Beulah murmured.

'You're not a spy, Mum.'

'If you insist on knowing every last detail, I bumped into that lovely lady who looks after the cottage, Rita. I was standing at the front door trying to get a phone signal to call you when she arrived with some eggs and said that you'd come here. It's only a few miles down the road so I thought I'd try to surprise you.'

'You've certainly done that,' Jules muttered.

'And isn't it a lovely place?' Beulah extolled, swivelling her head from left to right. 'Such fabulous energy.'

Jules rolled her eyes.

'And talking of energy, that cottage of yours is very special; the way it sits in the landscape with the hills on one side and the fields leading down to the water on the other. It nestles. Do move on to the bench, Julianna. You're making me anxious sitting there. I mean, it's obviously very grounding and you must need earth energy, but those ants look as if they might bite. This bench has plenty of room for the three of us.'

Beulah extended a hand and Jules allowed herself to be helped up to perch on the end.

'I can tell it's a healing place,' Beulah continued, 'although it's obviously got a way to go so far as you are concerned.'

'Thanks, Mum! You know just how to make me feel better.'

Beulah reached some sticky fingers up to Jules's face and stroked her cheek.

'I must come over and introduce myself to the spirits of Hideaway Cottage.'

'There aren't any spirits, Mum.'

Beulah frowned.

'That's not what Caroline told me.'

'I-I just told your mum about the blanket I found in front of the range and the tea caddy under the floorboards with the little lock of hair and the baby's rattle and...'

Sorry, she mouthed at Jules.

'Oh, there are definitely spirits,' Beulah insisted. 'Welcoming ones. I felt they welcomed me as I stood in the garden. They have welcomed you, Julianna. You just won't acknowledge it.'

'Talking of welcomes,' Carrie said tentatively, 'do you have somewhere to stay, Beulah? Guy and I have a spare room if you haven't booked in anywhere.'

'How kind.'

Yes, Jules thought, how amazingly kind.

Beulah threw Carrie her most beatific smile, the one which irritated Jules to no end because no one could fail to be charmed by it.

'You don't need to worry, either of you. I've made plans.'

Jules realised she was gripping the side of the wooden bench, the edge of the roughly sawn wood grazing her fingers.

'I've arranged to stay with my friend, Claudia... I mean Jo, as she is called now,' she said, her voice dropping to a whisper. 'It will be the first time I've seen her for years. We have a lot to catch up on.'

She turned to Jules again.

'So, I won't be crowding you, my darling, but I'll be just down the road whenever you need me. Won't that be wonderful?'

Jules felt her lungs expand a little.

'That will be... astonishing.'

Beulah beamed.

'I knew you'd be pleased to see me,' she said. 'Your sister said not to come, but a mother has to follow her instincts and here I am.'

'Yes, Mum,' Jules said with a wan smile. 'Here you are.'

'I thought she was going to be staying here,' Jules said as Carrie dropped her off at the cottage. 'Thanks for stepping in.'

'Turns out I wasn't needed anyway,' Carrie replied.

'Do you think she'll be here for breakfast?' Jules asked.

'Maybe. Jo gets up pretty early and heads to the Longstone most days.'

'That means Mum will be up with the lark, too.' She groaned. 'Why did she have to come?'

Carrie put an arm around her shoulders.

'Because she loves you, Jules. That's why. Don't be too hard on her.'

'I'll try not to be.'

'I'd get an early night though, just in case she's calling in here at some ungodly hour.'

'I will, but first there's something I need to do.'

'Phoebe. It's Jules.'

'Hi! Yes, I do recognise my own sister's voice.'

'Sorry, it's just a while since we've spoken and a lot has happened and...'

'We spoke outside your front door a couple of weeks ago. At least, I spoke and you refused to say anything apart from go away. Mum's been really upset.'

'Did you know she's here?'

Of course she knew. They told each other nearly everything.

'For what it's worth, I tried to dissuade her, but she's worried about you. We both are.'

'Your dissuading didn't work.'

Jules hadn't meant to sound snappy, but it came out that way.

'You know Mum once she's got an idea in her head. How are you?'

'Okay. Better than I was. Still up and down. You?'

Phoebe made a muffled sound at the end of the phone.

'Phoebes? Are you crying?'

Jules couldn't remember the last time she'd heard her sister cry. Was it at Dad's funeral when they'd both had to virtually carry Beulah down the aisle of the church as her knees sagged beneath her elegant crepe de chine black dress? Since then, if Phoebe had cried, she'd kept it to herself.

'Sorry. Stupid. My period's started. A bit over-emotional. We're trying for a baby, and every month is an utter nightmare.'

'Oh, Phoebe. I didn't know. I'm so sorry.'

'Really? I'm amazed Mum hasn't over-shared with you.'

'She hasn't. I promise. How long have you been trying?'

'Eighteen months. A very long eighteen months. I always thought I'd conceive really easily. Took it for granted.'

'Perhaps you ought to get checked out.'

'Been there. Done that. Both of us. Told everything is fine. Except it's not.'

'How's Giles?'

'Stoically bearing the brunt of my moods.'

'You're solid, you two, though.'

'I hope so. You never know until you're put under real pressure, do you?'

'Come off it, Giles is perfect for you. I knew it as soon as I met him.'

'Maybe,' Phoebe said, softly sobbing. 'Maybe if I can't give him a baby, I'm not perfect for him.'

'You mustn't think like that. Lots of people have difficulties and end up with families of their own. I see it all the time at work. Don't give up hope. Have you thought about IVF?'

'I'm not sure I can cope with that at the moment, and I know people who've been through it and ended up splitting because of the strain. Sometimes I think Giles would be okay if we didn't have children. He's talked about getting a dog and he's bought a new circular saw ready to build a chicken run. He's never particularly wanted animals before.'

'Well, maybe it wouldn't be a bad idea,' Jules said, gently. 'Take your mind off...'

'Nothing,' Phoebe said, vehemently, 'nothing will take my mind off it. It's there when I wake up, it's there when I go to sleep. It's like this massive black hole in my life, and do you know how guilty that makes me feel? I have this wonderful husband and a great job and a nice house and great friends and amazing holidays and I shouldn't complain, but it's a need, Jules, a yearning, and I can't ignore it.'

She paused to blow her nose.

'You've never felt like that, have you?'

'No.'

'I try to imagine you being with me when I give birth, but I'm just not good at visualising and I'm scared that means it will never happen.'

'It doesn't mean that at all,' Jules reassured. 'You'll work it out, Phoebes. Together. Like you always do. You're a team, you and Giles.'

'Thanks. I'm really sorry about Gavin.'

Jules bit her lip.

'I thought he might be the one. Just shows what a good judge of character I am.'

'Has it occurred to you that you've had a lucky escape?'

'If you'd said that a few days ago I'd have shouted at you, but now, after some time here, I do know that.'

'Are you okay over there, on your own?'

'I'm not on my own. I've got Carrie nearby and there's Rita just around the corner and her granddaughter, Tasha, and Lance who runs the pottery and his daughter, Erin, and The Major and Jo – and now I've got Mum just down the road. At least she's not staying with me, thank goodness.'

'Sounds as if you've got a whole sea of supporters.'

'I hadn't thought of it like that, but yes, I suppose I have.'

'I'm here for you, too, Jules, if you need me. I'm sorry about offloading when you've got your own problems.'

'It's fine. When I come back to the mainland, perhaps we could meet up, have some lunch, do some sisterly things?'

'I'd like that. And Jules, I know that Mum can be suffocating, but she does love us.'

'I know.'

'What are you doing this evening?'

Jules looked around the sitting room, at the squashy sofa, the pile of magazines on the coffee table, the fire laid and ready to be lit if the temperature dropped.

'The wind's getting up here and it's gone a bit colder so I'm going to snuggle down, see what's on the TV and have a nice quiet evening. Doesn't sound like party girl me, does it?'

'No, but it sounds perfect for where you are now,' Phoebe said.

'All part of the new me,' Jules replied.

'I'm going to pour myself a glass of something non-alcoholic and drink to that. The new Jules in the right place at the right time with the right people around her.'

And when she put it like that, Jules thought, it sounded incredibly settling.

FOURTEEN

Jules was showered and in her dressing gown and watching the end of a film when she thought she could hear crying. She turned the television down and sat for a moment wondering if she was imagining it, if it was one of those noises that Carrie attributed to ghosts, but for which she would be able to find a rational explanation. But no. There were definitely soft, muffled sobs coming from somewhere. She followed the sound towards the front door. Huddled in the porch, knees drawn up to her chin, hair falling forwards across her face, was Tasha. In her hands she cradled something.

'Tasha, what on earth has happened?' Jules bent down so that she was almost on a level. 'Are you ill or injured?'

A shake of the head.

'Then you can get up. Come on. You can't sit there. It's chilly for the time of year and the wind is blowing straight into the porch. That step must be freezing.'

She touched the girl's bare arm.

'Goodness, you're cold. And you're only in pyjama shorts and a strappy top. Let's get you inside.'

She helped Tasha to her feet and guided her to the sitting room, lowering her onto the sofa and wrapping one mohair throw around her shoulders and another over her legs. Instinctively she dropped a kiss on to the top of her head.

'I'm going to get you a warm drink.'

She passed her the television controls.

'I won't be a minute. Change channels if you want to.'

Deciding that hot chocolate was a better option than tea, Jules kept a close eye on Tasha through the doorway as she waited for the milk to come to the boil. She picked out a small floral tray, put a couple of biscuits on a plate, whisked the hot chocolate to a froth and headed back through.

'Here you are. Hold the mug for a while and it will warm you through.'

Slowly Tasha opened her cupped palms to reveal several pieces of broken pottery.

'Oh dear,' Jules said. 'What happened?'

'It was for you,' she said, the tears starting to flow again. 'I made it for Granny, but she's got loads of my jugs so I thought you might like it.'

'I do,' Jules said, as Tasha emptied the pieces into her hands. She turned the pieces of broken pottery over. 'Why don't we glue this? It will still be beautiful.'

'It will still be broken though.'

'In some cultures, they deliberately put flaws in things to remind us that life isn't perfect.'

'I know that, but this isn't deliberately done by me – it was ruined by her. She ruins everything.'

'Your mum?'

Jules put the pieces on the table and sat next to her. She felt a tightness in her chest. All those rows with her own mother came flooding back. Even now she thought it should hurt less each time they disagreed, but it never did. Every cross word from her mother felt like a betrayal. She turned her attention back to Tasha.

'Perhaps it was an accident.'

Tasha stopped crying and twisted to look at Jules, her eyes wide in disbelief.

'She took it from me and threw it on the flagstone floor because it was for you. She's jealous.'

'Of me? She doesn't even know me.'

'You're a rival.'

'For what?'

'Lance's affections.'

'That's ridiculous.'

'She saw you in the front of the car when he dropped me off. She was furious.'

'Well, she has no need to be and if you like I'll tell her that. Lance is a nice man, but my heart has been broken. I'm not about to dive into another relationship now or... well, not for a long time.'

'The thing is, Mum doesn't like not getting her own way. Any attractive female of the right age who enters Lance's orbit is a threat.'

'This is totally irrational. I most definitely am not – a threat, I mean – and to be honest I don't feel that attractive at the moment either. Being dumped does that to you.'

Tasha sniffed loudly and took a sip of the hot chocolate.

'Don't suppose you have any marshmallows, do you?'

'No, sorry.'

'I wouldn't know about being dumped and Granny is always saying that no one is that happy with their looks at fourteen and I shouldn't compare myself to celebs who've had the use of professional make-up artists and hairdressers and false eyelashes...'

'...and stylists and been airbrushed in photos,' Jules continued.

Tasha glanced up at Jules.

'Have you ever worn false eyelashes?'

'No.'

'You've got nice eyes, sort of grey green.'

'Thank you.'

'My eyes are too small and too close together and my nose looks too big in selfies.'

'Most people's noses look big in selfies. What *do* you like about yourself?'

Tasha went quiet and tucked her legs up underneath her.

'Nothing,' she whispered so quietly that if Jules hadn't been watching her lips she might have missed it.

She looked up at Jules with eyes which were neither too small nor too close-set and blinked, tears clinging to her eyelashes.

'Maybe,' she said with a fragile smile, 'it's because my mother's never really liked me.'

'Oh, Tasha,' Jules gasped, longing to wrap her arms around the girl, but knowing that if she did, they might both break down. 'What none of us realise at the time is that at fourteen we're all beautiful. All of those pouty people on social media are not real and most of them are not happy. Imagine the pressure to look like that all the time.'

'I sort of know that in my heart, but my head overrules it.'

'I do understand that, which is why I try to limit my social media to feeds that make me feel happy and inspired rather than dissatisfied or inadequate.'

'Mum's always on social media, but I don't think it makes her happy. She always wants what she can't have. That's why she's attracted to Lance, because he's unattainable.' She cast Jules a sly glance. 'You're way more his type.'

Jules felt a bit sorry for Lance although she was sure he could stand up for himself.

'Erin would really like him to meet someone. She's worried about him being on his own when she and Fitz leave home.'

'That's a way off. Anyway, maybe he's happy as he is. It's better to be on your own than with the wrong person.'

'But you don't feel better on your own, do you?'

Jules picked up a cushion and hugged it to her.

'It's early days and you know what, I think I'm getting there.'

'Most people want to be with someone else though, don't they? I want to meet someone when I'm older.'

'And hopefully you will.'

Tasha licked her lips.

'Is this full fat milk?'

'Yes.'

'Do you know how many calories are in full fat as opposed to semi-skimmed?'

'No. I just know that full fat tastes nicer and it's meant to be better for you.'

'Granny says that, too. I think you're both right. I won't have a biscuit though.'

'I'm really not sure how we got on to talking about me when it's you I'm worried about.'

'Oh, I'm okay now,' Tasha said. 'I'm used to bouncing back. Granny says that's the only way to be and she's right.'

Jules glanced at the clock.

'Does anyone know you're here?'

Tasha shook her head.

'We should let them know.'

She moved to the phone and Tasha flew up from the sofa, spilling some of the hot chocolate down the front of her lemon shorts.

'Please don't. Not just yet. They won't miss me. They'll think I'm in my room sulking. Just a few more minutes. I haven't finished my drink yet and your film's still going. We could sit and watch it together.'

'And then I'll walk you back.'

Tasha sat back down.

'You're like my guardian angel.'

'That's a lovely thing to say, thank you, but I don't want you to be in trouble.'

'I know, but when I've been here in this house and garden, and now with you, I feel that I can cope with anything. It gives me strength.'

Jules glanced around the room.

'It's strange how it does that to you,' she said quietly. 'I think it's beginning to give me strength, too.'

. . .

Rita picked up a torch from the windowsill next to the back door and shrugged on an old coat. It wasn't particularly cold, but she felt chilled to the bone, probably not helped by worry. She hadn't been able to eat a thing at supper, even though she'd cooked a nice chicken casserole with peppers and sun-dried tomatoes. It had been one of George's favourites and she could portion it up for the freezer, so she'd always got something for herself or a good warming meal when the children came back from school in the autumn. Instead, just as she'd been about to sit down, she'd heard all of that shouting coming from the yard.

'I shouldn't interfere,' she'd said to Hercules whose ears were pricked, a low growl coming from deep in his throat.

Then she'd heard Tasha screaming at the top of her voice and the cows had started to low in alarm.

'I wish you'd go away and never come back,' she'd shouted at Christabel. By now Rita had moved to the window and was standing half hidden by the velvet curtain so she could see them standing in the doorway to the bungalow. Christabel had something in her hand and from what Rita could see she just opened her fingers and dropped it to the ground. Tasha stood stock still for a moment.

'I hate you,' she shouted at her mother. 'If you won't go away, I will.'

At that Christabel had turned and headed back into the house as Tasha stooped to scrabble on the ground to pick up what had been broken. Rita put a hand to her chest. She should go and find out what was going on, try to calm everything down, but there had been so much stress recently. She sat down on the arm of the nearest chair and stroked the top of Hercules's head.

'It will blow over,' she said to the dog. 'It has before. It will now. She doesn't mean it. She'll go for a walk and then she'll be back.'

But Tasha hadn't come back. It was ten thirty now and Alastair was heading out in the car with Will.

He said they'd searched the farmyard and for Rita to stay where she was. But Rita had never been good at sitting still. She was pretty sure that Will knew where his sister hid when life got too much.

Tasha may not have been in the barn earlier, but she could be there now.

The weathered oak door to the big building was ajar. She slipped inside, Hercules at her heels, and closed it behind her. She'd crossed the yard by the light of the moon, her feet seemingly knowing just where to place themselves, her body changing direction instinctively to avoid a rut that might turn her ankle. Now in the blackness of the barn she reached for the torch in her coat pocket and turned it on. The scent of the hay was so much stronger at night, the shadows so much deeper, her heartbeat louder, pulsating in her ears. She shone the beam of light up towards the loft.

'Tashy,' she called, 'are you there, sweetheart? It's getting late. You really need to come home now. We can sort all of this out.'

Silence.

Rita put one foot on the bottom rung of the ladder and began to climb. The rungs were worn smooth from years of use. Hercules let out a little whine and balanced on his hind legs.

'You stay there,' she instructed. 'I'll be back in a jiffy.'

Rita paused at the top to listen. She heard a small rustling sound.

'Tasha, is that you?'

No reply. She really hoped that rustling wasn't a mouse or worse, a rat. She'd never liked vermin. They always made her edgy. Besides, they could do so much damage, eat through concrete, let alone wood and hay. They really ought to get another cat. George had said that every farm needed a cat, and he was right. She glanced down to where Hercules was waiting anxiously. If she could carry him up here, he'd soon flush it out. And suddenly, it must have been the looking down or the fact she hadn't eaten anything, but she felt dizzy. She dug her fingers into the boards at the top of the ladder and was about to haul herself up into the roof space when something launched itself at her. The worst of the worst, a rodent with wings. She'd found one hanging upside down from the inside pocket of her school blazer once. Her mother said that story about bats getting tangled in your hair was an old wives' tale, but Rita could never be sure. She ducked, feeling a swish of air as the bat's wings narrowly missed her temple. She lurched to one side. She felt her ankle give way. It had never been right since she'd torn some ligaments falling off her bicycle as a girl. That fall had ended abruptly in a ditch full of nettles. The fall now down to the redbrick barn floor seemed to take forever and all she could think about was not landing on top of Hercules who was barking furiously. And then George was there, at least she thought it was George, trying to catch her around the shoulders, cushioning her fall.

'I've got you,' he was saying. 'Everything will be all right.'

He always used to say that when there had been an upset. And it had been all right as long as he was there. And he was here now, catching her as he always had done. Except he hadn't quite got hold of her properly and Hercules was barking. She must not land on him, must not hurt him. She twisted in the air and landed face down on the barn floor. For a moment she felt nothing and then Hercules nuzzled the side of her face. There was something wet on the hem of her dress and then a searing pain from her knee which travelled up her leg and through her whole body.

'Oh, Hercules,' she murmured, 'that's not good.'

And then everything went black.

Jules heard a car screech to a stop outside the cottage and before she'd even reached the window to pull back the curtains there was a hammering on the door.

'Stay there,' she instructed Tasha.

There was an old wooden truncheon hanging on the wall next to the front door. She unhooked it and held it behind her back.

'Alastair,' she said, relaxing a little once she saw who it was. 'What's the matter? If you're worried about Tasha, she's...'

'It's not Tasha, it's Mum, Rita. She's had a fall. Can you come?'

'Of course. Give me a minute to get some shoes.'

'Dad.' Tasha was at her side.

'Tasha thank goodness you're here. We've been searching everywhere for you.'

'What's the matter with Granny?'

He rubbed his forehead as if trying to erase what had happened.

'She's fallen from the ladder in the barn and she's unconscious. Mum's called an ambulance, but we don't know how long that will take and I don't know what to do.'

Tasha started to shake and Jules put an arm around her.

'I'm going to go and help. Do you want to stay here?'

She shook her head.

'I want to come with you.'

'Over here,' Alastair said, almost running from the car across the yard towards a large redbrick building.

Jules stopped just outside and turned to put her hands on Tasha's shoulders.

'Just wait here for a moment, will you?'

'But...'

'You can come in shortly. I promise.'

Tasha nodded and pulled on the sweatshirt Jules had lent her before sinking on to the edge of the stone water trough. Inside the barn Christabel was pacing up and down while Will sat on the floor next to Rita's inert form and Hercules lay by her side, one paw in contact with her outstretched arm. Jules felt for a pulse and knelt down, putting her face close to Rita's.

'Rita, can you hear me? It's Jules.'

She turned to Alastair.

'Can you get some blankets so we can try to keep her comfortable and a bowl of warm water and some cotton wool so that I can wipe some of the blood off her face?'

He nodded as if grateful for something to do.

'And can you take Will with you?' she added. 'Will, can you make some tea, please? Plenty of sugar and if you've got any brandy that would be good.'

'She can't drink,' Christabel snapped. 'She's unconscious.'

Jules looked up and met the other woman's eyes.

'It's not for Rita. It's for us. Five cups, Will, and some cool water with a straw for Granny, please, for when she comes around.'

'What do you want me to do?' Christabel asked.

'Perhaps you could go to the end of the drive and wait for the ambulance,' Jules suggested, 'so they know where to come.'

'I've explained on the phone.'

'All the same,' Jules said calmly. 'Wouldn't want them to miss the entrance and get lost, would we?'

Christabel had stopped pacing and was standing firmly rooted to the spot, her feet planted wide.

'I can do that,' Tasha said, appearing in the doorway.

'This,' Christabel hissed, pointing a finger at her daughter, 'is all your fault. I wouldn't trust you with feeding the chickens at the moment, let alone looking out for a large vehicle with a blue flashing light.'

Tears started to pour down Tasha's cheeks. She looked as if she was about to turn and run again.

'That,' Jules retorted firmly, 'is definitely not helpful.'

She extended her arm behind her.

'Tasha, why don't you come here and sit next to Granny? It will be nice for her to see your face when she comes around.'

Christabel stared at Jules for a moment before marching huffily past. As soon as she had gone Rita's eyelids flickered.

'Good idea,' she murmured. 'Last thing I want is her fussing over me.'

'Welcome back,' Jules said with a smile. 'Look who's here.'

She urged Tasha closer.

'Best medicine in the world,' Rita murmured before her face screwed up in pain and she tried to shift.

'I need you to stay still,' Jules said, placing a hand lightly on her shoulder. 'There's an ambulance on its way.'

Rita blinked in assent, her eyes glittering.

'Tasha,' she said through gritted teeth, 'you're all right?'

Tasha was crying as she crouched down.

'I'm all right, Granny.'

'And Hercules?'

'He's fine. He's here, right next to you.'

The dog shifted closer and licked Rita's wrist.

'I'm so sorry, Granny, this is all my fault.'

Rita's eyes widened and she wiggled her fingers for Tasha to take hold of.

'Now don't you talk such nonsense. I've got nobody to blame, but myself.'

Tasha looked up to the top of the ladder.

'No thinking the worst,' Rita whispered. 'The Good Lord isn't ready for me yet.' She managed a smile through the pain. 'I'll be back in my kitchen before you know it. You see.'

Her eyes moved to Jules's face for reassurance.

'Absolutely,' Jules said. 'A quick check over in hospital and you'll be right as rain in no time at all.'

Rita looked grateful, but they both knew she was lying.

Jules lay in bed and stared at the ceiling. When she finally got back to the cottage after Rita was taken away in the ambulance she had been trembling with exhaustion and shock. She made herself a hot water bottle because her period had arrived – thank goodness – and put on a pair of socks to try and warm up her feet. Her grandmother always said it was important to keep your feet warm. She should have picked up the phone and let them know where Tasha was. If anyone was to blame, it was her. She tried to be very still, tried to close her eyes, but whenever she did her brain went into overdrive; flickering images of Rita lying on the barn floor, or her mother unexpectedly turning up, of those bewildering days after her father died and once again her whole being was transported back to her fourteen-year-old self. It was Phoebe who had taken on the role of dutiful daughter. A role she performed with much skill and not a small air of superiority.

'You always were more Mum's daughter than I ever was,' Jules had said to her once.

'I suppose it's convenient for you to think that,' Phoebe had shot back.

It had led to another row, not a shouting, letting-off-steam row, but a carefully controlled outrage of clipped sentences and modulated pitch steeped in bitterness. Did all children have to get divided up, she wondered, one to the father, one to the mother? She did see it often in the maternity unit and vowed that if she had children of her own it would not happen to her. She wondered if that had been the case with Lance and Sarah, but somehow she didn't think so. Lance was too sensitive to allow that to happen.

Be careful, Jules, she said to herself. *He's kind and funny and considerate. You could easily end up liking him a bit too much. And remember that a lot of people are not what they seem to be.*

She had come to the conclusion that the only person you could really get to know and trust was yourself and that was a lifetime mission. And Carrie, of course. She would always be able to trust Carrie, but most other people... better to be prepared for disappointment and then it wouldn't hurt so much. She reached for her glass of water just as a rush of air crossed the room, rustling the pages of the book she had left on the pillow next to her. She froze for a moment, even her breath stalling as she seemed to feel a waft of air playing with her hair. Surely, she was only half awake — imagining things?

She turned over, placed the book firmly closed on her bedside table, plumped her pillow and closed her eyes again just as voices filtered through the doorway. There was someone here. She propped herself up on one elbow and strained to hear words, but it was quiet once more. It must have been her own subconscious playing tricks, a lucid dream maybe. She lay back down and there it was again, a whispering of words; kindness, helpfulness, generosity, love. She sat up and pushed back the duvet before tiptoeing on to the landing but once more the house felt as if it was holding itself in. There wasn't anyone here from this world or any other.

If Carrie hadn't confided in her that the house possessed a presence she wouldn't have become so fanciful. That, along with the stress of everything else that had happened, had caused her to become susceptible. She'd never believed in spirits. If there was life after death, why had her father not made an appearance to her? Why had he not helped her to come to terms with her grief? Why had he not guided her in her relationships with men? Why had he not protected her from Gavin? No, there wasn't any such thing as an afterlife. Once you were gone, you were gone. And yet stupidly she half hoped that one day she might be proved wrong...

FEAR

Eliza had heard the scream pierce the night air. It caused the pigeons to flap from their roosting place at the top of the field maple. The scream rooted her to the spot for a moment and then she began to shake. She, too, had screamed like that once. Why would that be? What pain could have caused such a cry? At the back of the garden all the outside lights in the farmyard lit up the night sky. She could hear doors slamming, shouting and barking. She heard the rapping on the cottage door, saw Jules and Tasha climb into Alastair's jeep. She should go with them, but where was Isaac? She needed him to accompany her. She couldn't face whatever had happened alone. Eliza paced up and down the lawn. To go or not to go? To wait for Isaac? Not to wait for Isaac? And then he had appeared, striding across the grass towards her.

'Isaac, where have you been? What has happened? I heard this terrible noise and I didn't know what to do.'

Her whole form was trembling. He took both of her hands and led her to their seat beneath the willow tree.

'There has been an accident,' he said, pressing Eliza down on to the log. 'It is our beloved Rita.'

Eliza couldn't keep herself still. It was as if every part of her needed to move.

'Is she all right?'

'They called for an ambulance. There was blood, Eliza. She was unconscious for a time.'

He, too, was shaking.

'And now?'

'Now she is awake and our guest is tending to her.'

'Thank goodness. How did this happen?'

'She fell from the ladder leading up to the hay store. A bat startled her, I think. I tried to catch her,' Isaac continued, 'but...'

He lifted his hands momentarily from hers.

'My powers of protection are not strong enough. I grabbed her around the shoulders to prevent her from hitting the floor headfirst, but she twisted in mid-air and I couldn't stop her knee smashing into the floor. For a moment there was complete silence, Eliza. I thought...'

'Shh, my love.'

She put an unsteady hand to his anguished face.

'It was such a terrible scream,' Isaac said. 'I should have done more.'

'Oh, Isaac, but if you hadn't caught her, it could have been so much worse. What was she doing climbing up to the hayloft at this time of night?'

'I gather there was a disagreement with Christabel earlier in the evening and Tasha ran off.'

Eliza had gazed through the fronds of the tree, across the garden and the field to where the moon seemed to hang impossibly low in the summer sky.

'Why is it,' she whispered at last, 'that some people who are mothers don't deserve to be and others...?'

She gave herself a little shake.

'It is not the first time that Tasha has disappeared.'

'But this time she didn't return. I was taking my usual stroll around the farmyard, albeit a little later than usual. I was checking on the chickens, guiding Scattihen to a safe place when Rita came out to look for Tasha. That is why she was investigating the hayloft.'

'Tasha was here, Isaac. She arrived soon after you set out for your walk. Jules found her on the doorstep. She was upset, but safe.'

'I know that now,' he replied. 'I think she is going to be in a lot of trouble, Eliza. I fear for her state of mind.'

Eliza was silent for a moment before standing up.

'I must go to her and to Rita.'

'I think we should stay here, away from the commotion. It is not our place. There's nothing we can do.'

'Maybe not,' Eliza replied, 'but I'm still going.'

Isaac sighed.

'In that case,' he said, 'I'll come with you.'

Which is exactly what she expected him to say.

FIFTEEN

Carrie turned up at ten o'clock the following morning.

'Jules,' she said, putting her arms around her. 'What an awful thing to happen. Are you okay?'

'Yes, just tired and a bit shaken.'

'Guy's grandmother spoke to Alastair first thing and Rita's okay. They're operating on her knee later, but thankfully that seems to be the main damage. Everyone's very grateful for what you did, Jules. Al said you were a beacon of calm.'

Jules sank onto a kitchen chair.

'I didn't feel it, but thank goodness she's going to be all right. I'm partly responsible. She was obviously up there looking for Tasha who was safely ensconced here.'

'Don't be ridiculous,' Carrie replied. 'Rita doesn't just go up to the hayloft looking for Tasha, she takes herself off up there some-times to get away from everyone and I don't blame her. It's where she and George used to go for a bit of quality time together in their courting days as she herself so delicately put it! Later, when the farm and family began to get a bit too much, she said they'd take a flask of coffee and some homemade cake or sometimes a bottle of wine and go and get everything in perspective. To be honest, it's surprising she's not fallen off that ladder before.'

Jules knew Carrie was trying to be kind, but it didn't make her feel much better.

'Come on, get dressed and I'll take you to the beach. You look as if you could do with a gentle walk.'

Carrie took a left turn and steered the car down a narrow road bordered by a clear rippling stream and a neatly mown grassy area dotted with benches. She pressed hard on the brakes as a couple of ducks waddled across in front of them.

'The Pearl Centre is just a couple of miles in the other direction,' Carrie said as they reached a junction. 'We'll pay a trip before you go. They have some very pretty things.'

'I can't afford to treat myself. Gavin took most of my money, remember?'

'Then I'll treat you,' Carrie said. 'Call it an early birthday present.'

They were very close to the sea now. Jules wound the window down and sniffed at the air.

Carrie swung the car into a gravelly car park, opened the door and hopped out.

'Your mum rang. Wondered how you are?'

Jules felt her hackles rise. She was obviously more tired than she'd realised.

'Why did she call you?'

'Because you haven't given her the number for the landline and she couldn't get through on your phone and she's trying to be sensitive and not smothering.'

'It won't last.'

'She's very wary of upsetting you, saying or doing the wrong thing.'

'Like coming to the Isle of Wight.'

'She's partly come to see Jo. It's serendipitous that you are here, too.'

'Yeah, right. You believe that?'

'Yes, I do. Apparently one of Jo's daughters has been in touch. She wants to find her mum and wondered if Beulah knew where she was. This is a big deal. For her own safety Jo left her daughters in the middle of the night without so much as a goodbye kiss and she thought they would never forgive her. Now there is the possibility they could be reunited.'

Jules scuffed at a loose stone.

'Or it could be a trap, a way for Jo's ex to find out where she and Daniel are.'

'Your mum's well aware of that, which is why she wanted to come and tell Jo face to face. She's trying really hard to do what's best for everyone,' Carrie continued. 'The trouble is, in your case, what you think is best for you and what's best for her are not necessarily the same things.'

'That sounds like a criticism.'

'It's not meant to. I'm just trying to get you to see her side of it. She does know that you blame her for your dad's death.'

Jules stared unseeingly at the ground beneath her feet.

'Sounds as if you've had quite a conversation.'

'I'm sure that she blames herself, too,' Carrie said, touching the edge of Jules's blue windcheater.

'She wasn't there enough. She didn't make him go to the doctor.'

'Which is why she tried to make up for it afterwards.'

'It was too late.'

'For your dad, yes, but not for you and Phoebe. At least, that's what she hoped.'

'She was wrong.'

Carrie sighed and took hold of Jules's arm.

'Look at that view. Doesn't it make you feel more benevolent towards the world?'

Not particularly, Jules thought, aware that she was behaving like a recalcitrant teenager. And then she followed Carrie's gaze along the path, which sloped steeply down towards the beach and drew the eye across the shimmer of sea to the horizon.

'There's a world of infinite possibilities out there,' Carrie murmured, and Jules wasn't sure whether she was talking to herself or not.

'Breathe,' she said, throwing her head back and taking a gulp of air. 'It's invigorating, like a magic potion.'

'It's the ozone,' Jules said drily. She looked at Carrie with her translucent skin and glossy hair, 'and being in love.'

'And being here,' Carrie said. 'I love this tiny island more than I could ever have imagined loving anywhere.'

'You've found your place in the world. It's all come together,' Jules said, trying not to sound wistful. 'And I'm really happy for you.'

Carrie squeezed her arm.

'And you will, too, find your place.'

'My sister said something similar last night on the phone.'

'We can't both be wrong,' Carrie said. 'Now, come on, let's get down there and feel the sand between our toes.'

She slid her hand down and grabbed Jules's fingers, pulling her down the slippery path towards the beach.

Carrie had stopped for lunch and then hurried off to the gardens to meet up with Guy and check in on The Major. Jules was in the garden reading when she heard muffled voices followed by a familiar tinkling laugh floating over the thatched roof. She put down her magazine and, full of trepidation, wandered around to the front of the house. Beulah was standing with her best side towards Lance, one hand on her hip, the other attached to the long handle of a wheelie suitcase. She was still laughing, and he was smiling down at her. Jules felt a ridiculous pang of jealousy. How did she do that? Win everyone around so quickly when they had no idea what she was really like?

'Julianna, darling!'

Beulah moved as if to embrace her and then thought better of it, returning to her original position.

The air was suddenly swarming with awkwardness which irritated her even more than all those little gnats which flew about in the early evening and got caught in your throat and up your nose if you weren't careful. Lance didn't move, apart from to shift the parcel that he held under one arm.

'I was just getting to know your mother,' he said, in an obvious effort to lighten the atmosphere.

Beulah lifted her heels almost imperceptibly and swivelled on the balls of her feet so that she was standing alongside Lance and able to link a now-free arm through his.

'And we're already the best of friends,' she said, that laugh tinkling like birdsong through the summer afternoon air.

'What are you doing here?' Jules said.

'I've come to…' both Lance and Beulah replied in unison and burst out laughing.

Jules's nerves were becoming increasingly frayed, and Beulah had only been here for two minutes.

'Mum!'

Even Jules couldn't fail to spot that her mother gripped both Lance's arm and the suitcase handle a little more tightly.

'Julianna, darling, something awful has happened at Jo's.'

Jules felt her heart increase its tempo, her muscles tense as she imagined the worst. She didn't think she could cope with any more shocks. It was as if all the energy was leaving her body.

'What?' she whispered.

Beulah's eyes widened.

'Would you believe it, the water tank in the roof has sprung a leak and it has all poured through the ceiling into the spare bedroom.'

'For goodness' sake, Mum. Is that all? Why do you have to make such a drama out of everything? I thought it was much worse than that. I thought…'

'It's a miracle I wasn't drowned in my bed,' Beulah said with a theatrical flourish. 'You have no idea how much damage water can do, and poor Claudia's spare bedroom is ruined.'

'Jo, Mum. Her name is Jo.'

'Oh yes, whatever. Silly me. Always getting people's names muddled up. Very inconvenient for an actress.'

And very inconvenient that you're not sounding more convincing now, Jules thought, glancing at Lance, but he didn't seem particularly curious. Maybe only she thought her mother's protestations were completely lame.

'She's offered me her sofa, but Daniel gets up early, and the living room is just off the kitchen, and you know how I need my beauty sleep. I wondered...'

She was looking up at the cottage.

'You have a second bedroom here, don't you? It would just be for a couple of nights,' Beulah said, 'and I'll try not to be any trouble. You'll barely know I'm here, but if it's really not convenient I can try to find a bed and breakfast. I'm sure Lance could recommend one.' She frowned and pressed herself more tightly to him as if for reassurance. 'Although at peak holiday time it might be...'

'Of course you can stay, Mum.'

'Oh, Julianna, that is so generous of you,' Beulah gushed. 'I can see this place is doing you so much good. Your aura is looking much calmer and such a beautiful colour. Can you see that, Lance, the sea breeze colour of Julianna's aura?'

Jules cringed as they both gazed at her, Beulah wreathed in smiles and Lance – what was that expression on his face? Amusement? Pity?

'On one condition,' Jules added. 'That you stop calling me Julianna.'

'I thought she might be an actress, you see, like me,' Beulah explained to Lance. 'Such a dramatic baby from the moment she was born.'

Lance smiled politely.

'But she's gone on to do something so much more worthwhile. We're all so proud of her. I wish her father had lived to see it, but of course he does know.' She looked up at the sky. 'He is looking down on her full of admiration for what she has achieved, for what she is giving back to the world.'

'Mum!'

'Darling!'

'I'm going to put the kettle on and make a good strong cup of tea because I'm really surprised that you can't see that my aura is nowhere near sea breeze, whatever that is, but is distinctly battleship grey.'

'Oh, Julian...' Beulah said, as Jules turned to make her way back to the house, 'I'm so glad that the dreadful man, whose name we won't mention – do you know about the awful man, Lance?'

'Um...' he replied.

'Quite,' Beulah said with a nod. 'It's absolutely marvellous, Juli... that he has not caused you to lose your sense of humour. She's such a hoot, isn't she, Lance?'

Jules felt herself beginning to seethe. Much more of this and she was going to retract her very generous offer of accommodation.

'Indeed, she is,' he said, raising one eyebrow in Jules's direction.

'And for an extra surprise the gorgeous Lance has brought you a present, Jules.'

She turned to look up into his flushed face. Perhaps he had caught the sun. No, he was definitely blushing.

'Um, it's not really a present and it's not actually for you.' He looked disproportionately apologetic. 'It's for the cottage. Carrie commissioned it and said to let her know when it was finished. She told me you'd be here and asked if I could drop it in.'

'Oh, right, thank you.'

She held out her hands and took the parcel.

'And now your hands are free, Lance,' Beulah said with another of her winning smiles, 'perhaps you could be so kind as to take my suitcase. At my age I really have to be careful with lifting.'

'Mum, all of that yoga and Pilates has made you fitter than I am,' Jules retorted, 'and the suitcase is on wheels.'

'I have a twinge, Julia.' She placed her hand in the small of her back. 'And I really don't want to aggravate it.'

You have a twinge, Jules thought.

'I'll carry it in for you.'

'I'm sure Lance would like to see his fruit bowl in situ.'

'And I'm sure Lance has got better things to do. He has a pottery to run.'

'I've been hearing all about it from Jo. Marvellous it sounds and you've been in attendance. So therapeutic. Just what you need.'

She turned to Lance who was shifting from one foot to another, obviously not sure whether he should leave or not.

'She's really very creative, you know. Always drawing and making things as a child.'

Lance just smiled. Beulah tilted the suitcase towards him.

'Come along then, darling. What are you waiting for? Lead the way. I can't wait to see inside this cottage I've heard so much about. Already I can tell that it has an extraordinary ambience.'

Jules sighed. Her mother really was the most infuriating woman.

'You'll have to come around the back,' she said snappily. 'Tradesmen's entrance. The front door is locked.'

And off she marched, the rumble of the suitcase wheels behind her indicating that it was going to be a trying couple of days.

'I'm sorry,' Jules said as Lance appeared in the kitchen after having taken Beulah's suitcase upstairs.

'What for?'

'My mother.'

'She seems very nice.'

'Would you like her to come and stay with you?' she asked, leaning back against the work surface and raising an eyebrow.

His lips twitched. He had very nice lips, she thought.

'I thought not. Tea?'

He nodded.

'What have you done with her, by the way?'

'She's rearranging a few things to make the room more harmonious.'

'Ye gods!' Jules exclaimed, as thudding and scraping sounds came from upstairs. 'She couldn't lift a small suitcase, but she can shift furniture without a second thought for her twinge.'

She came and sat at the table and put her head in her hands.

'I know this will sound overly dramatic,' she murmured, 'but I'm not sure how I'm going to survive.'

'Tea might help a little,' he said, moving over to the boiling kettle and tipping water into the readily prepared teapot.

'Rita says that tea is a balm for most problems,' she replied, as he put a mug in front of her.

'That was another reason I called in,' he said, 'to ask how she is. I didn't want to bother Alastair and it's a bit difficult for me to call and speak to Christabel.'

'All I know is they're operating this afternoon.'

'It sounded bad.'

'She's totally shattered her knee, I think, but it could have been worse.'

'Erin told me that Tasha said you were amazing.'

'Not really. I just did what I could, what I was trained to do.'

'This could change everything for Rita,' he said, pouring tea into her mug.

'Scary, isn't it, how one misstep can do that, and you don't even have to be on a ladder?'

Lance cast a glance towards the hall where Beulah's singing of 'Oh! What a Beautiful Morning' was now filtering down the stairs.

'She does tend to churn up the atmosphere,' Jules said.

'I'd noticed. If you feel the need to get away you can always come to The Pottery for some creativity and calm.'

'Creativity and calm, that sounds wonderful,' Beulah said from the doorway, making both Lance and Jules jump. 'You haven't unwrapped the bowl. I would like to see Lance's creative genius.'

'I'm afraid you're about to be disappointed,' he said modestly as Beulah took the parcel from the island unit, placed it on the pine table, untied the string and peeled back the brown paper. The bowl was oval and glazed in a pale sage green, decorated with illustrations of cow parsley and red campion.

'I'm not disappointed at all,' Beulah said. 'That is very beautiful and made with such love. You are obviously extremely talented as well as handsome. I do like a man who's good with his hands.'

'Mum! You're embarrassing Lance.'

'Nonsense! I'm sure he's used to adulation.'

'Well, I wouldn't go so far as to...' he protested.

'If I was twenty years younger,' Beulah continued, sending him a wink.

Jules closed her eyes.

'But I'm not,' she continued, 'so I'll just have to settle for a cup of tea poured by those manly hands of yours.'

There was one thing about Beulah, Jules thought. She certainly took your mind off any other problems you might be having. She became the problem.

'Remember what I said,' Lance said, as Jules showed him out. 'You can visit The Pottery any time. Just come around to the back and let yourself into the studio.'

She looked behind her where Beulah was standing in the middle of the front lawn and saluting the sun.

'Thank you,' she murmured. 'I might just do that.'

He smiled and she wondered for a moment if he was going to touch her. Strangely she really wanted him to.

'Never a dull moment, hey?'

'No,' she said as he turned to go. 'Never a dull moment.'

'He's lush, isn't he?' Beulah said, when Lance was barely out of earshot. 'You could do worse, you know.'

'Mum!'

She glanced over to where Lance was getting into his car, but if he'd heard he didn't let on. Instead, he raised his hand and waved. Jules waved back tentatively while Beulah moved her arm backwards and forwards so energetically that her whole body swayed.

'This whole place is just adorable,' she said as Jules followed her back into the house, 'like a picture postcard. It feels such a happy place and definitely a sanctuary.'

She stopped suddenly in the hall and lifted her face slightly, her eyes moving from one side to the other.

'But there's something else...'

Here we go, Jules thought. Beulah turned her eyes, locking on to Jules's face.

'There's a sadness here.'

'The cottage is over two hundred years old, Mum. I expect there have been sadnesses.'

'It is well hidden,' Beulah said. 'It is a secret sadness.'

'Loads of people are walking around with those,' Jules said. 'Come on, I'm going to see what we've got for supper.'

'Have you spoken to the spirits, Julia?'

'No, I have not because you know that I don't believe in that sort of thing.'

'You should speak to them, darling. I sense that they are trying to help you.'

Jules moved through to the sitting room.

'Are you on or off cheese at the moment, because I might make a cheesy pasta bake?'

'You know that I can eat cheese in the summer, but not in the winter because of my sensitive sinuses.'

'I'd forgotten, but thank goodness it's summer.'

'I'll come and help you,' Beulah said. 'We can cook together. That's a bonding thing to do.'

Depends on who you're cooking with, Jules murmured to herself. Perhaps she would speak to the spirits after all. Perhaps she would ask them to help her find patience.

DANGER

Eliza stood in the doorway to the bedroom watching Beulah sleep. Isaac's hands rested on her shoulders, preventing her from moving closer.

'Another lovely visitor,' Eliza whispered in his ear. 'It is good that the cottage is so popular!'

'You need to come away, Eliza,' he said, pulling his wife back on to the little landing. 'I think this woman could be dangerous.'

'Oh, Isaac. You are worrying too much.'

She raised her hand and tried to stroke the stress from his face, resting her finger on the corner of his lips. The lips she had kissed so often with so much love. She would never tire of doing so.

'I do not like this new person being here,' Isaac continued.

Beulah stirred and turned over in bed, her face soft and relaxed.

'She looks harmless to me, Isaac, and if she is Jules's mother, she can't be bad.'

'I'm not saying that she is a bad person, my love, far from it. In some ways I feel that she is too good, too much in contact with more than her human form.'

'You mean, Isaac, that she may be able to see us?'

'It is possible.'

Eliza looked through the open doorway at Beulah.

'But I do not think she would cause trouble, even if she did.'

'She may not mean to, Eliza, but...'

Isaac let go of her and paced across the landing, head down, shoulders hunched, hands clasped together, seemingly unaware of the increasingly violent ripples of air he was creating. Eliza knew what this meant. He was trying to work something out, to foresee shadows in the future with a view to preventing them.

'Perhaps,' he said at last, spinning on the spot and turning towards Eliza, 'our latest guest could do with some of your assistance.'

Eliza's lips twitched.

'Surely, you are not advocating meddling, my love? I thought that I was banned from interfering?'

'Do not toy with me, Eliza. Please. Can you not see that I'm anguished and at a loss as to how to proceed. This situation calls for your touch.'

'When you put it like that...' Eliza replied, 'perhaps I could be persuaded. What is it that you wish me to do?'

She watched as Isaac frowned.

'I want you to get her to leave.'

'But Isaac,' Eliza said, raising her voice in shock, 'the poor lady has only just arrived. It is a time for her to bond with Jules. And how do you suggest that I do this?'

'I do not know,' he said. 'Frighten her, maybe; some wailing or ripping of her clothes or tipping her out of bed or all three.'

'Isaac, this doesn't sound like you at all.'

He took her hand.

'I'm afraid, Eliza. I have a premonition of something bad happening if she remains.'

'So you want me to chase her away?'

'We must. For our own safety. And your connection with humans is more refined than mine.'

Eliza snatched her hand away.

'I'm sorry, Isaac, but I'll have no part of this.'

Once again, she was defying him, but she couldn't allow him to push her into something such as this.

'Beulah seems like a wonderful woman: kind, helpful, generous and loving. I trust her.'

'You are misguided, Eliza.'

His features had hardened. Once again, he was distancing himself from her. She couldn't bear it if he ran away again. She clutched at his arm.

'Isaac, we know, don't we, because of our long time together, the importance of trust. We know that every one of us, whether in human form or spirit, are all inter-connected through time and space and that, with belief in the power of goodness, it multiplies.'

He didn't speak.

In the front bedroom Eliza heard Jules stir. She took Isaac's hand.

'I believe that it is important for Jules that her mother remains here for as long as is needed. We must not interfere with that process. Everything happens for a reason, Isaac. If there's trouble ahead, we will deal with it. Together. Come,' she said, taking his hand, 'we will go to the willow tree. That is where we go in order to gather our strength and do our thinking.'

She led him down the stairs.

'We must let our guests sleep now. I've wished them an extra sprinkling of hope. That always seems to encourage the full tranquillity of mind needed for restorative slumber.'

Eliza drifted through the rooms of their cottage, leaving a spiral trail of healing in her wake while Isaac did his best to quell his misgivings. Outside, in the soft but unusually cool summer darkness they settled in the place where they talked of their lives, the blessing of finding each other that day long ago on the beach, the sacrifices they had made to be together, of their good fortune at coming to Hideaway Cottage, the friends they had made, the support they had received and the fortune of a good marriage.

They talked of everything except the one thing that had been wiped from Eliza's memory, and which Isaac bore as a pain so deep that he couldn't allow it out into the open. But this one thing was there, always there, twisting and turning around within him and through their conversations both past and present. Eliza couldn't understand why she felt as if a knife had sliced her in two; she was sewn back together, but with something missing. But Isaac knew. He thought that he could bear it for both of them, that he could protect her with his silence. But since the box had been found... He was fond of Carrie, but if there hadn't been that misunderstanding between Guy and The Major, if Carrie hadn't decided to leave early, if Eliza hadn't felt the need to prevent her, the box would have remained beneath the floorboards – hidden.

Its discovery had pricked at Eliza's memory. He could see the questioning in her eyes, and feel the probing of the past as she retreated into silences along paths where he was afraid to follow. Eliza felt as if she was navigating a maze, each rumination leading to a dead end, taking her back to the beginning. She was starting to question whether the box was anything to do with her at all – whether, in fact, she was imagining the sense of loss that sometimes almost knocked her sideways with its intensity. Perhaps she was going mad. And yet... Isaac's reticence, his tension, his over-protection, all of these made her suspicious.

And guilty. Never before could she remember doubting her husband's motives. But she did now. If they were to pass over together, there must not be any secrets between them. Did he not understand that? She would find an answer, both to her own predicament and that of their guest. She was not one for giving up, never had been and she never would be. And now this new guest had arrived, and Isaac sensed danger. Perhaps he was right, but sometimes it was necessary to flirt with danger in order to reveal the truth.

SIXTEEN

'How are you bearing up?' Carrie asked when she phoned the next morning.

'To be honest,' Jules whispered, 'she's driving me up the wall. The first thing she said when she brought me a cup of tea at some ungodly hour because she'd been communing with the early morning birdsong, was "What shall we do today?" I hadn't even rubbed the sleep from my eyes.'

'Nice that she brought you a cup of tea though. What are the two of you going to do today?'

'I really don't know, but it's got to be something, or I'll go mad.'

'There are the botanical gardens at Ryde. They are amazing.'

'Too much time to chat,' Jules replied.

'What about the Roman villa at Brading? There are lots of things to read about and fascinating mosaics to look at so she won't be able to talk to you too much.'

'Apart from in the car on the way there and back,' Jules groaned, 'and over coffee and lunch and... You could come with us.'

'I could,' Carrie replied cautiously, 'except I don't think I should.'

'Why not?'

'Because, much as you're resisting, I think you should spend a bit of time on your own with your mum.'

'We did that yesterday until she fell asleep in front of the television.'

'I'll speak to you later to find out how you've got on. If you need me tomorrow, I'm available.'

'Some friend you are,' Jules said.

'Breakfast's ready,' Beulah called from the kitchen.

Jules put the phone down and walked through to the kitchen.

'Mum, I really don't need you to get me breakfast. I'm a big girl now.'

Beulah's face fell. She slumped down at the beautifully laid table with its jug of freshly squeezed orange juice, bowl of glistening strawberries, tub of yoghurt and jar of homemade muesli.

'All I wanted,' she said, her voice breaking, 'when your father died, was to protect you. But you always fought me and eventually I told myself that you needed to grieve in your own way. I tried to respect that. I'm only going to stay for a few days, but while I'm here, Julianna, please let me look after you a little. It might be good for both of us.'

Jules sighed.

'As long as you don't make me eat semolina or insist on sleeping on the floor next to my bed.'

'I only did that when you had that horrible virus, which the doctor subsequently suspected might be meningitis,' Beulah said. 'Thank goodness it wasn't. I live in absolute fear of losing you and Phoebe, too.'

She twisted her wedding ring around on her finger.

'You know Phoebe and Giles are trying for a baby?'

Jules nodded, ignoring Beulah's surprise.

'It's making her very stressed. I've told her to try and relax. I've sent her some breathing exercises and yoga poses, but...' She shrugged. 'They say that you're only as happy as your least-happiest child and it's so right.'

'And now you've got both of us being unhappy,' Jules said.

'I would do anything for you,' Beulah said, 'both of you. You do know that, don't you?'

Jules nodded. She did know that, always had. She just hadn't wanted to accept anything from her mother that she didn't have to.

'Perhaps we should stay here today, darling. You look very pale.'

'No, I'm fine. A bit exhausted, that's all. It comes in waves.'

'You have been through such trauma. It's bound to have taken it out of you. I wish it could have been me instead.'

And difficult as it was, Jules went over and draped her arms around Beulah's neck.

'I'm sorry, Mum. I don't always mean to be difficult.'

Beulah put both hands up to cover Jules's.

'I know how close you were to Dad, closer than you were to me. I was jealous of that, but when he died, all I wanted to do was to take away your pain with as much love as he would have given as well as my own. If I got that wrong, I'm sorry, too.'

And as she looked at her mother's hands stroking her own she felt as if something had begun to shift.

The Roman villa had been a good choice. Beulah was fascinated by the mosaics and the artefacts and the fact that the Romans had come to the Isle of Wight at all.

'What a wonderful location,' Beulah said. 'I suppose it meant they could travel to the mainland and to France fairly easily. They knew a thing or two, those Romans! Did you read that the Medusa mosaic is thought to be protective and ward off evil spirits?'

'I did,' Jules said as they sat in the café, each having a bowl of soup.

'Perhaps I could make my own Medusa mosaic to take home with me,' Beulah mused. 'Or we could go to Lance's pottery and make one together. Wouldn't that be fun?'

'Mmm,' Jules replied, taking a very long time to chew her piece of bread.

'I'm going to have dinner with Jo,' Beulah said later as she drifted around the sitting room adjusting the ornaments by millimetres and occasionally stretching up on her tippy-toes to touch the beams before folding in half and placing her hands flat on the floor. 'It will give you some space and give the spirits time to adjust. I sense that they are not entirely happy with my presence here.'

Jules looked around the room. The only unhappiness she could sense was her own.

'You don't have to,' Jules said half-heartedly, but already she was starting to make herself more comfortable, tucking her feet beneath her on the sofa, moving one of the cushions to make a soft support for her head.

Beulah shot her a piercing glance.

'I think it would be good for both of us although I don't want you here brooding.'

'I won't brood.'

Beulah picked up the tissue containing the fragments of Tasha's jug.

'Broken things create such a well of sadness inside me,' she said.

'It was a present or I'd have just put it straight in the bin. I thought I'd try to mend it, but I'm not sure how.'

'Kintsugi!' Beulah declared, jumping up and down on the spot. 'The Japanese say that nothing is ever completely broken, that our imperfections are part of our perfection.'

Jules stared at her mother.

'They mend their precious things with seams of lacquer and gold.'

'It might work, I suppose.'

'Of course it will work, and I know who will have just the materials you need. Come along!'

She moved around the back of the sofa and whisked the cushion away from Jules's head.

'I'll drop you off at The Pottery on my way to Jo's and pick you up later.'

Jules twisted up to a kneeling position and stole the cushion back, hugging it to her.

'I really don't think that's a good idea. I'll nip into Cowes tomorrow and get what I need.'

'I think it's an excellent idea. Didn't that nice man say you could drop by any time?'

'When people say that, Mum, they don't really mean it.'

'Some do and some don't,' Beulah said, 'and he was definitely one of the ones who do.'

She peered at Jules.

'You're looking a bit flushed now.' She put a hand to her forehead. 'Perhaps I shouldn't go to Jo's, after all. Perhaps I should stay here with you.'

'It's fine, Mum. I'll be fine.'

'I'd be so much more reassured if I knew you were with someone,' Beulah said, 'someone trustworthy who can keep an eye on you. You could start some sketches for our Medusa sculpture, too, while you're there.'

Jules placed the cushion back on the sofa. She knew when she was beaten. If she was going to get any peace at all this evening, she would have to do what Beulah wanted. She did so love to organise everyone 'in their best interests'.

'Now you will go in, darling, won't you?' Beulah said as she pulled up in The Pottery car park. 'You won't run away like you did when I dropped you off for that tennis tournament?'

'I was ten, Mum, and I didn't know anyone, and I didn't run away – I hid in the toilets.'

'For the whole day, darling. Such apologies I had to make when I came to collect you. People thought you had the most terrible upset stomach and the accusing glances I got from the other parents for sending you were enough to force my aura into hibernation.'

'I promise that I won't hide in the toilets here, Mum, and even if I did there aren't any parents to judge you.'

Beulah lifted up her sunglasses and gave her a beady stare.

'The trouble is, Jules, I can never make out whether you're being honest with me.' She checked her watch. 'But I'll have to give you the benefit of the doubt or I'll be late. I'll collect you later.'

Jules got out of the car and reached over towards the back seat to collect her basket containing Tasha's jug.

'Please don't, Mum. I can walk back.' She was braced for another battle. This was one she was determined to win. 'It's not much more than a mile down the road and I'm not planning to be here that long. It doesn't get dark until around ten.'

Beulah ran her hands around the steering wheel while she weighed up her response.

'If you insist, darling,' she said after what seemed like an age, 'but remember to walk facing the oncoming traffic.'

She dropped her glasses back down and tightened the knot on the multi-coloured silk scarf that covered her hair before blowing Jules a kiss. With a rev of the engine and a spray of stones, the little soft-top Fiat spun in a circle and headed for the exit, Beulah waving one arm extravagantly above her head. Jules winced and not just from the sting of the stones. How on earth did her mother get anywhere in one piece? It was a miracle.

She waited for a moment listening to the sound of the car's engine disappearing into the distance, wanting to be absolutely sure that Beulah had gone before heading back towards the road herself. Now, Jules could wander back to the cottage and have it all to herself.

'Jules? Is that you?'

She jumped at the sound of Lance's voice.

'And was that your mother I saw disappearing in a cloud of dust?'

She shifted from one foot to the other as if she'd been caught doing something wrong at school.

'It is and it was.'

'You should have let me know you were coming.'

'I'm not stopping. I realise it's inconvenient my turning up like this and...'

'It's not inconvenient at all.' He smiled broadly. 'Anything but. It's extremely serendipitous. I've got to go out – not far, just to Newport to deliver something – and Tasha's here with Erin. Alastair dropped her off earlier which was a bit of a surprise. Thought it might do her good to get away from the farm for a couple of hours. Obviously, the girls don't need babysitting, but Tasha's still upset and I was a bit concerned about leaving them both. If you're in the studio...' He paused, his eyes glancing at the basket. 'I presume that's why you're here and not for my scintillating company?'

'Yes, I mean, no. My mother made me come.'

She sounded totally pathetic. He raised an eyebrow.

'I've had some brush-offs in my time, but that's a first,' he said with a rich laugh. 'I presume the plan was to walk straight back to the cottage and that seemed easier than doing battle with her earlier?'

She looked up at him sheepishly.

'She's not an easy woman to negotiate with at the best of times and I just didn't have the energy...'

He came over and took the basket from her hand.

'Would you let me pour you a glass of wine and sit you in the studio with whatever it is you have in here while I nip to Newport? As soon as I get back you can either walk home, or I'll take you in the car.' He placed his palms together. 'You'd be doing me a huge favour.'

She nodded and with the lightest of touches he brushed her shoulder in thanks.

'You'll have to come around the back. The café's locked now so I get into the studio from the garden.'

She followed him through the gate at the side, across the patio that led from the kitchen, and through open double doors into the studio.

'Make yourself at home,' he said, turning on his heel and heading back towards the house.

Immediately Jules felt a sense of calm. The evening light spun patterns of gold on the whitewashed walls, and the whole place was bathed in stillness. She perched on one of the wooden stools at the workbench and took Tasha's jug from the basket.

'Rosé okay?' he said, reappearing with a glass in hand. 'I've got something else if you'd prefer it. Homemade elderflower cordial?'

'No, this is lovely. Thank you.'

'And I'd just made some bruschetta for the girls, topped with a broad bean dip.'

He placed an irregularly shaped plate in front of her with toasted bread topped with a coarse pate decorated with fronds of chervil.

'I thought you might like some to keep you going.'

'Thank you. That's so kind.' She blinked. 'I'm sorry. I get emotional when anyone is nice to me.'

'I shan't be too nice then,' he said seriously. He looked at the jug. 'And this definitely is not nice!'

'I thought it was beyond repair and then my mother mentioned Kintsugi, but perhaps it's too far gone.'

He leaned over and spread the pieces out in front of her. He smelled good, like freshly cut grass. She tried not to shrink away. She must not get into the habit of locking herself in when anyone got too close.

'I don't think so,' he said. 'I have something here which you can use to glue the pieces back together and then when that has dried you can gild it. I'll find what you need and tell the girls you're here. Then I'll get off.'

Jules was pleased with the way she'd been able to piece the jug back together and already she could see how the gilding would create something unconventionally beautiful. She placed it safely on a shelf to allow it to dry and wandered out into the garden. Bees and butterflies were still busy in the borders, and she followed Morwenna towards the little pond where the cat settled on a large flat stone at the edge and studied the darting fish. Jules perched next to her and kicked off her flip-flops.

'Hi, Jules.'

Erin leaned out of a bedroom window and waved.

She waved back.

'Are you both okay up there?'

'Fine. Are you staying for supper? Dad's going to pick up some crab from his customer.'

'I don't think so,' she called, 'but thank you for asking.'

'Another time then,' Erin said, seemingly unfazed. 'You could feed the fish, though, if you don't mind. There's a container in the shed.'

'What about Morwenna?'

'You don't need to worry about her. She just likes to watch them. She couldn't catch a cold.'

Jules wandered down to the shed at the bottom of the garden and found the fish food. She was crouching by the pond sprinkling granules on to the water when Christabel appeared through the side gate. She was immaculately dressed in a pale pink shirt dress and large, dangly gold earrings which sparkled in the early evening light. She stood stock still as if gathering herself.

'Don't you look as if you've made yourself at home,' she said.

Jules stood up and scrunched her bare feet into the grass.

'Hello, Christabel. I don't think we've been properly introduced. I'm Jules.'

Jules held out a hand while Christabel kept hers deliberately down by her side.

'How is Rita?'

Christabel blinked and twirled her sunglasses between her finger and thumb.

'Not good, I'm afraid.'

'Oh no! I thought the operation went well?'

Christabel shrugged.

'At her age it's difficult to say how she'll recover. One thing's for sure, she won't be as mobile as she used to be.'

'She'll have some physio in due course,' Jules said, 'and be given exercises to do at home so there's no reason to be too pessimistic.'

'The accident has completely sapped her confidence, and she's been a bit confused, bless her. Talked about George catching her as she fell off the ladder.'

'It could be the anaesthetic and the shock. It does that to some people.'

'Or it could be the start of cognitive decline,' Christabel said with a sigh. 'Poor Rita. She's very low. She seems to have aged overnight.'

'If she's up to visitors tomorrow I can stop by the hospital and try to cheer her up.'

Christabel shook her head, her glossy dark brown hair rippling across her shoulders.

'How kind,' she said, drawing out the words, 'but we wouldn't want to disturb your stay any more than it has been already.'

She fixed Jules with a stare. Goodness, this woman could have done a PhD in putting you on edge.

'This is a family matter and the family have it covered.'

That's told me, Jules thought. She placed the lid back on the fish food container and headed back towards the shed.

'Should you really have done that?' Christabel asked. 'Aren't you putting the fish at risk from that cat?'

'Apparently not.'

This had felt like a really happy place until Christabel arrived. She seemed to carry discontent with her.

'Where *is* Lance? Does he know you're here?'

Christabel had followed her and was invading her space. Jules banged her arm on the shed door, rubbed her elbow and smiled ruefully. Her mother would say the elbow was linked to adaptability and flexibility and that knocking it was a reminder of how she was letting go of resistance. Goodness, Jules thought, I may not believe in all this stuff, but I've absorbed it over the years.

'Yes, he does, and he's nipped out to make a delivery.' Lucky for him, she thought.

'Will he be long?'

'I'm not sure.'

He'd said less than an hour, but she wasn't going to tell Christabel that.

'And he's left you in charge?'

'It seems I'm deemed capable of supervising fish.'

'And the girls.'

'Not really needed. They're pretty sensible.'

'I'm here to collect Tasha who, as we both know, is less than sensible.'

Don't react, Jules said to herself. There's a lot you could say, but it's not your place.

'I think they're upstairs chilling out.'

'You think? You don't know?'

'I haven't got trackers on them although I don't think Tasha is expecting you.'

'No, she's not, but it's time she came home. She's been here all afternoon. A bit like you, by the looks of things.'

'I haven't been here long at all.'

She really didn't need to explain herself. Why had she said that?

'Of course you haven't,' Christabel replied with a not-so-sweet smile. 'Did you walk? I didn't notice a car. I can give you a ride back if you like.'

'My mother dropped me off and is picking me up later.'

Christabel wasn't to know that only half of that sentence was true. She glanced down at the pond where the fish were still scuffling over the last crumbs of food and Morwenna was washing her face.

'Lance built that pond for Sarah, you know.'

'No, I didn't.'

'There's a lot you don't know about Lance.'

Jules squared her shoulders. This was becoming tiresome.

'I expect there is. We've only just met.'

'Sarah used to sit by this pond when she was ill. She was the love of Lance's life. He'll never remarry.' She cast Jules a sly glance. 'May have the odd bit of fun. I mean, you can't expect him to be completely celibate, can you?'

Jules didn't deign that comment with a reply. She wanted to reach out and touch the back of one of those solid garden chairs for support, but they were too far away.

'He's that rare specimen – a one-woman man in the long term. And Sarah, lucky thing, was that woman.'

'Not that lucky,' Jules shot back, 'because she died.'

'No, obviously that was unfortunate.'

Jules felt a torrent of anger rise inside her.

'I think it was more than unfortunate. It was tragic. She left two small children.'

Christabel looked taken aback by Jules's ferocity.

'Perhaps I didn't express myself as well as I could have done.'

'Christabel, I think you pick your words very carefully and are capable of expressing yourself more than adequately if you choose. What *is* the point you're trying to make here?'

Christabel lifted her chin.

'There's no need to be so antagonistic. I'm only thinking of you. A lot of women come to the pottery and end up swooning over Lance. A woman likes a man who is creative, doesn't she?' She sent Jules a conspiratorial glance as if they were in league together. 'I was just trying to warn you that if you have any designs…'

'I don't. I'm here mending something. That's all.'

The words came out with such force that all the fish plunged from sight.

'Not that it's any of your business, but at this very moment another relationship is inconceivable.'

Christabel studied her for a few moments.

'That's such a relief,' she finally cooed. 'I wouldn't have wanted you to get hurt, Jules. We women need to stick together. And now that little matter is sorted, I'll go and retrieve my daughter, wherever she may be.'

Jules watched her go and raked her hands through her hair. That woman really was a piece of work.

SEVENTEEN

'Everything okay?' Lance asked, strolling in a while later, cool box in hand.

'Fine, except Christabel came for Tasha and she didn't want to go.'

'But she was meant to be staying for supper and then I was going to run her back later.'

'Change of plan apparently. Erin's pretty fed up, too.'

He shook his head in obvious frustration.

'My clients work in Bembridge and picked up some crab for me. It's one of Tasha's favourites.'

'That's kind.'

'She's fragile. Needs some TLC. Rita does her bit, but to be honest, Alastair isn't always there for her as much as he should be. I don't suppose you'd like to join us, would you? I know you might have other plans, and you might not even like crab, but I can rustle something else up to go with the salad if you'd rather.'

'I do like crab actually, but...'

She had a sudden feeling of panic.

'Your mother's waiting for you.'

'No. She's having supper with Jo. I'm just not very good company.'

'I totally understand,' he said, 'and I didn't mean to pressure you. When Sarah died people were so kind and they kept inviting us around for meals, but sometimes it just felt too much. I remember that feeling of wanting to sit at home without having to make polite conversation or make the effort to look as if I hadn't splintered into a thousand pieces. Take the crab home with you and eat it in peace.'

Erin slunk in through the doorway and went to stand next to her father.

'Sorry, honey,' he said, 'Jules told me what happened.'

'She's a witch, Dad,' Erin said as he put his arm around her. 'Tasha was so upset, and her mum wouldn't even wait to take the crab for her to eat.'

'I've offered it to Jules. She's going to take it home with her, so it won't be wasted.'

Jules looked at Erin's crestfallen face.

'No, I'll stay.' She glanced at Lance. 'If the offer still stands and you don't mind my grumpiness.'

'Dad can be grumpy with the best of them,' Erin chipped in.

She glanced at Lance.

'The offer might not still stand then.'

'It does,' he said with an unmistakably thankful smile.

'We could play cards after we've eaten,' Erin said to Jules. 'Do you play cards? Dad, Fitz and I play Go Fish sometimes.'

'I used to play rummy with my dad,' Jules said. 'Tell you what, we'll play both.'

'Loser has to do the washing up,' Lance said, laughing, and Jules could hear the relief in the timbre.

'Thank you so much,' Lance said, pouring two glasses of rosé. 'She gets so upset about Tasha, but what can you do?'

Jules looked through the window to where Erin was picking cut-and-come-again salad leaves from a raised bed.

'It seems to me that you do all you can to provide her with a bit of a sanctuary. She said to me how much she loves coming here.'

He clinked his glass against hers.

'And we love having her. Here's to sanctuaries wherever they may be. We all need them, don't we?'

'I'll drink to that,' Jules said.

She couldn't believe how quickly the evening passed. After supper of crab, salad and new potatoes garnished with fresh dill and parsley butter, Lance disappeared into the café and came back with three little tubs of ice cream.

'Honeycomb, chocolate and orange, or lemon and raspberry,' he said.

'Isle of Wight ice cream,' Jules said.

'Made with local milk and cream,' Lance said. 'There used to be over three hundred dairy farms on the island. Now there are only ten. You won't see that many cows around in the fields these days and this company is trying to keep cattle on the island and provide a livelihood for the farmers.'

'This is a very supportive place,' Jules said.

'It has to be,' Lance said. 'Any small community has to be supportive, or it won't just not thrive, it will die.'

'Mum used to say it was a magical island,' Erin said. 'Do you know what wight means?'

'No, I never really thought about it,' Jules said, 'but I presume it's an alternative spelling for white because The Needles are white. At least, they look white in photographs.'

'They're made of chalk,' Lance said, 'so they are white, but that's not the answer.'

'It means ghost or spirit,' Erin said.

Jules felt her heart beat a little faster and developed a clamminess at the nape of her neck.

'But it's had many different names over time,' Lance said. 'The Anglo Saxons called it Wiht which comes from their word for 'place of the spirits', but before that the Romans called it Vectis which people think might have derived from the Latin for conquered. The Vikings called it Wightland, and then it was Henry VIII who named it the Isle of Wight. Another theory is that wight used to mean a divide and of course we're divided from the mainland.'

'It is meant to be the most haunted place on earth. Mum used to call it the island of spirits,' Erin said. 'I like to think that. I like to think that Mum's spirit is still here somewhere. Tasha says there are spirits at Hideaway Cottage. Have you seen them?'

'No. I'm not sure I really believe in that sort of thing.'

'Don't you think it's got a special atmosphere though?'

'Yes, but that's not necessarily to do with spirits. It could just be the way the cottage sits in the landscape or perhaps how Guy has done it up with such care.'

Erin threw her a slightly pitying glance.

'Or it could be that the spirits of the people who lived there before are looking after it like Mum is still here looking after us.'

'Erin, you're going to end up scaring Jules. Why don't we choose an ice cream before they melt?'

He caught Jules's eye and held her gaze for a moment as if he was looking straight into her soul.

'Let me guess. You look like a lemon and raspberry person to me.'

She laughed, glad of the change of conversation.

'You're absolutely right.'

'What do you think Dad is?' Erin asked, pushing the remaining two tubs into the middle of the table.

Jules felt flustered. It's just an ice cream flavour, she said to herself. It really doesn't matter one way or the other if you get it right.

'This is my inscrutable face,' Lance said, leaning back in his chair.

'And it is impressively inscrutable,' she said. 'You don't look like you at all.'

And she blushed because it made it sound as if she'd been studying his every feature and really, she barely knew him. so how did she know what he looked like when he was in his own private space, when he was able to be his real self?

'I think you like both of them,' she said.

'That's opting out,' Erin said. 'You're not allowed to do that.'

'And you are right,' Lance said, teasingly. 'I do like both of them, but I like one slightly more than the other.'

'Come on, Dad, more than slightly. You're addicted to one of them.'

Jules thought back and tried to remember which cake he had eaten at teatime that day when she and Carrie had come on the course. It was only a few days ago, but it seemed much longer.

'You're overthinking this,' he said softly.

'I know.'

She felt like bursting into tears.

'Trust your instinct.'

But I don't trust my instinct anymore, she thought, and she looked up at him, her eyes pooling, aware of tears beading on her lashes.

'Erin, sweetheart, can you go and get some spoons?' he said, and she scraped her chair back and headed for the dresser. 'And while you're there, can you put a bit more food down for Morwenna?'

'Sorry,' he whispered to Jules, placing his hand over hers. 'It really doesn't matter. It's just a silly game we play with visitors.'

She felt the warmth of his skin against hers, looked at his nails and a small scab on one of his knuckles where he'd cut himself. She closed her eyes and suddenly felt safe.

'Chocolate and orange,' she said, flicking her eyelids open to find him still looking at her intently.

'Right first time,' he said.

'You'd have said that anyway,' she said, 'even if honeycomb was really your favourite.'

He shook his head.

'I wouldn't,' he said, 'because that would be deceitful and I would never want to deceive you, Jules.'

He was a good man, she thought. Christabel was right about one thing, after all. Sarah had been a very lucky woman.

'You can't walk now,' Lance said, 'it's getting dark. I've only had one small glass of wine so I'll run you back.'

Erin hugged her as she left.

'Thank you for staying.'

Jules dropped her head so that her lips brushed Erin's hair.

'Thank you for playing cards with me. It was nice.'

'Even though I beat you?'

'Maybe we'll have to have a rematch,' she said, meeting Lance's gaze over the top of Erin's head. 'Perhaps at Hideaway Cottage and see if Tasha is allowed to come, too?'

'That would be good, wouldn't it, Dad?'

'Let's see how much time Jules has left on the island before we start booking her up for card games.'

And irrationally she felt rebuffed.

They drove down the lane in silence as the shadows lengthened.

'When are you going home?' he asked, pulling up outside the cottage.

Such a difficult question to answer, she thought, because over the last few days this little house had felt like home, but of course it wasn't.

'I don't know.'

She had butterflies in her stomach at the thought of returning to Manchester, to the memories of Gavin, to the responsibility of her job. How long could she stay here tucked away from normal life? How long should she stay?

'Not that I'm trying to get rid of you,' he said with a half laugh.

'I'm sorry if I was a bit curt back there, but I don't want either of the girls to get too attached to you if you're not going to be here for long.'

'I've got to go back sooner or later. I can't hide behind trauma for ever.'

'Oh, Jules,' he said, 'you're not hiding behind trauma. You're learning to live with what's happened. You can't hurry that. If you go back too soon, to work, to normal life, you might have a relapse.'

His words felt like an enormous hug. She looked up at him, his eyes dark pools, his cheekbones highlighted by the moonlight.

'Did that happen to you?' she asked tentatively.

'The first year was incredibly hard,' he replied, looking straight ahead towards the cottage. 'The second year a little better. The third year...'

He shook his head.

'The third year was terrible. I had some grief counselling, which helped. I should have done it before, but I just ploughed on thinking I could deal with everything.'

'And now?'

He chewed his bottom lip.

'And now I'm in a pretty good place and I feel guilty for saying it, as if I'm betraying Sarah's memory.'

'But she wouldn't have wanted you to grieve for ever. She would have wanted you to get on and live your one precious life.'

He nodded.

'I'll be back, though, to visit Carrie and Guy and...' she paused, choosing her words carefully, '...hopefully catch up with everyone else who's been so kind to me. I'm not going to disappear up north, never to be seen again.'

He turned his face towards her and smiled.

'That's good to hear.'

For a brief moment she thought that he might lean over and kiss her, but after a couple of seconds he looked away and lifted his hand from the steering wheel.

'Is that your mother looking out of the window?' he asked, pointing towards the cottage.

'I can't believe she's doing that!' Jules exclaimed. 'It's not as if I'm fifteen and sitting in some randy sixth former's car snogging!'

He laughed out loud.

'I'm definitely way past being a randy sixth former, not that I ever was one, and there's no snogging allowed in this car. Fitz's rule.'

She blushed and wondered if he'd just made that up.

'I'd better go,' she said, reaching for the door handle, 'or Mum will come out in her nightie and haul us both inside for hot chocolate and marshmallows and an interrogation.'

'Has she got someone else with her? Jo, maybe? I thought I saw another figure at the window?'

'I don't think so. There's only one car here. Unless she's brought Jo and Daniel back to stay the night.' Her eyes widened in alarm. 'We'll be like sardines. I might even have to share the double bed with her.'

'Do you want to check? You can always come back with me. Fitz's room is spare at the moment.'

She reached for the basket on the back seat and accidentally brushed the collar of his shirt. She jumped away, but he didn't move.

'Sorry,' she said. 'Didn't mean to... you know. Just needed to get the basket. It's Carrie's, and thank you for the offer, but I'm sure it will be fine.'

Suddenly she couldn't get out of the car fast enough. He opened the driver door and stepped out, beating her to the gate.

'Thank you for a lovely evening,' she said, fumbling with the latch.

'Thank you for cheering Erin up and me, too,' he said.

'Did you need cheering?'

'We all do sometimes, don't we? You haven't glazed your bowl yet. Are you coming back to join the others for that?'

'I'm not sure.'

He looked as if he was trying to cover disappointment, but perhaps it was wishful thinking.

'Even if you don't, I'd like to think that somewhere you'll carry on working with clay. You have a real feel for it.'

'Thank you,' she whispered.

'See you soon,' he said. 'Sleep well.'

And then he was back in the car and reversing around to drive away up the lane. She turned to look at the cottage, the pink tinged moon low in the sky, a sheep baaing in the field, something small rustling in the border next to her. Inside was Beulah with all her years of pent-up maternal feelings and conversations. Jules didn't feel up to facing that yet, so she wandered around the side of the house and headed towards the willow tree.

'May I come in?' she asked, before parting the foliage.

It felt ridiculous, but she almost expected to see someone sitting there on that log. She stood and watched the tracery formed by the moonlight and the gently rustling branches. It was mesmerising, calming. She could have stayed there forever. Her mother and Carrie were right. There was something special about this place.

'Darling!' A voice brought her back to reality. 'There you are. I wondered where you'd gone. Almost wondered if you'd driven off with the wonderful Lance for a little cuddle.'

'Mum, no! He's far too much of a gentleman for that.'

'Shame,' Beulah said. 'That's probably just what you need.'

She spun around to look up at the vaulted space.

'I wonder who planted this tree, who lived in this house.'

'Rita's great-aunt lived here, I think.'

'Maybe even before that,' Beulah said. 'They are still around, the spirits of this place, their whispers float through the air like pollen. They are trying to care for you, to show you the way forward.'

Jules reached out and placed her palm against the strong body of the tree.

'When I came here only a few days ago I wasn't sure I could see a way forward but now maybe I can.'

Beulah reached for Jules's free hand and squeezed it.

'Something good will come of this,' she said. 'You just wait and see.'

Jules smiled and felt a gleam of hope infiltrate her palms, run up her arms and settle around her heart. Maybe her mother and Carrie were right after all, and hope was worth having.

EIGHTEEN

Rita's bed was right at the end of the small ward. The window looked out over a grassy bank which she stared at longingly.

'Rita,' Jules said softly, 'how are you?'

The older woman turned her head and smiled broadly.

'Aren't you a sight for sore eyes?' She twinkled.

Jules let out a little breath.

'I did call first,' Jules said, 'and the nurse said you were up to having another visitor if I didn't stay too long.'

Rita shuffled a little in the bed.

'You stay as long as you like,' she murmured. 'I'm bored to tears in here.'

Jules made a space on top of the crowded locker and placed a few magazines there.

'I wasn't sure what you liked so I bought you a selection and some chocolate.'

'Just what I need,' Rita said. 'Don't suppose you can use your influence to get me out of here, can you?'

Jules laughed.

'No, I can't. You've got to do what you're told if you're going to make a good recovery.'

'Oh, I will, and I am,' Rita proclaimed, 'there's no doubt about that.'

Jules settled back in her chair. This wasn't the Rita that Christabel had described at all.

'You look a lot better than I expected and your face is healing nicely.'

'I never would have won a beauty pageant even back in the day so not many looks to lose.'

'You have a beautiful face, Rita,' Jules said.

'My George thought so and that's all that matters. Shall we crack into the chocolate?'

Jules proceeded to open one of the bars.

'Christabel told you I'm at death's door, has she?'

Jules smiled, broke off a square of dark chocolate studded generously with dried raspberries and offered it to Rita.

'Not quite.'

'Going gaga then. She's going to use this, you know, to get me out of the house. I expect she's already measuring up for curtains as we speak.'

'I'm so sorry, Rita. I feel partly responsible for what's happened. I should have sent Tasha home straight away.'

'Not your fault, dearie. What's meant to be is meant to be. If it hadn't happened this time, it would have been another. Now take my mind off this place and tell me about you. Is your lovely mother still here? And have you been back to The Pottery? I think both of those things are really important for you.'

Jules sat back in her chair and told her about mending Tasha's broken jug and how guilty she felt regarding her annoyance that her mother had come over and how she'd now moved into the cottage.

'If it had been my father, I could have coped better,' she said. 'After all these years I still miss him every day.'

'The more you miss someone is a sign of how much you loved them,' Rita said. 'I still get a pain when I think about my George. Funny thing, it's as if he was there when I fell, trying to save me.

Perhaps doesn't want me joining him just yet. Not ready for my nagging in eternity!'

Jules reached for her jacket on the back of the chair and stood up.

'I ought to be going. I've stayed longer than I intended, and you'll be getting tired.'

Rita reached out her hand.

'It's been like a breath of fresh air. Next time you come could you bring Tasha and Will? I'm going to be here for another three or four days according to the powers that be.' Her eyes swivelled to the side. 'Uh oh! And talking of powers that be, here comes one of them now. Better put on your crash helmet.'

Christabel strode down the ward, her heels clicking with military precision on the vinyl tiles.

'You again!' she said, totally ignoring Rita. 'Considering you don't even live on the island you get everywhere. I thought I told you this was a family matter.'

Jules opened her mouth to speak, but Rita got in first.

'Where are your manners, Christabel? You should be thanking Jules for helping out in an emergency. I know I'm eternally grateful and before you say anything else derogatory, I asked Jules to visit.'

She turned her head slightly so that Christabel wouldn't see the slight wink she made with her good eye.

'And how did you do that?'

Rita picked up her phone and waved it in the air.

'I'm not too stupid to send a message. Irene's coming in later, too. And I've asked Jules to bring Tasha and William next time she visits.'

'And what are you eating?'

'Chocolate. Do you want some?'

Christabel shook her head and snapped her head towards Jules.

'I'm sure you don't want to spend any more time in a hospital ward. You must have enough of that in your everyday life. I can take over now.'

'I was about to go anyway.'

Jules turned to Rita who blew her a kiss.

'Bless you for coming,' she said. 'Done me the power of good.'

'I'll walk you out,' Christabel said.

'I think I can find my way.'

'I'm sure you can, but I want a chat with the ward sister anyway.' She turned to Rita. 'I'll be back soon.'

That's what I'm afraid of, she mouthed at Jules.

As they walked out together, Christabel carried on past the reception desk until they reached the outer doors which led to the main staircase.

'I'm sure Rita appreciates your visit,' she said, as Jules pushed the exit button, 'but as you're the reason she's in here the best thing you can do is go back to where you came from and sort your own life out.'

And with that she turned on her heel and walked away.

'Christabel was vile,' Jules said to Carrie as they walked up through the woods to the Longstone later that afternoon.

'She's not the friendliest. I'm sorry if she upset you.'

'Actually not, she's just made me really angry. I don't know how Rita tolerates her.'

'From what I hear most people think that.'

'What on earth did Alastair see in her?'

'She can turn on the charm when she wants to, apparently, and she is attractive. According to Irene, Guy's grandmother, Christabel has delusions of grandeur. When she met Alastair and heard about the farm and saw the farmhouse, which is undeniably beautiful, she thought she'd be taking on a lady of the manor role.'

'Sounds as if she'd be better with The Major's son.'

'Oh, I think she's fluttered her eyelashes at him a few times in the past, but he's never here for long enough for her to really work her charms.'

'It can't be a happy marriage.'

'How do you define a happy marriage? Maybe it suits both of them. I don't know. She comes and goes pretty much as she pleases and Rita's always around to look after the children.'

Jules picked up a stick from the path and threw it for Wilbur.

'I know that Christabel has the lives of both the children mapped out,' Carrie said.

'That's a mistake.'

Carrie grinned.

'You don't have to tell me that. My mother's still reeling from me staying here and not heading back to Manchester to try and get another job in a big PR company. In fact, she's so distraught that they've extended their world tour. I feel a bit guilty because they ended up staying with my brother in New Zealand for a lot longer than planned.'

'But you said your dad's lent you some money to tide you over?'

'Yes. He's been great actually. Much nicer than I expected, but I'm not to tell Mum about the money. It could cause a problem if she finds out.'

'Do you think many people have happy marriages without secrets?'

'Everyone has secrets, don't they? Things they're ashamed of that they don't want other people, even the people who love them unconditionally, to know about. But yes, I do think there are happy marriages, although I also think there has to be a lot of compromise on both sides.'

They reached the top and Jules looked out across the valley. Dark clouds were gathering to the west. It felt as if there was a storm coming.

'Life is a compromise, isn't it?' she said.

'Up to a point, yes,' Carrie said. 'That's the benchmark of a civilised society. But compromise doesn't always have to be a negative thing. It can lead to contentment.'

'That's what I'm looking for,' Jules said, 'contentment. It sounds less exhausting than happiness.'

'You'll find it,' Carrie said.

'Yes,' Jules said with a nod. 'Yes, I will.'

They both heard the crash from the kitchen.

'Oh my, what was that?' Beulah exclaimed.

'It sounded like something breaking,' Jules said, bolting through the sitting room, across the hall and up the stairs.

She stood in the doorway of her bedroom and stared at the angular shards of her mother's magnifying mirror scattered over the floor.

'I forgot I'd left that on the sill,' Beulah said, appearing behind her. 'I was using the better light in here to pluck my eyebrows.'

'And you opened every single window back and front when the wind's getting up,' Jules accused.

'It's luften, darling.'

'What?'

'Luften,' Beulah replied, with an apologetic smile. 'It's German. It means to let air in. It's all about letting the old, stale air out and new fresh air in. Very important for wellbeing, especially in an old property like this.'

'Except it's not going to be very good for my wellbeing if I cut myself to ribbons picking up pieces of broken glass.'

'I can't have fixed the window latch properly. Oh dear, I am a bit slapdash about things like that. The mirror must have smashed against the radiator on the way down. Let me clear it up.'

'No,' Jules said, raising her voice. 'The last thing I need is blood all over the carpet. I'll do it. I've already had to deal with one injury with Rita next door, I don't want to be tending another one.'

She went downstairs to find an old newspaper and stood next to the hearth trying to compose herself. This is what happened when she spent time with her mother. Just when things seemed to be getting better between them something happened to make her churlish and impatient. Did she really want to go through the rest of their lives having this reaction? She reached into the log basket and retrieved some paper. She could change her attitude right now if she chose, or at least try to.

Beulah was standing in the same place when Jules returned to the bedroom. She was twisting her thin gold wedding band back and forth, a crestfallen expression consuming her face.

'I'm so sorry.' She sniffed. 'I can't seem to get anything right.'

Jules went and put her arms around her.

'It's fine, Mum. It doesn't matter.'

'Except I really don't want either of us to have seven years' bad luck, Jules.'

'Me neither,' she said, bending down to spread out the news-paper and gingerly place the mirror pieces on the sheets, 'so it's good that I don't believe in that sort of thing. Who on earth made that one up anyway?'

'It comes from the Romans, too. I've been reading more about them since we went to the villa. They thought that humans go through a process of renewal every seven years, in all areas, spiritu-ally, physically, emotionally. They believed that a mirror reflected your soul and if you broke a mirror your soul would be broken.'

'Already been there, done that, got the T-shirt courtesy of Gavin,' Jules murmured, 'so you don't need to worry on my behalf, Mum.'

'But I do worry, darling, all of the time.'

Jules looked at her mother's carefully pedicured bare feet.

'The main thing you have to worry about is getting glass splin-ters in your feet. I'll get the vacuum out, but there might still be some bits that escape so I'd put some shoes on while walking about up here.'

She took the parcel down to the bin in the kitchen with Beulah following close behind.

'Wait,' Beulah said as Jules placed her foot on the pedal. 'You can't put that in there. You have to bury it.'

Jules's hands hovered in mid-air.

'In the garden. You have to bury the mirror, preferably under the light of a full moon.'

Do not snap, Jules, she said to herself. Remember your new benevolent attitude of only a few minutes ago.

'O-kay, except I think the full moon was a couple of days ago and I'm not hanging on to a broken mirror for another month while I wait for the next one.'

'No, no, no, that wouldn't do at all,' Beulah said, 'and the light from the moon will still be strong so I'm sure it will be almost as effective.'

I have to be patient, Jules thought as she stared at the parcel of broken glass. I can be patient.

'The thing is, Mum, this isn't my garden. Someone might dig it up later on and injure themselves.'

Beulah moved to the half-open stable door and looked out.

'We must be able to find a spot where that's not likely to happen. What about there, beneath that willow tree? Nobody will try to plant anything beneath that, will they?'

'No,' Jules said, resigned to her fate, 'I suppose not.'

'Then as soon as it gets dark,' Beulah said, 'that's where we will bury it.'

Jules stood and watched.

'We probably should have come out and dug the hole before it got dark,' she said.

'It's fine,' Beulah replied. 'I can see perfectly well. The moon is guiding the space.'

'Aren't willows shallow rooted?' Jules asked. 'Won't it be difficult to find a place to dig deeply enough?'

'No, no, this is a good place,' Beulah replied, 'and we could put a large stone over the top or even move this fallen tree trunk forwards.'

'No!' Jules said, surprising herself. 'Not the tree trunk. We can't move that. It looks as if it's been there forever. It should stay in the same place. It would be too heavy for us to move anyway.'

'Why don't you go and look for a suitable stone?' Beulah suggested.

Jules placed the newspaper on the ground and parted the fronds to step back on to the lawn. She took a deep breath. It had felt so claustrophobic in there and strangely distressing, not calm like last night. She was amazed that Beulah hadn't picked up on it. But perhaps it was bringing back memories of Gavin and how upset he had got when she broke the phone. Coercive control, she thought. That's what he had used on her and even though she'd seen evidence of it with others she'd never realised she'd become a victim herself until now. How stupid she had been. How desperate for him to love her. He had made her feel weak, had tried to isolate her from friends, had subtly fed her discontent with her mother and sister instead of encouraging rapprochement. She walked around to the front garden. She could take one of the large stones lining the path and then move some of the others around so that it wouldn't look as if anything had changed. But suddenly everything had changed, and she realised with absolute clarity what a lucky escape she'd had.

Jules chose the squarest piece of stone she could find and prised it from its place. Beulah was taking a rest when she returned, leaning on the spade. Immediately Jules stepped back inside the confines of the branches she felt breathless and clammy. This time it wasn't just a sense of distress she sensed, it was something more menacing than that.

'I'm all hot,' Beulah said, wiping her forearm across her forehead. 'I'm getting too old for digging.'

'Then perhaps we should leave it,' Jules said. 'Tasha, the girl next door at the farm, says that this is a special place. She comes and sits here sometimes, says she feels protected. I don't need to bury this mirror to move forward without fear, Mum.'

Beulah threw her a curious glance.

'No, I can see that.'

'The weather's getting worse,' Jules persisted as the branches of the willow creaked above her. 'Let's go back inside and just put the mirror in the bin.'

'Yes, yes,' the tree seemed to whisper to her. 'You do that.'

'Did you hear that?' she asked, whipping around to look behind her.

'Probably just the wind,' Beulah replied, but her eyes were dark with apprehension.

'No, Mum, it's more than that. We shouldn't be here. Someone or something doesn't like it. Can't you feel that? You're meant to be the ultra-sensitive one. Oh! Something just brushed against my face.'

'And mine. It will just be a bat. One of those ones from the farm which upset your friend Rita. Bats are good. They encourage us to embrace change. A couple of inches more and that will be plenty deep enough,' Beulah said, plunging the spade into the hole once more.

'What *is* that?' Jules asked, as something pale gleamed in the moonlight.

'Probably just a bit of root,' Beulah said.

Jules moved closer.

'I don't think so, Mum.'

Beulah fished her phone out of her back pocket and switched it on.

'You're right. I must have disturbed some animal bones. A cat maybe or a small dog.'

Jules didn't reply. Her heart felt as if it was in her mouth. She took Beulah's phone from her hand and shone the light into the hole.

'What can you see?' Beulah asked, grabbing her arm.

'Something.'

'Perhaps this wasn't the right place to dig, after all.'

Jules shot her a withering look.

'Now you say that!'

Above them the willow branches began to swish backwards

and forwards, the whole trunk of the tree seeming to be straining against the wind.

'Let's go back inside,' Jules said, 'and leave this until the morning.'

'I can't leave it until then,' Beulah protested. 'Goodness knows how much more bad luck that will attract.'

'It'll be pretty bad luck if a tree falls on us,' Jules snapped.

Seething with irritation, she dropped to her knees and reached down into the hole. The ground was soft and crumbly beneath her hands, as if someone at some time had dug here before. She used her fingertips to brush the soil away from something solid. As she worked her way around the edge of the hole, she almost felt as if there was someone else there, too, someone who was looking down into that space alongside her. Jules knelt back on her heels.

'Is that what I think it is?' Beulah gasped, as the beam of light from her phone fell upon something curved.

'Yes, Mum. It's a skull.'

'It's not a cat or a dog, is it?'

'No.'

'It's very small.'

Jules looked up at her in shock.

'That's because it belongs to a baby.'

Eliza had been pacing up and down the lawn fretting about Isaac when she'd spotted Jules and Beulah walking towards the willow tree. The older woman carried a rake in one hand and a spade in the other whilst Jules held some form of paper parcel with outstretched arms as if whatever it contained might bite. Immediately Eliza felt a sense of alarm as if something terrible was about to happen. Where was Isaac? Why had he not returned from his walk? He knew how she hated storms. She watched as Jules let go of the parcel with one hand and tugged at Beulah's sleeve, causing her to pause.

'I'm not sure we should be doing this,' Jules said.

Then don't, Eliza willed. If only she could say it out loud. Maybe she could whisper it in Beulah's ear.

She was meant to be attuned to matters beyond the normal limited view of existence. But no, Eliza could see that it would be futile. Beulah was far too wrapped up in concern for her daughter and any intuition would have left her; stress, worry, trying too hard to please, robbed you of the gift of sensing so much more. The woman who Isaac had rightly warned her about took a step forward and parted the fronds, invading their sacred place. Eliza ran across the upper lawn, down the steps, skirted the magnolia and slipped inside the canopy of the willow at the back. Beulah was standing in the centre of the space looking around while Jules hovered at the edge, unwilling to take part in this strange human ritual. And for a moment Eliza had hope that everything would be all right. Whatever was about to take place would be abandoned. The women would return to the cottage and all would be well. Except it wasn't. Eliza watched in horror as Beulah began to rake away layers of fallen leaves before reaching soft loam. Then she picked up the spade, pushed it into the earth and began to dig.

Eliza needed Isaac here, by her side. He would know what to do. Men always went missing just when you needed them most. Could he not sense that she was distressed? That the remains of their beloved dogs, which they had so carefully laid to rest beneath this tree, were about to be revealed. Those dogs had been more than companions, they had filled a void, had seemed to sense her every mood and always offered comfort. She would not have them disturbed. These women were desecrating her space, Isaac's space. She could not allow it. She wafted her arms around, she rustled the weeping branches of the willow, she even brushed her hand against Jules' face. She didn't want to alarm her but what else could she do? Maybe the Beulah woman wouldn't dig too deeply. Maybe they would place whatever it was in a shallow hole and then Jules's mother could go and leave them in peace once more. But as she watched, as she moved closer to the darkness of the hole, something shifted in her memory and began to reveal itself and she knew that she would never feel peace in this place again.

Eliza had never run so fast. Her feet barely touched the ground. It almost felt as if she were flying. If she hadn't been so distraught it would have been a wonderful sensation. As a girl, much to her mother's dismay, she had lain on the grass in the orchard and watched the birds high in the sky, wishing she could join them.

'I despair, Eliza,' her mother used to say, 'your frock will be ruined. I have a daughter who likes nothing better than to climb trees, roll around on the grass in an unseemly fashion with her hair completely awry and a son who spends all his time inside drawing and reading poetry. I really don't know where I went wrong. I'll have to go and lie down.'

Her mother had spent a lot of time lying down, Eliza thought. What a waste when you could be running, jumping, skipping and feeling the wind and rain and sun on your face. Sometimes she had escaped the confines of their walled garden and run down through the village of her youth, not with a view to counting her steps like Carrie – whosoever had heard of such a thing – or trying to become fitter or relieving stress, but for the pure joy of it and the heady sense of freedom it gave her. She would laugh and wave to people as she passed by. Now there was no freedom, there would be no more waving, no laughter, just grief.

'Eliza!'

Isaac was striding across the field towards her, but she was determined not to stop. She would just keep running as if he didn't exist.

'Wait,' he called as she raced past.

He put out a hand and grabbed at her arm, but couldn't hold her properly. She felt an improper sense of triumph that she had eluded him. She had always been the faster runner. He would not be able to catch her now except she had been thrown off balance. She stumbled and he caught up, grabbed hold of her.

'Eliza, what is it? Where are you going?'

She tried to fight him, to wrench herself from his grasp, which became stronger the more she resisted.

'Stop!' he said, his voice raised so that the sheep looked up from their sheltering place beneath the hedge. 'Tell me what is troubling you. Is it the storm? I went further than I intended, and I heard thunder in the distance. I was hurrying back as fast as I was able.'

She couldn't bear to look at him. He took her firmly by the shoulders and suddenly all the fight went out of her. He looked back towards the house where lights now shone brightly from every window.

'They have been digging,' she said quietly, 'beneath the willow tree.'

She felt his fingers tighten around her.

'Why would they do that?'

He seemed to be speaking to the ominous sky as much as to her.

'To bury a broken mirror,' she replied. 'Apparently it prevents bad luck if it is buried.'

Now she had the strength to look up at him.

'And do you know what they found, Isaac?'

He didn't reply, but she felt his fear. Be gentle, Eliza, a voice seemed to echo in her ear, but she could not. Compassion had left her.

'They found bones. Not one of our beloved dogs, as I first believed.'

She paused, not knowing she could be so cruel.

'They found the bones of a baby. Our baby. You see, I remember now.'

He released her and she took several steps backwards.

'All of these years I've struggled to remember, knowing that there was something missing, something important, something vital to my wellbeing. How could you let me go through that, Isaac? How could you not have told me what it was I needed to know?'

His whole face contorted in anguish. She would not stroke those lines away.

'I was trying to protect you from pain. We had been through so much.'

'But you stopped me from all the memories of motherhood, that I had finally carried a baby to full term and, for a few precious months, nursed her. You denied me all of that joy as well as the pain. Did that not occur to you?'

'We had struggled for so long to have a baby. To lose her felt like a punishment from God. It was the worst of times, and I nearly lost you, too. You were ill for weeks with the consumption, Eliza, barely conscious for much of that time, and when you began to recover you were so weak. Any setback would have been dangerous so it seemed to be a blessing that you had forgotten.'

'But I dreamed about her. I thought she was the baby I had never had. That it was my mind playing tricks because of the longing. But she was real.'

Isaac let go of her and collapsed to his knees.

'Yes, she was real. She was the most beautiful baby I've ever set eyes on and just like her mother.'

'And you buried her beneath the willow tree?'

'I wrapped her in the shawl you had knitted and laid her to rest here. I wanted her close to us in the garden where I used to carry her and point out the flowers and the birds and let her hear the sound of the wind rustling in the trees. I would show her the gleam of the sea in the distance and promised to take her in our little rowing boat one day.'

'And the articles beneath the floor. You placed those there, too?'

He nodded, unable to look at her, lost in his memories, which she could tell were as painfully fresh now as hers.

'Her little bonnet, apricot like her curls which were just beginning to blossom, the rattle which I bought even before she was born, and her name.'

'Philly,' Eliza whispered, 'my precious Philly. But I didn't recognise that as your handwriting, Isaac.'

He shook his head in shame.

'I disguised it just in case you should ever find the little box.'

'When you said that you had gifted that tea caddy to a friend I often wondered why. And her crib? What happened to that?'

'I gave it away. I cleared out everything that would be a reminder. It has been such a burden, Eliza, to keep all of this from you.'

She should have felt sorry for him, but he was a different man to her now.

'I didn't think we had any secrets between us, Isaac. Everything has changed.'

He fell to his knees.

'Please do not say that, Eliza. You know I am nothing without you. I was so afraid that you would pass over first. That I would be left alone.'

He was right. She was the strong one. She'd had to be. She had to be now.

'I would not have gone without you, Isaac. But where is Philly's spirit? It is not here in this house, in the garden, dancing on the wind or weaving in and out of the tree branches. I can't feel it anywhere.'

He sobbed and still couldn't look at her as he spoke.

'Gone. I had left the window open by mistake, and I saw it leave her body. I tried to hold on to it, but it was so small and wriggly.'

He looked up and reached for her hands, pleading for compassion.

'I saw her pass over, Eliza, and it was a bright smiling light. She was no longer in distress, I promise you. We can go to her now. Together. Leave all of this and be reunited with our daughter.'

And Eliza got a tantalising glimpse of release and new possibilities.

'That would be wonderful, Isaac.'

And suddenly he looked like a young man again, as if all the strain had fallen away from him. She looked back towards the cottage.

'You have done more than enough here, Eliza. It is time to go. Come, all we have to do is to let go of the ties that have been binding us here.'

Maybe he was right. Maybe now was the time. But not with her husband. She would go alone and be reunited with her daughter.

NINETEEN

Guy and Carrie had arrived late.

'There's not much we can do tonight,' he said as they sat in the kitchen drinking hot chocolate laced with brandy. 'I'll call the police first thing in the morning, but we'd better cover the remains back up and I'll put some stones over the top to stop the foxes disturbing it.'

Jules and Beulah stood at a respectful distance the following morning as two police officers studied the little bones and took photographs.

'They'll send the photographs to a biological anthropologist to determine roughly how long she's been there,' Jules said to Carrie on the phone, 'but they're pretty sure it's a long time.'

'And what then?'

'It has to be reported to the coroner's office obviously, but if she's of no interest to the police she will become the responsibility of the county archaeologist.'

'You keep saying *she*.'

'Because surely it's Philly? The rattle and the bonnet in the tea caddy must have belonged to this baby.'

'I've been back through the census records and there aren't any children mentioned who were living at Hideaway Cottage. Isaac and Eliza Cooper lived there from 1841 to 1900. Then there's a bit of a gap, after which it was sold to Rita's great-aunt and she never married.'

'That doesn't mean she didn't have a baby. It did happen even in those days.'

'Maybe we'll never know.'

'Someone knows. The energy here is all stirred up.'

'You sound just like your mum! How is she?'

'Subdued. Jo is here and they are making a little shrine in the garden: flowers, crystals, shells from the beach, some willow weaving. It's beautiful.'

'I've got to go into Cowes this morning and collect some plants for Guy which are coming over on the ferry. Fancy coming with me? We could take Wilbur for a walk on Tennyson Down afterwards. That's if your mum doesn't mind being left on her own.'

'They'll be busy for ages, and a walk is just what I need.'

'Tennyson used to walk up here almost every day, whatever the weather,' Carrie said, keeping Wilbur firmly on the lead because of the cliff edge. 'Sometimes he used to pull his wife, Emily, in a little carriage.'

Jules trailed her fingers over the railings which surrounded the tall granite monument erected in honour of the great poet.

'He lived on the island for thirty-nine years,' Carrie said, 'and he was incredibly famous in his day. He had a bridge built over the road so that he could walk directly from his beloved garden at Farringford House on to the High Down without having to fend off his adoring public.'

'He sounds like a modern-day celebrity.'

'Absolutely. He was considered almost as famous as Queen Victoria or the prime minister, William Gladstone. Did you know he wrote "Tis better to have loved and lost/than never to have loved at all"?'

'No, I didn't.' Jules threw back her head and let the wind ruffle her hair. 'Do you think the parents of that baby would think that?'

'I don't know,' Carrie said, as she stared into the distance. 'Some people seem to get more than their fair share of pain, don't they?'

Jules thought about Lance and Erin and Rita and Tasha and how resilient they were. You could learn such a lot from how others coped with adversity. She stood next to Carrie and linked their arms.

'Thank you for bringing me here,' she said.

'You've already told me that,' Carrie replied with a smile.

'I know but this time I really mean it. Thank you for bringing me here to this island, to the cottage, to these people.'

When they returned to the cottage Lance's car was parked outside.

'Looks as if you've got a visitor,' Carrie said.

'Mmm,' Jules replied. 'I wonder what he wants.'

'Only one way to find out,' Carrie laughed, half pushing her out of the car.

'He might want to see you,' Jules said, aware that she sounded panicky.

'I very much doubt it,' Carrie said.

'You're coming in, though?'

'Sorry, I need to get these plants to Guy. Besides, you've got a chaperone right here.'

Jules groaned as Beulah came rushing out of the front door, a large bunch of sage in her arms.

'That walk looks as if it's done you the world of good,' Beulah said. 'Blown some of your cares away. You have some colour in your cheeks at last.'

She winked at Jules.

'We have a visitor in the kitchen pacing up and down like Mr. Darcy in Pride and Prejudice when he was about to tell Elizabeth Bennett how ardently he admired her.'

'Have fun!' Carrie called through the open window, before heading back up the lane.

'I wouldn't get excited, Mum,' Jules said drily. 'I very much doubt he's come to propose to a spinster not of this parish.'

'Oh, Jules, you are such a hoot. I must take a walk on Tennyson Down myself if it's so good for one's sense of humour. Lance has a very good sense of humour. That's so important in a man, don't you think?'

'Oh, Mum, what have you been saying?'

'Cross my heart I have been the soul of discretion and normality.'

'Mum, you have never been normal.'

Beulah beamed.

'That's one of the nicest things you have ever said to me, darling.' She leaned closer. 'Lance was very agitated when he arrived. I've made him some of my lemon verbena tea to calm him.'

Jules glanced at her reflection in the hall mirror. The walk had given her a glow. A lot of the inner anxiety she had been feeling, and which had manifested all over her face, seemed to have vanished. In spite of everything she looked better, felt stronger. She tucked a stray wisp of hair back into her ponytail and slipped off her walking shoes.

'Lance,' she said, walking into the kitchen, 'what a surprise.'

He came straight over to her and took her hands.

'Oh!' she said as her fingers met his and a spark of electricity ran through her.

'Are you all right?' he asked, bending forwards a little.

'Yes, I'm fine, thank you.'

'I heard what happened. Not what you need on holiday.'

'No.'

He dropped her hands and waved his arm around.

'I hope it hasn't made you feel differently about the cottage. Made you want to leave. Guy wouldn't want that.'

'No, strangely not, although I'll have to go back to Manchester soon. I can't hide away here forever, and I've made a decision to report my... Gavin to the police. There might be other women in my situation. I don't want anyone else to go through what I have.'

He pulled out a kitchen chair from the table and sat down suddenly.

'That's a relief. Not the going back. I mean the not going back, at least not just yet. And I'm glad that you're going to report him.' He looked at her. 'You sound different. As if...'

'As if I'm over him?'

'No, no, of course not, just coming to terms with what's happened.'

She smiled.

'I think I am.'

He pressed his fingers to his forehead.

'This is difficult, and the timing might be all wrong, but I didn't want you to go until...' He lifted his head and sniffed the air. 'Can I smell burning? Is something on fire?'

'That'll be my mother,' she said with a strained smile.

'Your mother's on fire? Should we rescue her?'

'She's smudging; burning sage to purify the atmosphere and promote healing for the cottage and us.'

'Oh!'

'When I was a child, I'd often come home from school to find her wafting around the house with some sage, chanting as she went. As you can imagine, I didn't ask many friends back for tea!'

'My mother's a neat freak so I wasn't allowed to ask anyone back for tea. Small boys tend to make a lot of mess.'

'Watch out for the salt bowls as well. They're meant to promote calm and relaxation and restore harmony, but they don't always achieve that when they're left in places where you can trip over them, such as doorways.'

'She's an interesting woman, your mother.'

'I always think "interesting" is such a loaded word. As a child, you don't always want your parents to be interesting, do you?'

'Maybe not too interesting,' he said with a smile. 'Talking of interesting...'

He paused.

'You may not be interested in this at all so don't feel you have to say yes. I won't be offended.'

He shifted on his chair, his right hand clenched into a fist resting on his jeans.

'An acquaintance of mine is opening a gallery over towards the middle of the island and she's having a launch party, and I wondered if you'd like to come?'

The question hung in the air as she tried to find an answer. Something had changed and she couldn't work out what. His composure, that's what it was. His attitude towards her before had been relaxed and now it was tense.

'When is it?'

She was playing for time and he knew it.

'Tomorrow. Very short notice, I know. You've probably got something else arranged or after last night just want a couple of quiet evenings.'

Jules felt as if she was on the edge of something unknown. She turned away, moved over to the sink, ran the tap, took a glass from a nearby cupboard and filled it.

'I'm sorry. I can't.'

'That's a shame, but it's fine. I mean, it is short notice, and I didn't really expect...'

Except it obviously wasn't fine. He stood up abruptly.

'I'm really sorry,' she said.

He smiled, but it didn't reach his eyes.

'Me too,' he said, 'but I do understand. Too soon.'

'Yes.'

And he marched out, kicking over the salt pot her mother had left on the threshold as he went.

<h1 style="text-align:center">TWENTY</h1>

Tasha appeared in the garden clutching a posy of feathers tied together with lemon ribbon.

'Some people say that finding a feather means an angel has passed by,' she said to Jules.

'Or a chicken,' Jules replied. 'That looks like one of Scattihen's feathers.'

'It is. But this one isn't.'

She touched a small downy white feather curling around the bow.

'This one just floated down as I was walking up the lane. It landed on my hand. It felt like a sign.'

Jules sighed.

'You'd get on well with my mother.'

'I saw her and Jo this morning when I was in the farmyard collecting the eggs. They said they were making a shrine near the willow tree. I thought I'd put these there.'

'That's a lovely thought, Tasha. You do that and I'll get us a cold drink.'

. . .

'Can Erin come around and bring something?' Tasha asked as she sipped her iced tea.

'Of course she can. Carrie said a few people from the village would like to bring something as a tribute.'

'She wasn't just dumped, was she, the baby?'

'No. She was put there quite carefully, I think.'

'And now she has been discovered, she'll be loved all over again. People want to show that, even though she is no longer here, she is cared for. That's good, isn't it?'

'Very good.'

'Sometimes life seems so cruel and horrible and if you read the news, you think that everyone is at each other's throats. It upsets me, overwhelms me. I don't know what's going to happen to me or my family or friends or the world. I lie awake worrying about it.'

'Me too. We each have to do what we can in our own small way. We have to look after each other. There's kindness to be found, Tasha. I've found it here.'

'Your mum seems kind.'

'Yes, she is. Annoying, but kind.'

'Erin can be annoying.'

'All friends can be annoying, but when you love someone, you make allowances and hope they make allowances for you.'

'Erin thinks you've upset Lance.'

'Why does she think that?'

'Because he came to see you and when he got back, he was very quiet and then he snapped at her. Lance never snaps.'

Jules pushed a piece of lemon away from the side of her glass.

'You could do worse than Lance, you know. He's very honourable and kind and...'

'Tasha, stop!' Jules said. 'That's just what my mother said. I know you both mean well, but please stop. It's complicated. I'll hurt him. I'll hurt Erin and Fitz even though I have never met him. I have hurt so many people in the past. I can't get anyone's hopes up. I can't commit because it will probably all go wrong because of me. And now, thanks to Gavin, I know what it's like to be really hurt.'

She took a deep breath and closed her eyes.

'Carrie says that it's your pride that's hurting with Gavin.'

She opened them again and looked straight into Tasha's concerned face.

'Does she indeed? Nice to know my personal life is the talk of the village.'

'It isn't. Granny used to say when I fell off my pony that the best thing to do was to get straight back on again. She also says that there are only so many times that things can go wrong before they start to go right. Perhaps Lance is your chance for things to start going right.'

'What are you going to be when you leave school, a relationship counsellor or a producer of romantic films?'

'I might be a psychologist,' Tasha replied. 'I've read that people with difficult parents often make very good psychologists.'

'I'm surprised there aren't more of them around then.'

'Did Lance ask you out on a date?'

'No, he didn't!'

Tasha tilted her head to one side.

'Are you sure?'

'I think at my age I'd know.'

'In my experience a lot of adults know very little.'

'Already such a cynic! You didn't inherit that from Granny. If you must know, he asked me to go to the opening of a gallery tomorrow night.'

'That's a big deal.'

'Really? He didn't make it sound like it.'

'Well, he wouldn't. He's Lance the Modest. The woman who's set up the gallery is an interiors influencer and she's going to stock some of his bigger, more expensive pieces. She's got squillions of followers on Instagram and London contacts. Erin's really excited about it, but Lance is worried that it'll all come to nothing. He hates Erin to be disappointed.'

'So, not a date then, in your opinion?'

Tasha shook her head. 'More like a cry for help and you rebuffed him.'

'Don't say that!'

'He probably just wants someone to give him some moral support, that's all. Anyway,' she said, with a sly glance, 'would it be too terrible if it was a date?'

'Yes, it would.'

'Why?'

'Because I'm not ready.'

'Granny says we're very rarely ready for things. She says the trick is not to plan too far ahead or look too far behind. Try to live in the present. She also says don't give up on the important things.'

'Easier said than done.'

Tasha frowned.

'I've said that to her, but she just gives me that look as if I need to look inside myself and find some fortitude.'

'And do you?'

'I try. I don't want to disappoint her. I can live with my own disappointment in myself but not letting her down. Granny says you're not a giver upper. She says you're going to be okay.'

Somehow hearing that Rita thought that gave her a real boost.

'If you'd known it wasn't a date, would you have said yes?'

'Possibly.'

'I bet your mum would make you go. Where is she, by the way?'

'She's upstairs having a rest. The responsibility of shrine making is exhausting apparently.'

Tasha stood up and walked towards the sitting room.

'Tasha, don't you dare go and get her,' Jules said, half laughing.

'Erin worries that Lance has spent too much time going to things on his own.'

'I presume she'll be there tomorrow?'

'Mmm, but it's not the same, is it? I'm hoping to persuade Mum to let me go, too. I might wrangle it. I thought I was grounded because of Granny, but I have a secret suspicion that Mum now thinks I might have done her a favour, and she'll be able to oust a crippled Granny out of the big house.'

'Tasha, that's an awful thing to say about your mother.'

'True, but I'm under no illusions. No point burying your head in the sand, as Granny says. Something to do with ostrich, I think. Comes from Pliny. Have you read any Pliny?'

'No.'

'Me neither. He's on my list.'

'You are an extraordinary girl.'

'Geeky, you mean.'

'No! I mean extraordinary, amazing, beautiful, funny, wonderful, so full of potential.'

Tasha blushed and swished her hair across her face.

'I'm none of those things.'

'You are all of them and so much more. I hope one day you realise it.'

'If I'm allowed to go tomorrow, will you come as well? I know you're not going to be here for much longer and I'm going to miss you.'

'I'll miss you, too.'

'So, you'll think about it?'

'Yes, I'll think about it.'

'What is there to think about?' Carrie asked as they walked along the beach. 'Just come and enjoy yourself. Guy and I are going. I would have asked you, but wasn't sure if the numbers were restricted.'

'I'm worried it will be sending out the wrong message.'

'And what message is that?'

Jules looked out to sea. A boat was passing by. She wondered where it was going, where Gavin was now. If he was trying to manoeuvre his way into another gullible woman's heart and con her out of her savings. As soon as she got back to Manchester, she was going to try to put a stop to that.

'That I'm available.'

'Well, you are, aren't you?' Carrie said, skimming a stone across the water. 'If you want to be.'

'I'm not sure I want to risk getting close to anyone again, especially so soon.'

Carrie sighed.

'Not every good-looking man is a potential partner.'

'Is that what I've been doing? Weighing all men up as to their suitability?'

'I don't know. Is it?'

Jules sifted absentmindedly through the stones beneath her fingers looking for a fossil of some sort.

There were meant to be thousands, tens of thousands, of them on this beach, but to be honest she didn't really know what she was looking for. She could pick up a piece of fossilized bone or wood and not have a clue that it was anything special. Subconsciously, was she assessing each single man as to his suitability as a husband, a father even if her biological clock suddenly started ticking, someone she could spend the rest of her life with? Goodness, that sounded desperate, like someone who was looking for another person to complete them, which was a heavy burden for anyone to bear.

'What I've learnt,' Carrie said, 'since you packed me off here, is that you have to accept that you are good enough as you are. And if you don't feel that you are, then you have to do something about it, but gently, slowly.'

'You don't think that other people can make you a better version of yourself?'

'I think they can inspire you to want to be a better version of yourself, but only you can do it. I also think there's a lot of pressure to improve ourselves all the time and it's important to accept that most of us are dealing with life the best we can at any given moment.'

'I feel so weak, not physically, but emotionally. With the mums in my care, I spend so much time building up their confidence, especially if they are on their own, but really, I'm a fraud.'

'You're not a fraud. You are resilient and kind and wonderful, but you do tend to overthink things. So far as I know Lance has never seriously dated anyone since Sarah died. He's just devoted himself to Erin and Fitz and the business. There's no reason to think that's going to change. Why don't you just come along tomorrow and have a nice evening and if it gives Lance a bit of extra moral support then that's all good, isn't it? One of the things you're really good at is moral support. You've just said so yourself.'

Jules nodded. Maybe she'd think about going to the gallery opening after all.

She'd borrowed Beulah's car and gone into Yarmouth to buy herself a new dress. It was ankle skimming and floaty with little covered buttons down the front and a tie at the back, which cinched the floral fabric in at the waist. Jules swayed backwards and forwards in front of the full-length mirror. It was the perfect summer dress. She let her hair dry naturally in the afternoon sunshine and used her fingers to tease out the waves. Her toenails were painted a pretty carnation pink and she'd borrowed some gold sandals from Carrie. As she stood looking at herself, she dropped her shoulders, lifted herself up from the hips and took a deep breath. This would be the most amount of people she had been with for weeks. Suddenly she wasn't sure how she would cope. If she could just go under her own steam and be free to leave when she wanted to, she'd be all right.

'Oh, don't you look beautiful,' Beulah said, popping her head around the door.

'Thanks, Mum. You look pretty glam yourself.'

Beulah beamed and did a little twirl.

'I've been wanting an excuse to wear this hand-painted silk

blouse forever. It's vintage. I got it in a charity shop in Chichester, and I'd already got these trousers.'

'It's very you.'

'Thank you, darling. I think your father would have liked it. I always think about his tastes when I buy something special. I always wanted to look nice for him. I still do.'

'But you still dressed for yourself, didn't you?'

'Of course, but then your father never wanted me to be anybody apart from who I was.'

'That's nice. I think Gavin tried to turn me into a version of his perfect woman.'

Beulah came over and placed her hands on Jules's forearms.

'Jules, my precious, to those of us who love you best, you are perfect as you are.'

Jules blinked away tears.

'I'm so sorry for being such a difficult daughter, for letting you down, for not being there when you needed me.'

Beulah tightened her grip and adopted a fierce expression.

'Do not say that. You have never ever let me down. We've both dealt with what life has thrown at us in the best way that we could and I'm more than aware that I'm not the easiest of mothers. Now, please do not cry because you'll set me off, too.'

'I don't think I'm up to going tonight. All of those people...'

'Which is what I thought you would say.'

She reached for her clutch bag and fished a small brown bottle from inside and waved it in front of Jules's face.

'Rescue remedy. Marvellous stuff. It's got me through stage fright on many occasions. Open your mouth.'

She dropped some of the liquid on to Jules's tongue.

'Now, come on, I'm going to drop you around to the farm and I'll see you there.'

Jules smiled. Trust her mother to have wangled an invitation through Jo. She was glad though. It felt surprisingly reassuring to know that she was going to be there.

'I could come with the two of you.'

'Oh, darling, would that you could, but Jo's car's on the blink so I said I'd pick her up and I really don't want you squashed into the back seat of the Fiat in that gorgeous dress. Besides, from what you've told me Tasha could do with some moral support as well.'

'Dad's too busy to come and Mum's thrown a wobbly so she's redoing her make-up, but I've got to go with her and Will,' Tasha said when Jules arrived at the farm. She checked her watch. 'Lance and Erin will be here soon. Oh, here they are.'

The old estate car pulled into the farmyard and instinctively Jules retreated behind a planter filled with an extremely tall dahlia with orange dinnerplate-sized flowers.

'Look who's here,' Tasha said, as Erin stepped out. 'Jules, where have you gone?'

She stepped out feeling doubly foolish.

Erin pressed her hands together.

'Jules! You look amazing! Look, Dad, Jules is here.'

The driver's door opened and he stepped out dressed in a crisp white shirt and olive-green chinos.

He smiled half-heartedly, she thought.

'Hi!' she said, shyly lifting her hand. 'I changed my mind. Hope that's okay?'

'Of course.'

'Dad, I'm going to go with Tasha if that's all right?' Erin said.

Jules felt a gulf of panic begin to open up inside her. Erin beckoned them all closer and lowered her voice.

'The thing is, if I'm here Christabel will have to take me. Otherwise, she might decide at the last minute to pull out.'

'This woman is mega on social media,' Tasha said. 'I'm pretty sure Mum will move heaven and earth to be there, but thanks.'

'Jules, you don't mind going with Dad, do you?'

She shook her head, thinking she couldn't look particularly convincing. Lance opened the passenger door for her.

'Sorry,' he whispered, as she swivelled into the seat. 'That feels a bit like a set up. Nothing to do with me, I can assure you.'

He stooped to scoop the hem of her dress up into the car and closed the door. From the way he pressed his lips together she was sure he felt as uncomfortable as she did.

They drove through the lanes in relative silence, Lance occasionally slowing to point something out to her. Jules had never felt more self-conscious and he, too, seemed unusually uptight.

'Tell me about where we're going,' she said, after a silence that felt as if it would go on for ever.

'A big house almost in the middle of the island. The husband works in finance in London and the wife, Gabriella, is an interior designer. She's been all over the world, had features in national newspapers and glossy magazines plus of course a devoted following on social media. She's converted this barn in the grounds and wants to showcase local artisans.'

'Sounds as if it could be very promising for you.'

'It needs to be,' he said, his mouth set in a grim line. 'I met my accountant today and...'

He fell silent as they stopped at a junction.

'I'm not sure how much longer I can carry on,' he said.

'Oh, Lance. I'm sorry. I had absolutely no idea. The car park has always seemed busy when I've driven past.'

'That will be for the tearoom, which is what really keeps us going. When Sarah was alive, she ran that with just a bit of help. Baked most of the cakes herself. Any artistic venture is a risk, a precarious way to make a living, and Covid destroyed so many niche businesses, so many dreams. It nearly finished us. We'd already had to tighten our belts because of buying in cakes and employing more people, which cut into our profits, and now with business rates going up, higher wages and people being a lot more cautious about what they spend their money on...'

He looked momentarily defeated. She wanted to lean across

and cover his hand on the steering wheel, do something to comfort him.

'Isn't there anything you can do?'

'The only money I have saved is from Sarah's life insurance. It isn't much and I really wanted to ringfence that for the children.'

'That's laudable.'

'It's what she would have wanted.'

'But from what you've said, she'd have wanted you to keep the pottery going, too.'

'Yes,' he said slowly. 'I think she would, although it was more my dream than hers. She was very supportive even though her parents were horrified. I think they blame me a little for what happened.'

'How?'

'Stress. They believe the stress of running the pottery caused the cancer.'

'That's ridiculous and very unfair to say so.'

'Oh, they haven't actually said it out loud, but I'm pretty sure that's what they think. The place was very rundown when we moved over here. We did all the renovation work ourselves, even down to making the kitchen cupboards. It's amazing what you can learn from YouTube! It was exhausting, though, and Erin was little so we tried to make sure she settled in. Maybe we did take on too much. Sometimes the constant worry wears you down. Sorry to offload. Bet you wish you'd gone in the car with Christabel.'

'Um, no!'

'Please don't say anything to anyone. The last thing you want customers to know is that a business or its owner is struggling. It's the kiss of death. To be honest, I'm more worried about the children than the business. I can start up again somewhere else doing something different, but Erin loves it here and Fitz has ADHD so he would probably find it really hard to settle into a new school and make new friends.'

'And Tasha would be devastated if you all left.'

'I know. She's like another daughter.'

He turned the car into a driveway flanked by tall iron gates.

'Here we are,' he said, turning to look at her for the first time. 'I hate things like this. "You need to sell yourself, darling," Gabriella said to me when I came over last week, but I'm no good at that stuff. I just want to sit in my studio and create.'

'Then I'll do it for you,' she said. 'Point me in the direction of the right people and I'll sell you and your beautiful artefacts.'

He looked doubtful.

'You don't believe me? I can be really positive if I put my mind to it. It's time I rediscovered that positive person instead of wallowing in self-pity. Look at it as a quid pro quo if that makes you feel any easier. You've helped me out since I came here. Now it's my turn to do the same for you.'

Side by side they walked up a tree-lined path towards the barn; little lanterns, already lit, had been placed on the ground ready for when darkness arrived.

'This place is stunning,' Jules said, looking down towards a lake where swans glided lazily across the water. Outside the barn were a plethora of terracotta pots filled with every shape and size of perfectly clipped box bushes. Draped beneath the eaves of the barn itself were festoons of fairy lights and from inside came the clink of glasses and chatter of voices.

'Deep breaths,' Jules said as they paused outside the open doorway.

She felt the tension radiating off him and reached for his hand.

'You've got this,' she whispered. 'We both have.'

And as she shifted closer, he curled his fingers gratefully around hers.

Towards the end of the evening Jules slipped out of the barn and made her way across the manicured lawn. It was one of those rare English summer evenings when the warmth still wrapped around you and there was no hint of a breeze. High in the darkening sky the moon glowed brightly, silhouetting the tree canopy on the other side of the lake. Almost hidden by bulrushes a small wooden jetty jutted out over the edge of the water. Jules settled at the end of it, took off Carrie's sandals, which were pinching a little, and dipped her toes into the coolness as she watched swans shepherd their cygnets towards the safety of a small island. A sense of safety, that's what she had craved ever since her father died, and it had always eluded her. Since coming here, she had realised that chasing after safety was like chasing after a rainbow. It would always elude you, but you could find something different: feeling content with the present. Sitting here, swirling her feet around in the water, even batting insects away from her face, she felt content. She wished she could capture the feeling and hold on to it, but emotions weren't like that. They came and they went, up and down like a roller-coaster, and that's how it was meant to be.

'Here you are!'

And it was gone, that feeling of contentment to be replaced by fluster.

'Sorry! I made you jump.'

She looked up at him, smiling tenderly down at her. Please don't look at me like that, she thought. I don't deserve it.

'I was miles away.'

'Are you all right?'

He made no move to sit down beside her and for that she was grateful.

'Exhausted.'

He stared out across the lake and rolled his shoulders.

'It gets a bit much after a while, doesn't it, all of the noise, the effort of talking to people you don't know?'

'I used to be good at that.'

'You still are from what I could see.'

He had been watching her, but if she was honest, hadn't she been watching him, too? Always looking to where he was in the room, craning to hear his steady voice above the others, feeling the need to have him near.

'Has it been useful?' she asked.

'Mind if I sit down? My back is aching, and my brain is completely scrambled. I've bought you a soft drink, something grapefruity, I think, although to be honest I can't remember.'

She moved to one side as he sat down, knees crooked, and handed her a paper cup. 'I've got your pashmina as well.'

He held out an arm with her wrap folded carefully across it. 'You might not need it. It's pretty sheltered down here.'

She took a sip of the drink, trying not to think about how close he was, how his arm was almost, but not quite touching hers. He closed his eyes and sighed. He looked exhausted, too.

'It is grapefruit. It's nice. Thank you. Do you want a sip?'

He nodded and she passed him the cup. Sharing a drink felt so intimate, something you did with someone you knew well, and she didn't know him that well at all.

'You need to take your shoes off,' she said, looking down at his brown brogues and green striped socks. 'Dip your feet in the water. It's really refreshing.'

'But then you'll see my feet,' he said.

'What's wrong with them?'

'They're pretty bony and ugly. Rat feet, my mother calls them.'

'I'm a midwife. I'm pretty sure I've seen worse things than your rat feet, but if it makes you feel better, I'll avert my eyes.'

He glanced at her.

'Promise?'

She laughed.

'I promise.'

'You have a nice laugh,' he said as he handed her back the cup and began to unlace his shoes. 'You ought to do it more often.'

'It's meant to be good for you, isn't it? I've read that some people claim to have laughed themselves well from illness. Perhaps I could make it one of my second half of the year resolutions.'

'Do you do that?'

'Not usually, but I thought it might be a good thing to start. After all, January is a terrible time of the year to commit to things; you're tired after Christmas, probably a bit vulnerable health-wise because it's the middle of winter, and a whole year is a long time to commit to something. Whereas summer is a much more optimistic time, unless you've just been dumped and cheated on, of course.'

He began to peel off his socks.

'You're looking.'

'Only at your face.'

'I suppose that's marginally better than my feet. What do you think?'

He made a rat face, and she laughed again.

'Your feet have got to be better than that!'

'I wouldn't count on it,' he said, placing one hand to block her eyes.

She could feel the warmth of his palm radiating between her eyebrows and smell the fabric conditioner from his shirt. The metal from his watch strap glinted in the moonlight.

'Oh, that's good,' he said, splashing his feet into the lake, removing his hand and leaning back, his arms half stretched out behind him, palms flat on the jetty. 'I'm not great at standing for long periods. Too tall. People say it's wonderful to be tall, but it has its downsides.'

'Like hitting your head on low door lintels.'

'That as well.'

'You didn't answer my question. Have you met some useful people?'

'I don't like to think of it like that. It feels so mercenary.'

'You're too nice. Do you prefer interesting?'

He smiled at her.

'I've met some very interesting people, not all of them interested in pottery.'

'But some of them are?'

'I think so. I hope so. I've learned in the past that the people who sound most enthusiastic are the ones you often never hear from again.'

'I've got some useful contacts for you.'

She reached for her bag and fished out half a dozen business cards.

'These are all worth following up, I think. There was one lady in particular who has a gallery in London that sounds particularly promising.'

'Oh, I met her. She came to find me.'

'Maybe a trip to the big city beckons.'

'We could meet up,' he said softly. 'How long does the train take from Manchester?'

'Just over two hours on a good day.'

'Doable then.'

She was quiet. His feet touched hers briefly as they moved them around in the water.

'Yes,' she said, after what she hoped wasn't too long. 'Very doable.'

He smiled, closed his eyes and tilted his head back.

'This is nice,' he said.

Yes, it is, she thought, looking at his profile, and she had the sudden overwhelming desire to kiss the base of his throat.

'Let's stay here for ever,' he said.

And she didn't answer because she would have been happy to do that.

TWENTY-ONE

'Did he kiss you?' Carrie asked as they sat having a coffee in The Manor gardens the following day.

'No, of course not. Besides, Erin was in the car on the way home.'

'Bet he'd have kissed you if she wasn't.'

'No, he wouldn't.'

'He wanted to.'

'How on earth do you know that?'

'Because I saw him watching you all evening. His eyes were following you around the room.'

'That's probably because he was looking to see who I was talking to, so we didn't double up.'

'Nonsense!'

Jules bit her lip.

'I've decided it's time to go back to Manchester.'

'Why? I thought you liked it here.' Carrie cast her a sly glance. 'I thought you were beginning to like Lance.'

'Of course I like him. He's kind and gentle and thoughtful and I love the way that bit of hair on the back of his head won't lie flat and the fact that his nails are always so immaculate even though he works with paint and clay.'

'Oh dear, that sounds serious.'

'I know – and that's why I've got to go. It's not just Lance, it's Erin, too. I can't risk hurting her.'

'You're running away.'

'Yes.'

Jules turned her vintage teacup around in its saucer.

'*I wanted to kiss him.*'

'Ah!'

'And he makes me feel safe. I never felt safe with Gavin. I've never thought I wanted to feel safe in a relationship before. I always thought it would be boring.'

'And now?'

'Safe feels...'

How did it feel? She tried to recapture that contentment from sitting next to him on the jetty, their feet making circular patterns in the water.

'...accepting. Lance accepts people for who they are. That's why they feel at ease with him. Gavin wanted to change me. I wanted to change myself for him to be more glamorous, more erudite, more cultured, more organised, more everything.'

'Sounds like hard work.'

'It was. I was always running to catch up and never feeling good enough.'

'And Lance makes you feel good enough?'

'I think he could if I let him.'

Carrie leaned over and gave her a hug.

'Why not stay a bit longer and let him do that? Let us all do that?'

'I can't. It's not fair. I'll let him down. I let everyone down.'

'No, you don't.'

'I'm not certain if how I feel is real or if it's just because I'm desperate for someone to love me. And I'm not certain how he feels about me or how long a relationship would last or...'

'If you're looking for certainty, you won't find it,' Carrie said, feeding some of her cake crumbs to the robin at her feet. 'Uncertainty is part of life, but surely that's a reason to take a chance on something or someone because we never know what's around the corner?'

Jules heard the rumble of a wheelbarrow and saw Guy walking along the path towards the vegetable patch.

'You were certain about Guy though, about staying here.'

'As certain as I could be, but not totally. Don't forget I'd been hurt, too. I was worried that Guy might be a rebound choice, probably like you are. What's that saying from the Bible? "Do not worry about tomorrow for tomorrow will worry about itself", or something like that. Rita would know the exact wording and where it's from.'

'I'd like to see Rita before I go.'

'If you're really determined to leave, I can't stop you.'

'But you could take me to visit Rita. Now she's on the mend you can ask her a bit more about Philly.'

'Have you told your mum you're going back?'

'Not yet.'

'She can stay in the cottage if she wants to.'

'That's really kind, but you need to be letting that out now. I think she'll probably want to go home soon and see my sister.'

Carrie drained her cup.

'Shall I pick you up this afternoon to visit Rita?'

Jules nodded.

'Are you going to tell Lance you're leaving?'

'Yes.'

'Face to face?'

Jules nodded.

'In fact, there's no point in putting this off. If you can drop me at the pottery now, I'll see if he's free.'

'Poor Lance,' Carrie murmured. 'I have the feeling you're just about to ruin his day.'

Lance was in the studio setting out pieces of paper and coloured crayons on low tables. Jules stood in the doorway watching him for a moment, the little crease of concentration between his brows as he stooped, the carelessly rolled up sleeves of his linen shirt about to unravel towards his wrists.

She could imagine his arms wrapped around her waist as he pulled her closer. She blushed as he looked up, sensing that he was being watched.

'Jules! This is a nice surprise.'

His whole face lit up, the crease between his brows smoothed away to be superseded by wrinkles radiating like the sun's rays from the sides of his eyes.

'Children's party later. It'll be organised chaos, but hopefully they'll enjoy it.' Just as quickly his smile faded. 'Is everything okay? Is it Rita?'

She realised that she must have looked so serious, distraught even, as if someone had died.

'Rita's fine. I'm going to see her this afternoon.'

She paused. Morwenna jumped off the windowsill and sauntered over to twine around her legs. She bent down to scratch behind the cat's ears.

'To say goodbye,' she said quietly.

He looked stunned.

'Is this a sudden decision? I mean, last night I thought... you gave no indication...'

'No, sorry. I decided this morning.'

She looked around the studio space and tried to memorise everything; the vintage jars crammed with pencils and paintbrushes, the multitude of aprons hanging on an assortment of pegs, red geraniums on the windowsill, some of their petals adorning the floor like bright confetti.

'When are you going?'

'Tomorrow morning.'

'No time to glaze your bowl.'

'No. I thought I'd give it to Tasha to do. She'll choose beautiful colours.'

'Have you told her?'

'No, not yet.'

He sat down on a child's chair. He looked ridiculous, all legs and arms.

'I thought you'd come back and spend more time here with us, meet Fitz, spend time with me. When you were in here the other evening and I was doing some paperwork, that was – nice. I know we barely spoke, but just to have you here made me feel happier than I have in a long time.'

She placed her hands across her chest.

'This isn't easy, but the longer I stay the more difficult it will be to leave.'

He looked up.

'Then don't! There must be midwifery jobs here and definitely some on the mainland; Portsmouth and Southampton are only just across the water. You would be able to get a job there.'

'You make it sound so simple. I have a home in Manchester, friends, a life...'

'You have friends here and from what I saw last night you could make more easily. You could rent out your Manchester place while you see if things work out.'

She didn't know what he meant, while what worked out?

'And where would I live? I can't stay at the cottage indefinitely and I can't move in with Carrie and Guy, although I know they'd offer.'

'Here, you can stay here.'

'Lance, I can't.'

'Why not? We have a spare room.' He held up his hands. 'No strings. No pressure. Just to see where it goes.'

She moved towards him and crouched down.

'I'll hurt you. I'm not a long-term relationship person. I get scared of commitment. If Gavin hadn't done what he did I'd probably have sabotaged that in some way, too.'

'I'm willing to take that risk.'

She took his clasped hands and cupped them within hers.

'I know you are, and I'm really flattered, but I'm not going to let you do that.'

She reached up and held her hand against his cheek.

'One day you will meet someone who is worthy of your love and who won't let you down.' She stood up before dipping down to kiss him on the cheek. 'One day you'll look back and think you had a lucky escape with me.'

And she turned her back on him and walked out as quickly as she could so he wouldn't see the tears beginning to stream down her face.

Beulah's bags were packed and by the front door when she returned to the cottage.

'Oh, my darling girl. What has happened?'

Jules couldn't explain so she let Carrie do the talking and just listened. She felt desperate, even more desperate than when Carrie had first brought her here such a short time ago. But she was doing the right thing. She was definitely doing the right thing.

'I got a call while you were out,' Beulah explained. 'My audition has been brought forward, but I'll call and tell them I can't make it.'

'No, don't do that,' Jules said. 'You must go, Mum. This is important to you.'

'But you are more important.'

'I'll be fine. I'm leaving tomorrow myself.'

'Why don't you come with me now?' Beulah said. 'You can get a train to Manchester from London.'

It was tempting, but Jules shook her head. She looked around. She needed a little more time here on her own.

'I want to visit Rita this afternoon and check how she is.'

Beulah looked unconvinced.

'I'll stay with her tonight,' Carrie reassured.

'And you'll call me tomorrow?' she asked Jules. 'When you get back to Manchester? I really don't like to think of you going back there on your own.'

'I don't either,' Carrie said, 'so I'm going to go with her and stay for a couple of days.'

'Oh no, you're not,' Jules said.

'Oh, yes, I am,' Carrie replied, 'and I'm not going to take no for an answer.'

'It feels so quiet,' Jules said, when Beulah had finally gone, after several false starts because she'd forgotten shoes and hats and to give Jules an extra kiss for protection.

'She certainly brings a certain amount of chaos with her, your mum,' Carrie said, as she prepared some sandwiches for a light lunch.

'It sounds almost wrong to say it, because of what's happened, but it has been good to have her here.'

'I'm pleased.'

Carrie stopped spreading a little French mustard on the sourdough bread and looked around the kitchen.

'I think the house is pleased that she's gone.'

'How strange you should say that. I think so, too. After we found the baby there was so much turbulence in the atmosphere, all of that peacefulness which makes this a special place disappeared, but after Mum and Jo made the shrine, it's started to come back. There is forgiveness in the air.'

'And we all need a little more of that,' Carrie replied.

HELP

Isaac was panic-stricken. He scoured the house and garden for Eliza. He scanned the distant fields in the hope that she would appear. He investigated every corner of the farmyard and almost ran to The Manor gardens to see if she was sitting in the rose garden or blowing seed from some of the plants in the herbaceous borders. He couldn't smell the scented trail that followed her. There was only one place left where he could think to look – if she was not there, he could only conclude that she had passed over without him. He had ruined everything and had only himself to blame.

Isaac strode along the holloway, pressing himself to one side as a couple passed with a dog. The animal stopped and growled, and Isaac felt like growling back, but the owners tugged it away before he got the chance.

Caution, he reminded himself. Caution at all times. This is not your world anymore. You have over-stayed your welcome and to remain you must take care. Had he not told Eliza this over and over again? That they shouldn't be here, that they must be subtle. The cottage hadn't been theirs for over a hundred years, yet Eliza still thought of it as her home. He did, too, if he was honest, but that was wrong. It was time to disentangle themselves from its threads.

He traversed the last part of the holloway and towards the top. Even though it was high summer, he smelled that mixture of violets and primroses which was uniquely hers. He had found her at last. Maybe he could begin to make amends, but first there was something he must tell her.

She was sitting on the fallen stone staring out across the valley. He stopped for a moment, taken aback by her loneliness.

'Eliza,' he called tentatively.

She didn't seem to hear him, and he was afraid to approach her.

'Eliza,' he called again.

This time she looked towards him; such a disconnected look that it almost broke his resolve. He should leave. She obviously didn't want to be disturbed, especially not by him. He would have to work out what to do on his own, but he wasn't sure he was capable of that.

'What are you doing here, Isaac?'

'I came to find you.'

'Well, here I am.'

She turned her head away again.

He didn't recognise this cold and aloof woman. Where was his beloved wife? How could he ever forgive himself for what he had done to her?

'You didn't tell me where you were going,' he said. 'I was worried.'

'Maybe I didn't tell you because I wanted to be alone,' she replied.

He moved a little closer.

'And I'll leave you alone shortly,' he said, 'but something has happened. I thought you ought to know about it.'

'If it is to do with the world of mortals I'm not interested,' she said. 'They are not my concern anymore.'

The breeze caught at her hair, ruffled the hem of her dress, caused her whole form to ripple like water.

'The Beulah woman has already gone, and Jules is leaving, too.'

She didn't stir, her normal curiosity seemingly stifled.

'Good.'

'The house will be ours again, Eliza, for a time at least. We will be able to sit in the garden undisturbed and talk like we used to. We will be able to inhabit the house without fear of being spotted.'

'Undisturbed,' she echoed, raising her voice. 'I'll never be able to sit in that garden undisturbed, as you call it, again. The house will never be ours again, Isaac. You were right. We've remained for too long. It is time to let go, to let everything go.'

Isaac felt a slice of pure fear, like a hot blade dividing him in two. He needed to find a way to bring her back to him, back from this place of grief and anger and indifference which had claimed her whole being.

'Eliza, I do not think Jules is ready to leave.'

She flashed him a callous stare.

'We shouldn't take it upon ourselves to make decisions for others. If our guest thinks she is ready to leave, then who are we to prevent that?'

Isaac tiptoed forwards and perched on the edge of the stone, his hands steepled together as he spoke.

'But you didn't say that about Carrie. When she was leaving you tried to delay her, to allow her more time to discover her true feelings for Guy and his for her. I may not have supported you as I should at the time, but with hindsight it was the right thing to have done. You brought two good people together and added much happiness, not just to them, but to their friends and families and to our little community here. You have always said, Eliza, that the happiness of each individual has the potential to spread out far and wide into the world and make it a better place.'

Eliza lifted her chin.

'I seem to remember you accused me of meddling.'

He would take her hand if he dared, but his courage failed him at the last moment.

'I'm sorry for those words, but I now know that you are much wiser than I on matters of the heart.'

Now she turned to him.

'And are not most things connected to the heart?'

'Yes, yes, they are, and I fear that our guest is not giving herself the chance to heal her heart because she is leaving someone who is becoming very fond of her.'

'You are talking of Lance.'

'Yes.'

'And you know this how?'

'I can't help but hear things, Eliza; conversations on the telephone between Jules and Carrie and I may just have happened to be at The Pottery when she told Lance that she is leaving.'

At last, he had aroused her curiosity.

'You, at The Pottery? How did you get there? Did you walk?'

'I may have secreted myself in the back of Carrie's automobile.'

Her eyes widened.

'Isaac, you didn't?'

He nodded, gave her a tentative smile.

'Did it go very fast?'

'Like the wind racing in from the sea on a winter's day.'

'How thrilling! I wish I had been there.'

For a moment she was his Eliza again, full of wonder and courage.

'Lance has waited so long for the right person...' he said.

'And you think Jules is the right person?'

She was testing him.

'W-w-well,' he stuttered. 'I wonder if she might be. She cried all the way back to the cottage and why would she do that if she was not the one for him and he for her? But you are so much better at this sort of thing. Maybe I've misunderstood?'

She was mollified. He could see it in her eyes.

'No, Isaac, you have not.'

'But she is afraid to love him. She is afraid of becoming too attached to Erin, to Tasha, to the island. She is running away from a wealth of wonderful possibilities.'

'And you think that keeping her here for a little longer may help?'

He nodded.

'But I don't know how to do that, Eliza. You are the one who comes up with plans, the one who creates solutions. You are the one whose destiny it is to bring happiness to others. That has always been the way.'

She sat quietly for a few moments, staring once again into the distance.

'Where is Jules now?' she asked at last.

'Still at the cottage. Carrie is making her lunch although I doubt that she'll eat much. This afternoon, when she has composed herself, Jules wants to go to the hospital and say goodbye to Rita in person and tomorrow she'll leave.'

She stood up, smoothed her dress and lifted her chin.

'Do you have a plan?' he asked.

'No, not yet, but I'm sure that by the time I've walked down through the woods and communed with the trees something will have occurred to me.'

She set off back towards the holloway at pace.

'Come, Isaac!' she called over her shoulder. 'Do not dawdle. There's not much time. We must get back to the cottage before they leave for the hospital.'

As Isaac skedaddled after her, he sent up a silent prayer of thanks. This was his Eliza. She was restored to him. At least for now.

TWENTY-TWO

'Absolutely not!'

Rita's voice boomed down the length of the ward. A couple of people in the adjoining beds smiled wryly at Jules and Carrie.

'Perhaps we should wait,' Carrie suggested, tugging at Jules's sleeve, 'or come back another time. You'll come and visit me in the future. You can come and see her then and, in the meantime, you could always give her a call or write her a card.'

'Perhaps you're right,' Jules said, standing still. 'I don't want to bother her if she's upset.'

Something nudged her in the small of her back and she took a step forwards.

'Was that you?' she asked Carrie.

'Was that me what?'

'Pushing me.'

Carrie lifted her hands in front of her.

'Not unless I've got a third arm I don't know about.'

'It definitely felt as if someone pushed me.'

'You're imagining it,' Carrie said. 'Come on, let's go.'

'Alastair, you can't make me.' Rita's voice reverberated. 'I'm not listening to any more of this.' She put her hands over her ears and began to sing in a wavery contralto. '*Eternal Father, strong to save,*

Whose arm hath bound the restless wave,
Who bid'st the mighty ocean deep
Its own appointed limits keep;
O hear us when we cry to Thee,
For those in peril on the sea.'

As she paused to take a deep gulp of the antiseptic air the whole ward burst into applause.

'We really shouldn't get involved,' Carrie said.

'No, we shouldn't,' Jules agreed before marching down the ward towards the end bed.

By the time they got there Rita was making a start on 'All Things Bright and Beautiful' and Alastair was raking his hands through his hair. The doctor who stood hesitantly by the window was looking extremely stressed, but Jules suspected that was probably his default expression and not necessarily a reflection on Rita.

'Mum, will you please stop singing?' Alastair said in a raised voice. 'You'll end up being sectioned, not just sent into respite care.'

But Rita ignored him. She was sitting in the chair next to the bed, her leg propped up and her eyes cast down, the lids slightly red and puffy. On her lap lay an open prayer book. Jules wasn't sure if she was clasping it for comfort or was ready to throw it at someone if they got too close.

'Each little flower that opens
Each little bird that sings.'

Jules bent over and touched Rita's shoulder. She looked up.

'Oh, Jules. Aren't you a sight for sore eyes? And Carrie, too. What a treat.'

Rita gave them both a wobbly smile.

'We just came to see how you are,' Jules said, perching on the side of the bed, briefly including the doctor and Alastair in her gaze.

'I *was* all right,' Rita said. 'Looking forward to going home. The doctors and nurses say I'm doing well.'

'Are you Rita's daughter-in-law?' the doctor asked Jules.

She opened her mouth to answer, but Rita got there first.

'No, more's the pity. I expect it's because of *her* that you're both plotting to put me into this home.'

'We're not plotting and it's not a home, Mum,' Alastair said, wearily. 'It's respite care. Just for a couple of weeks until you're properly on the mend.'

'And once I'm in there I'll never come out,' Rita replied vehemently. 'I've seen it happen. My friend Valerie went into one of those places for two weeks because her family didn't want to have to worry about her while they went swanning off on some long-haul holiday and two years' later, she's still there, poor soul. You're not doing that to me. When I leave here, I want to go home.'

'I'm sure no one has any intention of keeping you in there longer than necessary,' the doctor began.

'People are full of intentions,' Rita interrupted, in a tearfully furious voice, 'and they're not always upfront about them. "Be very careful, then, how you live – not as unwise, but as wise, making the most of every opportunity," Paul says in Ephesians and some people's opportunities are other people's disasters.'

'Mum,' Alastair said, a desperate tone weakening his voice, 'I really don't see that you have any choice.'

He cast a sideways glance at Jules, his eyes looking for some support.

'Too old to have a choice now, am I?'

Rita dabbed at her eyes with an overly damp tissue. Jules rummaged in her bag and found a clean one.

'Here you are,' she said.

'Someone at least knows how to look after me,' she said accusingly to Alastair.

'You'll need someone to look after you for a few weeks,' the doctor said, 'not just in the moment. You'll need help getting around, in and out of bed, to the toilet, maybe cook some meals for you.'

'I've got a freezer full of meals,' Rita said. 'Enough to keep me going and before you say anything I have a granddaughter and friends who will rally around and a daughter-in-law who can help out.'

'Mum, I really don't think it's fair to expect Christabel...'

'Not Christabel, Alastair. You must think I'm losing my marbles. I wouldn't expect such a thing of her in a million years. No, Rosie, your brother's wife, just in case you'd forgotten. They're coming back from holiday in France to see me tomorrow. She won't mind staying for a while.'

Alastair massaged his temples.

'Of course I haven't forgotten. I've been speaking to him regularly since this happened.'

'Well, that's something, I suppose. If there's one good thing to come out of this, it's that you're on speaking terms with your brother again. I was beginning to think that the next time you communicated would be at my funeral.'

Alastair rolled his eyes.

'You're a long way off that, Mum, and in case you didn't know Rosie's just got a new job. She can't take time off now.'

Rita slapped her hand on the side of the chair, her wedding ring glinting under the glare of the hospital lights.

'If your father knew what you were trying to do!' she said. 'Trying to force me out of my own home first and now put me in some care place where half of the residents probably don't know their own name and can't wipe their own bottoms.'

Tears were streaming down her face. Jules took hold of her hand.

'Shh,' she whispered.

'Mum, this really isn't like you,' Alastair soothed.

'It's probably the painkillers,' the doctor said. 'I'll check she's not having a reaction to them.'

'I'm here,' Rita said. 'I'm not dead yet, although it would probably suit some people if I was.'

'Rita,' the doctor protested, 'I don't know where you've got all of these negative ideas from, but...'

'It's Mrs. Tompkins to you. All of this familiarity making it seem as if you're on my side when you're not. You'll have to take me out of this bed kicking and screaming unless I know for sure that I'm going home and that's not going to look good in the local paper, is it?'

She turned her head towards Alastair again.

'Why can't we have someone in to look after me? There are companies who specialise in this sort of thing.'

'Do you know how much they cost?' Alastair asked.

'I've got a bit saved,' Rita replied. 'I was going to leave it to the grandchildren, but...'

She gulped and let out a huge sob.

Jules couldn't bear it any longer. It really wasn't her place, but who cared?

'Rita, you really mustn't upset yourself like this.'

She knelt down and handed her another tissue, saw the raw fear she was trying so hard to contain.

'I've been upset ever since my George went.'

'I know you have.'

Rita looked down at her, tears spilling on to capable hands which twisted and turned the tissue.

'You understand me better than my own kith and kin.'

Something tickled Jules's ear. She pushed her hair back. There was a little whoosh of air as if someone was breathing against the side of her face and then a voice, faint, but steady. *Go on*, it said. *You know it's the right thing to do*. Jules shook her head.

'That's not true,' she replied both to Rita and her brain, which was obviously playing tricks on her.

Rita completely covered her eyes with the tissue. She was silent for a few seconds apart from small involuntary sobs.

'One of the nurses can give you the name of a couple of places we recommend,' the doctor said to Alastair.

Something prodded Jules in her side.

'Stop it!' she said, surprising herself with the force of her voice.

Everyone looked at her expectantly.

'I'll do it,' she said. 'I'll look after you, Rita.'

Carrie came and put her hand on Jules' shoulder.

'Jules, you can't.'

'Yes, I can,' she replied, 'at least for a couple of weeks.'

'It will need someone with some knowledge,' the doctor said.

'I'm a midwife. I think I can cope.'

'Oh, dearie,' Rita said, moving the tissue so one eye was visible, 'thank you, but no. I can't let you do that.'

'The occupational therapist estimates you'll need someone on hand for four to six weeks, Mum,' Alastair interrupted. 'Two weeks isn't long enough.'

'But it will get Rita home,' Jules said, 'which is the most important thing for her recovery in my opinion and will give us time to sort something else out going forwards.'

'I'm not sure your opinion counts,' Alastair retorted.

'Alastair!' Rita admonished, suddenly sounding like her old self. 'Where are your manners?'

'I'm sorry if you think I over-stepped the mark,' Jules said, 'but studies have shown that following hip and knee replacements people recover more quickly at home.'

She looked to the doctor for support, and he nodded.

'This may not be a knee replacement, but it's still surgery and I think Rita has already shown that she would be much happier back at home. If you are happy in your environment and you have the right care, your body stands a much better chance of healing more quickly.'

'You don't need to worry, Alastair. I'm not going to take Jules up on her very generous offer,' Rita said, suddenly looking totally defeated again.

Jules leaned in closer.

'Why not?'

'Because it wouldn't be fair, lovey. You're here to recover from your own problems, not take on all of mine.'

'Sometimes,' Jules said, softly, 'the best way to navigate your own problems is to help someone else with theirs. I would be honoured to look after you, Rita, and it's not entirely altruistic. I get to stay on the island a little longer and keep the real world at bay.'

Rita leaned forward herself so that their foreheads were almost touching.

'It would really annoy Christabel,' she whispered. 'She'd be spitting feathers.'

'All the more reason to say yes then,' Jules whispered with a conspiratorial smile.

'You are an absolute angel,' Rita whispered.

'Wait until I've been looking after you for a couple of days before you bestow me with a halo.'

'The Lord works in mysterious ways. I thought he had forsaken me.'

Jules squeezed Rita's hand.

'Not you, Rita. He would never forsake you.'

The following morning Jules was packing up some things to take to Orchard Farm when Wilbur came bounding up the stairs.

'Wilbur, what are you doing here?' Jules asked, giving him a pat.

'Sorry, he knows he's not meant to be coming upstairs,' Carrie said breathlessly, appearing at the bedroom door, 'but I think he's as excited as I am.'

Jules looked down at Wilbur who was now lying on his back, all four paws in the air, tail thudding against her foot as he waited for a tummy rub.

'He looks really excited!' she said dryly.

'We've found her,' Carrie said, almost jumping up and down on the spot.

'Who?'

'Philly, and we've found her parents, too.'

'That's amazing! Who's we?'

'The Major and I. We've been online. At least, I've been online with him looking over my shoulder. He said that all the birth, marriage and death records from 1837 to 2010 are held at the Lord Louis Library in Newport. We found an Eliza Louise Henderson who was married to Isaac Bartholomew Cooper on June 21st 1839 at Old St. Boniface Church, Bonchurch, and we found a Philomena Grace Cooper who was born on 18th July 1852.'

'But how do you know they were linked to the cottage?'

'Because Eliza and Isaac are recorded on the census as living at this cottage for over fifty years.'

Jules's hands flew to her chest.

'And The Major, bless him,' Carrie continued, 'has been out at the crack of dawn scouring the churchyard and he's found their graves.'

'So Philly can be buried with her parents?'

'He's looking into that possibility.'

'That's amazing. And you're sure it's the same Philly?'

'There's no death certificate for some reason, but there's no record of her on any census form for the cottage either so she can't have lived that long. It has to be her, Jules.'

Jules looked at the floor where in a little tea caddy below the boards rested a rattle and an apricot silk bonnet and a lock of baby hair.

'And her belongings? What will you do with those?'

'What do you think?'

Jules stood quietly and listened for guidance, but none came. She got a sense of the room – in fact, the whole house – holding its breath, waiting for her decision. She wanted to make the right one.

'This is where she lived and where she died. I think they should be left where they are.'

'Agreed.'

And suddenly a feeling of peace filled the room, a scent of primroses and violets and a whisper of a breeze which, when it landed on Jules's cheek, almost felt like a kiss.

. . .

The Major dithered at the top of the drive and ground his stick into a dusty pothole. With tractors coming up and down all the time it was a never-ending job keeping up with repairs. It would only get worse in the winter if it wasn't dealt with. He wouldn't mention it to Rita now though. She needed to concentrate on her recovery. Silly of him to come and see her. He could have just had some flowers delivered. It was Irene who had persuaded him. Guy's grandmother was a persuasive woman. He'd bumped into her outside the small supermarket in the next village.

'Are you eating properly?' she'd asked, leaning forwards to give him a small peck on the cheek.

He only allowed her to get so close because she'd been such a good friend to Honoria. He suspected she knew that, and it amused her.

'Of course,' he'd replied gruffly.

'What have you got in there?' she asked, trying to peer into his canvas bag.

He pulled the bag back, so it was almost behind his knee.

'You can't live on ready meals, Andrew.'

The wretched woman was some sort of psychic.

'It's about time you learned to cook.'

'I'm too old and I'm not interested. Honoria was a good cook. I could never match up to her.'

'Nonsense! You can do most things if you put your mind to them, even at our age.'

'You're not as old as me.'

'I'm not far off it. Here...' She reached into her basket and pulled out a pink and white striped paper bag. 'Two lamb chops from the butcher. You take them and cook them for yourself tonight and get some vegetables from that lovely garden of yours. I noticed plenty of courgettes and potatoes the other day.'

'Been spying on me, have you?'

The woman totally ignored him. She would not be riled.

'Honoria's cookery books are still on the shelves in the kitchen.

They will tell you what to do or you can look on the internet or' – she tilted her head mischievously – 'I could come over and show you.'

'I'll manage,' he said.

'I thought you would,' she said with a chuckle, before checking her watch. 'I must be going. I'm off to visit Rita. Have you been?'

'No, not yet.'

'I'm sure she'd love to see you.'

'Maybe.'

'It's the least you can do after all those meals she's cooked for you over the last few years.'

She had the lightest of tones, but he wasn't stupid. She was being subtly censorious.

'Look at those roses,' she said, turning towards a bucket of flowers outside the florist. 'Pink is Rita's favourite colour. You could take her some. That would cheer her up.'

She stood on tiptoes and kissed him again.

'I'll tell her you'll drop by tomorrow, shall I?'

He was about to resist, but she'd quickly turned and was heading across the road with a jaunty wave, leaving him feeling extremely put out. Somewhere at the back of his brain he heard Honoria's voice.

'Andrew, if it wasn't for people like Irene, you'd be a total curmudgeon. And why shouldn't she kiss you on the cheek? Touch is very important. You need to stop being so grumpy and make more of an effort.'

She was right, of course. Always had been. A miracle that she'd married him and a miracle that he could still hear her voice. He didn't always listen to what she said now she wasn't here in person, but perhaps he should.

Rita was sitting in a high-backed armchair in the living room, Hercules curled up in a brand-new basket next to her.

'Here she is,' Jules said, ushering him through.

'Andrew, what a lovely surprise. I didn't know you were coming.'

He looked at Rita, wreathed in smiles, and immediately felt guilty. Astonishingly she looked genuinely pleased to see him.

'Are they for me?' she asked, gesturing to the flowers. 'They're beautiful. Pink's my favourite colour, you know.'

'From the garden,' he muttered.

'Garden flowers are always the best,' she said, burying her nose in the soft petals.

She gestured to the chair next to her. He sat down, unbuttoned his blazer and laid his stick on the floor, then fished in his pocket for a treat for Hercules who came and lay across his shoes.

'You look very smart,' Rita said.

He made some sort of an appreciative noise. Rita was of the generation who recognised effort. He liked that.

'Tea?' Jules asked.

'Yes please, dear. And cake, and would you mind putting these flowers in water for me?' she said, then asked, 'Are you eating properly, Andrew?' as Jules left the room.

'Why does everyone harp on about that?' he grumbled.

'Because it's important and you don't,' Rita retorted. 'I've got various single portions of main meals in the freezer if you want to take them.'

He squared his shoulders. This would surprise her.

'That's very kind of you, Rita, but I've decided this is a good opportunity for me to learn to cook a few things.'

Her eyes widened gratifyingly.

'Last night I made a rather good job of cooking some lamb chops, if I say so myself.'

'Well, I never!' she exclaimed.

'And I dug up a root of potatoes from the vegetable patch and pulled some carrots.'

'Goodness me, Andrew. I am impressed.'

He felt himself expand a little with pride.

'I haven't quite got the measure of gravy. That was a bit lumpy, but...'

'Gravy isn't always easy. When I'm up and about I'll come over and show you how to do it.'

'I'll look forward to that,' he said, and the thought of it, Rita bustling around his stark kitchen, giving it some life, made him feel lighter. He looked around the room at the stone fireplace filled with houseplants for the summer, the bookshelves crammed in a higgledy-piggledy way with books on just about everything, the gilt-edged mantel mirror with its foxed glass and the oak table in front of the window full of family photographs jostling for their own space in sparkling silver frames.

'I haven't been in this room for a while,' Andrew said. 'I'd forgotten how charming it is.'

'I don't use it very often now. Living in the kitchen seems easier and warmer in the winter.'

For the first time her face fell.

'Such Christmases we used to have in this room when the children were growing up and when I was a girl. Do you remember the parties, Andrew, the fun, the laughter?'

'I remember the drink,' Andrew said with a chuckle. 'Goodness me, it flowed!'

'George never wanted anyone to have an empty glass. Some people never made it home the same night. Just used to find a cosy spot around the house and I'd cook porridge for everyone in the morning to sober them up. Couldn't do that nowadays.'

'Probably a good thing, too,' he said.

'I miss those days,' she said, 'the people who have left us.'

She blinked, fingered the newspaper on her lap.

'And now we're alone,' he said softly.

'Yes.'

She reached out her arm, her fingers thickened from years of physical work, but her nails painted a delicate shade of cyclamen pink to match her lipstick.

'It's hard, isn't it?'

He nodded, felt his eyes begin to water.

'You have your family around you,' he said.

'The Lord has blessed me. It is more than I deserve.'

'Why would you say that, Rita? It is exactly what you deserve.'

'I am a wicked woman, Andrew. I am breaking the tenth commandment.'

Andrew wracked his brains.

'Thy shalt not covet your neighbour's house...?'

'I don't covet anyone else's property,' she whispered, 'but I covet this. It's never really been mine. Like you, I've always been looking after it for the next generation, but I can't seem to let it go. Are we foolish, Andrew, rattling around in our big old houses when we could be having an easier life somewhere smaller and more modern?'

He didn't answer and was relieved when there was a tap on the door.

'Are you ready for tea?' Jules asked, balancing a tray with two Crown Derby cups and saucers, a silver teapot, two plates, some little napkins and cake forks.

Rita beckoned her in.

'Jules is insisting I use my best china,' Rita said.

She held out her wrist and fingered a gold bracelet interspersed with pearls.

'In fact, she's insisting I use the best of everything. George bought me this for our thirtieth wedding anniversary and I don't wear it much because I'm worried about damaging it.'

She looked at Andrew.

'But what are we saving all these things for, Andrew? If we don't enjoy them now, when will we?'

The Major looked at Jules and smiled.

'A wise girl,' he said, affectionately. 'I knew it as soon as I met her. A girl with strong opinions, too. Perhaps we ought to ask her about our housing dilemmas?'

He watched as Jules blushed charmingly at the flattery.

'I think,' she said, placing the tray in front of The Major, 'that instead of putting me on the spot, you should be mother and I should go and get the cake.'

He chuckled and reached for the teapot. He'd been right to come after all. This little outing was doing him good.

TWENTY-THREE

'What you need,' Jules said after a couple of days, 'is a social secretary and a florist, not a nurse.'

Rita chuckled.

'I do seem to have a lot of people phoning and wanting to visit. I'm astonished.'

'You shouldn't be. You are a much-loved lady.'

'Have you seen those cane toppers that Lance has made me?' Rita asked.

Even the mere mention of his name made Jules's heart jump.

She pointed to three ceramic flower shapes on the table in the corner.

'Aren't they beautiful? Came all nestled in a little box of lavender clippings.'

Jules couldn't resist picking one up and cradling it in her hand. It made her feel close to him and far away all at the same time.

'He popped his head around the door yesterday afternoon for a few minutes when he was dropping Erin off. You missed him. You'd nipped back to the cottage for your afternoon respite.'

Jules was aware that Rita was watching her keenly.

'Tasha told me he'd been.'

'I reckon he was disappointed that you weren't here.'

Jules didn't reply, but placed the sea green cane topper back on the table.

'Said he thought I'd have more than enough fresh flowers and he's right. Probably won't get as many as this when I die,' she said with a laugh. 'And Christabel knows that I hate lilies. Do you think you could put those in another room, Jules? The scent is so cloying. It reminds me of a crematorium.'

Jules picked up the large cut-glass vase of deep red lilies and crossed the room.

'I'll put them in the hall,' she said.

'Thank you, dear, and would you mind finding somewhere for Lance's gift? I don't want them to get broken.'

'Why don't I place them on top of the canes supporting the dahlias? You'll be able to see them through the window from your chair.'

Rita nodded and leaned forwards to rub her knee.

'Lance says they'll stop me poking my eye out when I get back to my weeding which won't be long now. He's a very thoughtful person. He thinks a lot of you.'

Jules paused by the door.

'You could do worse,' Rita said.

'Than the dahlias?'

Rita threw her a frustrated look.

'I think you're being deliberately obtuse. You could do worse than Lance.'

Jules sighed. She'd been successfully avoiding this conversation for several days, but Rita wouldn't be deterred.

'I know I could, Rita. Most of the people I've been out with aren't a patch on Lance.'

'But you don't fancy him?'

Jules half laughed.

'I don't know why you're laughing. It's an important factor in a relationship. I fancied my George rotten.'

'Of course I find Lance attractive.'

'What's stopping you then? You're young, both of you. Have some fun. It doesn't have to be a lifelong commitment. The Good Lord put us on this earth to enjoy ourselves and as long as you're not hurting anyone else, give it a go, I say.'

'The trouble is, I might hurt him and Erin. I like them both too much to risk that.'

'Some risks are worth taking. My George left a good job and a steady salary to come and help me run this farm. We didn't know whether he'd like it or if we could make enough money to support ourselves, but he took to it like a duck to water and we've done all right. Even took my surname, you know, so that it was still Tompkins' Farm?'

'No, I didn't know that.'

'Quite unusual back in the day. Brave even. Lance is brave.'

'I know he is.'

'Reminds me of my George. He wouldn't let you down.'

'No.'

Rita yawned. 'Anyway, you think about what I've said. We oldies do know a thing or two about life.'

'I will. You're tired now. I think you should have an early rest.'

'All of this sitting in a chair doing nothing takes it out of you.'

'You're hardly doing nothing. I'm having to fight off people wanting to visit! Socialising can take it out of you, too. Do you want to go back to bed?'

'No, thank you, dearie. I think I'll stay here.'

Jules placed the lilies on a side table and went to adjust Rita's cushions and place a blanket over her lap.

'Rest is very under-valued. I tell my new mums to rest as much as they can, not race around tidying the house or cooking meals. So many people have a baby or an illness and try to get back to normal too quickly.'

'It is a very inconvenient time to be laid up,' Rita fretted, 'with harvest taking place.'

'I think any time in this house would be inconvenient,' Jules said with a smile.

'You're not wrong there,' Rita said, rubbing her eyes. 'It's good for you to go back to the cottage each day and have a break while I take a nap. The cared-for must look out for the carers, too.'

Jules moved the phone so that it was within easy reach. She kissed Rita gently on the cheek.

'Tasha's in the kitchen if you need anything and I'll see you later,' she said.

By the time she had collected the vase of lilies and closed the door softly behind her Rita already had her eyes closed.

Tasha was standing by the table nibbling on some cheese and biscuits while sorting eggs into boxes.

'Are you heading back to the cottage?' she asked.

'Just for a couple of hours, if that's all right?'

'You're early.'

'Your granny's tired today. I think I might have to curb some of her visits and phone calls.'

'Do you miss the cottage when you're not there?'

'Yes. I do.'

'It's the sort of house you do miss, isn't it?'

'Mmm, I suppose so.'

'Will you miss it when you're back in Manchester?'

'Yes.'

'And the island, too?'

'And the island.'

'And me?'

'Especially you.'

Jules picked a feather off the top of one of the eggs and stroked her palm.

'Will you be sad?' Tasha said, stopping what she was doing to look at her directly.

'I'll try not to be, but when you miss people, you are a little bit sad, aren't you?'

'Erin says Lance is sad.'

'Ah!'

'Why don't you like him? He's a brilliant person.'

'Oh, Tasha, I do like him. I'm a bit of a mess at the moment on the romantic front...'

'He knows that. He could make you happy again.'

'If only it was that simple.'

'I think you're making it more complicated than it is.' She placed the egg cartons in a big box. 'Can you drop these off on the table at the top of the drive on your way past? There are also some punnets of raspberries in the fridge which Erin and I picked yesterday and a few courgettes.'

Jules nodded. 'There are some figs, too. I picked loads off the tree earlier and Rita's not going to be making jam or chutney anytime soon, so she said to put those out as well. Is Erin coming around later?'

Tasha nodded.

'In about half an hour. We're going to do some baking. I think we'll make an apricot and almond cake. There's still some jam left from last year and it's one of Granny's favourites.'

'You're such a star, Tasha.'

She beamed.

'Granny does loads for me. Now it's my turn to pay her back. It's not all about me, is it? You showed me that.'

'Did I?'

'By saying you'd come and look after Granny when I know you were planning to head back up to Manchester.'

Jules frowned.

'How did you know that?'

Tasha picked up a piece of cheese and studied it.

'I sense things. Mum says I'm hyper-sensitive and she makes it sound like the worst thing in the world.'

'It can make life hard.'

Tasha nodded. 'But it's not always a bad thing. It does have its advantages. I can empathise. A lot of people can't do that, or they shut that part of themselves down. I'm not going to do that any longer. Some of us need to cry or take ourselves off for some quiet time more than others.'

Jules smiled. 'That's very true.'

'In the nineteenth century they said tears were heart-improving.'

'I'll remember that. My heart definitely needs some improving.'

Tasha took a bite of the cheese.

'I'm trying to eat a bit more, too.'

'I'd noticed.'

'I'm not anorexic. There are people at school who are, and I know I'm not.'

'I never thought you were.'

'I got these viruses last year, one after another, and I couldn't seem to pick myself up. Post-viral syndrome, the doctor called it. Mum and Dad argued a lot about whether I should go to school on days when I was really tired. When I'm stressed out, I find it difficult to eat.'

'I can understand that.'

'You understand a lot of things. Granny does, too. I want to get strong for her.'

Jules moved around the table and wrapped her arms around Tasha's thin frame. She smoothed back her hair and kissed her on the forehead.

'And she wants to get strong for you and Will and your dad and between the four of you, you'll get there. Granny's a determined lady. She'll be almost as good as she was before, but no more climbing that ladder to the loft. You'll have to put a stop to that. I think she'll listen to you.'

Tasha nodded and Jules pulled away a little.

'You'll call if you need me?'

'We'll be fine. Mum's just across the yard. Not that she's much use in a crisis, but at least she's there and Dad and Will are in the near field. I can see the combine from the yard.'

Jules picked up the box of produce and headed for the door.

'Jules,' Tasha called after her, 'thank you for being here, for being my friend.'

Jules smiled.

'Always, Tasha,' she said. 'I hope we'll always be friends.'

Jules was stacking up the empty egg cartons and arranging the full ones on the table when Lance's car turned into the top of the driveway. Erin waved from the passenger seat, but Lance looked straight ahead. She felt completely deflated as she emptied the honesty box and put all the money into a little leather purse to give to Rita later.

'You have done the right thing, Jules,' she said to herself as she arranged the courgettes in an artful pile and tilted a couple of the raspberry punnets so they were easily visible from the road. If it hadn't been for Rita and that rash decision to look after her, which she didn't regret for one moment, she would have been back in Manchester and the whole situation would be out of sight, out of mind. He wouldn't be just down the road, and she wouldn't be lying awake at night in Rita's spare room thinking about him, wondering if he was also lying awake thinking about her. Except love didn't work like that, did it? It didn't go away just because you changed location.

'Jules!'

The sound of his voice calling her name sent a jolt right through her. He was striding up the driveway, kicking up dust and stones in his rush. The sun was beating down and she hadn't got a hat. Why did she always leave her hat behind when she needed it? There was an extremely irritating wasp circling her basket of figs, too. She batted it away. There wasn't room on the table for the basket. She should have put it there first. She was going to have to rearrange a few things and she felt irrationally hot and flustered.

'How are you?'

He had reached her now, but thankfully wasn't standing too close. She didn't think she could bear that. He was wearing a linen jacket over his shirt. He must be hot, too, but he looked pale and drawn.

'I'm okay. You?'

'Bearing up.'

There was an awkward silence.

'Are you on your way home – to the cottage, I mean?'

'Yes. I go back every afternoon around two when Rita has her rest.'

Of course he knew that, which was presumably why he'd been dropping Erin off at the farm a little later so as to avoid them bumping into each other.

'You're early today.'

'Rita's tired. She's had loads of visitors and phone calls.'

'I've got another appointment with my accountant later so thought I'd drop Erin off early, too.'

'Hope it goes well.'

He swallowed, looked at the ground, toyed with a stone using the side of his shoe. Anything to avoid looking at her, she thought.

'I've had quite a few enquiries since the party at the barn,' he said.

'That's good.'

She moved the raspberry punnets but there still wasn't room for the basket. She swayed it backwards and forwards to try and deter the wasp.

'Let me,' he said, and she stepped back to watch as his hands dexterously moved things around to create a much better display than she could have done, with a perfect space at the side for the basket of figs.

'Can I walk with you back to the cottage?' he asked, looking directly at her for the first time.

She felt the breath stall in her chest. This was the moment, she thought, the moment to say no, that it wasn't dark and it wasn't far and it wasn't the nineteenth century, she'd be fine on her own. This was the moment when what she said would make a real difference, would make him realise that she meant what she said the other day.

And she was about to say no, she really was, when the wasp dive-bombed towards her foot and stung her right on the end of her big toe.

'Ouch!'

'Ouch!' Lance echoed. 'I saw that.'

She hopped up and down and he took the basket from her, placing it at a safe distance.

'Sit down,' he instructed.

'I'm fine,' she said.

'It was a huge wasp. That must be painful.'

'It's not too bad,' she lied.

The sting was starting to take hold.

'You're not allergic?'

'I don't think so.'

'Thank goodness for that. I'll go and get the car.'

'Please don't. I'm fine. Really. I'll walk. I've got some antihistamine cream at the cottage.'

'You can't walk on your own. Look, it's already swelling up.'

Jules looked down at her toe, which had turned bright red, a white halo encircling the puncture wound.

'I'm getting the car. Sit down here.'

He led her to the grass verge and pressed her down.

'Do not move,' he said.

'Can you bring a net for the figs?' she called as he began to bolt back down the drive towards the farmhouse. 'In the dresser drawer, top right.'

Without turning he raised his right hand and gave her the thumbs up sign before alarming the sheep with the speed at which he ran alongside their field.

'Antihistamine cream from Tasha,' he said, the tyres of the Mercedes skidding to a stop in front of her a few minutes later, 'in case you couldn't find yours, and a net for the figs.'

'You're a fast runner,' she said.

'Teenage cross country county team,' he said. 'Didn't know I'd still got it in me. You're not feeling faint, not going into anaphylactic shock?'

'No, it's just my toe that's throbbing, but I'm not sure this is necessary.'

He helped her up and she could feel the heat of his hands against her skin and through the back of her dress. She had tried to forget how she felt when he touched her, but now it all came flooding back.

'It'll make me happier to see you home,' he said, as she settled in the passenger seat and he wound all the windows down. 'Air con's on the blink and I can't afford to get it fixed at the moment.'

'I like the fresh air coming in,' she said. 'Air con makes my nose run.'

'Me too,' he said, a sudden smile lighting up his face.

That was good, she thought, seeing him smile. It made her feel safe and warm before a wave of guilt washed over her. She watched as he covered the basket of figs with a net.

'You can have some if you like,' she said when he got into the car. 'There are loads more on the tree. I'm sure Rita wouldn't mind.'

She put her head back and closed her eyes, feeling the air rushing over her face, lifting her hair and cooling her temples. It felt good to be sitting beside him even though the drive barely took two minutes. If only she'd met him at a different time in her life...

'Here we are,' he said, stopping the car at the front of the cottage. 'Home!'

And for some unaccountable reason she burst into tears.

And he was twisting in his seat and holding her, not too tightly, not too gently, but in a way which was just right. He stroked her hair, leant his head against hers.

'Shh!' he murmured. 'It's all right.'

Over and over again he said those words, like a lullaby, a balm which seeped into her pores and travelled through her body.

'I'm so sorry,' she said at last, pulling away. 'I don't know what came over me.'

He looked at her for a moment.

'Come on, let's get you inside.'

In an instant he was opening the door for her, offering her his arm, releasing the latch on the gate and taking the key from her hand to unlock the front door. He led her into the hall and stooped to carefully remove her sandals.

'Best thing to do is to put this in some cold water to reduce the swelling and then apply some vinegar followed by the antihistamine cream.'

'You sound like an expert on wasp stings.'

'Anyone who has a café on site has to be an expert on wasp stings. They're a nightmare at this time of year and sometimes they just take against you for no reason.'

'I *was* holding a basket of figs, which I suppose is like heaven on earth to a wasp.'

'But you weren't holding it with your toe.'

'No.' She half laughed. 'That would be a feat! It was weird the way it dived like that, almost as if it had been blown in that direction.'

Jules sat on a chair in the kitchen while he filled a washing up bowl full of cold water.

'Soak for five minutes,' he said, lifting her ankle and gently lowering her foot into the water. He remained crouched in front of her, swirling the water around. 'Maybe I'll get some ice. That always helps.'

She reached out and touched the top of his head. He looked up, startled.

'Thank you,' she whispered. 'Apart from Carrie I can't remember the last time someone took care of me like this.'

And she leaned forward, cupping his chin with her hand, before kissing him lightly on the lips. She felt a sweet thrill ripple through her, not the fireworks she'd felt with Gavin, but something better than that, deeper, potentially more long lasting, something to build on gradually, respectfully, tenderly. But maybe she had blown it the other day. Maybe he didn't feel the same anymore. He may have been looking at her, but he wasn't giving anything away. Without speaking he reached for a towel and dried her foot, then applied some vinegar to a tissue and applied it to the end of her toe.

'Can you stand?' he asked at last.

She nodded but a flood of disappointment made all her limbs feel weak. He was obviously ready to leave.

'Good,' he said, moving the bowl before standing up to enfold her forearms, 'because it's difficult to kiss you properly like that.'

And slowly, questioningly, he drew her closer, but she didn't resist. She let him wrap his arms around her and she tilted her head back for her lips once again to meet his.

'I can't believe this is real,' she said later as she lay on the sofa, her head in his lap. looking up at his face.

Me neither,' he said. 'Better check, just to be sure.' And he leaned forwards to kiss her again. 'Yes, it's real!'

Momentarily he rested his forehead against hers.

'I thought I'd lost you for ever and then I heard that you'd offered to look after Rita so you'd be here for a bit longer and I wanted to hope but I told myself that you weren't staying for me.'

She smiled up at him.

'I couldn't bear to leave the island.' She dropped her voice to a whisper. 'And I couldn't bear to leave you. It was as if someone knew how I really felt and put those words in my mouth at the hospital to make me stay.'

'I'm glad they did.'

She looked up at the beams.

'It feels calm in here again, the way it felt when I first arrived.'

'Could that be because your mother's gone?' he said with a smile.

'Maybe, or maybe it's because we've identified Philly and once she's returned from the County Archaeologist, The Major says he's going to make sure she's reunited with her parents.'

'I wonder why they weren't buried together in the first place.'

'That is something we'll probably never know.'

'Do you think the spirits of the cottage are happy again now?'

'As happy as they can be,' she replied.

'I thought you didn't believe in that sort of thing?'

'Maybe my mother has performed some mind-altering spell on me,' she said with a laugh.'

'She called in at The Pottery to say goodbye.'

Of course she did, Jules thought.

'And to ask me to keep an eye on you.'

'Oh! That's a bit out of order. I'm sorry.'

'Don't be. She knows how I feel about you.' She bit her lip.

'There are so many things you don't know about me, Lance, things I'm not particularly proud of, things which might make you change your mind about us.'

'I doubt it, but I'm willing to take that risk, if you are. There are things you don't know about me, too, remember? I understand how hard it might be for you to have a relationship with someone who isn't exactly financially stable, but I promise I'll never ask you for money.'

'I know that. I trust you. I'm sorry you've had to rearrange your appointment with the accountant.'

'I'm not. This is more important.'

'I've always wanted my relationships to be perfect, not just romantic ones, all of them. I've put so much pressure on myself and other people. I don't want to do that any longer. I'm exhausted by it.'

'We're not going to be perfect, Jules. No couple is.'

And she felt something release, as if her whole body had breathed out and relaxed.

'What are you smiling at?'

'The imperfect couple. It sounds perfect!'

He laughed.

'Like the imperfect pot, which reminds me...'

He lifted her head and went through to the kitchen where his jacket was hanging over the back of a chair.

'I brought this to give to you.'

She sat up and unwrapped the dark blue tissue paper.

'Tasha's jug!'

She turned it around, letting the gold tracery catch the light.

'It's beautiful. Thank you.'

'You can take it back to Manchester when you go so you don't forget us, any of us.'

'As if I could ever do that. This place has been one of the best things that ever happened to me. I'll have to go back for a while, though. I need to sort out my job and I need to report Gavin.'

'I know.'

'Manchester's a long way from here.'

'Nowhere would be too far for me.'

'That's one of the nicest things anyone has ever said to me.'

'And I know you'll come back.'

'You sound as if you've always known that.'

'I've always hoped. Besides, you've got a bowl to glaze and Erin refuses to do it for you.'

'She's sneaky, your daughter,' she said with a smile. 'So many people have helped to bring us together, seen and unseen. I don't want to let them down. I don't want to let you down.'

'You won't.'

He sat next to her as she cradled Tasha's jug and savoured her good fortune.

'There's something or someone good in this house – a strong spirit of love,' she said. 'Can you feel it?'

'I can,' he replied, the tip of his nose touching the tip of hers, 'and at the risk of frightening you away, I love you, Jules.'

He backed away slightly and placed a finger to her lips.

'You don't have to say you love me back. I knew you were someone very special the first time I saw you and I'm prepared to wait for as long as it takes.'

She kissed the end of his finger. She could say it now. She was pretty sure she would mean it, but she had to be absolutely sure. He was too precious to mislead.

'Thank you for that,' she said. 'I don't think you'll have to wait long.'

He traced his finger around her lips.

'Step by step. We have the rest of our lives.'

She nodded. He was right. They did. And the next step was to kiss him again.

GOODBYES

Eliza's work was done. One swift waft of air and the wasp hadn't stood a chance. It had been blown towards Jules's foot instead of her hand and Eliza's mission was completed. After that it was up to the people themselves. She could do everything in her power to bring them together, but the final decision was theirs. She couldn't impose her own wishes upon them. Free will was always going to be paramount.

She watched from the window as Jules and Lance walked arm in arm up the path flanked by lavender and squeezed side by side beneath the honeysuckle arch as they made their way towards the car. Jules turned as Lance closed the gate and she blew a kiss towards the cottage or perhaps it wasn't just for the house... Perhaps their guest could see her gazing at the two of them remembering when she and Isaac had been like that, their love transcending all the struggles of life and death. She had believed that devotion would be for eternity.

Now she had the cottage to herself once more and she drifted through the rooms trailing her fingers across the mantelpiece, the deep windowsills and the uneven walls. She reached up to touch the roughly hewn beams and stooped to place her hand flat upon the slate flooring in the porch. Of course, the cottage looked so different now to how it had been in her day when she had hung dried flowers from the large central beam in the kitchen and oil lamps had created light rather than electricity. She had cooked on a range, but nothing as beautiful and benign as the duck egg blue one which their guests used. Hers had been black and temperamental, often smoking or refusing to get up to the required heat. Her life had been hard in many ways. They hadn't had much money, she and Isaac, that had been determined the day they decided to run away together, and her family had cut her off both emotionally and materially. But it hadn't mattered. They'd had so much love for each other. That had got them through – until now.

She left the kitchen and walked through the garden past the willow tree. She couldn't bear to sit beneath it anymore. Now she would rest on the bench at the end of the lawn looking out over the water. She would gaze up at the sky and the clouds and anticipate the next stage.

'Eliza.'

Isaac stood behind her, his voice tremulous, his body language now permanently contrite, not that it made any difference.

'You have worked a miracle,' he said. 'I saw our guest and her beloved arriving back at the farm. Thanks to you all shall be well with them. I'm sure of it.'

Eliza shrugged.

'It was nothing.'

Before Carrie arrived in the spring, the prospect of welcoming guests to their home had been so exciting, so full of promise. How ironic, she thought, that against the odds she had brought two couples together only for it to cost her own relationship. Tentatively Isaac came to sit beside her.

She shuffled to the far end of the bench.

'I hope one day, Eliza, you will be able to forgive me.'

Would she? She of all people, who had preached forgiveness all of her days, was now being put to the ultimate test and failing.

'I am leaving, Isaac,' she said.

He nodded.

'The time is coming. We agreed to complete this one more mission.'

She looked at him directly.

'I'm leaving now, Isaac. Directly. Today.'

He leaned towards her.

'But Eliza, what about Philly? She has not been returned to us.'

Eliza tried not to think about the day those people had come to take their beloved baby away. Jules, Carrie and Guy had stood silently as her little bones were released from the soil. The vicar had said some prayers and then her daughter had been placed in a small box to be taken to a building in Ryde.

'It could be weeks or months before that happens, Isaac. Besides, those are just her mortal remains. Her spirit is elsewhere, waiting. I'm going to her.'

'Do her mortal remains not mean anything to you, Eliza? They do to me. Can you not wait a little longer, my love, and we can go together?'

'No!'

Isaac steepled his fingers together and placed them to his lips.

'I can't come with you. I wish to see Philly laid to rest. The Major is making arrangements. He and Carrie have ascertained that she belongs to us and soon we will all be reunited in the churchyard.'

'And then she'll be forgotten again.'

'She has never been forgotten, Eliza. I think of her every day, and your heartstrings have always been connected to hers. Look at all the flowers that people have brought to lay beneath our tree. Her short life is being honoured by people who never knew her. That gives me comfort and hope. Carrie and Guy are in the process of persuading The Major to hold a garden party to raise funds for a headstone for her. I wish to stay and see these plans come to fruition and I wish you to stay with me.'

She shook her head.

'I'm sorry, Isaac. That is not possible.'

He was silent, looking out far into the distance.

'Then we must go our separate ways for now,' he said, at last. 'I couldn't protect our child in life, but I'm determined to watch over her final journey on this earth. This is one of the last things I can do here. It is my duty as her father. I won't shirk it. Perhaps it is for the best, you with her spirit and I with her mortal remains. Always remember, Eliza, that I love you. I have from the first moment I saw you on the beach and I always will, just as I have always loved Philly from that moment you first told me that you were carrying her.'

Eliza shivered despite the warmth of the late afternoon sun. It used to be her favourite time of the day. She would stroll around the garden dead-heading flowers, doing some gentle weeding or watering, picking vegetables to be cooked for their supper. And for a few short months Isaac would be there with Philly, walking beside her, their precious child wrapped in a shawl, the apricot bonnet covering her fine hair. Isaac would point out the birds and the bees and his favourite blooms. When she got fractious, he would produce the silver rattle and tinkle its little bells to soothe her. He had been the best of fathers, the best of husbands. She turned to look at the cottage. This had been the best of homes. Isaac stood up before leaning to kiss Eliza on the forehead.

'When I'm ready to leave this world, I'll come to find you, Eliza,' he said, looking down at her with that gentle, but strong face which she had loved for so long. 'It will be up to you to decide whether we're to be permanently reunited. The choice will be entirely yours.'

And he walked away without her even able to say that she loved him. Those words that had come so easily for all of these years had withered like the fallen leaves beneath the willow tree. Isaac would take his evening stroll around the farmyard, checking on the animals, no doubt inspecting the yield from the harvest, finding a safe place for Scattihen if she hadn't been shut away, looking in on Rita and sending goodwill for her convalescence. He was a good man, a good man who had made a mistake, for reasons she could acknowledge, but not understand, nor condone. One day maybe she would be able to. But not now. Now they must go their separate ways.

She sat waiting for the sun to go down, listening to the sounds of her garden; the grasses blowing in the breeze, the creaking from the barn on the other side of the hedge, the scurrying of small creatures in the undergrowth. Behind her Hideaway Cottage stood firm, giving her strength as it always had. The love she had bestowed upon it seemed inadequate compared to the blessings it had imparted to her. Leaving it would be one of the hardest things she had to do, almost as hard as saying goodbye to Isaac. But the perfect moment would be here soon. And when it came, she would leave Hideaway Cottage and her beloved Isle of Wight, never to return.

A LETTER FROM THE AUTHOR

Dear reader,

Huge thanks for reading *The Whispers of Hideaway House*. I hope you were hooked on Jules's journey. If you would like to join other readers in hearing all about my new releases and bonus content, you can sign up here:

www.stormpublishing.co/alexandra-barber

If you have enjoyed this book and could spare a few moments to leave a review, that would be hugely appreciated. Even a short review can make all the difference in encouraging a reader to discover my books for the first time. Thank you so much!

If you would like to connect with me on social media, I'd love to hear from you.

Alexandra Barber

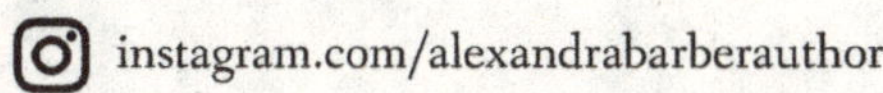 instagram.com/alexandrabarberauthor

ACKNOWLEDGEMENTS

Looking back the creation of a book always seems to me like something of a miracle! The way a single idea can grow until I am compelled to take that leap of faith which with tenacity, resilience and not a small degree of patience will hopefully result in a fully formed story which someone will want to read. That process, from the first sparking of an idea to the last full stop and then with the blessing of serendipity the holding of a book in your hand involves teamwork. My team involves my family, my friends and everyone at Storm especially my editor, Kathryn, and I offer them all my heartfelt thanks. The support, encouragement, reassurance, trust and attention to detail from these special people means more than I can say. I would also like to say thank you to my readers. You are the reason I write. It is my hope that in sitting down with this book you have been gifted a short breathing space within what can feel like an increasingly pressurised world.